It's 1932 and middle-class Malcolm lives with his mother in Highgate. Though confident and capable at work, he is tormented by "beastly inclinations"—a strong attraction to young men. One drunken evening at Charlie Brown's pub in Limehouse he meets Alfie, a working-class docker—and the most beautiful young man Malcolm has ever seen. Alfie is friendly, kind and changes everything by making Malcolm's inclinations seem considerably less beastly—but in 1930s London, this can surely have no future. Alfie is younger, apparently "normal", and from the Isle of Dogs, far from Malcolm's cosy world of quiet privilege.

Nevertheless, Malcolm launches himself into Alfie's world of rough pubs, a dance club, and even a football match. Resigned to a platonic friendship, he is thrilled to find that Alfie has other ideas. But by offering him something he hadn't even dared wish for, fate may have called his bluff and he fears his own naivety and sexual inexperience will see him squander this unexpected shot at happiness. After some excruciating but sound advice from a more worldly friend, the relationship becomes sexual, and more emotional, but remains an unsuitable attachment that cannot last forever.

When Alfie is nearly killed in a fire at the docks, and war planes on maneuvers growl over the Docklands skies, both are reminded that life is too short to worry about "forever". During a police raid on an illicit West End club, Alfie's heroism saves Malcolm from ruin, convincing him that whatever the future holds, this boy loves him now. The disapproval of families and friends, a hostile society, Malcolm's insecurity, and Alfie's belief that he'll eventually get married because "that's what young men do" cannot thwart a love that grows in unpromising ground and endures no matter what is thrown at it.

UNTIL THE REAL THING COMES ALONG

CHRIS SIMON

A NineStar Press Publication
www.ninestarpress.com

Until the Real Thing Comes Along

First Edition, May 2024

ISBN: 978-1-64890-760-9

Also available in eBook, ISBN: 978-1-64890-759-3

CONTENT WARNING:

This book contains sexually explicit content, which may only be suitable for mature readers. Depictions of homophobia, homophobic slurs, a deceased parent, suicidal ideation, references to suicide, and no HEA or HFN.

To Peter

Part One

Don't Tell a Soul

Chapter One

Grubby Angels

August 1922

THIS WAS WEALTH. This was power. This was the world in which Malcolm Trevelyan must make his mark.

A line of black cranes dipped and swung over the cobbled north quay of the Western Dock, as they lowered crates and barrels towards the waiting men below. Once landed, the goods were loaded onto handcarts and spirited away into the transit sheds nearby. The noise of the crane winches and the shouts of men drowned out any words of explanation from the guide escorting the small group of six trainee import clerks of which Malcolm was a part.

Beyond the transit sheds stood ancient brick warehouses, bulging with cigars and raw tobacco, grain, fragrant spices, ivory, and ostrich feathers. He breathed in the aromas of the nation's store cupboard, awed by the sheer scale of the warehouses and by the range of goods he saw in them. Beneath their feet lay a labyrinth of cool vaults packed with puncheons and hogsheads of port, brandy, and wines. The London Docks were an organised chaos and just about the most exciting thing that sixteen-year-old Malcolm had ever seen.

But it wasn't just the goods. Out on the quayside an even greater impression was made on him by the flat-capped, waistcoated dockers, concentration straining their features, skin glowing with their exertion. They worked in gangs, intimidating clutches of masculinity, strong and foul-mouthed. Most were middle-aged, weather-beaten, worn and scarred, but there was a handful of younger men among them. They were cocky lads— a different breed from any Malcolm had seen before and he was drawn to them. Strong, lithe, and energetic, they laughed and joked together with an easy familiarity he envied.

The dockers paid little heed to the gaggle of pale-skinned trainee clerks observing them. They would spare them attention only if the party looked like they were getting in the way, at which point a youngster would be sent to shoo them off, as though they were scavenging gulls circling over a consignment of raw sugar.

As the visitors weaved tentatively through the busy crowd, a sudden violent hailstorm lashed down on the quayside. Everyone ran for what shelter they could find, apart from the crane drivers, who watched the scurrying smugly from their cabins. Malcolm found shelter in the narrow covered doorway into a warehouse. It was padlocked and he had to share the brick arch with two young dockers and endure the bittersweet sensation of having them pressed up against him. Having their hard bodies and the smell of their sweat so close would no doubt have repelled some people. Not Malcolm. The sweat was fresh, the result of honest toil. And the bodies— well.

The young lads were deferential to him, in case he was someone important, toning down their profanities and allowing him as much space as they were able to. In adjusting his stance to try to give Malcolm more room, one of them yelped as a hailstone the size of a quail's egg struck his bare arm. His face, close to Malcolm's, blushed engagingly and he laughed.

"Ow! That bleedin' hurt!"

"Don't be such a jessie," jeered his mate. "Wotcher stick yer arm out for anyway, yer fathead."

"I was trying to give this gentleman a bit more room, weren't I? Yer don't want 'ailstones getting on yer nice duds, do yer, guvnor?"

Malcolm smiled weakly but was unable to utter a single word, let alone form a sentence. This lad of around his own age had called him "guvnor" just because he was wearing a suit, yet he was the tongue-tied one.

The hail lashed down for five minutes before stopping abruptly, allowing the young dockers to return to their labours.

As the clerks filed back out of the dock gates chattering about what they'd seen, Malcolm was disconsolate, because his desperate longing had undermined the excitement he'd felt at having seen the Port of London working at close quarters for the first time. He was no longer incarcerated in boarding school. There were plenty of girls for him to look at, in the streets and in the typing pool at work, but nothing had changed. Boys still preoccupied him and none more than these working-class lads. They were so different from him and the boys he'd known at school—and nowhere was safe, because the streets of London teemed with them. He wouldn't even know whether the two young dockers would have been considered handsome or not. Their faces had yet to have years of hard labour etched upon them, they'd yet to sustain scars or lose teeth, their complexions were unravaged by the drink to which they would probably turn for comfort. Their youth and vitality, their common clothes and flat caps, the hair cut short at the napes of their necks and their choirboy faces tormented him still.

He could tell himself his inclinations would shift towards women in due course, but he knew it wasn't true. In a week or two, he would have forgotten about these two particular lads, but there were legions of grubby angels dressed as thugs to fill him with a burning longing for… Well, he wasn't quite sure for what.

What could he do about it?

The answer was obvious. He must put all his energy into his work and see how far it would take him. It was his duty to achieve wealth and power to ensure his mother would live the rest of her days in comfort, and above all, he mustn't allow himself to indulge in any behaviour that would bring disgrace down upon her. He must not merely put aside his unnatural feelings but bury them absolutely and forever.

*

HE HAD BEEN a disappointment to everyone, of that he had no doubt. He certainly disappointed his ill-tempered father. The war had made them strangers and ahead of the Michaelmas Term of 1919, for both their sakes, Malcolm had been taken out of Hornsey County School and packed off to Wendells, a modest boarding school in Shropshire.

The school was over a hundred and fifty miles away from their leafy street in Highgate, but although she was horrified by her husband's decision, his mother hadn't been able to put up much of a fight against Malcolm's exile. She fussed and sniffled a bit as, clutching his suitcase, he climbed into a taxi bound for Euston station, but that was about it. Malcolm hadn't been bitter because he'd come to feel that he didn't fit in anywhere. He was an only child at home, a loner at the County School, and he was sure the new place would be no different.

At first, it was strange and disconcerting. The thing that had the greatest impact on him at Wendells was not loneliness, not hard work, not the bullying he feared, but nudity. Never before had he seen so much flesh, let alone been in amongst it. The boys did their physical training either in the gymnasium or outside wearing only white shorts and pumps and there were the showers to contend with, which involved being completely naked unless one wished to be mercilessly ribbed. There were no cubicles and even the individual ceramic baths stood six abreast on either side of a narrow gangway. Apart from the midwife who had delivered him, only his mother and father had ever seen him naked until this point and he was self-conscious about it. He felt small, white, and puny as he compared himself to the biggest, strongest boys, overlooking the many more whose physique and complexion were closer to his own than to the handful of dormitory Adonises.

There was also the matter of that most private of private things, which he had always called his "winky" on those infrequent occasions it had been necessary to refer to it at all. He learned quickly that it had many more names and indeed his own name for it was likely to elicit hoots of laughter from his dorm-mates. He decided that if pressed, he would refer to it henceforth as a "cock". He was increasingly concerned that many in his dorm were already better endowed than he was, because like all boys, he knew this was how men were ultimately judged.

*

HIS NARROW IRON-framed bed had been one of forty arranged in lines on either side of a long high-windowed dormitory, which stank of new green linoleum. Each night as he lay in it, he found himself dwelling on the nakedness problem. His feelings were uncomfortable and disconcerting, but he grew to realise with some reluctance that he rather liked seeing some of the older boys' bodies. In fact, he liked it very much. When confronted with any nudity at all, his mother had always taught him to look away, but increasingly, he found he didn't want to. Malcolm knew that Robbins in the bed next to him shared this appreciation, because the wretched boy hardly ever shut up about it. When they talked of it in hushed tones after lights out, it would leave him so excited that he was unable to sleep. He had to pretend to have fallen asleep, just so Robbins would shut up.

Malcolm was thirteen, so of course he'd had erections. They were frequent and distracting, but he had never masturbated as no one had ever told him such a practice existed, let alone showed him how to do it. The chaplain often issued dire warnings of the evils of "self-abuse", but they were lost on him. The term had him picturing Henry II flagellating himself, as he was meant to have done in atonement for ordering the murder of Thomas a Becket. He'd heard references to "bashing the bishop", so that must be it. Perhaps it was all right to do it if you'd inspired the murder of a senior clergyman, but not under any other circumstance. Being averse to pain, he concluded that flagellation wasn't the vice for him.

All the hormonal adolescent chemistry was still bubbling away in his body, but he was doing nothing to ease the pressure and he sometimes felt he would explode. During the early hours of one morning, as he dreamed of being rescued from drowning by David Garfield from the Fifth, explode he did, with sticky inevitability. He half-awoke as he felt it building, but it wasn't to be stopped whatever it was. He was mortified by the mess on his sheets and the pyjama bottoms that clung to his skin, for which he had no explanation, but the thought of compounding his disgrace by going to Matron about it left him close to tears.

He lay in this mess paralysed with fear, desperately seeking an explanation or excuse as to why after all these years he'd come to wet himself, but with some kind of pus rather than piss. Perhaps he was ill. Supposing it was a cancer or his bones were turning into liquid or something! He dreaded hearing the door of the dorm being opened by whichever prefect was on the rota. Hemmingway, Lake, or, God forbid, the sadistic Lascelles who would revel in his misfortune.

Inevitably, the door opened, and his dorm-mates leaped from their beds and scampered away, toilet bags swinging, towels under arms. Malcolm stayed in bed as though his shameful emissions had glued him there.

"What the hell is up with you, Trevelyan? Get a move on! Showers! Chop-chop!" barked Lake, who, through a small mercy, was the duty prefect. He set about hurrying the other stragglers up until they were the only two left in the dorm.

"I say! Whatever's the matter?" he asked not unkindly.

Malcolm sobbed, although he was trying desperately not to make the situation even worse by being an appalling cry-baby in front of Lake.

"Come on, old boy! It can't be as bad as all that can it?"

"I—I think I've wet the bed."

"Oh, dear. Never mind. Better show me."

Malcolm pulled back his sheets to reveal his shame, with a discernible bleachy smell that Lake must have caught a whiff of completing his humiliation. He could barely look at the older boy for fear of seeing the revulsion and disgust that must surely register on his face. But to his surprise, after recoiling slightly with a wince, Lake smiled and ruffled Malcolm's hair.

"It's all right, Trevelyan, you haven't wet yourself *per se*," he said kindly. "That's spunk, old chap. You've had a wet dream."

Malcolm must have looked bewildered because Lake flushed and gave a small, embarrassed cough.

"It's all part of growing up. It's nothing to be ashamed of. Happens to us all. It's to do with…with sex." He ran his fingers through his blond hair, obviously uncomfortable. "Look, hasn't your old man told you *anything* at all about this sort of thing?"

Malcolm quickly and emphatically said he hadn't, mortified by the thought of discussing anything like this with his father, of all people.

"Have I to take my sheets and pyjamas to Matron, please, Lake?" he asked wretchedly.

"Ha! I shouldn't. Make your bed up and it will dry in no time. It'll be a bit crusty, but nowhere near as crusty as Matron. It will be relatively inoffensive once it's dry. Putting up with it for a few nights will be far better than having to discuss the sordid little episode with her."

Malcolm felt like blubbing again but this time from sheer relief and because of Lake's kindness.

"Run along and get washed, Trevelyan, or you'll be late for breakfast."

*

DURING SUMMER TERM in the fifth form, Malcolm looked forward to entering the Lower Sixth in the autumn term and becoming a house prefect, where perhaps he could offer the same kindness Lake had afforded him to some other poor wretch. Lake had become a mentor, but in three years Malcolm hadn't made any close friends. Then Freddie Latimer was catapulted into his life.

Freddie came to the school mid-term due to a family crisis, and their House Master Mr Mannion asked Malcolm to help the new boy to acclimatise. His solitary nature made him reluctant at first, but as soon as he set eyes on the utterly forlorn looking newcomer, he agreed. By this time, he knew he was queer, but had he needed any affirmation, the impact that Freddie's fresh handsome face, auburn hair, and hazel eyes had on his senses was conclusive. Like Malcolm, Freddie had grown up alone, having spent the last few years on a tea plantation in British Kenya, and the boys hit it off right from the start.

Freddie was a keen cricketer and an excellent spin bowler which meant he would soon make other friends. He became more popular in three weeks than Malcolm had managed in three years. Malcolm feared being dropped altogether, but despite his burgeoning popularity, his new friend remained obstinately loyal. Their walks in the grounds continued, and he got to share the contents of lavish hampers from Fortnum & Mason that Freddie received each month. Although it liked to pretend it was a public school, Wendells was not accustomed to such luxuries, and when Malcolm commented on their opulence Freddie dismissed it as a symptom of his mother's guilty conscience.

One precious moment after a cricket match held such romantic promise. Freddie was ebullient after starring in an overwhelming success against a bigger more highbrow school. That glorious evening, breathing in the sweet scent of newly mown grass, Malcolm listened to an over-by-over account of the match and was touched that even in all the excitement, without any sign of reluctance, Freddie had stuck to their plan to go for a walk. He had been tactile and affectionate, and his eyes danced with possibilities.

Malcolm had been badgered for sex by a few boys, particularly a pest named Parnaby, but he hadn't been tempted because they weren't a patch on Lake. But this new friendship promised to engage the loins *and* the heart. Malcolm hoped so, for his head was full of Freddie and he could hardly wait for their next tryst.

But that tryst would never come.

*

EACH JUNE, THE fifth-formers were told what their Lower Sixth role would be at the beginning of the next school year, and Malcolm was not surprised or apprehensive when he was summoned to the Headmaster's study. Mr Mannion intercepted him in the corridor, draped an arm loosely around his shoulders, and accompanied him, which should have alerted him that something unusual was afoot.

Mannion knocked on the door of Mr Pritchard's study and they entered when prompted. A woman in black sat before the Head in the wood-smelling, book-lined room. It was Malcolm's mother. Grace Trevelyan opened her arms, and her son permitted an embrace and a soft kiss on each cheek, thankful that none of his peers were there to see him doing something so wet.

"Hello, darling," she said in a strained and unfamiliar voice.

"Mum! What on earth are you doing here?" He was bewildered. There were several weeks of term left, so she could hardly be there to collect him. His parents never did that anyway; it was always the trap and the train for him. "And where's Dad?"

"Darling, I'm afraid I have some very distressing news for you. It's difficult, so I'll just come right out and say it." Her voice trembled as she said, "Yesterday evening, your father passed away."

Everything and everyone dissolved and became unreal. He was stunned, as though he'd taken a physical blow. So, they were "widow's weeds". He should have known, for black was not a colour he associated with her. The Head's secretary brought in a cup of sugary tea and as he sipped it and tried to collect himself, the adults began a muted conversation, the sense of which he was oblivious to. He was a diffident boy, usually reluctant to interrupt adult conversation, but there were things he felt he must know.

"How? How did it happen?" he blurted out suddenly.

His mother hesitated. "Never mind that now, dear. All in good time."

"I want to know *how*," he insisted. When he broke the news to Freddie, he'd be sure to ask.

Grace exchanged an anguished look with the Head, who said, "Malcolm, it's too soon for the authorities to be absolutely certain of what happened, and until they do…"

"The authorities? With respect, sir, what's that supposed to mean? I take it that my father didn't just drop dead then. Was he attacked? Was he…*murdered?*"

"No, dear, of course not. It wasn't like that at all," said his mother, narrowing her eyes at the Head's indiscretion.

"Well, what *was* it like then? Surely you can tell me something?"

"Look, Malcolm, this is very difficult for your mother," began the Headmaster, but she held up a black-gloved hand to stop him doing any further damage.

"It's no use, Mr Pritchard. We can't spare him this, I'm afraid." She turned to her son and clasped his hand tightly. "Malcolm, it looks as though Daddy was cleaning his old service revolver and it went off. A horrible, horrible accident."

Once again, he was stunned into silence for a moment as he tried to make sense of it. He found he couldn't.

"I—I don't believe it. He was a *soldier*, for goodness' sake! He wouldn't have tried to clean a loaded gun—and it can't have gone off on its own. It isn't as though it was some old antique or anything. It was only from the war!"

"He went upstairs to one of the spare rooms and the gun went off. He was alone so we can't really know how it happened. I'm so sorry, darling."

Malcolm sat shaking his head in bewilderment and denial. This was not the sort of thing that happened in Cranmer Avenue. It just wasn't! They were a stupefyingly ordinary family. Perhaps they were even dull. And there was no way in the world his father would have tried to clean a loaded revolver, of that he was quite sure.

"He did it on purpose, didn't he?" he said quietly.

"No, of course not, darling," his mother protested shrilly. "We can't know that."

"Well, of course he did. Dad was in the army for years. He wouldn't clean a loaded gun. He just wouldn't."

No one seemed able to find any words that would challenge his hypothesis, which convinced him he was right. His father had ended his own life, and he had no idea how he should feel about it. Would they expect him to collapse? To cry? He had no desire to do either of those things. After all, his father had been a remote figure for the last eight years, practically half of Malcolm's life. Major William Trevelyan had spent five years away because of the war and Malcolm had been packed off to boarding school soon after his return.

No, he wouldn't cry.

Nor, for his mother's sake, would he let on how little he found he cared about this as the initial shock of the news wore off. It wasn't that he didn't care at all, he just didn't care as much as he felt he ought to. But *she* must have loved him, he supposed, and he would share the grief with her.

Having concluded that his father's death had been no accident, as awful as this was, he began to accept it. This was far worse for his mother, and he must always bear that in mind. For the first time in his life, he must behave as an adult, for her sake. He pretended to accept that it might have been a tragic accident, even offering spurious reasoning about a faulty safety catch to support a theory that would make it all a little less sordid. *He* was comforting *her* now.

He knew his time at Wendells was over. His friendship with Freddie was over too, before it had properly begun, as surely as though Freddie himself had been shot dead. This was the loss he would mourn. He found it hard to forgive his father for that, but he already had quite a list of grudges against the man. He was determined not take it out on his mother.

*

ANY HOPES GRACE Trevelyan had harboured that the shooting had been accidental were extinguished by the coroner's verdict that her husband had taken his own life "while the balance of his mind was disturbed". She could see what the war had done to poor William, but her grief was tainted by fury. How on earth could he have acted with so little thought for her—and for their son's future? He had made provision for his family—but there was no money available to allow Malcolm to stay on at boarding school, nor to go on to university. He would have to find work if they weren't to scrimp and save.

Fortunately, the British Atlantic Trading Company, where William had worked either side of the Great War, held him in high enough esteem for them to offer his son a position as an imports clerk. The British Atlantic arranged for the import and export of goods through the Port of London. Malcolm had no other thoughts of what to do and was aware that his mother needed him to become established as soon as possible, so he took the job and would do his best to make a success of it.

During his first week, he was plunged into a building full of strangers, all of whom knew each other, leaving him feeling an outsider once more. Tristan House, an Edwardian edifice on Eastcheap, not far from the Monument, with five floors containing a maze of offices full of wooden desks and filing cabinets, was a scene of frantic activity as its army of clerks went about their work. He found it easy enough to rub along with people and he was the new boy for only eight days. Under great pressure to succeed, he listened attentively and absorbed as much knowledge as he could, as rapidly as possible.

He was assigned to a branch headed by a fussy and unpopular little man named Arnold Cuthbert. By observing and respecting all his foibles and making sure he never made the same mistake twice, Malcolm learned to indulge the whims of a man who was notoriously hard to please. The branch arranged warehouse space and transport to disperse imports from South America, much of it frozen meat passing through the refrigerated warehouses at the Royal Albert Dock. It wasn't a complex task, but nor was it as simple as putting some furniture or a crate of books into storage. The different cargoes coming through the port could not all be managed in the same way. London's five dock systems made it the largest port in the world, with thirty-five miles of quays and thousands of bonded warehouses. The British Atlantic also worked with the older wharves and quays along the river. It was dull work, not the kind of thing to get a schoolboy's pulse racing, but had Malcolm craved excitement, he would have joined the army.

Chapter Two

The "Bolshevik" on the Board

Tuesday, 4 May 1926

IN THE FOUR years since leaving school, Malcolm had worked hard to make his mother proud of him. She would regularly visit her sister Hannah in Folkestone and she helped the church ladies with flowers and fetes, but her life was mainly dedicated to looking after her son. He was well-fed, his wardrobe was well-stocked, and his clothes immaculately laundered. She tried to be a friend to him by walking with him, listening to the same wireless programmes, sharing books, and taking tea together, for she was concerned about his solitary nature.

He became the British Atlantic's best import clerk, and his prospects were excellent—but in the May of 1926, he put all this in jeopardy. The Trades Union Congress called a General Strike, and it had a dramatic impact on everyday lives, particularly for those who lived in London. On the first day of the strike, all transport stopped, and he was unable to get to his office on Eastcheap. He would need to find a way on subsequent days, because his employers might see his continued absence as support for the strike, which would have led to his dismissal. If he had to rise at five and walk all the way, then so be it.

Fortunately, many City workers lived in Highgate, and he was offered lifts with a neighbour who worked at the Stock Exchange. It wasn't a comfortable arrangement because the man sounded like a broadcast edition of the *British Gazette*, the emergency paper printed to put the government side to the people. He was terribly gung-ho about overcoming the TUC's "treachery" and Malcolm resented the assumption that he might agree with this bumptious fellow—but he was grateful for the lift.

The Port of London was paralysed. The export of goods ceased, and although imported goods continued to arrive, the cargo remained on the docked freighters with no one willing to handle it. The British Atlantic management worried about goods they had already arranged warehousing for, about mountains of perishables being left to rot in ships' holds and about warehouses being looted as food supplies ran out.

Many members of staff became volunteers, intent on helping break the strike. Malcolm supposed he was a Conservative as his father had been, but he sympathised with the coal miners whose plight had sparked the emergency. He could think of nothing worse than spending the long day in darkness a mile underground and doing such hard and dangerous work. A lot of the miners' spare time was spent trying to scrub every trace of coal dust from their bodies, while being aware they couldn't scrub it from their lungs—which was often to be the death of them. It upset him that men had to work in those conditions, and he believed those who did so should be well rewarded, because the country and the Empire relied on the filthy stuff. The railways that connected the nation, the industries that forged its wealth, the ships that helped Britannia "rule the waves" would all come to a halt without coal. When times were hard, somebody needed to tighten their belts, but it should not be these people. Yet it always was.

His Head of Branch, Arnold Cuthbert, rose to the challenge of the strike and relished co-ordinating the common effort. He approached the clerks with a roster on a clipboard, bluffly assuming they would all be eager to help the nation in its hour of need. "That's the spirit!" he brayed as the clerk at the next desk signed up for duty with an empty stab at enthusiasm. Cuthbert wasn't so much co-ordinating as recruiting and Malcolm wouldn't have been surprised if he'd carried a pocket full of white feathers to hand to anyone unwilling to participate. So far, no one had been brave enough to refuse him.

Until Malcolm himself did.

"I'm sorry, sir, but in all conscience I can't. I shall continue to do everything in my power to get into work, of course, but I feel I can do no more than that."

"Good God, man!" blustered Cuthbert. "Why ever not? Surely we must all do our bit. It's a national emergency, don't you know?"

"As I said, I'm sorry, sir, but my understanding is that thousands of miners who do vital, dangerous, and filthy work have been told they must have their wages cut by twenty-five per cent. I don't mind telling you that if the British Atlantic tried a stunt like that with us, I'd be straight out of the door. If a General Strike is the only way to make Mr Baldwin listen, then I believe it's justified."

Cuthbert turned as pink as the British Empire on a map of the world. "*Justified?* How can it be *justified?*" he spluttered. Malcolm tried to ignore the unpleasant sensation of the man's spittle spraying his face. "Holding the country to ransom like this! Look at all the disruption it's causing ordinary decent people."

"With respect, sir, there'd be little point in it if it didn't," he said calmly.

"Don't be impertinent!" snapped Cuthbert. He waved a finger close to his young clerk's face. "I knew your father, my lad, and I can tell you he would be ashamed of you today. D'you hear me? *Ashamed!*"

Malcolm swallowed hard but remained calm. "I can't deny that any more than you can claim it, because he isn't here to speak for himself, is he, sir?"

Cuthbert hissed, "Whatever the wage levels here, my lad, you may well be out of that door sooner than you think. I've always seen you as an upstart, but until today I didn't have you down as a damned Bolshevik!"

For days, Malcolm was haunted by the spectre of dismissal, often thinking *I should have kept my mouth shut or offered to drive a bloody bus or something.* But his stock had risen with many of his peers because of the confrontation and that did a lot to assuage his concerns. Cuthbert was widely disliked and for standing up to him, Malcolm became respected as a young man of principle who would stick to his guns even when backed into a corner.

Just as he'd begun to hope the matter had blown over, Sir Lionel Haynes, another Head of Branch, passed Malcolm in the foyer and said, "Ah, Trevelyan, I hear you're a Bolshevik agitator now."

Malcolm's face fell. "If you're alluding to my exchange with Mr Cuthbert, sir, I just like to see fair play, that's all. I hope I shan't be punished for saying what I think."

Sir Lionel smiled benignly. "Not at all, dear boy. I wish more people would do just that. I daresay old Cuthbert is still smarting, but not enough for him to sack one of his better men. Indeed, I wish he *would* give you the push. I'd take you on in a flash if he did."

Buoyed by Sir Lionel's words, Malcolm continued to thrive at Tristan House. A reorganisation of the company led him to work for Sir Lionel anyway, in Continental Imports, and when he moved, Cuthbert, far from being glad to see the back of the "young upstart", was most unhappy with the arrangement. Malcolm had come a long way in a short period of time, and by 1928, at the age of twenty-two, he became the youngest ever Senior Clerk in the company.

*

Monday, 16 September 1929

ON THE FRANTIC floors of Tristan House, Malcolm Trevelyan was a serene presence. His calm, reasoned approach was appreciated in an area where even experienced staff could become flustered. Whether it was to be a good day or a bad one could depend on the tides, or the competence or otherwise of colleagues inside and outside the organisation. Malcolm couldn't be ready for every eventuality, but he ensured he was as well prepared as he could be and that he learned from every experience, particularly the bad ones.

While he was still an import clerk, a cargo of Indian bauxite had become a headache for a colleague, Cyril Palmer. Something as mundane as importing bauxite could become a drama if you had nowhere to put it and no one to take it to wherever it was supposed to go. You couldn't dump a cargo like that just anywhere. By no means all the many wharves and docks in the Port of London could accommodate mineral ore—and those that could were sought after by all importers of the stuff, not just British Atlantic.

"I don't even know what bloody bauxite is," lamented Palmer, as the accommodation he'd arranged for it fell through. "The ship carrying the blasted stuff from Bombay is due to dock tomorrow morning, and I have no idea what it is, let alone where to put it."

"It's an ore," explained Malcolm. "They make aluminium out of it, I think."

He didn't think, he knew—but he also knew that no one liked a know-all. Palmer was some way older than him, but when the chap covered his eyes and slumped in his seat in despair, Malcolm added, "I think there may be a shed at the East India Docks that will take it. They took some iron ore for us last week and from what the man was saying, it sounded as though they had capacity there. Would you like me to give them a call for you?"

Palmer at once straightened up in his chair. "Would I? I should say so!"

Malcolm reached for the telephone stick, picked up the brass receiver, held it to his ear, and dialled. Palmer leaned towards him in his seat, the docket scrunched in his hand and his eyes fixed on Malcolm.

"Hello, Operator. May I have Stepney Green 472, please? Yes, the East India Docks… Hello, is that Mr Travis? It's Malcolm Trevelyan from

British Atlantic again… Yes, not so bad—and you…? Good, good. Look, you know you took that iron ore for us last week, well, could you handle some bauxite? I think it's roughly the same tonnage… You can? That's excellent. At the same rate…? Thank you, sir. You're a gentleman." He pulled the docket from Palmer's eager hand and scanned the page. "All being well, it's due in the London Docks tomorrow morning at around eleven, so it should be with you mid-afternoon—will that suit…? Thank you, sir. Good day to you."

Palmer was left with the paperwork to do, but he didn't care, as his bad day had been instantly transformed into a good one.

"You're a ruddy marvel, Trevelyan," he said gratefully. "You've just solved all my problems at a stroke—and not for the first time, I might add. Don't think I haven't noticed. I owe you a drink, old chap."

Malcolm would never collect the promised drink as he always went straight home to his mother in Highgate at the end of each day, but the goodwill he had earned would serve him well.

*

A MONTH OR so later, Mr Cuthbert was forced to retire because of a heart complaint, scotching once and for all the rumour that he didn't have one. Malcolm was summoned "upstairs" and despite his relative youth, he reckoned he'd been performing well enough for them to consider putting him temporarily in charge until a new man could be recruited. The process for filling senior positions was often notoriously protracted, so this could mean quite a few extra pounds landing in his pocket. He was saving up to buy a motor car in which he could take his mother for runs in the country, so the money would be most welcome.

By the time he was sitting outside Sir Lionel's oak-panelled office, Malcolm feared he'd been getting ahead of himself. Even as a stopgap, they were sure to choose someone older, with longer service. He worried about the real reason he'd been summoned. He thought he was good at his job, but supposing the management didn't agree. An unwelcome cold sweat began when it occurred to him that he might have been unconsciously indiscreet when "appreciating" a male member of staff.

In ten minutes, the dictograph buzzed and after lifting the receiver the secretary said, "Sir Lionel will see you now. Please go through."

Sir Lionel Haynes sat behind the largest desk in the building. It was built of rich red-brown mahogany and had a maroon inlaid leather surface upon which his papers, inkwells, and the telephone and dictograph receivers were spread out. He couldn't look anything less than very important sitting behind it. He rose as Malcolm entered and the warmth of his greeting suggested there would be no reprimand.

"Come in, come in, my boy. Take a seat, won't you."

"Thank you, sir." He did as he was told, and Sir Lionel followed suit.

"Well, Trevelyan. Have you any idea why I've asked to see you?"

"No, sir. Well, not really. I've speculated, of course, but I came to no firm conclusions."

"Quite. Quite. Well, I shan't beat about the bush. I want to offer you the Head of Branch post vacated by Mr Cuthbert."

First Malcolm felt a surge of relief, but when he realised a reaction was expected from him, he said, "Ah. That was one thing I'd considered but I thought I would be too… Still, for temporary cover while you find someone, yes, I…"

"Oh, for heaven's sake stop blathering, man! You're not being offered it on a temporary basis while we "find someone"! We've found someone. You!"

"Me, sir? Be Head of Branch? But…"

"Yes, of course. You're far too young. I won't lie to you; that has been said in some quarters. But after taking all options into consideration, Malcolm, the board has decided to take a risk on you. Now I'm Chairman, my only concern is that we do the work and do it well. I don't give a fig for seniority and the idea that if you stay where you are for long enough, you'll eventually get to the top. I'll do what I think is best for the British Atlantic and I think you're the right chap."

"I—I don't know what to say."

"There's only one sensible thing you can say, my boy. Say yes."

"Well, thank you, sir. The answer is yes, of course! It will be an honour."

"Excellent. And before you leave here—a word to the wise. You've risen so far so quickly, you must take some time to enjoy your success, otherwise what on earth is the point of it? I think you'd be well-advised to give more of your attention to other matters."

"Like what, sir?"

"Well, after the flush of this current triumph has passed, it's sure to dawn on you that you could one day be sitting behind this very desk, Malcolm. No guarantees, of course, but you've suited British Atlantic so admirably thus far that you're sure to be a contender. But don't forget, ability alone won't get you here. In order to be in contention, you need to be exemplary."

"I'll do my level best, sir."

"I don't doubt it, but as I say, it isn't *all* down to ability. Not to put too fine a point on it, you'd do well to look around for a suitable wife. A good marriage will prove essential if you're to get to the pinnacle. You're young, so there's no need for you to rush. But keep an eye out for the right one. And whatever you do, don't go ruining everything by falling in love with a showgirl or an actress!"

"Don't worry, sir, I shan't. I can promise you that much."

The elation didn't hit him until he'd closed the door to Sir Lionel's office behind him. To have become a Branch Head so soon was beyond his wildest dreams. His father had never risen that high. He knew he would soon fret about his ability to do the job, not to mention Sir Lionel's advice to find a wife, but for now he meant to enjoy the thrill of this unexpected success. Most of all, he looked forward to telling his mother about it.

*

THE SURPRISE CHOICE to be Cuthbert's successor didn't go down well with everyone. At the age of just twenty-three, he was responsible for a large staff—and at the British Atlantic this was unheard of. But whenever someone grumbled about Malcolm being promoted into management ahead of so many more senior colleagues, Cyril Palmer, and others to whom he had been helpful, spoke up for him. Even though they were among those overlooked, they accepted that he was simply the best man for the job. He wasn't "pushy", but he had the knack of getting others to work with him without them even realising they were being organised.

He was given Cuthbert's office—a room big enough for him to play tennis in—and he quickly became better acquainted with the wood-panelled corridors, the plush carpets, and mahogany furniture of the executive floor. Rather dauntingly, he was also given Cuthbert's secretary, the terrifying Miss

Hassell.

On his first day in the new position, Miss Hassell said, "I daresay it will seem a bit strange, Mr Trevelyan, but don't worry, I'll show you the ropes."

"I'd be obliged, Miss Hassell," he replied. "But once I know them, don't be surprised if I move them."

She smiled. He might be young, but she thought he'd do very nicely. After seven years of Cuthbert, Malcolm Trevelyan might prove a breath of fresh air.

Chapter Three

Imported Meat

Tuesday, 11 March 1930

MALCOLM WAS PERCEIVED by many at work to be an odd sort of fellow who kept himself to himself. He wore dark suits with starched wing-tipped collars which gave him a dour Edwardian appearance but his approach to the work was progressive and modern.

Not everybody settled as easily as he did into the cut and thrust of the import world. Peter Burkett, who started in Henry Bellamy's office, was a fresh-faced young man with cornflower-blue eyes and golden hair. The younger secretaries chattered excitedly about him, and he caught Malcolm's eye too. Sadly, it was soon talk of his apparent ineptitude that dominated the company tea rooms. It was said his days were numbered, and Malcolm was sad to hear it, but in an office full of young men it was easy for him to brush thoughts of Peter aside. One evening, however, having stayed late to complete a return for the board, Malcolm was approached by Miss Hassell who'd already put on her coat and hat, ready to leave.

"Mr Trevelyan, I'm a bit worried about that young clerk of Mr Bellamy's. They seem to have left him rather in the lurch and he's in an awful funk. Could you have a word perhaps—just to see if he's all right?"

Malcolm sighed. As if he didn't have enough on his plate. Still, he was tickled to see that the formidable Miss Hassell had a compassionate side.

"I'm nearly done here," he told her. "I'll look in on my way past if he's still there."

Burkett was still there all right. Malcolm found him sitting alone under a solitary lamp in Henry's dark empty office, slumped at his desk, one hand covering his eyes. There was no sign of activity.

Malcolm hesitated at the door. "I say, Burkett, are you all right?"

Peter turned and looked at him. His face was drawn, no longer handsome for the moment, his usually vivid blue eyes dulled and desperate.

"I was meant to find warehouses for all of these"—Peter swiped a hand at a daunting pile of dockets—"but I put them aside and forgot about them. I haven't got anywhere, for any of it." His voice was uneven, and Malcolm suspected he didn't trust himself not to cry.

"Well, there's absolutely no point in you carrying on at this hour, Peter. All the people you're trying to phone will have gone home long ago."

"Then I'm done for," Peter choked. "Mr Bellamy said I needed to clear these today or I'm finished here."

Resisting the urge to put a comforting arm around his shoulders, Malcolm sat down beside him and leafed through the paperwork that was proving such a burden. He couldn't help but think that no one should have been sunk by such a straightforward task, but it would have further demoralised Peter to have said so.

Instead, he swiftly reordered the dockets and said, "Dates, oranges, olives, and tomatoes—all fruit. I'm sure you can find a wharf that would take the lot. That's assuming the dates are fresh rather than dried, of course. You'll need to check that because it isn't clear on the docket. Bananas can stay in the West India. And these spices—turmeric, molasses, cinnamon, and nutmeg—they can probably all go in the West India too. It's only three warehouses you need, you know. Four at most. Were you looking for nine?"

"Well, yes. I'm a bloody fool! But it's too late now."

Malcolm paused for thought. "Not necessarily. Transport might be tricky this late in the game but… Look, we can't do anything about it tonight, but Henry doesn't usually get in until nine, does he? Most of the wharfingers and warehousemen get in early so there's a chance. If we could both get in for seven-ish, we'd have the best part of two hours to find homes for this stuff and I could call in a favour regarding the transport. Can you be here that early?"

Hope flickered in Peter's cornflower-blue eyes. "Well, yes, of course."

"Right-oh. Let's do that then, shall we? I can even send a message asking Henry to come and see me at nine-fifteen about something or other, which will give you a little more time to sort out any loose ends."

His face transformed by sheer relief, Peter was once again the handsome boy who had first caught Malcolm's eye. "Oh, Mr Trevelyan, thank you so much! But—well, why ever should you go out of your way to help me like this?"

Malcolm didn't wish to dwell on his ignoble motivation. "We all work for the same firm, Peter. Maybe one day you'll be able to help me with something, eh?" It was difficult to picture what that might be, because handsome though he undoubtedly was, Peter appeared to be a bit of a clot.

Turning to go, he saw that Miss Hassell had been loitering in the doorway all along. A faint smile played on her lips, and she winked at him before heading for the lift and her delayed journey home.

*

OVER THE FOLLOWING months, Peter's struggles continued. Henry Bellamy prided himself on having the most dynamic clerks in the building. When his boys phoned a warehouse, they would not allow the call to end until their goods had been accommodated. They were encouraged to bully. A lot of their threats were empty, but because they were delivered with such emphasis, most of the time they worked.

Peter shrank away from them from his first day. It was "dog eat dog" and Bellamy saw no future for this timid pup as he floundered for five more months until late August. The Branch Head was from the old school, an ex-army officer. If the board had decided that Peter should be put out of his misery, he would happily have shot him. After the weekly meeting of Branch Heads, he called the boy into his office with a terse flick of his head. It was Friday, the traditional day for giving people the push, and the other clerks smirked knowingly at each other.

"Come in, Peter. Shut the door behind you, there's a good chap."

Bellamy sat behind his desk but did not indicate that Peter should be seated too.

"Well, I shan't drag it out. You're just not cutting it here, I'm afraid. We can't carry you any longer."

"I'm sorry, sir." Peter seemed resigned to his fate. There are few things as demoralising as persisting with something that you're no good at, so he wasn't inclined to plead. The experience of the last months had practically emasculated him as it was.

"Yes, yes, I daresay you are, but it's no use, is it?" said Bellamy dismissively.

"No, sir."

Even Bellamy wasn't unmoved by his bleak demeanour. "Don't take it too hard, old man. Not everyone is cut out for this work. And it could be worse, you know."

"Could it, sir?" Peter asked dejectedly. "What could be worse than this? How am I to tell my old man that I've got the sack?"

Bellamy leaned back in his seat. "The sack? Oh, but you haven't. Look, I'm honestly convinced that this isn't the job for you, Peter, but for some reason Trevelyan appears to think otherwise. He argued long and hard to keep you, so you're being transferred to his office and Alan Miles is moving here—from Monday morning. I'm sorry if I led you to believe… Well, just do your best to take the second chance that's being offered you. That's all. Off you go."

*

ON PETER'S FIRST morning in his branch, Malcolm welcomed him into his office for an introductory chat. He was ashamed that his interest in Peter's welfare had been prompted by the fellow's good looks, but Peter would have no reason to suspect his motives and he resolved to try to get the best out of the lad. He delivered all the platitudes and clichés involved in office welcomes, but his new clerk looked uncomfortable and lost.

Malcolm stopped and asked, "All right, Peter? What's on your mind?"

Peter sighed. "I'm grateful to you for fighting for me, sir, truly I am. You've been so wonderful towards me that I shall remember it always. But perhaps Mr Bellamy is right, and I'm just not cut out for this. I only went for it in the first place because jobs are so scarce at the moment. But here, I'm the proverbial square peg in a round hole."

Malcolm smiled indulgently. "All we need to do is shave those corners off, Peter. Then you'll fit into the round hole, won't you?"

"No, I mean it, sir. I start every day feeling sick with worry. Every time one of those dockets hits my desk, I have to swallow back the panic. I look around at other people getting on with things, knowing what they're about, laughing and joking with each other in between telephone calls and the panic in me gets worse. They probably look at me and think, what the devil does that idiot think he's doing?" He added wretchedly, "I'm a misfit, sir. I don't belong here. After all you've done for me, Mr Trevelyan, I'm terribly afraid of letting you down."

Malcolm mulled over Peter's words. It had been honest of him and brave too, to explain how he was feeling. Perhaps he wasn't such a clot, after all.

Peter waited for help or dismissal, no longer caring which. Even his father's disappointment could not make him more miserable than he had been in recent months, sick of the rising panic that virtually immobilised him every day.

"Peter—don't worry about what the other clerks are doing and still less what they may or may not be thinking. At work, as in life, everyone tries to put a brave face on, even if they're struggling. I can tell you categorically that you're far from being the only man in Tristan House who's finding it hard going. There are many people in this office who hadn't ever thought of becoming import clerks before they came here. For heaven's sake, no child ever said, 'When I grow up, I want to be an import clerk.' It isn't really a vocation and as you say, jobs are scarce."

"But I'm really bad at the actual work. You saw that for yourself the other week."

"I saw the panic you're talking about. Your planning and organisation could use some work. But I also heard you on the telephone and I thought you sounded good. You were polite and professional."

Peter was dubious. "Any fool can speak on the telephone."

"No, Peter, any fool can't—not to my satisfaction at any rate. Look, would it surprise you to know that if you'd spoken to the wharfingers on the telephone in the manner adopted by the clerks Henry favours, then I wouldn't have wanted you in my branch at any price?"

"Well, yes."

"There you are then. The work of this branch is much the same as what you saw in Henry's office, although you'll be dealing with more imports from South America rather than the Colonies. The approach, however, is totally different. Henry tends to think that all those who work in the warehouses are somehow inferior to us and we're doing them a favour by bestowing our bounty upon them. He served in India and boy, does it show! Don't concern yourself with looking at his clerks and thinking they're good at their jobs, because they aren't."

For the first time, a smile broke out on Peter's handsome young face. It had been worth waiting for.

Malcolm went on, "We aren't like that here. Henry would have it that we're 'bowing, scraping and begging' for transport and warehousing, but he can call it whatever he likes. I think people react better if you treat them as equals and are civil with them. It should be the least they expect from us, don't you agree?"

"Yes, as a matter of fact I do."

"Good. Then you're halfway there already. When you phone up the docks or wharves, I want you to forget everything you've heard in Henry's office. I want you to be polite. I want you to be pleasant. I want you to sound as if you care about them and what kind of day they've had. In fact, assume they've had a bad day and treat them accordingly. And if they end up saying they can't fix you up with what you need, thank them, tell them you quite understand, and politely wish them a good day. That way, they'll remember you. They'll remember that you weren't too pushy, that you gave them no lip, no trouble at all, in fact. And believe you me, they will want to do business with *you* rather than someone more abrasive and rude from Henry's office or from another firm."

He looked Peter in the eye. "I've listened to you, don't forget. I *know* you can do this well. The rest will come with experience and a little help. That is, if you decide to give it a go, of course. Come on, give yourself a chance, Peter. What d'you say?"

Peter smiled again, nodded, and said, "All right. I'd like that."

"Good man! I'm going to sit you next to Archie Davies. He's been doing this for years and he's used to helping other people settle in. I still go to him for help myself sometimes even now."

"I'm surprised you need to, sir. I mean, you're a Branch Head at your age. You know everything."

Malcolm smiled at the compliment. "Peter, no one knows so much that they never need to ask for help. It may also surprise you to learn that I've spent a large part of my career sick with worry as I travel in each morning." He tapped the side of his head. "There's a voice inside here that says, 'Today might be the day they find you out, Malcolm'."

Peter looked puzzled. "What could they find out?"

"That I'm actually no good at my job at all. I don't really believe it, of course, but the tiny voice in my mind likes to taunt me with the idea. I think lots of people have that element of doubt in them. We just need to ignore it and get on with the day."

But Malcolm had blushed while he spoke, conscious that there actually *was* something for them to find out.

*

OVER THE FOLLOWING days, when passing, he listened discreetly to Peter's calls, and although initially hesitant, Peter's demeanour improved dramatically as he relaxed and shared his lovely smile more often. A week or so after he started, Archie Davies came up to discuss a problem with a Surrey Docks timber warehouse and Malcolm took the opportunity to check on the newcomer.

Archie pursed his lips and nodded before saying, "He's coming on pretty well, I'd say. He's a pleasure to have around, in fact."

"You're not just telling me what I want to hear?"

"Mr Trevelyan! When have I ever not told you what's what? Yesterday it looked as though he had nowhere for all that Argentine beef due in on Thursday, but while he was telling me—and he made it sound as though someone had died, by the way—Ellis Watts from Collyer's Wharf phoned him to say they could take it, after all. Now, he must have made a good impression on Ellis for him to do that. Ellis isn't an easy man to deal with a lot of the time."

When Archie left the office Malcolm thumped his fist on the desk in celebration. His instincts had saved the career of a boy he liked and given his branch another good clerk.

Chapter Four

Beastly Inclinations

Summer 1930

HE MAY HAVE achieved the wealth and power he needed but away from the office no one would have mistaken Malcolm for a happy man. He was pale, not much given to smiling, and appeared to many to have something sad about him. There was love in his life, for his mother surely loved him, but a mother's love can only take a young man so far.

His ambition receded, leaving his "beastly inclinations" to resurface, stronger and harder to suppress than ever. He even came to rue the opportunities he'd missed at Wendells. He remained bitter about the loss of Freddie Latimer, but he was even sorry he'd resisted Parnaby.

There were some lovely girls in the office, and he knew that some of them had him in their sights. Yes, he was a little old-fashioned, but he was young and personable and promised to deliver a great standard of living to whichever wife he chose. But girls, however beautiful, were of little interest to him and never would be.

Reading aside, he had no hobbies. He would walk around for hours tormenting himself with reckless thoughts because despite its size, solitude was not difficult to find in London. Just across Highgate Hill lay the ornamental Waterlow Park which sloped delightfully down towards the cemetery gates. A little further away were Highgate Woods and the vast wilderness of Hampstead Heath.

Sometimes he would walk the streets, where a bittersweet melancholy would steal over him. He liked to see ordinary people, particularly ordinary boys, going about their business. He would watch a van being unloaded and envy the men as they laughed and joked, making light of their burdens. To Malcolm their lives seemed gloriously uncomplicated.

If the handsome bus conductor had known how Malcolm valued his smile and his cheery greeting, he might have thought more of himself. So might the postman, the assistant in Burton's Tailoring, the younger clerks at his branch of the Midland Bank and the Post Office, the boy who swept hair from the floor of the barber's, the grocer's delivery boy, the butcher's assistant who managed to look alluring in an apron liberally smeared with gore—in fact, any personable young man who was prepared to treat him with unthinking kindness for a precious moment during the course of the day.

He was less comfortable with road-workers and labourers because usually they would not pass the time of day with him or indeed acknowledge him at all. But his eye was still drawn to the younger, fitter ones, stripped to the waist, lost in their task so that he could study them unobserved, enjoying what he could see and torturing himself with what he couldn't. He preferred "nice" boys and he liked to tell himself that he wanted nothing from them other than their smiles and their courtesy. They were the thick red blood coursing through the arteries of London, a constant source of pulsating temptation and torment for a frustrated and confused young man.

He'd imagine their "uncomplicated" lives by investing them with families and pastimes. He'd picture the young cockneys laughing in the pub, enjoying the races, cheering at football matches, playing illegal betting games at the kerbside, and having a jolly time around the "old Joanna". Then he would chide himself for his bourgeois fancies. He could not picture their reality because he knew them no better than he did the tribes in the far-flung jungles of Africa. As for their lives being "uncomplicated", surely every human being had their own worries, their own frustrations, their own hopes. They might not suffer from his "beastly inclinations", but all of them would have some struggle or other. He didn't think the working classes he so admired would have any time for his sort. Like the young dockers, these were nice decent lads and not at all the types available to him, he was sure of that.

One day, someone would take offence and give him a good hiding, but so far, whenever his stares had been intercepted, they had only ever elicited a smile or a friendly wink. He'd almost have preferred the hiding to the torment these lovely youths unknowingly inflicted upon him. If there were a God, he'd both thank and curse Him for making so many of these wonderful creatures and ask to be delivered from the curse of loving them, if love it was.

God had cast the shadow of guilt over his childhood, but in early adolescence Malcolm had rejected religion and its morality. In spite of that, he was sure his inclinations were against nature and therefore wrong. The boys he longed for surely longed in turn for girls, which was the natural way of things. He even felt guilty about the impure thoughts he'd harboured in the warehouse doorway. He'd stolen the heat from those young men's bodies and had violated them with his indecent thoughts, despite them being unaware of it. In God, he had at least felt that he had something or someone to turn to. Now he had nothing and no one.

If one of the young men he so admired would hold him, just for a moment, and tell him everything would be all right, then he imagined that in an instant he would become the happiest man in the world. He could wish for no more than the embrace, but it seemed more likely that a man would one day walk on the moon than that he should ever get it.

There were other men inappropriately attracted to their own sex, and from walking around the West End, Malcolm knew where to find them. There were antique dealers, theatrical types, and effete young men of presumably independent means, who he imagined might help him satisfy his inclinations. They could be found in cafés and public houses in some of the streets behind Piccadilly Circus, on the Soho side. He had been. He had seen. But he had found nothing in those places to inspire him. His abject loneliness still sometimes drew him there, and, occasionally, he even came close to speaking to someone, but he recoiled from any clumsy overtures and fled. Those people were not like Freddie Latimer and the boys at school. They were nothing like the lads loading vans, nor the young dockers sheltering in the warehouse doorway. If they were his kind, he judged them harshly, seeing little in them to love.

His days, his weeks, his months were all the same. Each morning, he would walk down the hill to Highgate underground station or brave a tram if it was wet. He would buy a *Daily Telegraph* from the boy at the entrance before stepping onto the moving stairs and descending to the platform deep below to get the train to Bank station. The paper served as a screen to protect him from any unwanted attention, although this was seldom a problem on the underground, where an unspoken vow of silence seemed to have been taken by its passengers.

He wasn't one for small talk anyway, nor did he wish to listen to others making it. The newspaper usually deterred any attempt, but he could still peer over it whenever the carriage contained an attractive young man. Given his taste for the commonplace, there was a plentiful supply of them on the Edgware to Morden Line and it was unusual for him to finish reading a single article most mornings. The young men nodded their heads, not in acknowledgement or agreement and sadly not in consent, but through the rocking motion of the carriage. The strap-hangers swayed with it, oblivious to how well they looked performing their unwittingly erotic dance. Sometimes a strap-hanging boy would stand close enough for Malcolm to breathe in the smell of his shaving stick and the soap with which he'd washed his body. He would picture him standing stripped to the waist at the bathroom sink, absorbed in scraping lather away with a cut-throat blade, oblivious to his own allure, until it became too much and he had to tear his thoughts away.

These young men were unaware of their "peril", and he became adept at scrutinising them intently without them ever cottoning on. He would dismiss young men with facial hair, favouring the clean-shaven, and he didn't like a man who was carrying too much weight. When subjected to scrutiny, some who initially made a favourable impression were found to be simply too young. One could appreciate potential, but it wouldn't do to dwell on them even in a fantasy. He wasn't the sort to chase telegraph boys no matter how flattering their uniforms.

Once his "victim" had been selected, Malcolm would savour every detail of him that he could see and would extrapolate those he could not. The colour and volume of a man's eyebrows might give a fair indication of the colour and density of the crisper hair growing in more intimate places. Armed with that image, Malcolm could imagine him undressed. He was less confident that the length of fingers, shape of noses or size of feet were reliable indications of endowment, but keen and persistent observation of the crotch area in most cases would offer clues about that sooner or later, even in the fashionably loose trousers known as "bags". It was difficult to admire a face and a crotch at the same time and even in Malcolm's strange world of sexual fantasy, it was faces he valued most. Tormented though he was by them, on the occasional day when there were no attractive youths in his carriage, he viewed his fellow travellers with impatience and irritation.

He wondered whether he should feel guilty about subjecting young men to this scrutiny, which, if perceived, would almost certainly have been unwelcome. Indeed, it would more than likely have resulted in his arrest, or even earned him a damned good thrashing. But he wasn't doing them any harm, provided he didn't ever touch. And they would never know that for twenty or so minutes until it was time to alight at Bank station, they were the "Underground Boys" and they belonged to him.

There were scores more slim bodies and clean-cut handsome faces to torment him on the moving stairs up from the tube and still more on the walk to Eastcheap. It was the City, the land of the proverbial "stuffed shirt"—and some of the shirts were very nicely stuffed. On each floor of Tristan House were scores of good-looking young men with sharp haircuts glistening with pomade or brilliantine, scrubbed clean and smart in their suits. Because of his status, many of them were eager to please Malcolm Trevelyan—apart from in the ways he most often imagined.

Malcolm continued to keep an eye on Peter Burkett. His reasons were no longer even remotely altruistic. Now Peter was more relaxed, he twisted in his chair with the suppressed energy of a tethered colt. He would stretch languidly, his white cotton shirt pulled taut over his chest and hard flat stomach for a few moments, showing the definition of his muscles. Now it was summer he wore no vest, and his dark nipples sometimes showed tantalisingly through his white cotton shirt.

Malcolm felt guilty about the fantasies he had about him. He might torment himself with thoughts of Peter smiling at him, kissing him, even standing undressed before him, but Peter would never know of it. His only role in repaying the debt he owed to Malcolm was that of an oblivious figure in a fantasy that would harm only the fantasist himself. And it did harm him.

Peter Burkett was only one of the young men about whom Malcolm became sentimental but could never have. The oft-quoted line from Coleridge's "The Rime of the Ancient Mariner" seemed appropriate: *Water, water, everywhere, nor any drop to drink*. Would that it was only water he was after.

As each day ended, he would bring vivid memories of that day's boys back and try to ease his beastly urges. He did so with slow deliberation, partly through preference and partly so the creaking of the bed didn't alert his mother to the fact that something she'd consider rather unpleasant was going on. It was a big house, yet her room was only a few paces down the landing. In the fantasies that brought him to his messy climax, the young men would be naked, they might be aroused, he might run his fingers over their smooth skin, but it was never any more than that. Apart from masturbation, Malcolm had no idea what on earth two men would get up to together. If one of the objects of his desire were to show willing to collude in his depravity, what would he do, lamentable little virgin that he was. Despite all the guilt that weighed him down so heavily every day, he was in his own way an innocent.

Exhausted by his own futile longing, he was tired of forbidden fruit, and sick of his obsession with male youth and beauty. Most of all, he was sick of himself, a desperately lonely man, imprisoned in a chamber of solitude from which he must never allow himself to escape even if he could.

He knew he could stop it. He could step into the path of an omnibus. He could throw himself into the Thames off London Bridge, where a treacherous current flowed beneath its narrow spans. Or he could retrieve the other revolver. The police had taken the one that had done the job for his father, overlooking the fact that he had a second. Inevitably, Malcolm's conscience would intervene. He would need to have been far more desperate to do that to his mother, and this made him push these thoughts of self-destruction aside.

Part Two

Don't Say Goodbye

Chapter Five

Not the Marrying Kind

Spring, 1932

THE WOMEN WORKING at the British Atlantic were mostly secretaries and typists, and they were well aware their careers would only last until they found themselves a husband. They had no choice in the matter because it was company policy not to employ married women. Most of the women who worked there were resigned to this and saw their jobs as something to furnish them with pin money until some personable chap came along and whisked them away to a mock-Tudor semi-detached house in "Metroland".

Doris Finch was pretty and dressed so well that many young men thought she'd look good on their arms. She was a natural blonde, although some uncharitable older colleagues jumped to the conclusion that she'd used peroxide and was therefore "no better than she ought to be". She was proud of her hair and kept it in a Marcel Wave, tight enough to endure any of her collection of cloche hats to be jammed onto it without being compromised. Some office wags speculated as to whether she had at one time been a gangster's moll, because her hair was set so hard there seemed every chance it was bullet-proof.

There were more than enough male clerks, overseers, and junior managers with whom Doris and the other girls could play a courting game that with luck would result in a walk down the aisle and a decent house in the suburbs. Malcolm didn't hold it against them. Women might have won the vote, but society still made it difficult for them to have a decent future not tied to that of a man. He was well-placed to appreciate that, even in this stuffy office, there were plenty of modern young men, sharply dressed and beautifully groomed, who were the prospects most likely to attract the young ladies. His own eligibility would be ranked much lower than his position in the hierarchy of the company, and this was a matter of some relief to him.

Doris, however, wasn't a girl to be distracted by a dazzling smile or the neat parting of a sharp haircut, however brightly it glistened with oil. At twenty-five, she was running out of time. She dreaded being left on the shelf to become an old maid, but this wasn't going to happen if she had anything to do with it. From the moment she joined the company, her gaze swept the assembled desks and offices like that of a lioness poised beside an African waterhole, ready to pounce on the most succulent beast she encountered. It alighted on Malcolm. He was surprised to find how often he caught her gaze and how frequently he seemed to encounter her while going about his business. She had seen that his position carried an extremely generous salary. Her colleagues in the typing pool dismissed him as a dull mummy's boy who was likely to remain a confirmed bachelor, but despite their sniggering, he remained top of her list of potential prey. She sought a way to escalate their acquaintance.

Some of the staff would socialise after work, particularly on a Friday, but Malcolm never joined in. He was never asked. It was more for junior staff anyway, but one day Peter Burkett surprised him by inviting him along. Part of him desperately wanted to go, but he was so weighed down by decorum that he declined the invitation and a number of subsequent ones. When he mentioned it to his mother, she encouraged him to accept. More to please her than himself, the next time he was asked he agreed, and he was gratified to see Peter's features flush with apparently genuine pleasure. It wouldn't be just Peter on his own, Malcolm told himself, so what harm could it do?

*

AFTER WORK, ONE Friday evening in April, he walked with Peter, Doris, and a small group of others to the tiny East India Arms on nearby Fenchurch Street. There they joined a crowd, which grew over the course of the evening to some twenty people, all drinking and talking and laughing in the loud, tightly packed, smoky public house until closing time. He had endured a sleepless night and during the day had barely been able to work because of the anticipation of getting to know Peter better. Perhaps this was to be the beginning of a deeper friendship and beyond that, who knew? But he was cautious enough to realise it might just as well prove a huge mistake.

He felt duty bound to buy the first round and was to fork out for several more before the night was done. His usual drink of choice, dry sherry, was the wrong thing for a man to have in this company and so he ordered a pint of mild instead. What possible harm could something described as "mild" do? It had to be a safer choice than something called "bitter". Peter was inclined to look after him and offered Malcolm another before he was even half done. A pint seemed a tremendous volume of liquid for someone unaccustomed to drinking and it made him feel bloated and slightly nauseous. He wasn't even convinced that he liked the taste of the stuff. Nevertheless, it proved to be indispensable as a social lubricant and he found himself able to relax a little. Over a period of two or three hours, he consumed three or perhaps even four more.

He didn't have much to say for himself at first but was content to listen to the chat about people in the office he barely knew, films he hadn't seen, dances and the popular tunes of the day he hadn't heard, and football and boxing about which he knew nothing. One gloomy individual even tried to start a conversation about Herr Hitler, the permanently angry little chap on the rise in Germany, but no one was in the mood for British politics let alone anything foreign.

As people left their seats to go to the lavatories or to the bar, those remaining shifted around and so it was that Doris ended up sitting beside him. She evidently found what little he did say very witty indeed for she was quick to laugh and occasionally laid her hand on his forearm, as though to warn him that if he continued to be so funny, he would leave her in a state of distress. It left him feeling that he might have underestimated his abilities as a raconteur.

When he decided that he could drink no more and he must leave, he was gratified that one or two people, Doris among them, were kind enough to protest. Fearing that the unfamiliar ale may have led to unpleasant consequences had he continued, he was adamant, and he walked out into the chilly April night feeling pleased with himself for once. He had indeed felt part of the gang and it had been good. He was perhaps not as different from other people as he had always believed himself to be. When he got home, he still had a smile on his face, and his mother was delighted.

"There you are, you see, dear? I knew you would have *heaps* of friends if you'd only give people a chance."

"Steady on. I've spent one evening in a pub with a handful of colleagues. It hardly makes me Sibyl Colefax."

"No, but it's a start. With you having got so high up at such a young age, these people are most probably a bit in awe of you, dear."

He snorted at the idea.

"And I suppose that some of your colleagues are young ladies?" she continued hopefully, at which point he bade her goodnight and went to bed.

The unfamiliar effect of the drink lulled him to sleep before he was able to savour whatever Peter had said to him over the course of the evening.

*

SIX MONTHS WENT by. Spring turned to summer, then to autumn. The weekly visits to the East India Arms became routine, and Malcolm looked forward to them. He found he could comfortably sink more beer and, as a consequence, was better able to contribute to the conversation. He preferred it when the group broke up into smaller pockets, particularly if he was able to chat to Peter, who seemed flatteringly curious about him. His mother may have been right about the "awe"—in his case at least.

Because the pub was loud, he and Peter would sit close enough for him to catch the pleasant fragrance of whatever soap his young colleague used, and occasionally he'd feel the heat and the firmness of a well-muscled thigh against his own. He treasured these moments. He didn't deceive himself that Peter was his way inclined and saw his interest for the hero-worship it most probably was. Given the disparity of status within the company and the fact that Peter worked directly for him, he was conscious of the peril in it. But the boy's company was more intoxicating than the beer and he found it impossible to step back.

The Friday-evening routine had become so much a part of his life that it was noticed by his peers and even the more senior managers in the company. They were no strangers to the pub themselves, but they were unlikely to hobnob with the hoi polloi in there as Malcolm was doing. Some raised an eyebrow while others praised him for working on good relations with the junior grades. He was aware of all this but ignored it as he basked in his new and unexpected popularity.

Doris made sure that she never missed a Friday, never missed a syllable of Malcolm's conversation, and never missed an opportunity to get just a little bit closer to him when she could manage it. Her manoeuvring had not escaped the notice of their colleagues, who observed the pursuit as though it were a sporting fixture. One interested party was a man named Donald Sutton, a middle-aged clerk from the Accounts department. He was always the first to arrive and the last to leave the East India Arms, for he was a very thirsty fellow. Malcolm suspected he was as partial to Doris as he was to his drink, but Sutton was too old for her to consider him.

Malcolm knew what her game was and had mixed feelings about it.

He didn't want to mislead her, but he imagined it was his prospects that attracted her rather than his soft fair hair and his hazel eyes. Sir Lionel had strongly implied that he could not expect to get any further up in the British Atlantic without a wife. If he had to have one, then surely Doris would serve as well as any. She was pretty enough and would get his mother off his back. He would no doubt have to negotiate the horrors of providing her with children, but it would be a mutually beneficial alliance, and as a businessman, he was all in favour of those.

*

THEN ONE WET October evening, his better judgement having been corroded by Scotch whisky, Donald Sutton had uttered the few words that brought Malcolm's new social world collapsing down in flames about him like the wreckage of the *R101*, the airship that had crashed and burned two years before.

Doris's pursuit had seemed particularly desperate on this final evening. Her exaggerated laughter in response to anything Malcolm said that was remotely humorous grated, as did the way she'd cornered him and leaned into him so that a great deal of contact was unavoidable. She placed a small hand on the front of his thigh and left it there, which would have been considered brazen behaviour by many, even if they'd been walking out together.

Malcolm was uncomfortable both socially and physically. Peter sometimes looked away, part amused and part embarrassed both for Malcolm and for Doris. Donald too seemed increasingly exasperated by what he was witnessing. To drown his irritation, he had been knocking back the whiskies at a faster rate than usual, but it seemed rather to be making him even more irascible. Eventually, as Doris shrieked with laughter at a mildly amusing anecdote Malcolm had shared to distract her from her mission, the worst happened.

"Oh, give it up, Doris, for goodness' sake!" Donald said rather too loudly.

Doris's laughter was instantly extinguished, and she glared at him icily. "I have no idea what you're talking about, I'm sure."

Donald indicated Malcolm with a sweep of the arm. "Oh, come on, love. The whole Trevelyan thing, it's bloody ridiculous."

"What are you implying?" she sniffed.

"I'm 'implying' that you've set your cap at him, and you've got no ruddy chance. No ruddy chance at all, love."

"You don't know what you're talking about, Donald, and no one else knows or cares what you're talking about either." She was visibly flustered and glanced around for expressions of support from those colleagues who were within earshot.

"Is that right?" Swaying on his heels a little, he turned to those assembled, who had been stunned into silence and asked, "Is it?"

"Shut up, Don—you've had more than one too many," said someone, to a murmur of agreement.

"All right. I'll tell you what I'm talking about then, shall I? I believe in plain speaking, after all."

"Oh, God! Not plain speaking," said one of the crowd. "That never ends well."

"It usually just means 'rude'," added another.

Donald ploughed on undeterred. "Do you honestly think that he comes in here to sit gassing with you, love? Really? You weren't the one who first asked him to come along, were you? It was Peter. Trevelyan is here because of Peter."

"Whatever does it matter who asked him to come along? He's here now, isn't he?" snapped Doris.

"Yes. But he's here for Peter, love, not you. You may have put young Peter up to asking him, but he doesn't know that. He thinks Peter likes him, so he sits here with you oozing all over him like syrup running down a stone wall. And you've got no chance with Trevelyan because he just isn't the marrying kind."

"That's a wicked lie!" squeaked Doris, trembling with indignation.

"No, it isn't. What's wicked is you chasing him like this." He turned to address Malcolm directly for the first time. "Did you know, Mr Trevelyan, that Doris paid for Peter and his sweetheart to go to the pictures as a bribe for asking you along? *Grand Hotel*, I think it was they saw. Of course, Peter would have much preferred *Tarzan the Ape Man*, as I'm sure you would too, but discretion is the better part of valour, isn't it?"

In one fluid movement, Doris stood up and stung Donald's cheek with an almighty slap that unfortunately carried sufficient force to knock his dentures clean out of his mouth. It sent their awful pinkness skidding across the beer-puddled floorboards until they came to rest at the feet of a nonplussed Peter as he returned from the bar with another tray of drinks.

"You bitch!" exclaimed Donald drunkenly, before diving after them. Absurd as this scene was, more from shock than concern for him, no one laughed as he scrabbled on the floor to retrieve his broken grin.

Malcolm abruptly stood up, upsetting two half-full glasses as he did so. Leaving his coat and hat behind, he barged his way through his colleagues, out of the pub, and into the soaking night. His only thought was to escape this intolerable humiliation.

Heedless of the deluge, he hurried past the Monument and onto London Bridge, without consciously deciding to go there. He stopped midway between two of the lamp standards illuminating the bridge, as far away from the light as he could manage. Leaning against the balustrade, he stared down at the Upper Pool, with its brisk traffic of tugs and barges. Lighters moored mid-stream shifted and clanked in the darkness, the forest of cranes on either side barely visible against the night sky and Tower Bridge silhouetted in the distance. Further downriver, ships sounded their melancholy horns, oblivious to his misery as he stared at the sinister black water that offered an escape from his wretched life.

He was bitterly angry with himself, with his own stupidity for compromising the one stable element of his life—his job. How foolish, to have believed young Peter had liked him enough to ask him to go for a drink! Good God, he'd even begun to imagine sharing confidences with him and daydreamed about finding that his interest was reciprocated. The memory of those dreams made him writhe inside. Was it a cruel practical joke—and if so, how many other people were in on it? He would be a laughing stock throughout the British Atlantic. And why? Because he'd been stupid enough to think people might actually like him.

A police constable walking by gave him a watchful but kindly, "Good evening, sir," and he managed to gather himself to move away from the balustrade and to reply. He began to walk towards the underground station. Even the fiercest of storms has its lulls and so it was with his anger. *Why should they like me, after all?* he eventually asked himself. He had done little to inspire any affection by being aloof and perhaps unapproachable. His first emotion had been bitter disappointment as his fledgling hopes had been smothered, but gradually cold fear crept over him as it dawned on him that embarrassment might be the least of his worries.

Those few simple words, "not the marrying kind", could be the ruin of him. This was where the real danger lay. What if the British Atlantic was suddenly to become aware that it had a man like him in the office? A whiff of scandal like this could lead to him losing his position in such disgrace that he would find it impossible to get another. Donald Sutton's use of that bloody phrase clearly suggested he knew—unless he'd taken a wild shot in the dark and scored a direct hit with it.

Fear and humiliation, aided by alcohol, had sent Malcolm deeper into his dark humour and left him contemplating escape. But it had just been contemplation, because his fevered mind always took him back to the inconvenient complication of having a much-loved mother, and his father already having "taken his own life" as they put it. That was where his mind had been before common sense and maybe even the courage to face the music had brought him back to the world.

Chapter Six

Avoiding Mother

ON SATURDAY MORNING he was out of the house before his mother had the chance to put her face on. He refused to spend the day fending off her questions about how his evening had gone. She would see right into his misery, for he was a hopeless liar, and she would fuss around him trying to make him feel better but instead making him feel worse. He had avoided her interrogation the previous evening by nursing a few more pints in a corner of the Crown on Highgate Hill and only returning home at close to midnight when he was sure she would be in bed.

Last night, he'd come closer than ever before to ending it. Today, he needed to think—and to do that, he needed to walk. It was chilly under a sky carrying an ominous grey threat. Standing on Archway Bridge, he paused to look down at buses, trams, and lorries as they laboured up the hill towards Highgate, but then he remembered this was a popular spot for suicides and hurried on his way. He walked on to Crouch End and trudged over the hill to the early-morning bustle around Finsbury Park station. It had begun to rain in earnest, so he took the Piccadilly Line into the West End.

Sitting on the underground was good for thinking. He knew he was suffering from something known to the medical profession as "homosexuality". It was a disease—a "disorder" according to *Everybody's Family Doctor*, the hypochondriac's bible. The information on it was terse, although helpfully cross-referenced with the entry for *Inflammation of the rectum*, where "immoral practices" were listed as a potential cause. He didn't understand how a chap's rectum could become inflamed just because he was attracted to other men, but rectal inflammation could be treated. There was no detail on the homosexuality itself, no proposed treatment, and no suggestion that those suffering from it were worthy of any sympathy. Yet why should anyone feel guilty for being afflicted with a disease?

His solution to most problems was to read books about them but finding information on this particular condition proved difficult. Outside of reading about disgraced men in the newspapers' court reports, the terse entry in *Everybody's Family Doctor* was all he had to go on. He wasn't aware of another book that might enlighten him and although he often walked across the park to Highgate Library to return his mother's murder mysteries, he certainly wasn't going to ask about it in there. The elderly librarian, Miss Frinton, would have been lunging for her smelling salts. He had considered making an appointment with Dr Sherwin, for many years their family practitioner, so that he could lay the affliction before him and have the great relief of being told what action he should take that might offer him hope of a cure. Sadly, he couldn't bring himself to say such things to the grey-haired old chap who'd sorted out his measles, his mumps, and his chicken pox. Nor did he expect there to be an ointment that would instantly soothe his homosexuality and clear it up entirely in a fortnight.

If abstinence was the solution, then he was doing well. For all his flights of erotic fancy, he had never in his life touched the intimate parts of anyone's body other than his own. Even at school where everyone was at it, he had remained chaste despite often being propositioned. He hadn't managed to lose the habit of masturbation and was embarrassed that he still did it so often at his age.

*

FROM LEICESTER SQUARE station, he wandered into Soho to continue his melancholy ruminations over a drink. Everything the world had to offer was to be found somewhere in London's streets. The air crackled with possibilities, even for someone as hopeless as he was. This was why he walked so much, to see some of those possibilities playing out in the lives of his fellow citizens. In the tight, cosmopolitan streets of Soho, he saw that not everyone sharing his affliction was intent on finding a cure. Some seemed happy to explore the symptoms with unseemly relish.

Even his mother had heard of "that sort of person". Grace had warned him as a child to avoid Mr Wren, a curate at their church, because she feared he might be "one of them". Of course, Malcolm had been instantly fascinated and had wanted to know more, but all she said was, "Never you mind, and just do as you're told." Mr Wren had seemed perfectly pleasant, but Malcolm did as he was asked, good little boy that he was.

The Lyons Corner House on Coventry Street notoriously boasted an extraordinary concentration of exotic creatures who dubbed it "the Lilypond". There, painted young and not so young men sat beside the potted palms in an unofficially reserved area away from curious tourists and clucked like a yard full of histrionic poultry. It could be deafening at times as the restraints of a world that was cruel to them were loosened for an hour or so. Some had tinted hair, just a hint of rouge, and radiated a fragrance that was some way short of "manly". The image didn't appeal to Malcolm in the slightest, but he admired their courage. Sporting that look in the West End was brave enough, but some of these fellows probably lived in places like Acton, Plumstead, or Holloway, where they wouldn't easily blend into the crowd.

Braying and shocking and amusing, they were a small, conspicuous minority, surrounded by more conventional-looking men who, although more discreet about it, were also lovers of their own sex. At the weekends in particular, the crowds in Coventry Street, Leicester Square, and Piccadilly Circus were laced with men promenading back and forth, hoping to make a connection. Whenever anything of the sort had been attempted with Malcolm, he had always looked away but would wonder later how it might have played out, had he gone along with it. He concluded that a trip to the Police Courts would have been the most likely outcome, followed by a fine, dismissal, and ruin.

There were a few public houses that tolerated a homosexual clientele because capitalism would seldom allow morality to get in the way of making a profit, and even a clandestine club or two. He'd occasionally visited one for a terrifying hour or so, but he wouldn't have wanted to become a regular in any of them. They were difficult to track down anyway unless one was in the know, and going to them was risky. Any such drinking establishment, even if not frequented by homosexuals, was illegal and so liable to be raided by the police and closed down. It would open again only days later at a new location. Their solution was to keep moving, but if they were caught, the entrepreneurs responsible would pay a little fine, serve a little time, and start all over again.

He would go into the pubs every now and then, because despite low expectations, there remained a flickering flame of hope within him, like the stubborn pilot light in a gas boiler. It was quickly extinguished on every visit, but it would always flicker to life again in a week, or a month, and he'd be back again. He'd get a number 15 bus from Eastcheap as far as Charing Cross station, a good place for him to begin exploring debauchery.

There were certain public conveniences where sordid relations were reputedly the thing. He went to see. He seldom stayed for long, certainly not long enough for anything untoward to occur. The whole idea was repellent to him, nauseating even. Some of these conveniences were Victorian and had once been grand, with tall porcelain urinals, brass pipework, and high cast-iron cisterns, but most looked as though they hadn't been cleaned properly since the old Queen had been on the throne. Beside the once gleaming porcelain urinals, dark figures in respectable clothing would stand in absolute silence. Heads would turn with furtive downward glances. Hands would reach over and there would be a rhythmic movement of arms. All would melt away in an instant if a policeman were to enter or, more rarely, a lavatory attendant. Malcolm would never find any answers in those stinking places, but most of the men in there did at least *look* like "normal" men.

Women held no attraction for him, but the flamboyant queens in the

Corner House, courageous though they were, held still less. They flashed like a warning light, screaming, *"You do not want this! You are not like this!"* What if, despite his revulsion, people saw him as being like that? He didn't think he was effeminate at all, let alone as big a whoopsie as some of them were, but was he really the best judge of that?

He had desperately unfulfilled sexual and emotional urges and he knew it would be better altogether if he could lay them aside, find a nice girl, settle down, and get married. Young women looked so appealing, so clean, bright, gentle, and…dull. What he wanted smelled of shaving soap, tobacco, or beer, spoke with a deep voice, and might be inclined to kill him if they could read his mind.

In certain places, there were men available who he *did* find attractive. He watched them intently, and, in many cases, it wasn't hard to fathom that they weren't homosexual at all but simply needed cash. For them, it would be easy money when they were a bit short—if they could stomach it. Evidently, they could, because they kept on coming. He had heard that soldiers would often oblige to supplement the King's Shilling. Not in the queer places obviously, because their uniforms were too conspicuous. You needed to go to ordinary pubs or parks in the vicinity of a barracks if you wanted to pick up "a bit of scarlet". They were young and fit. They looked appealing and masculine in their smart tunics, and more practically they were invariably clean and healthy, so there were unlikely to be any unpleasant medical consequences from going with them. This made them extremely popular. He would like to have become acquainted with a soldier; the prospect excited him, but not on those terms. He was strangely moral about it.

With a few drinks inside him, he wanted sex all right, whatever it entailed, but he wanted more than that—something he didn't really believe existed for the likes of him. He wanted love, from another man. From a normal-looking young chap with a normal job. A clerk, a bus conductor, an electrician, a grocer, a coalman. If he could only find an ordinary man who'd love him, then all the confusing sexual stuff could be worked out. This was why he believed himself doomed to be miserable for the rest of his days. Men like that did not want other men. He was sure of it.

He took no vestige of the confident young executive he was into these pubs, and became instead a drab wallflower, crippled with embarrassment. Despite how well he'd done and how much he earned he felt ugly and socially inept. When someone in one of the queer places tried to strike up a conversation with him, he would clam up. However, he did occasionally speak to a man named Godfrey Chalmers. The latter had persisted with his attempts at conversation each time they met, even though he seldom got much more out of Malcolm than mundane pleasantries.

Tonight, Malcolm opted for one more drink in a queer pub in a basement bar on Gerrard Street, and there was Godfrey.

"Hello, Malcolm dear. Frightful weather we're having."

"Yes, it's horrible."

"I'm glad you're out and about though. I always say you should get out and about more, don't I?"

"Do you?"

"Well, yes."

And that was it. Malcolm knew he exasperated Godfrey. The last time they'd bumped into each other, Godfrey had sunk a few gins too many, and they'd inspired him to deliver a stream of unsolicited advice on Malcolm's non-existent love life.

"Malcolm dear, you really need taking in hand, you know. You are actually quite a nice-looking boy, so there's no excuse for you being so bloody gloomy all the time. You may be a bit bookish and bespectacled, but there are plenty of chaps drawn to that type, you know? You do rather dress as though your mother still chooses your clothes, but you have a lovely head of hair, beautiful teeth, and nice skin."

Malcolm blushed and, unused to praise, he mumbled a thank-you, which was briskly waved away.

"I haven't finished! Honestly, Malcolm, any would-be suitor will soon give up on you because you're far too much like hard work. You're like a pale-grey sky with dark clouds gathering. Any likely fellow will flee before the downpour begins!"

He didn't know whether Godfrey even recalled that last encounter, but finding Malcolm no more outgoing than usual, Godfrey soon excused himself and went in search of more congenial company. Left to drink alone, Malcolm found he couldn't finish his pint. He was tired of the place and how it made him feel. Sick of the brooding desperation of all the men who stood around in there pretending not to care. Men like himself.

Chapter Seven

Charlie Brown's

THE DRIZZLE HAD turned into heavy rain, but he didn't dash for the shelter of an underground train home. Instead, he walked through Covent Garden market, past huddles of wet fruit porters, treading carefully to avoid the slime of discarded produce. He continued along High Holborn, struggling through a forest of umbrellas and the scramble for buses and taxi cabs outside Gamage's department store, then crossed the viaduct and eventually passed the great dome of St Paul's, shrouded in the gloom, before turning down Cheapside in the direction of the Bank.

Avoiding Fenchurch Street, the scene of his recent humiliation, he hastened down narrow medieval City lanes and found himself at Aldgate. From there he began to walk along Commercial Road, one of the arteries running into the East End, and towards the docks. It was unfamiliar territory, and he wandered along it in a daze, having no particular destination in mind. Whenever the rain fell more heavily, he lingered under bedraggled shop canopies.

This grubby thoroughfare was leading him away from everything he knew. He was sprayed once by an omnibus and several times by large lorries coming in from the East and West India Docks as they laboured by, roaring like wounded beasts. His raincoat and hat were splattered with reeking mud and wringing wet. He was tired, he was cold, and he was hungry, and Commercial Road was not a place that was likely to lift his or anyone else's spirits.

He finally came to a place where the traffic forked into the two Dock Roads. To avoid crossing, he veered onto the West India Dock Road and headed towards the cranes he could make out through the sepia gloom. Approaching the dock gates, he happened upon a public house. First, he heard laughter, then he saw its warm light reflected on the glistening pavement as the rain once more began to hammer down. The pub stood beside a bridge that carried the elevated London & Blackwall Railway and the sign above its door, creaking back and forth in the wind, read "The Railway Tavern". The place appeared warm and inviting, and somehow reassuring.

Aware that he looked a mess, he turned into the Public rather than the Saloon Bar. His spectacles misted up as soon as he entered its warmth, and he pulled out a handkerchief to clear the lenses.

The evening session had only just started, and it wasn't yet busy inside, so he found a chair away from what other patrons there were, but from where he could observe them. He draped his sodden raincoat over the back of it, dumped his dripping hat onto the table, and went to the bar. A glass cabinet on the counter displayed pies and uninspiring-looking sandwiches of indeterminate age. Having not eaten for twenty-four hours he was ravenous, which enhanced the appeal of the modest fare. A barman in a crisp white apron took his order of a pork pie, a cheese and pickle sandwich, and, attracted by the colourful label, a bottle of Newcastle Brown Ale.

Malcolm let his eyes wander around the bar as his order was being dealt with.

It was like no other pub he had ever seen, let alone entered. The walls were half-tiled, their upper halves covered with framed pictures and ornamental plates. In similar fashion, any shelves or dressers were loaded with lamps, china or stone busts, clocks under glass domes, porcelain figurines, stuffed birds and animals—and all manner of other curiosities. It was like ordering a drink in an antiques shop.

"This is quite a place," Malcolm commented.

The barman glanced up, smiled, and seemed inclined to chat. "Never been before, sir? This is Charlie Brown's, famous the world over."

"I thought it was the Railway Tavern."

"You're right, it is, but no one calls it that. It's been Charlie Brown's for donkey's years now. Nearly forty, in fact."

"Who *is* Charlie Brown?"

"Not is, sir, was. He was the landlord. I'm afraid he passed away a couple of months back. His daughter Ethel runs the place now."

"Oh, that's a pity. He must have been quite a character. What *is* all this stuff?"

"The curios? They're treasures, sir. Charlie's treasures from the Orient, India, Africa—you name it, we've got something from it."

"How did it all get here?"

"Well, there's some what are gifts from sailors, but Charlie collected most of the things hisself. He knew what he wanted—anything out of the ordinary, particularly if it had a bit of a yarn behind it. This is handy for the docks, see, and sailors make a point of coming here. They may want to go to the Tower and Piccadilly Circus, but they don't really feel they've been to London at all unless they've sunk a few pints in Charlie Brown's."

Malcolm was now so hungry his stomach ached, and he took his drink back to the table to scoff his food while taking in the bewildering treasures around him. Some of them looked like the kind of things you might find at a fairground or a seaside fancy goods shop, but closer inspection showed there were many nice pieces in the room. Should there be a bar-room brawl, God forbid, a plentiful supply of missiles was available.

He devoured his crusty, salty pork pie, then his cheese sandwich, in a manner that would have drawn a tut from his mother, and he swigged his brown ale with lip-smacking relish. The bar filled up rapidly with evening trade. To Malcolm, the patrons seemed as exotic as the treasures on the shelves. There were black men from the Caribbean and Africa and Lascars from the Indian subcontinent, Chinese from the Orient or more likely from London's "Chinatown"—Limehouse Causeway or Pennyfields across the road. Dockers were meeting up after finishing their shifts, men who had probably not ventured far from the surrounding streets all that often in their entire lives. He saw women meeting their men. Jaunty dance music came from a wireless behind the bar, tuned to the BBC National Programme where Henry Hall was doing his stuff with the BBC Dance Orchestra.

Malcolm thought it a magical thing that he'd been drawn into Charlie Brown's. The place had lifted his spirits and diverted his thoughts from his fear of what he might face on Monday morning. Not only that, but the customers were so diverse he felt he didn't stand out in such a crowd. Indeed, there were two men at a table nearby who may well have shared his affliction, because they gazed at each other with affection and occasionally their fingers brushed. He found this more stimulating than anything he'd ever witnessed in those West End places he despised. If they indeed shared his affliction, they didn't seem to share his despair over it.

There were couples in the room where the woman was white and the man was not, and no one paid any attention. He supposed the men were seamen who had found love of one kind or another with local girls while in port. His own misery receded as he became warmed by the happiness of others.

As he ordered another brown ale, he said to the barman, "This place is…marvellous!"

The fellow beamed at him indulgently, as though such proclamations were not uncommon. "Thank you, sir. It's like all of London should be, innit? Like all the world should be really. It's a special place."

The crooner on the wireless was singing the song "Don't Say Goodbye", the words of which sounded less trite to Malcolm now than they might usually have done. His foot tapped along to it.

This is *how the world should be,* he thought. Everyone happy, everyone getting along, nobody judging or frowning with disapproval. Charlie Brown's was wonderful. Newcastle Brown Ale was wonderful too. He was content just to soak up the atmosphere, breathe in the cigarette smoke and the smell of beer—and if he wanted another three brown ales, then he would jolly well have another three brown ales. He exchanged pleasantries with strangers who wanted to know about him. To some of them, Highgate was as exotic a place as Zanzibar or Madagascar.

He had consumed little food, consumed it hurriedly and late, and he'd washed it down with so much drink that as he rose to fetch his fifth brown ale he stumbled and would have fallen flat on his face had his shoulders not been seized by the steadying hands of one of a group of young dockers standing nearby.

"Whoa, steady on, mate! Did no one tell you that the floors move in 'ere?"

Malcolm looked up at his rescuer, but his words of thanks died before they reached his lips. Before him was quite simply the most beautiful face he had ever seen in his life. The young man's complexion was flawless, his teeth immaculate in a smile designed to break a heart. His eyes were a glistening midnight blue behind almost feminine lashes. There was nothing remotely feminine about the hands that steadied him though. They were rough and brutal looking, with long blunt fingers. These hands and his surprisingly deep voice were what betrayed the boy as a man, although he surely couldn't be more than twenty. He was dressed like pretty much every docker, in stout brown boots and dark trousers of a heavy material, which, although baggy, failed to hide from Malcolm's practised eye that underneath them, all was as it should be. His moleskin waistcoat had seen better days and was shamed by the polished silver chain of his pocket watch. A white collarless shirt with the sleeves rolled up revealed strong smooth forearms. A navy-blue paisley scarf was knotted around his neck, a flat cloth cap jammed onto his head at a rakish angle. Beneath it lay dark brown, almost black hair, cut typically severely, short and crisp at the back and sides. He smelt of carbolic, and the chill of the outside emanating from him suggested he'd only recently arrived.

They stood like that for what seemed an age until the young man noted, "Blimey, mate, you're wet through! You sit dahn again. I'll get yer brown ale fer yer, don't you worry yerself."

And so he did. A good-humoured young cockney boy was ready to buy a drink for a comparatively well-to-do, slightly inebriated drowned rat he'd never met before. The women who'd been sitting at the table next to his rose like a flock of startled pigeons to flutter across the road to the Blue Posts. The boys who'd been so friendly to Malcolm pounced on the vacated seats. One of them shouted after the departing girls, "Thanks for warming the seats for us, darlin'! If you wanna come back, yer can always sit on me knee!" The remark was rewarded with the briefest of smiles before the door swung shut behind them.

The other two lit up cigarettes as soon as their backsides hit their chairs, but Malcolm's saviour did not. They didn't try to talk to him, perhaps believing that he might not be up to conversation. They spoke of boxing and football and paused when a cheerful march heralded the sports bulletin on the wireless. They weren't happy that West Ham had been beaten 4-1 by Preston North End that afternoon, but when the barman twiddled the knob to find a continental broadcast so that the dance tunes resumed, their high spirits were revived.

As he wasn't engaged in the conversation, he was free to observe. There were more profanities in it than he was accustomed to, but this was their patch, their world. These were the sort of boys who always drew his eye, even though they would be more likely to mock him or beat him up than give him what he most wanted. They were good-natured enough now, but that could change. This was the East End and to many who'd never set foot there it meant deprivation, violence, and crime. But not that evening in Charlie Brown's, where the young man had bought him a drink.

This one boy, who'd caught him more than just physically, seemed a confident lad, but there was no hint of arrogance about him and he seemed quieter than the others. His cap came off. His dark hair had been parted and slicked with oil earlier in the day but now a few locks at the front occasionally tumbled free and he had to push them back from his forehead. He soon tired of it and jammed his damp cap back onto his lovely head. His mates teased him about some girl they'd have killed for. She was sweet on him, they said, but he protested. He blushed a little, which enchanted Malcolm further.

"Havin' Nora runnin' after yer! You're a lucky bleeder, Alfie, honest to God," said one.

Alfie—so that was his name. Why had it never occurred to him before what a lovely name Alfie was? How privileged they were to have a friend with such a lovely smile, such a lovely manner, such a lovely everything. Malcolm was sure they would not appreciate it as he did.

Eventually, the boys rose to move on. It seemed they'd half-promised to meet some girls in another Limehouse pub. Malcolm's heart plummeted although he'd feared they might not be there for the night. He found enough of a voice to make a protest.

"Hang on, you can't go yet! I owe you a drink!"

They reassured him that he didn't need to return the compliment just because they'd bought him one and told him they were running late already. But one, the smaller, wirier one named Frank, said, "Go on, Alfie, you can stay and have another. You was the one what bought the gentleman a drink, after all. If yer really set on avoiding getting earache from Nora…" He gave a scarcely perceptible wink as he said this.

There was a show of reluctance before young Alfie caved in. "Oh, all right, go on then."

This was the best possible scenario. This young god was to stay with him. Alone. Less than twenty-four hours after his great humiliation in the East India Arms and his desperate vigil on London Bridge, Malcolm Trevelyan found himself sharing a drink in a wonderful East End pub with the most beautiful boy he had ever seen. As unlikely as it seemed, it was as though his suffering was being rewarded and the thrill of it gave him goosebumps.

"It's probably best I don't go with that lot tonight. There's this girl, see? Nora. I ain't interested no more but she won't take no for an answer and it fair wears me out, it does. She goes on at me all the time. So, I'm all yours, mate, for a few hours anyway."

Malcolm smiled weakly. He hadn't much liked talk of a girl, but he wouldn't allow anything to spoil this unexpected tryst.

"You don't say much, do yer?" said Alfie with a bemused smile that unfairly seemed to improve upon perfection.

"I'm sorry. It's been a long day and I'm not used to drinking this much," Malcolm replied honestly.

"S'all right. Was it 'appy drinking or sad drinking?"

Malcolm paused for thought before answering with slow deliberation, "Well, it started off as sad drinking, but it's ended up as happy drinking."

"That's 'cos you've met me, I expect," said Alfie with a twinkle in his eye. He was just being cheeky, rather than arrogant.

"Well, it certainly hasn't hurt," conceded Malcolm, "but mostly it's this place. It's wonderful. Did you know this Charlie Brown fellow?"

"Yes, I did as it goes. He was a decent bloke, old Charlie. He was always good to me. A real character. I was proper upset when he went. He had a good send-off, mind. It was like a royal funeral round here. The streets was lined wiv thahsands of people from here to Bow. They buried him in Bow Cemetery, where me dad is. It was in the papers an' everything. But hey, seeing as you're down here and it ain't your manor, d'you fancy going to a few other local boozers? Charlie's son runs the Blue Posts across the road—there's more weird old junk in there you can look at. I can give you the Cook's tour if you like."

Malcolm had eyes for only one treasure and would have agreed to any destination, even a pub at the Gates of Hell, were that treasure to go with him. The Blue Posts was followed by the White Horse, then by two or three others on Poplar High Street. They always went into the Public, full of smoke and raucous laughter, the floors covered in sawdust to soak up the slops, the piano well used in one of them, with old music-hall staples belted out by almost everyone in the crowded bar, including his young companion. In each of these pubs there was someone or other to greet Alfie in a "hail fellow well met" sort of way. He was a popular chap, and why wouldn't he be?

Malcolm was wide-eyed to start with, like someone visiting a foreign country for the first time. He couldn't get over how loudly many of the patrons were speaking, as though they wanted the whole pub to hear their jokes, but he had to admit that many of the exchanges were genuinely funny.

He loved this unexpected East End evening but, having drunk more than twice as much alcohol as he had ever done in one go before, he was getting drowsy. He would need to make a move towards home soon if he was realistically to get there. Like a child who desperately wanted to stay up late with his new friend, he could barely keep his eyes open.

As though reading his thoughts, Alfie asked, "How the hell are you gonna get home, mate?"

"Oh, I'll just get a cab."

"O' course you will." Alfie chuckled wryly. "Money gets what money wants, dunnit? I'll give one a shout for you, shall I?"

Poplar High Street seemed not to have any taxis, so they walked through the narrow shabby stretch of Pennyfields, past Chinese who observed them without curiosity, back onto the West India Dock Road. Seeing a cab in the distance, Alfie put his fingers to his mouth and his piercing whistle drew it swiftly to the kerb beside them. He looked pleased with himself. Malcolm heard him tell the driver, "Take him up to Highgate station and I'm sure he'll be able to work it out from there, mate."

"Here, he ain't gonna spew 'is guts over me seats, I 'ope?"

"Nah, course he ain't, mate. He'll be fine, I promise." Alfie turned to Malcolm with mock solemnity and pointed his index finger at him in silent warning.

As the cab edged into the still heavy traffic, Malcolm twisted around and looked through the tiny rear window to watch his young companion walk back into Pennyfields. He wondered if he'd ever see him again and sadly concluded that he wouldn't. At least he'd have the memory of how his feet had taken him deep into the East End, to a pub that was a kind of paradise and to a date with a young god in a flat cap.

"Had a good night, sir?" asked the cabbie, in the hope of a decent tip.

"Yes, thank you," said Malcolm wearily.

The rain was still torrential and the windscreen wiper in front of the driver was flapping back and forth, ineffectually for the most part. Its rhythmic whine, coupled with his exhaustion and inebriation, meant he soon nodded off. What felt like seconds later he was being shaken awake by the driver as the taxi idled outside Highgate underground station. He paid the fare and walked unsteadily up the hill towards home.

Chapter Eight

Malcolm's First Hangover

Sunday, 23 October 1932

"OH, GOOD LORD! What on *earth* has happened to you?" asked Grace Trevelyan as the wreckage of her son shuffled in and slumped down at the kitchen table. "Darling, are you ill?"

Malcolm felt as though his eyes were banging on their lids, trying to break out of his head. His mouth was dry, his tongue rasped against the roof of it like sandpaper. He was desperately hungry, but his appetite was punctuated by waves of nausea. The headache gripping him was a wrap-around affair, encompassing his neck and even his shoulders.

"And where have you *been*?" she went on. "I didn't see you at all yesterday. I was looking forward to hearing about your night out on Friday."

"Not now. I'm feeling rather poorly," was all Malcolm could manage.

"Stuff and nonsense. You have a hangover, that's all."

Seeing that she'd get no more sense out of her son, Grace was galvanised into action. After some clattering about, two slices of dry toast and a cup of black tea were placed on the table beside him. She also gave him a tumbler full of water into which she dropped two large white tablets from a glass tube. The water clouded and fizzed for a bit. With the authority of a nurse she said, "Drink that, they're new. Then eat your toast and go back to bed. I'm glad we're not overly religious because I'm sure the Good Lord would take a dim view of you being in this state on a Sunday morning."

Grace did, in fact, like to go to church. Malcolm, who no longer went with her, had teased her by saying that if she concentrated on the parts of the service she enjoyed most, she might just as well go to the park with Marjorie, a box of cakes, and a bottle of sherry, and have a good old sing-song. How she had laughed at the sheer naughtiness of the thought.

Having taken his Alka-Seltzer and eaten his toast, Malcolm obediently went back to bed, where he slept for a few more hours. When he awoke, he felt better although he was still afflicted with an unfamiliar lethargy, accompanied by a pointless but persistent erection. He attended to it swiftly and brutally. As he lay in his pit, he listened to the rain beating against the window and tried to piece together his recollections of the previous afternoon and evening. Many episodes and conversations came to mind, although he couldn't have arranged them in chronological order. Of course, he remembered Alfie, the beautiful youth, but not as clearly as he would have liked.

Cringing, he also recalled making a fool of himself by asking the boy for his telephone number. "We don't have a telephone, mate. No one on my street has a telephone," had been the dry response. To meet someone so lovely and spend hours in his company only to lose him again was harsh, but perhaps it was just as well. What was he likely to get from any prolonged friendship with a handsome docker other than more torment and misery?

The docks were dangerous, and he had been foolish to venture there alone. They'd even walked through Chinatown, and everybody knew what that was like. Alfie could have taken him to an opium den where he might have been robbed and even murdered, dumped through a cunningly concealed trap door into the river. Not that Malcolm believed all the lurid tales told in *Limehouse Nights* and the "legends" of Dr Fu Manchu, but there might be some truth behind the fiction—and fate should not have been tempted.

His mother had returned from church, and he could hear the clink of crockery as she prepared their Sunday lunch. He smelled the roasting beef and licked his lips. Her roast potatoes would make any day better. The telephone rang and she answered. Any calls were always for her. She had friends, he didn't.

After a few moments she called up the stairs: "Malcolm! Telephone!"

"Who is it?"

"Well, I don't know, I'm sure. Why don't you come down and see, dear?"

He descended the stairs gingerly and picked up the ivory receiver from the hallstand. "Hello?"

"Malcolm? It's Alfie. I just wanted to check that you got home all right."

Hearing that deep masculine voice sent the adrenalin coursing through him. "*Alfie!* However did you get my number?"

He heard a chuckle at the end of the line. "You gave me your card, you fathead. I ain't surprised you don't remember though, the state you was in. It is all right me telephoning now, is it?"

"Yes, of course it is. I was just surprised, that's all."

"Was that your mum?"

"Yes, it was. Look…I really enjoyed last night."

"I know, it was a lark, wunnit?"

"Where are you calling from?" Malcolm put his hand to his head. What on earth did it matter where he was calling from?

"Telephone box outside the East India Dock gates. That's why it's so bloomin' noisy here."

There was a pause as they struggled to find anything to say. Malcolm toyed with the braided cord, desperately searching for some words, something that would bring them a little bit closer to the intimacy they'd shared the previous evening.

"What are you up to?" was the pathetic best he could manage.

"I've just been swimming. Poplar Barfs. I like to go a couple of times a week if I can."

This put images of the handsome boy unclad into Malcolm's mind, so the question had been worth asking, after all.

Alfie went on, "I've got a ship in this afternoon so I'm off to work now."

"Oh. Marvellous." Scintillating, Malcolm. Scintillating

"Look, I'd better go 'cos I can't hear you very well in all this racket. I ain't really used to telephones to tell you the truth so I ain't got nuffink much to say anyway really. I just wanted to, you know, see you got home all right an' that."

"Well, I did. It was kind of you to check." Oh, God, even to his own ears he sounded like a maiden aunt thanking a child for her birthday flowers. "Will…will I see you again?"

There was the briefest of pauses then, "Sure. If you want to." He sounded as though he didn't mind one way or the other.

"When?" Malcolm didn't want to sound desperate, but frankly he was. Despite concluding only minutes ago that further contact with this young man would be folly, put to the test he knew it was what he wanted, more than anything and no matter what.

"I dunno. Friday night? Me, George, and Frank'll probably go to the White Horse. Remember that one? Just at the end of Poplar High Street by the Chinese street?" Alfie gave a chuckle. "You can't really miss it—there's a big 'orse on a pole outside."

"Yes, I remember it. You say 'probably'…"

"All right, if you're coming, I'll definitely be there for around seven. Will that do yer?"

"That'll be perfect. Thank you."

"Wotcher thanking me for? It's just a few drinks, innit? Look, I'd best be off because that was the last of me coppers."

"Of course. Goodbye. See you Friday."

He had phoned! *He had phoned!* Malcolm was elated. He couldn't conceal it because the smile on his face wasn't to be suppressed any more than his earlier erection. If anything, the smile would be harder to get rid of.

"Darling, I've finished *Have His Carcase* if you'd like to read it. It's a Lord Peter Wimsey. It's quite involved, but it's awfully good."

"Yes, I'd love to." He looked more delighted at the prospect of

Dorothy L. Sayers than his mother would have expected.

"You've certainly perked up a bit, dear. Who was that?"

"A friend."

"What—someone from work?"

"No, actually."

Grace Trevelyan beamed. "Well, you have suddenly become gregarious, haven't you? I *am* pleased."

"So am I." A weekend of extremes had ended more happily than had ever seemed likely. There were all sorts of worries ahead of him, but for now he felt strong enough to deal with whatever he was to face at work the following morning.

*

SIR LIONEL DIDN'T summon him—and if anyone at the British Atlantic was laughing at his expense, they were doing it in secret.

Donald Sutton's Saturday-morning hangover had been accompanied by the horrific recollection of his own words, which gradually rolled over him, line by line. He understood that, if his drunken remarks were taken in the context he had intended at the time, then he had slandered Trevelyan in front of at least fourteen witnesses. He hadn't alleged that Malcolm was homosexual but had strongly implied it—and on the flimsiest of evidence. Now he was sober, he had no real conviction that it was true. Just because the young bloke didn't bound around like Errol Flynn, it didn't make him a Nancy boy. Donald would have been happy for the earth to swallow him up, and when he recalled his dentures sliding across the sticky floor, he thought it might have looked as though it was trying to.

A few drinks at lunchtime on Sunday had calmed him down, and by the evening, he felt he had nothing to apologise to anyone for. By Monday morning, all his fears had returned, but they would be banished again later using his tried and trusted methods.

Doris had been left to rue the mistakes she had made, and the spectacular collapse of her romantic ambitions. She had drunk just a little too much and tried just a little too hard. For the moment she could think of nothing that could repair the damage and get her back on course with Malcolm, and although she couldn't exactly claim to be broken-hearted, she was genuinely sad. He was a nice man and she had never meant to hurt him. Her pursuit of him was over and she must find herself someone else. As for Donald, she was glad she'd knocked the wretched man's teeth out and regretted not having had the presence of mind to stamp on them until they were beyond repair.

Once Peter Burkett had been told what had happened during his brief absence, he was mortified that the truth behind his invitation had been exposed. He spent the weekend fretting about what lay in store. He feared it could be the sack, which would be the very devil to explain to his father after things had at last begun to go well for him at work. More than that, he had been genuinely glad he had invited Malcolm to join them even if Doris had put him up to it. He'd come to like him. Malcolm respected his views about the things they discussed, and Peter was gratified that someone of high stature in the company took the trouble to listen to him. He was a sensitive boy, and neither his sweetheart nor his family could drag him out of his despondency.

Among the first to arrive at the office to start the week, without any attempt at delaying the inevitable, he took Malcolm's abandoned hat and coat straight to his office. Miss Hassell hadn't arrived yet, so he rapped sharply on the gold-lettered glass and entered when invited.

"May I please have a word, Mr Trevelyan?"

Malcolm gestured towards the chair facing him, and Peter perched on it as though he might need to make a quick escape. Malcolm didn't show signs of being in any particular humour, good or bad. He simply raised his eyebrows expectantly. Peter offered up the items.

"You left these in the pub on Friday night," he said, then he blurted out, "Look, I'm so sorry for what happened."

"Oh? Which part?"

"Any part that hurt your feelings, but particularly my part in it."

"Well, I hope Doris paid up. You did keep your part of the bargain, after all, Peter."

The young man squirmed in his seat at this. "Oh, for the love of Mike! I may be a bit short a lot of the time, but I can usually afford a couple of fourpennys at the flaming pictures! Can I just say that the only reason I'd never asked you to join us in the pub before was I didn't think you'd ever come. What's more, I would have been too frightened to ask. Doris's 'bribe' just gave me another push to do it. Honestly, Malcolm. You've been really good to me. You've saved my bacon on more than one occasion, and you've made me, I hope, reasonably good at my job. I would never do anything to hurt your feelings or injure you in any way. I'm mortified about taking part in Doris's game and I'll bear you no ill will if you sack me because of it. It's what I deserve."

"Steady on! Did you honestly think for a moment I'd have sacked you over this?"

"Yes, I did. I've been worried about it all weekend. But honestly, I'm more worried about you thinking badly of me. Truly I am."

"Put the confounded coat down. You look as though you're trying to sell it to me."

Peter draped it over one end of the desk.

"Look," Malcolm went on, "it was a damned silly thing to do, yes, but nobody died, Peter. I didn't fight hard to keep you here just to get you fired over something as silly as this. And yes, I *have* made you good at your job, so I don't want to start from scratch with some other young nincompoop, do I?"

"But they told me you were really angry! I saw you storm out."

"I was, and I did. It was most embarrassing, and I was disappointed, I suppose. I'd really enjoyed those evenings in the pub with you…all, and suddenly it seemed as though my presence had just been tolerated for Doris's benefit."

"That's not true. Doris is genuinely fond of you, I think, but I was really glad of your company. So were most of the others—everyone but bloody Donald and his preposterous insinuations. Quite frankly, he's the one who should have cleared off, not you."

"What—and leave me at the mercy of Doris?"

For the first time, Peter smiled sheepishly. "Well, there is that. But look here, Doris is all right. She's a nice girl once you get to know her. You could do worse."

"I'm sure," said Malcolm carelessly. "Look, Peter, I'm genuinely sorry if you've lost any sleep over it all. I wasn't happy, but it's all done with as far as I'm concerned. Let's never discuss it again, all right?"

"Oh, thank you for being such a good sport. I hope you'll still come out with us."

Malcolm shook his head emphatically. "I think not. Maybe on a special occasion, but not back into the old routine, I'm afraid. Once bitten and all that."

"I understand. Would you consider having a drink with just me on occasion?"

"Yes. I'll consider it. Now do run along or I *will* sack you."

Part Three

Until the Real Thing Comes Along

Chapter Nine

Anyone Would Love To

Friday, 28 October 1932

AFTER WORK, MALCOLM pushed through the City crowds to Aldgate and caught a 67 tram along Commercial Road. It was chilly, but under the flaming autumn sunset, the area didn't appear as wretched as it had done the weekend before. The offices, factories, and shops remained shabby, but the colourful sky and his improved state of mind made it all look better.

The tram slowed and groaned to a halt outside the Star of the East pub. He hopped off and crossed the road towards the West India Docks. Anxious not to be late, he had arrived ridiculously early. If he walked directly around to the White Horse, he would have nearly an hour to wait. He would have felt self-conscious sitting alone in an unfamiliar East End pub, particularly dressed for work, and he'd run the risk of being half cut by the time Alfie and his friends arrived. He decided he'd pop into Charlie Brown's to see whether it would live up to his fond memory of it. No one could look out of place in there, whoever they were or whatever they were wearing.

At the door, he stood aside to allow a group of tourists to file out onto the pavement behind their guide, whose words were lost to the rumble of a goods train on the viaduct. Many East End tours included a half pint of beer at Charlie Brown's before a stroll through Chinatown to gawp at the long-suffering Chinese, while regaling the customers with lurid fictions. Even Thomas Cook was running tours now, which lent the myths an air of legitimacy they scarcely merited. He'd read that, at night, "bright young things" in dinner suits or more outlandish garb flocked to the area seeking opiates and excitement, and treating the locals as though they were bit-part players in their dramas.

There weren't many Chinese in Limehouse, but the papers revelled in sensations about opium and abduction—the so-called "Yellow Peril". Inspired by these scandalous stories, Scotland Yard had conducted raids around the area, uncovering about as much criminal activity as they would have done in any dockland neighbourhood, and little of it involving the handful of Anglo-Chinese. The more responsible newspapers explained that this so-called "Chinatown" was no sinister warren of opium dens run by pigtailed Tong warriors. Still the tourists came, and as each party left Charlie Brown's, the locals rolled their eyes at their gullibility.

This time, Malcolm wandered into a different room from the one he had enjoyed on his earlier visit and waited his turn at the bar. He'd have an hour to drink a pint before the short walk to the White Horse. While he waited, he listened in to a conversation going on close by.

The barman had just served about ten halves to another tourist group and a detective sergeant from Limehouse police station over the road was being served.

"As a Chinaman, Danny, don't you get a bit narked about these bleedin' sightseers gawping at yer all the time?" the barman asked.

"Nah, Wally, it don't bother me. Me mate Jimmy Sung's got a shop on the Causeway. He's making a fortune selling 'em 'authentic' Oriental knick-knacks wot he gets from a factory in Dagenham. He can't stop 'em, so he may as well make money out of 'em, he reckons."

"Exotic but cheap, eh? I'll have to remember that when the missus's birthday comes round next."

"Only if you wants her to leave you, Wally mate. It's absolute tat! Anyways, you shouldn't grumble. These tourists must bring a lot of money into this place."

"Not as much as you'd think. We get two or three groups a night. They get herded in, have an 'arf while they look round the treasures before being shooed out again. I daresay many a punter is put off by them being here and goes elsewhere." Wally wiped a splash of beer off the bar. "You wanna get more of your lot in 'ere."

"My lot? Coppers, you mean?"

"Oh, my Gawd no! I mean Chinamen. You must have some influence."

"Sorry, mate, but you're asking the wrong bloke. It's funny, 'cos I think that's what the Force thought when they posted me to Limehouse. I must be a terrible disappointment to 'em. I was born and brought up in Bethnal Green. Me dad was Chinese, but I never met him. I think me mum only met him the once. As far as I'm concerned, the 'Mysterious East' is Clacton, 'cos I ain't never been there."

"Yes, well, don't you trouble to get more coppers in 'ere, Danny boy. Enough of the buggers come over anyway. They come in the one door and half our custom goes out the other. If yer really want to do us a favour, get 'em to stick to the Oporto. Tell 'em there ain't no sense in them crossing a busy road to get a drink." Wally turned to Malcolm. "What can I get yer, sir?"

He ambled around, pint in hand, taking a closer look at the treasures from all over the world. It was like the British Museum with beer. The pub had been extended under the railway arches, so it was much bigger than it looked from the outside. There was even a dance floor with a low curved brick ceiling. He thought the dancers must get awfully hot in there. As he wandered back to the more cluttered rooms, the curiosities distracted Malcolm from the cocktail of anticipation and apprehension being shaken vigorously inside him.

While excited at the prospect of seeing Alfie again, he was afraid that this time it might not go as well. He had been drunk when he first met the young dockers, so supposing he didn't recognise them, or mistook one of the others for Alfie? He remembered thinking him the most handsome lad he'd ever seen, but he couldn't picture his features clearly. When Malcolm had been exposed to a smiling young face, to consideration, to kindness and companionship—perhaps drink, fatigue, and a day of solitude had made Alfie look perfect.

He'd barely slept during the week as his mind had played out different scenarios. He was afraid of being stood up of course, but most of all he feared Alfie's indifference. What if all this anxious anticipation came to nothing but a solitary drink? Malcolm decided he would return to Charlie Brown's if that happened, have a few more drinks and see what else developed. He was determined not to slink away home to lick his wounds. Not this time.

At five to seven, almost reluctant to tear himself from the warm embrace of Charlie Brown's, he walked along Pennyfields past children playing noisy games in the street. Intriguing exotic aromas wafted out of Doe Foon's restaurant and Quong Yuen Sing the butcher's shop. Drawing closer to the High Street, he spotted the unmistakable effigy of a horse on a column bearing the words *Truman, Hanbury, Buxton*. No wonder Alfie had been confident that he couldn't miss it.

By now, Malcolm was nervous to the point of agitation, but he had no time to work himself up any further because Alfie and he almost collided at the pub doorway. Before a word was exchanged, Malcolm congratulated himself for braving the ordeal. In the golden light of the lantern over the door, this boy was breathtaking. Alfie took his arm and steered him away from the Saloon Bar entrance, pulling him into the Public instead.

"We ain't spending a penny a pint more to slop our beer over a carpet," he said with a smile that drove every thought out of Malcolm's head and turned him into a blithering idiot.

Alfie got the first one in, and as he chatted amiably with the landlord, standing at his elbow, Malcolm was able to appraise the young docker. If anything, the boy was even more beautiful on second sight. It wasn't only the way he looked, it was the assured, masculine way in which he moved and the rich sound of his surprisingly deep voice. Scrubbed clean, glowing with health, he wore a smart dark-blue serge three-piece suit under a grey mackintosh, his cap worn to one side as before. His clothes were of a surprising quality considering his humble background. He wouldn't have looked out of place in the Saloon Bar.

They carried their pints to a rough table with a wooden bench seat which stood vacant in a corner. Malcolm asked where George and Frank were.

"I told 'em eight. I thought everyone at once might be a bit much for yer, with you not knowing us that well. Gives us a chance to chat for a bit, dunnit? Is that all right with you?"

Obviously, it was. He was touched that his new friend had been so considerate.

"You look very smart, Alfie. Are you going on somewhere afterwards?"

"Nah, mate, not really. I always make an effort when I'm out of an evening—you never know who you're going to bump into, do yer? I got to look nice in case the girl of me dreams pops in, ain't I?"

"Of course." He felt a pang of disappointment, even though he hadn't entertained the notion that a lad as normal-looking as this one might share his inclinations.

"As for the whistle, I got some of me cousin's clobber when he died. Me family couldn't of afforded nuffink like this, that's for sure."

"Oh, I'm sorry. How old was your cousin?"

"Nineteen. He was me Uncle Tommy's son. Tom's head of the gang—of stevedores, that is, not an Al Capone sort of gang, don't worry. So, he has a bob or two, see? Edward weren't gonna follow the family business anyway, he was brainy. He was gonna be a lawyer or sumfink and everyone was dead proud of him, but then he went and died just like that. Pneumonia."

"That's a great pity. Were you close?"

"I can't say we was, no. Well, I was a few years younger than him, so our paths didn't cross all that much. But when I did see him, at family dos an' that, I liked him. He was a quiet sort of bloke. Even though I was only a kid he'd talk to me proper, you know. As if what I thought mattered." He glanced down at his jacket with approval. "Good job I'm the same size as he was, innit? Me sister said she'd feel funny wearing her dead cousin's clothes, but I like it. It's gonna make me sound nuts but I feel that the suits help me, that they're always on my side." Alfie smiled a rare kind of smile. "Don't you go telling no one any of this, mind. They'll be sending me down the funny farm like me Great-Uncle Bernard."

Malcolm decided not to pursue the fate of Great-Uncle Bernard. "It's good of you to let me join you and your friends like this."

"Nah, it ain't good of me at all. It's good of you to come all this way. I ain't really sure why yer doing it though."

Malcolm was prepared for that question. He knew he'd need a story and, in a way, it was the truth. "It's going to make me sound a rather sad case, but I don't really have any friends of my own, you see? My life has been all about work so far, so I have colleagues instead of friends. For a moment, I made the mistake of confusing the two things and…well, you saw the results for yourself last weekend."

"Well, you was 'appy enough when we bumped into yer."

Malcolm smiled. "Yes, I suppose I was. I have Charlie Brown to thank for that."

"You should have one over the eight more often, mate. It suits yer."

Malcolm blushed. It was not the sort of comment he would have expected from another man, let alone this one.

"And so does that." Alfie laughed gently at his blushes, but there was no mockery in it. In fact, there was just the hint of a reciprocal blush.

Malcolm struggled to suppress his disappointment when the towering figure of George arrived with his brother Sid in tow, and Frank not far behind them. The other boys were as smartly dressed as Alfie, without wearing anything of matching quality. At least in his own suit, Malcolm didn't look as conspicuous as he'd feared.

The idea that he could have mistaken any of the others for Alfie was ridiculous. In childhood, George must have eaten half of his brother's meals because he was a good few inches taller and far more powerfully built. Even his nose and mouth were bigger than Sid's although they shared the same dark, slicked-back haircuts. Sid's features were more refined, which made him look intelligent, but he had a distracted air about him. Frank was fair and his wavy hair was parted almost, but not quite at the centre. His face was in its own way remarkable, for when he smiled and the warmth reached his pale-blue eyes he could look an attractive youth, but in Malcolm's limited acquaintance with him, he often sported a scowl that made him look like an angry weasel.

Sometimes the evening became a bit louder than he'd have liked, but he was happy to soak it up and remain as unobtrusive as possible. It gave him the chance to study Alfie and to savour it. The sharply cut dark hair…surely anyone would love to run their fingers over the crispness at the nape of his neck. The sensuously shaped lips that surely anyone, anyone at all, would love to kiss whether they cared to admit it or not. The white teeth, all present and correct unlike many of his peers. The shining eyes, an uncommon shade of dark blue with whites that were just that, white, with no dilated vessels. The way he moved, unthinkingly graceful, an animal secure in its own habitat.

Malcolm appreciated it would be bad form to monopolise him all night. He tried to talk to the others, however inept a conversationalist he felt in this company of younger men of a background outside his experience.

"He's a good-looking boy, our Alfie, ain't 'e?" said Frank, catching his eye. "I'm sure you'll 'ave noticed."

"I suppose he is, yes."

"There ain't no suppose about it, mate. All the gels is after him, I can tell you that for nuffink." Something about Frank made Malcolm feel he was on to him, could see the worst of what lay inside him.

Sid came to the rescue by asking, "How d'you know Alfie then?" and when their meeting a week earlier had been explained, "I did wonder how you fitted in. You're a bit posh for us—no offence. Why was you slumming it in the East End in the first place?"

Malcolm gave them the gist of the East India Arms affair, omitting the "not the marrying kind" aspect. When Frank heard there was a woman at the bottom of it, all his apparent wariness evaporated and for the moment he became an ally.

"I can't stand scheming women like that," he railed. "Someone ought to give her a bloody good hiding, I reckon."

"Oh, shush!" said Alfie, joining the conversation once more. "If there was any gel in here mug enough to think about taking you on, she'll 'ave changed her mind hearing that, won't she?"

"I've got plenty of women!" protested Frank, puffing out his chest.

"Really? Well, give me the keys so's I can go and let 'em out then."

Frank punched Alfie's shoulder. "Fucking pretty boy!"

The argument, if you could even call it that, petered out and George steered the conversation towards politics. Earlier that week in Trafalgar Square, some hunger marchers had clashed with Mosley's Blackshirts and George's sympathies did not lie with the fascists. The boys were all in accord, which was awkward for Malcolm. He had no time for the British Union of Fascists who were nothing but uniformed thugs, but he was also wary of the hunger marchers, because they were surely Communists, or at least the *Daily Telegraph*'s correspondents seemed to think so.

"I had a good mind to go up West and join 'em," said George, striking the palm of one hand with the fist of the other. "Them Fascists need a dose of their own medicine. It's the only thing they understand."

"Don't change nuffink though, does it, George?" said Frank. "The Blackshirts are still putting Jews' windows through, and the hunger marchers are still hungry." He turned to Alfie. "Have Mr and Mrs Grodzinsky had any bovver, Alf?"

"If they 'ave they ain't told me. I do worry about them though. They're a nice old couple who are never anythink but kind to people and they shouldn't 'ave to worry about them bastards. It ain't right." Realising that Malcolm had no idea who the Grodzinskys were, Alfie explained, "Mr and Mrs G run a newsagent just off the High Street. They sort of took me under their wing when I was a nipper. They've been good to me."

"There's trouble all over," Sid said gloomily. "There was a bit of a ruck up by the Seamen's Rest over Jeremiah Street last week."

"Blackshirts again?" scowled George.

"Nah, unemployed geezers complaining about the Means Test. Prince George was there to open a new wing or summink. They had a fight with the coppers and three of 'em was arrested."

"At least the poor blighters might get a decent meal down the nick," George said, "What kind of country do we live in, eh? There's people with no work having to do a test to show they've got nuffink before they get any help at all. And Gawd knows that ain't much. Fuckin' tokens just to make sure that everyone knows to look down on 'em. And they're talking about sending unemployed blokes to work camps now! I don't like the sounds o' that. It's degrading, innit? I wasn't a fan of the workhouses but this new system seems no better to me. It's no wonder the sight of Prince bloody George poncing around opening things rubbed 'em up the wrong way. There's people starving, for Gawd's sake!"

"People like 'em though, don't they. A lot of people round here just love the King and the Royal family," Frank put in.

"Well, I don't. The sooner we 'ave a revolution in this country the better. It's coming too, you mark my words."

"You reckon George Lansbury's gonna start a revolution?" Sid's scepticism was written all over his face.

"He's not been in charge of the Labour Party for a week, give 'im a chance, Sid," laughed Alfie. He turned to Malcolm and said, "I got me middle name from him, you know."

"What—George?"

Alfie chuckled. "Nah. Lansbury for me sins. Alfred Lansbury Atwood! Would you bleedin' credit it?"

Frank poked Malcolm's shoulder sharply. "Yer honoured. He don't normally let on to anyone about that little secret."

"Why Lansbury?" Malcolm asked.

Alfie sighed. It was obviously a question he'd been asked many times before. "Me mum was a bit of a suffragette and she saw George speak a few times." He shoved his mate's shoulder. "George Lansbury that is, not this idiot. A bit before I was born, he was sent to prison for speaking out for the suffragettes. He was accused of 'inciting violence' or some such nonsense in a speech at the Albert Hall, because he said it was all right for 'em to break a few windows."

George chipped in bitterly, "There weren't no trial, mind. No charge and no trial, but they put him away for months because he refused to guarantee his future conduct." He slammed his fist down on the table, slopping a little of everyone's pint. "That's yer so-called British justice for yer, that is!"

Malcolm never thought he'd be relieved when a conversation turned to football, but he was, because he didn't feel these young East End lads were likely to vote Conservative. For all there were three of them, his opinion counted for more because they weren't even old enough to vote yet. Perhaps they'd see things differently after they'd turned twenty-one. He couldn't abide snobbery and class distinction, but he assumed that he was a Tory and had voted for them in 1929, then for the National Government in 1931. He also considered himself a loyal subject of the King. Now here he was in a Red area, and he was uncomfortable. He dreaded anyone, particularly George, asking him for his views.

Fortunately, this time Frank unwittingly rescued him by insisting that they must all go to a football match the following afternoon.

"I tell you what, we gotta beat Burnley tomorrow," he said, shaking his head gravely. "Things are getting really bad for the Irons now."

"Should be all right." George shrugged. "We've picked up at home, we ain't lost since Bradford City done us back in August, have we?"

"Nah, but we've lost every single away game," Alfie put in. "Every single one. We can't carry on like that and expect to stay up."

"Blimey, six-nil at fuckin' Lincoln, George. You gotta admit that's embarrassing," said Sid with a pained expression. "Battered at Preston an' all. Syd needs to sort it out."

"We'll stay up, boys, I'm tellin' yer," insisted George, exuding confidence. "Syd King always comes up for us in the end. He's West Ham through and through. It's only October and there's a long way to go."

"I ain't disputing that," said Frank, "but we're in a relegation battle again and like you said, it's only bleedin' October! Maybe Syd has had his day."

"Garn! Get away wiv yer! We've always been able to rely on old Syd."

As the debate wore on, Alfie darted Malcolm the odd glance and at one point got the chance to ask, "Are you all right?"

"I'm fine, honestly. I'm learning a lot. West Ham football team isn't quite living up to expectations, I gather."

Alfie laughed darkly. "Nah, they're living down to expectations."

"Who's Syd King?"

"He's the manager. He's been the manager of West Ham since before I was born. I don't suppose you 'ave a team, do you, Malcolm?"

"Not really. The Arsenal are my local club but I don't take much of an interest. I've never even been to a match."

"Blimey. If you turn your nose up at the Arsenal there's no point me offering to take you round West Ham, is there?"

"I didn't turn my nose up exactly. My father was more of a rugger man and…well, we weren't terribly close."

Alfie nodded sympathetically.

"Were you going to?" Malcolm said. "Ask me to go to a football match, I mean."

"Maybe. I was thinkin' about it. I mean, if you wanna be one of the lads I 'ave to take you up the Boleyn, don't I? That's the ground, in case you was wondering."

Alfie smiled his lovely smile as he said this, and he had a twinkle in his eye. Malcolm blushed again, because he realised there was a double entendre in there somewhere, even though he didn't understand it.

And so a middle-class, boarding-school-educated professional from Highgate sat in the Public Bar of a pub on Poplar High Street with four young dockers discussing the fortunes of West Ham United. He was enjoying every moment of it. The way these young men got on touched him for he had never experienced anything like their easy familiarity. Much of their conversation consisted of boasts, arguments, threats, and the issuing of unsolicited advice to each other, but he noticed how often they touched. A friendly shove, an arm around the shoulder, pulling one another's caps down over the eyes—it was all laddish stuff, and they all understood what it did and didn't mean. Apart from the odd handshake at work and exchanging dry kisses on the cheek with his mother and aunt, Malcolm touched no one and no one touched Malcolm. These four had grown up together and knew one another inside out. They probably loved one another but would never have said as much. He'd had school chums, acquaintances, and colleagues, but never what he'd call real friends, never anything approaching this comfortable intimacy. He felt he'd been allowed a glimpse of something special, something that didn't occur in his privileged middle-class world. It made him sad. As the alcohol took hold of him, he had to stop himself from getting too sentimental about them.

Suddenly, the temperature dropped as the door was flung open and an explosion of girls waltzed in, clucking like startled hens and chattering nineteen to the dozen. They wore bright floral print dresses, with vivid shades of lipstick and perfume that was not of the best quality. They were Lily, Mabel, Phyllis, and Nora and they were half expected. Nora pointedly squeezed in next to Alfie and was relentlessly vile to him for ten minutes. He was clumsy, thoughtless, and stupid. He thought he was cock of the walk, but he wasn't worth the dirt under her shoes. Why was he talking about football when nobody else was interested? These may not have been her actual words, but it was the gist of what she was saying. She became a more physical nuisance by snatching his cap off his head because he was "in the presence of ladies" and didn't "have the manners he was born with". All the boys were wearing their caps; it wasn't done to take them off in a pub, "ladies" or no, not if you wanted to leave with the one you came in with.

No wonder Alfie'd stayed in the pub with him last week instead of going to meet *this* girl, Malcolm thought. Yet his young friend remained placid. After she began to appreciate that her tactics were getting her nowhere, for tactics they surely were, Nora calmed down a bit. She said that "being as she was such a nice person," she'd let him take her along to Alexander's later for a dance.

"I can't tonight, Nora—I'm with me mate."

As Alfie nodded in his direction, Nora turned and looked at Malcolm properly for the first time. It was as though someone had pointed out some dog mess.

"Who's he? I ain't never seen him before."

"Nora, this is Malcolm."

"Pleased to meet you, I'm sure," she said, then pointedly turned her back on him and faced Alfie again. "Ain't he got a gel he can dance with?" She glanced back at him. "No, I don't expect he has. He looks a bit of a—"

"Fuck off, Nora!" Alfie snarled.

It was the nastiest moment of the night, and Malcolm feared that his face was betraying him. Frank was his unlikely saviour again.

"Yes, fuck off, Nora! You think any bloke what don't fall at yer feet must be a pansy, dontcha? You may have a pretty face, gel, but it's ruined by the ugly gob on yer!"

"Alfie, are you gonna let him talk to me like that?" she squealed.

"Don't light the blue touch paper if you don't want the bleedin' firework to go off, Nora," snapped George.

Moments later, the altercation seemed forgotten, but Malcolm and Nora exchanged resentful glances like two dogs eyeing the same bone.

*

MALCOLM HAD NEVER been to a dance hall, and he was curious, but he wouldn't have suggested it after Alfie had been so adamant that they wouldn't go. But despite not wanting to oblige Nora, he saw Malcolm was curious and said, "Come on, then. We can go up Alexander's for a bit, seeing as how you ain't been to one before."

Alexander's was no Kit Kat Club. Sited on the East India Dock Road, it had once been a not terribly glamorous music hall before being cheaply converted. They had tried to achieve an Art Deco, Odeon-style effect, but they had been hampered by the once grand Edwardian ornamentation. The orchestra pit had been removed and a twelve-piece dance band sat behind two rows of monogrammed music stands facing the audience, their polished brass instruments flashing under the lights. An easel beside them bore cards indicating whether the next number was to be a foxtrot, a quickstep, or a waltz. There were tables around the edge of the room, but the space was mostly given over to a dance floor where an endless whirl of couples wheeled around, enjoying one of the few opportunities men and women had to touch in public in a respectable way. It was a sea of flannel suits, with the women supplying all the colour.

Many of the tunes were familiar to Malcolm, because his mother had taken to listening to dance music on the wireless. Initially she had disapproved of jazz and "crooning", but when the BBC had grudgingly allowed short dance music programmes to be broadcast, she'd soon come round. He paid scant attention to it when she did, because all the words seemed trite. Where they made any sense, they were all about love and longing; where they didn't, they were nonsense. The magic of the previous Saturday in Charlie Brown's had made him re-evaluate some of them, especially "Mad About the Boy". Noel Coward had captured his feelings about Alfie well. It remained to be seen whether there was anything of "the cad about the boy".

There were two bars at the side of what had once been an auditorium, one for alcohol and a smaller one for teas and coffees. They found seats close to the larger bar, with Alfie and Nora sitting as far apart from each other as they could manage. Despite the music, Malcolm found it easy to hear all the conversations around him whether he wanted to or not.

George waited until Nora went up to the bar to look for someone to buy her a drink before joining her.

"You never learn, do you, gel?" Malcolm heard George tell her.

"I dunno what you mean, George Mason," she sniffed.

"Oh, yes, you do. Why you think that being a pain in the backside's gonna get you Alfie, I'll never know."

"Well, if you've got a better idea…"

"I 'ave, as it goes. Look for someone else. Get yourself a library card—run away and join a bleedin' circus. I don't care what you do, gel, but leave Alfie alone. He ain't interested. Not in you."

Nora's voice quivered with suppressed emotion as she replied, "You don't know that. You don't know the 'arf of it!"

"Yes, Nora, I do. I'm his best mate. I know you been after him for years. I know there's been a bit of how's-yer-father in the past, but it's done with. 'Orrible as you are to him, he's usually as nice as pie with you, but today, you made him swear at yer. What does he 'ave to do for you to get the message, eh?"

Without waiting for an answer, George left her standing there biting her lip and headed off to the Gents. Lily took his place at the bar.

"'Ere Nora, what you 'aving? I'll get this one."

"I'll take a port and lemon, ta," she said, before adding with a sob, "Oh, Lil, what am I gonna do?"

"I dunno, Nora, honest I don't."

"I love him so much. It's been Alfie for me, ever since I first set eyes on him. He's been in my thoughts and even in my dreams so much that it's like I know him."

"But you don't, darlin'. You don't know him. And I can't think of one thing he's ever said or done to encourage you."

Nora looked askance at her. "What? Apart from what he did with me up Mudchute, you mean?"

"You didn't give 'im much choice, Nora, did you?"

"He's been very kind to me at times."

"Yes, he has. He's a nice boy. He's got a nice way with him. He's like that with everyone, but tonight you provoked him enough for him to tell you where to get off in public. Not only will you never get to be with him, you're gonna have him hating yer, darlin'. You don't want that, surely?"

Nora's temper flared up again. "Normally us girls stick together, don't we, Lil? But not when it comes to Alfie, oh no! Everybody loves bleedin' Alfie and no one will have a word said against him."

"Darlin', he causes bleedin' havoc, I'm not saying he don't. But you must see that it ain't his fault. Looking as he does, he'd do well if he *was* a bastard, but seeing as he ain't… Well—havoc like I said. You've just got to find someone else, Nora. Yer not short of admirers yerself, gel."

Back at the table, Frank grumbled, "We was having a good night until the skirts turned up. Bloody women! They're more trouble than they're worth."

"It was only Nora, Frank, the others didn't do nuffink wrong," said Sid.

"What must Malcolm think of us, eh? I bet it ain't like this up Highgate."

"I really wouldn't know," said Malcolm truthfully.

The boys danced with the girls. Sid gallantly took Nora on to the floor, leaving Alfie and Malcolm alone.

"I expect you're used to a bit grander than this dive," remarked Alfie.

"I'm not used to anywhere at all other than my home, my office, the East India Arms, and a handful of teashops and grills favoured by my mother. This is quite an adventure for me. Honestly."

Alfie smiled but said nothing. He seemed distracted. He excused himself but promised it was just for one dance with Lily. Malcolm nursed his drink, let the brass and clarinets wash over him, and watched the dancers. Happy, competent couples span around the hall, but others shuffled around like it was a duty. Alfie was good at it, not missing a step even though he and Lily were deep in conversation. Having dismissed dance bands as hotel restaurant fripperies enjoyed by vacuous rich people, Malcolm found himself having to think again. This East End crowd had worked long and hard to earn enough for their night out and took their enjoyment seriously.

The band played American music with a British accent. Three of the musicians were black, he noticed, or was it more that he noticed how no one seemed to care. There were plenty of non-white faces in the East End, so why would they care? He had never given any thought to whether he was prejudiced. He hoped not. Alexander's, like Charlie Brown's, seemed to have a much healthier mix of people in it than the uptight little places he went to with his mother.

He was beginning to appreciate the power of the music. Some of the melodies were sumptuous and began to tug at his heartstrings. The rising sound of clarinets carried a swell of emotion and when the trumpets periodically overwhelmed the other instruments as if escaping from captivity, it was…sexy. Watching Alfie dance was sexy too. He would never be able to listen to this kind of music again without thinking of this wonderful boy.

Alfie was as good as his word, and when he came back, he said, "I just wanted to check with Lil that Nora's okay."

"And is she?"

"Oh, I'm sure she will be. I think she understands she pushed me too far tonight. She ain't a bad gel, you know. It ain't her fault that she fancies me—you feel what you feel, dontcha? But the same applies to me, and it ain't my fault that I *don't* fancy her. Every time we meet nowadays, she carries on, but tonight…" He sighed ruefully. "Anyway, I'm sorry you 'ad to put up with it, that's all. You'll probably think twice about coming out with us again, eh?"

"Not at all. I've had a jolly good time. Really, I have. Am I invited again?"

"Of course. If you can put up with tonight, you can put up with anything, mate. I'm glad you want to come again." That smile spread across his face. "So, d'you fancy going to a match wiv us or not?"

"Well, as they say, I'll try anything once. I can't tomorrow though."

"In a few weeks maybe. That gives you a bit of notice, dunnit?"

*

HE CAUGHT A bus back into central London, not wanting to seem too moneyed in front of his new friends. It was full of people who'd had a night out and the bus rocked from side to side as some stepped off and more clambered on. No doubt some had enjoyed a good time while others hadn't, but apart from the odd banal conversation most of the passengers were sleepy, swaying and nodding with the movement of the bus.

Malcolm had a double seat to himself and was glad to be alone with his thoughts. After that night, he would remember every detail of Alfie's face forever, even if they were never to meet again. Alfie may have looked dazzling, but he also seemed a genuinely nice person, which made him even more attractive. They were to meet for a football match of all things. He didn't expect that he would care about the match, but he would be with Alfie and that was all he wanted from life at that moment…whether it was a good thing or a step down the road to disaster.

Chapter Ten

Tribal

ALFIE STUCK TO his promise and although Malcolm was in two minds about it, he told his astonished mother he would be going to the match. Once she'd got over her surprise, she fussed.

"Shall I make up a small picnic for you and your friend?"

"No! You don't take a blasted picnic to a football match!"

"Well, how do you know, dear? You've never been to one. I daresay the food on offer won't be very nice. Your friend might appreciate a few nice sandwiches and perhaps a slice of cake."

"No picnic, Mum. No sandwiches and no cake."

"Well, please yourself, of course, dear. But make sure you wrap up warm. It must get awfully chilly standing out in the open like that, and I do hope you don't get hit by the ball."

For Malcolm, the first thrill of the invitation had worn off and he felt unworthy of the friendship. What was he playing at? What sense was there in going to a football match just to be close to a lad he could never have? He'd torment himself and subject Alfie to indecent scrutiny, imagining the body under the clothes. It was a disgraceful way to behave towards a boy who for some reason found something in him to like and who offered a simple, uncomplicated friendship. But here he was, waiting outside Upton Park station for "the lads" as though he was a normal man rather than a sneak-thief ready to steal as much of one of them as he could.

Alfie had tried to help Malcolm understand that there was more to a league football match than twenty-two men kicking a leather ball around in the mud for ninety minutes. But listening to Alfie and his friends, you'd think they hated rather than supported the Hammers. They reckoned all the players were rubbish either because they were past it or because they'd never been any good in the first place. When Malcolm put this to him, Alfie chuckled grimly. "We *do* hate 'em in a way. Why wouldn't we? No other club causes us as much pain as they do, that's for sure. We love 'em too, mind."

After West Ham had lost 3-0 to Bradford Park Avenue on Bonfire Night a couple of weeks before, their long-serving manager Syd King had been relieved of his duties. Ever loyal, George took pains to point out, "He's been moved sideways, not sacked. He's too big a part of the club for that. Syd's been manager for all of our lives and he played for the club for years before that, right back to when we was the Ironworks. He's Mr West Ham United, Syd is."

Frank was less sympathetic. "Well, I think it's a bloomin' good job he's gone. I heard that he turned up pissed at a board meeting! I reckon old

Syd has gone clean round the bend."

Alfie explained that things were looking up at last. Under the new manager, Charlie Paynter, they'd beaten Grimsby 5-2 and drawn at Stoke City, who were up near the top of the table. Today it was Charlton Athletic, who had only managed to scrape a point more, so if West Ham were to win, they would pass the indignity of lying bottom of the table to their visitors.

Alfie was the first of the boys to meet him. When they were all gathered, they walked down Green Street, and Malcolm was surprised at his growing sense of anticipation. It was far removed from any other experience he'd had in his life—all these people walking to the same place, all hoping for the same thing, a West Ham victory. They passed Green Street House, or "the Boleyn Castle" as it was known, a crenelated folly from a time before these streets were built. It now served as a social club for West Ham fans. Scarves and rosettes of claret and blue were being sold by hawkers shouting, "*Get* yer colours! *Scarves, rosettes!* *Get* yer West Ham colours!"

The crowd was mostly men, many of whom were already sporting theirs, and here and there were a few wearing the red and white of Charlton Athletic, the opposition from over the river. Wooden rattles of the sort used during the war to warn the troops of gas, but painted claret and blue, were on sale. Nearer the ground were the official programme sellers. The boys didn't usually bother with them, but Alfie, eager to ensure that Malcolm enjoyed his first ever match, fished a warm penny from his trouser pocket and bought one for him to keep as a souvenir.

They walked among the modest throng down to the end of Green Street and into the Boleyn Tavern. Furnished with beer, the boys were brimming with optimism. After all, they had a new man at the helm, and they hadn't lost under him yet. It was only two games, but it was a start. Today's match was their sixteenth game of the season and there would be twenty-four more so there was time for Charlie Paynter to sort it out, but they had to win today to extend the run and get off the bottom of the table.

They entered the ground from Priory Road into a low covered stand with wooden terracing. Alfie told him it was the East Stand, nicknamed "the chicken run", but he wasn't able to explain why. As Alfie had predicted, there was plenty of space. They hung back in the middle of the stand, away from the cluster of people drawn to the whitewashed wall around the perimeter of the green and brown rectangle of the pitch.

Alfie said, "Most of the idiots wiv rattles goes down there. You don't wanna be listening to that racket. You don't wanna clout on the earhole wiv one neither."

He reckoned the ground would hold about 45,000 people but it was still no more than half full with fifteen minutes or so to go before kick-off.

A brass band from Beckton Gasworks entertained the swelling crowd. Malcolm didn't know most of the tunes although he did recognise "Lady of Spain" and "I'm Forever Blowing Bubbles". As the latter song was played, he found himself being buffeted by his companions as they, and all the fans around them, began to sway from side to side in unison as they sang along. He had no choice but to move with them, and he felt a little foolish, until the sensation of having Alfie's body pressed up against his overcame it. He didn't care about the match; this alone was enough to make the afternoon a great success. Alfie's body was fit and hard; he was a docker and easily strong enough to hurt Malcolm if he was minded to. It was hard to imagine because he seemed such a gentle boy, but it gave Malcolm a small thrill to think he had the physique to do it. As it was, Alfie seemed to be using his greater strength to shield Malcolm, as though he were made of bone china.

A much larger stand in two tiers stood opposite them. He correctly supposed that it backed on to Green Street and housed the club's offices. To the left was another low stand, the roof of which was emblazoned with the words WEST HAM UNITED F.C. in white paint, and there was nowhere near enough roof to keep everyone on the terrace dry should it rain. To the right, closer to them, was a large open terrace, the North Stand, punctuated with iron crush barriers and backed with advertising hoardings for Claymore Whisky, OXO, the *News of the World,* and the *Daily Herald.* That was where they usually stood, Alfie told him, but they thought the chicken run would be safer for Malcolm's first visit.

On the North Bank, the open terrace filled up and the barriers became obscured by spectators wrapped up against the cold, almost all wearing caps. Small boys were being passed overhead to sit at the front and get a decent view of the game. "That was me when I was a nipper," said Alfie with a smile. "I used to love it better than any fairground ride."

Malcolm was excited by how overwhelmingly masculine the crowd was. The smell of cigar smoke hung in the air, having drifted across the pitch from where the directors sat.

At twenty-five minutes past two, out onto the pitch filed the two teams to enthusiastic applause. The claret-and-blue-clad Hammers' captain and his white-jerseyed Charlton counterpart watched as the referee, in shorts and blazer, tossed a coin. West Ham would kick off and the teams would remain at the ends they'd run to.

Football hadn't been played at Wendells, but Malcolm was intelligent enough to understand the basics of the game, if not the details of the offside rule. He didn't know when or whether he'd ever attend a match again, so he hoped it wasn't going to be a dull affair.

He needn't have worried.

The crowd roared its encouragement when West Ham attacked. It sounded intimidating, but it was more urging and imploring rather than anything aggressive, and as all those around him were willing the home team to succeed, Malcolm too became drawn in. It was tribal, but for the time being at least, he was part of the tribe.

West Ham won an early corner, and from it, Arthur Wilson nodded the ball into the net for the first goal, receiving enthusiastic but controlled applause as he jogged back, head bowed modestly. When Malcolm expressed surprise that there hadn't been a greater roar, Alfie explained this crowd had suffered too many disappointments for it to be seduced by a single goal—or even two goals, because less than a quarter of an hour later one of the Hammers players was tripped in the Charlton penalty area and Jim Barrett converted the spot kick for 2-0. The crowd response was again restrained even though Barrett was a local hero, according to Alfie. They were pleased, but they weren't about to get carried away.

Malcolm liked the look of Jackie Morton, a fair-haired, wiry young forward, but with Alfie standing next to him, there was no cause to look at anyone else. Morton it was who got a third goal for West Ham and the home supporters' celebrations became more raucous as belief flowed into them. Three goal leads weren't often squandered.

"See? I told you Charlie Paynter's the man to turn it round for us," said a beaming Sid.

Even though many people were shouting, a young lad with a corncrake voice made himself heard above all the cheers and the rattles: "*Come on, 'Ammers! Come on, let's 'ave another!'*

Just as things seemed to be going so untypically well, the wind was knocked out of their sails as Cyril Pearce, the Charlton centre forward, quickly pulled a goal back, and shortly afterwards another for 3-2—and even though they'd scored three and their wingers were constantly torment- ing the Charlton defenders, anxiety was creeping back into the crowd. This had an effect on the players. Passes were misplaced. First touches were heavy. The ball seemed to stick in the mud at inopportune moments. Alt- hough they were still ahead, just, it didn't feel like it. West Ham had already leaked a lot of goals that season and the mercurial Pearce was looking lethal all of a sudden. Arthur Wilson settled their nerves by ending the half as he'd started it by planting the ball into the Charlton net for 4-2 and that's how it stood when the players trooped off to be replaced by the Gasworks Band. Alfie said that on occasions when things weren't going so well, many an uncharitable supporter had suggested the band stay on and play the sec- ond half, but there was none of that kind of talk today. Alfie then disap- peared, to relieve himself in the spartan toilets.

Malcolm had enjoyed the game so far more than he'd expected to, but Alfie aside, the crowd and their reactions had really captivated him. Now that the turnstiles were shut, George reckoned there were 18-19,000 fans present, not even half the ground's capacity, but it was still the largest assembly of people Malcolm had ever been a part of—and he did, by now, feel part of it. Each time West Ham had scored, the cheering had been louder—and when the fourth had gone in, the general relief had been such that he found himself surrounded by grown men jumping for joy. He could reason to himself that it was only a game and the result didn't matter, but right now, it felt like the most important thing in the world. He desperately wanted West Ham not only to win, but to tear the opposition apart.

Alfie returned carrying a bottle of pale ale with another four stuffed awkwardly into his jacket pockets; he then shared them out. During the match, Malcolm hadn't noticed the bitter cold, but it was starting to bite now. He was surprised that none of the boys wore an overcoat, relying instead on their caps and scarves tucked into heavy jackets. When asked, Alfie explained that he did own a coat, but seldom wore it and left it at that. Sid quietly told him that Alfie's coat was "much too posh for a football match" and none of them would wear one anyway because Frank didn't own one and it would set him apart. Malcolm was touched by this.

Alfie was cautious about the first-half performance. "We'll have to see what happens in the second half before we can judge if that was a good half or not," he reasoned. "But it was better than it has been of late, I'll give you that."

"Gawd! There's no pleasing some people," said George, shaking his head in exaggerated bewilderment before shoving his friend a few steps down the terrace.

Shortly after the second half kicked off, Alfie's caution looked to have been justified as Cyril Pearce completed his hat-trick, bringing Charlton to within a goal of the Hammers once again. The long-suffering West Ham fans had cause to fret—and fret they did. Before the match, much of the talk had been about veteran forward Vic Watson, who had scored more goals for West Ham than anyone so far that season, but he'd hardly had a sniff of the ball during the first half, not where it counted anyway. The threat of a further Charlton revival galvanised him into action, and as all great players can do, he took the game by the scruff of the neck. He skilfully put through the winger Tommy Yews to score a fifth for West Ham.

They had already been shown the danger of resting on their laurels, so they did not ease off and wave after wave of claret and blue attacks, led by Yews and Morton on the wings and Watson in the centre, surged towards the Charlton goal.

"Skin 'im! Skin 'im! Come on, Irons! Let's 'ave another!" screamed their stentorian neighbour, whose undernourished frame did not look robust enough to hold such a mighty voice.

The Charlton keeper prevented an avalanche, but in the end, he couldn't stop the increasingly influential Watson from ending all resistance and triggering scenes of jubilation among the West Ham faithful by scoring another two goals as twilight stole over the Boleyn Ground. The first of Watson's goals earned Malcolm a hug from Alfie while the second resulted in another hug and an arm being left draped over his shoulder until the final whistle.

When the referee blew it, the youth with the corncrake voice let out a bellow that nearly took the roof off the chicken run, leaving Alfie looking pained. "Oh, gorblimey! Can you imagine what it's like living with 'im in-doors?"

"I bet there ain't a scrap of plaster left on their walls, that's for sure," said George.

They returned to the Boleyn Tavern, where everybody was cock-a-hoop. Away from the cauldron, Malcolm was astonished by how much these people cared about a football club. His companions were bouncing off the walls as they sank pint after pint. He could hardly keep up with them. He saw again the rough affection between them, whether it was a hand on a shoulder, a clutch of a lapel, or a fist to a chin threatening a fight that would never happen. When they'd calmed down a bit, they seemed to notice him again.

"Don't be thinking it's like that every time," warned a beaming Alfie. "It ain't often seven-three, I can tell yer. Especially not to the 'Ammers."

"Don't tell 'im that!" protested George. "He's got to come along every time now. He's our lucky charm, ain't he?"

Chapter Eleven

Tangerines

MALCOLM HAD NO intention of going to every West Ham match, but under the influence of one too many pints of beer, he agreed to go to the next home game on the tenth of December against Manchester United. He even suggested to Alfie that they should go on the North Bank so he could experience its even more vibrantly masculine atmosphere. Unfortunately, his plans were scuppered by something as banal as a hold full of tangerines. A huge consignment of them arriving for Christmas needed to be redirected to another Wharf due to water damage at the one booked for it.

The wharfinger had no alternative to offer so Malcolm went into work and spent all afternoon with the British Atlantic's directory of wharves and docks in one hand and the telephone receiver in the other. The freighter was already off Gravesend and was due to dock at the Royal Victoria Dock in an hour or two. The office clock ticked ominously and the latest time he could leave for the match came and went.

He was agitated. These tangerines were from Spain, not South America, yet somehow, he had been lumbered with them. He hated letting his new friends down when his clerks should have been able to deal with this without him. However, it was a Saturday, so few of them were in the office and none of those present had his range of contacts, or experience.

What worried Malcolm most was that he had no way of letting Alfie know he wouldn't be turning up. Had it been his mother or one of his few acquaintances, a simple telephone call would have sufficed, but as Alfie had said, no one in Glendale Street had a telephone. Alfie would have been at work all morning, but Malcolm doubted that the West India Dock Office would appreciate a call saying he couldn't make a football match. Had he needed to find a home for dried or tinned fruit it wouldn't have been a problem, but as it was, having arrived at noon, it was getting on for six o'clock before he got Chester Wharf over in Westminster to agree to accommodate the tangerines—and that was after he had driven down to speak to them in person. It wasn't handy for Covent Garden, but there seemed no other option.

The match had long since finished, but he was desperate to explain his non-appearance. The lads might be offended and never ask him again. Worst of all, he might never hear from Alfie again, because they had made no arrangement to meet beyond this match. It brought home to Malcolm how fragile this friendship was, that had already come to mean so much to him.

He decided to go first to the Boleyn Tavern in the hope that the boys were still in there. As he had the motor car, it should have taken him no more than twenty minutes, despite the traffic and the unfamiliar roads. As he'd worked himself up into such a funk by then, it took him the best part of ten minutes to start the engine. It was always a palaver, and his efforts at starting the motor with the starter button resulted in horrible grinding noises. "Blasted car!" he growled as he cranked it to life with the starter handle. Once he did get on the road, he stalled the car several times, with the added humiliation of having an audience drawn by the Humber's infernal noises. He cursed himself for not buying an Austin 7 or a cheaper model that was easier to drive. "Fucking tangerines!" he exclaimed more than once in his leather-upholstered cocoon.

Much later than expected, he reached the vicinity of the football ground and parked the motor on Barking Road. He got out, slamming its door in disgust. His glasses misted as soon as he entered the warm pub, still busy with Hammers fans discussing the match. When the mist cleared, he could see that the boys weren't there. His panic grew as he faced the prospect of losing his friend through circumstances not of his making and about which he could do nothing. He didn't know Alfie's address, apart from Glendale Street being on the Isle of Dogs. He walked disconsolately out of the pub and immediately collided with someone on the pavement. It was Sid Mason.

"Oh, 'ello, Malcolm. You stood us up today, didn't yer?"

"I know. I'm so sorry. There was an emergency at work, and I had to go in. I was trying to find Alfie to explain." His excuse sounded feeble, even though it was the truth.

Sid tutted and said gravely, "Well, I don't think he'll want to see you, mate. He was very put out, I don't mind telling yer." Then, appreciating from Malcolm's stricken expression that his words had been taken more seriously than he'd intended, he slapped him on the back and went on, "I'm only pullin' your leg, mate. Don't look so worried. He's right as rain. He said it would be work, most prob'ly."

The relief was overwhelming, but he had to see Alfie just to be sure, and asked Sid where they'd gone.

"The Star of the East on Commercial Road, just near where the Dock Roads fork. If they ain't there, try the Eastern or Charlie Brown's. They'll be out all night, so you'll be sure to find 'em round there somewhere. I wish I could come but I promised me old mum a night out. I ain't going wiv her, like—I'm looking after me younger brothers and sisters for her so's she can catch second house at the pictures."

Malcolm nodded and smiled. Sid was a nice chap, but at that moment, he couldn't have cared less if he were to go home and mow his siblings down like Jimmy Cagney in a gangster picture. All he wanted to do was to put things right with Alfie.

In the haven of the car, he collected himself and headed off to the more familiar territory of Limehouse. It was a mercifully straightforward run along the East India Dock Road, but even on a Saturday evening, the traffic was heavier than he liked. It never stopped around the docks. Up until now, his driving had been confined to the deserted City at the week-end, tree-lined North London suburbs, and Sunday outings to the country-side.

He found them in the warm fug of the Star, which glistened with newly hung paper chains and other Christmas decorations. The group looked like any other, a table of dark-clad men in flat caps, each with a pint pot on the table in front of them and two of them with fags in their mouths.

But one of the dark figures was Alfie, who embraced him like a long-lost friend, which was both embarrassing and lovely. He smelled of cigarette smoke, but somehow, it wasn't so bad coming off him. He seemed genuinely pleased to see Malcolm, much to the latter's relief. They had downed a fair few pints already and as the Hammers had beaten United 3-1, they were in high spirits.

"Yer missed a corker, Malc. Vic Watson scored twice in the first half, and they got one back just before half time. But then Vic hurt his leg and had to go off injured. We had to play most of the second half wiv ten men," Alfie recounted breathlessly.

"I thought we were done for," grunted Frank.

"Me an' all. But we held on and then Wilson sealed it at the death."

West Ham were now five games undefeated so even Syd King loyalist George was beginning to concede that Charlie Paynter was turning their fortunes around. Once the afternoon's action had been described to him in detail, Malcolm explained how he had spent his afternoon.

Alfie seemed impressed. "Aw, mate, you're a bloody hero. Plenty of Christmas stockings round the East End won't have much in 'em, but at least they might 'ave a tangerine, thanks to you."

So, on that basis, a pint of mixed was hastily bought to reward him for his service to the deprived children of the East End. He settled wearily into a seat and was content to listen to them chat about all sort of things, having exhausted all their thoughts about the match.

George said, "Have you seen how much the GPO is losing from people robbing telephone boxes? Three hundred nicker a month, in London alone. It's what…tuppence a call?" He did some mental arithmetic, his head bobbing from side to side as he calculated. "That's thirty-six thahsand calls they ain't getting the money for every month—in London alone! It's a wonder they think it's worth having the bleedin' things. I ain't never even used one."

"I have," said Alfie, laying a hand on Malcolm's shoulder. "I know you use a telephone every day, Malc, but when I went to a box to call you to see you'd got home all right that night, it was the first time I'd ever used one. I was proper scared of making a fool of meself in that box, I can tell yer. That bleedin' operator lady was terrifying."

"That's because the Alfie magic don't work if they can't see yer, mate," laughed Frank.

Malcolm only had two more pints, but they made him lightheaded enough to regret having the car outside. He was nervous about it being parked on Commercial Road anyway, given the nature of the traffic that rumbled back and forth on it, particularly double-decker buses and the larger lorries. These could easily clip it and would certainly ensure that it was covered in a layer of grime. He wasn't a dedicated motorist, but he was fond of the car as an object, certainly fonder of it than his attitude earlier that evening had suggested. It was a blue 1929 Humber 9/28. He spent more time polishing it than he did driving it, and it had only a few miles on the clock. The only times it ever went anywhere were for weekend emergencies like this or for a Sunday drive into the countryside with his mother.

As it approached ten o'clock, Alfie said that he was tired, he'd had more than enough to drink, and he'd be heading home. He had further to go than the others, and so Malcolm offered to give him a lift home.

"Well, if you don't mind. I'm fair jiggered, I don't mind telling yer."

Alfie made appreciative noises when he saw the car, taking in the immaculate blue bodywork and oxblood leather seats. When he climbed in, he stroked the walnut dashboard with reverence.

"Blimey! It's proper swanky, Malcolm. It musta cost a bob or two."

"Three hundred and twenty pounds. I scarcely use it, but I've little else to spend my money on, I suppose. And I certainly couldn't have managed without it today, that's for sure. Can you drive, Alfie?"

"Me? Nah. When I was working on the quay, I used to drive an electric bogie every now and again, but that's no harder than driving a dodgem at the fair. There's no sense in me learning to drive 'cos I ain't never gonna be able to afford a car anyway. Three hundred and twenty nicker! Fuck me! I suppose Uncle Tommy might let me use his Morris but…nah."

"Well, maybe one day we could find a quiet stretch of road somewhere and you could have a go with this one? Just to see what it's like."

He felt like a vile seducer for suggesting it, but Alfie momentarily sobered up and was wide-eyed as he exclaimed, "Really! You wouldn't mind?"

"Of course not."

"Oh, mate, I would love that. Thank you."

Daringly, Malcolm swung a U-turn on Commercial Road and drove towards the East India Docks where he turned for the Island. The roads were restricted by the docks and the London Blackwall Railway, so making a wrong turn could take you miles out of your way. Alfie's calm instructions ensured that didn't happen, and the Humber got to Prestons Road without difficulty. Despite the December cold, driving in the dark on the unfamiliar and intimidating route made Malcolm perspire so his shirt clung to his back. He didn't so much fear going miles out of his way as he did making a wrong turn and having the car plunge into a graving dock or even one of the main docks. When he voiced his concern Alfie laughed.

"It's an 'Umber, not a tank! How many newspaper reports have you ever read about cars falling into the docks?"

"Well, none."

"There's a reason for that, yer fathead."

As they approached the bridge across the entrance to the South Dock, they were stopped because it was about to swing open to allow a ship through. Rather than wait in line, Alfie told Malcolm to turn down Coldharbour and park the car. There was precious little room in the close, cobbled terrace, but he managed to park, and they got out. Alfie led him down a dark alley beside the Gun pub, and suddenly they were looking out onto the river just as a large freighter was being manoeuvred into the West India Docks from Blackwall Reach by a couple of steaming tugboats. Its lights glittered, and as its bow towered over them, they could make out the name *Baron Felix*. As if to greet them, its horn sounded a melancholy, baritone sound.

Alfie laughed quietly and said, "Me mum'll be cursing 'im."

"Who?"

"Whoever gave the order for her to make that racket. Mum's lived round the docks all her life, but she still gets startled by the ships. She's daft as a brush."

"What will it be carrying, do you think?"

Alfie shrugged. "Search me, mate. She could be carrying anything. My guess would be tea."

"Let's hope it isn't bloody tangerines, eh?" quipped Malcolm. "Living and working with all these ships, from all over the world—aren't you curious about what it's like to sail on them?"

"I was when I was a boy. I used to imagine all sorts of adventures—

fighting pirates and the like." His brilliant smile flashed in the dark. "But not so much now. Ain't no point in hankering after sumfink I can never afford. I could work on 'em, I suppose, but I'm a skilled worker so I get good money. Getting a job on a merchantman would be a step back for me. Besides, I doubt me mum'd like it." He turned to Malcolm. "'Ere, are you trying to get rid of me?"

"Good God no!" Malcolm exclaimed too vehemently.

"It's all right. I never really thought you was. I'm only joking, mate."

Alfie smiled at him sweetly. It was dark and bitingly cold, and he was dressed in a heavy black jacket and cap so that he almost merged with the night. His white shirt and knitted claret and blue football scarf were mostly hidden so all there seemed to be at that moment was his beautiful face, like a vision from a better world. His eyes, black in the darkness, had a glint in them that was probably down to the beer. His breath was steam. They stood close together and Malcolm felt that something unbelievable was going to happen. Something wonderful. Alfie might be about to kiss him.

Alfie pulled a hand from deep in his jacket pocket and placed it firmly on Malcolm's shoulder. He hardly dared breathe. Alfie gave it a squeeze and said, "Come on. Let's get back to yer car. It's fuckin' perishin' out here."

As they walked back to the Humber, Malcolm was again glad of the dark masking his embarrassment. His face burned. How could he have imagined that this perfect youth would be interested in kissing any man, let alone a pasty little pipsqueak like him. Thank goodness he hadn't anticipated the kiss and tried to instigate it!

Alfie got Malcolm to drop him on Manchester Road where it met Glengall Grove. Malcolm tried to insist on driving him to his door, but he wouldn't have it. He liked a bit of a stroll to clear his head, he said. It was quiet. The traffic was light and the pavements were empty because the pubs had another half hour before they turfed their patrons out.

When the car pulled up at the kerb, at first he made no move to climb out. He turned to Malcolm and said, "We'll 'ave to sort out a drink before Christmas, yes?"

"I'd like that. When will I see you again exactly? You know, if I hadn't been able to find you tonight, I might never have seen you again."

"Why not?"

"Well, I don't even know your address or anything."

"But I know your telephone number, don't I, yer daft bugger. You don't escape from me that easy, don't you worry about that." Alfie smiled and shook his head briefly. "You're a funny one."

"Really? In what way?"

"I dunno. I ain't quite figured it out yet. But I will do, don't you worry."

With that he opened the door, letting in a blast of cold night air, climbed out, and slammed it shut behind him. He touched the peak of his cap in farewell and walked slowly away, his footsteps echoing around the dark empty streets of Cubitt Town. Malcolm sat quietly for a moment, listening to the melancholy hooters and horns from the river traffic, to steam locomotives puffing and clattering nearby and to a piano and drunken laughter from an unseen pub. He couldn't decide whether he wanted Alfie to work him out or not. He had thought that being in Alfie's company would be enough for him, but now he wondered whether he'd been wrong. He'd be like the old woman who lived in a vinegar bottle, asking more of fortune after each wish was granted, only to end up back in the vinegar bottle.

Chapter Twelve

The Balance of His Mind

Saturday, 14 January 1933

MALCOLM ENJOYED MORE nights out with the young dockers in the run-up to Christmas, filled with beer and chat. They questioned him about his life, and he was embarrassed to discover it was so sparsely populated with people and events. Anecdotes about missing consignments of frozen beef were hardly likely to thrill them, but apart from the odd eccentric act from his mother, he had little to draw on. His car at least was something. They all enjoyed a ride in it, but the offer of having a go behind the wheel was kept exclusive.

Alfie proposed they go to the third round of the FA Cup to give

Malcolm his first taste of a cup tie because they had an altogether different atmosphere from league matches. West Ham had been drawn away to the Corinthians, a famous amateur club. Early in the New Year, the match was to be played in the shadow of the Crystal Palace in Sydenham. The boys didn't normally travel to away matches, but as it was in London and against unfamiliar opposition, they arranged to meet at Wapping station to journey south of the river.

Malcolm arrived early and loitered outside the station watching goods being shifted between the waterside warehouses of Gun Wharf and those across the road. He didn't stray far from the station entrance, partly to avoid impeding any of this frenetic activity, but also to avoid missing his companions. He expected the others to arrive together from the West India Docks where they'd spent the morning working, so he was surprised to see Alfie turn up alone.

"I'm sorry, Malc," he said, "but there's been a change of plan. We ain't going to the match no more."

"Oh, I see. Why ever not?" He at once assumed that *he* was the problem. Perhaps the others hadn't wanted him to tag along. Perhaps they resented the way Alfie had drawn this outsider into their circle. It was a concern that visited Malcolm often during their nights out, particularly when he caught one of them, usually Frank, looking at him unsmiling. On this occasion at least, he was wrong.

"A very sad thing has happened, and we don't fancy it no more. Specially not George."

"He hasn't had a death in the family, I hope?"

Alfie shook his head. "Nah, not exactly. It may sound daft to you, but do you remember us talking about Syd King?"

"The West Ham manager?"

"Yes, that's right. I'm afraid he's passed away. He only officially retired the other week, but now he's gone and died."

"Oh, dear. That *is* sad."

Alfie seized the sleeve of Malcolm's overcoat and put his mouth close to his ear to be heard over the clatter. Malcolm's skin tingled under his warm, moist breath. "I had to come just so's you'd know what was happening. I could have tried you on the telephone but…look, let's go to the pub and I'll tell you all about it. As much as I know, anyways. I could do wiv a drink, to be honest. I've been working all morning loading carpet slippers, of all things. You'd never have thought a load of bleedin' slippers could be so heavy!"

Alfie led him along the narrow pavement between the warehouses and past the River Police Station at Execution Dock until they came to a long narrow pub beside Wapping Old Stairs. This was the Ramsgate. Long ago, Judge Jeffreys had been apprehended there by the authorities, disguised in a sailor's clothes. Today, many genuine seafaring men were in there as the Saturday lunchtime trade was brisk. Without consultation Alfie got them each a pint of mixed which had become Malcolm's drink of choice. When he returned, he continued the sad story.

"It gets worse, I'm afraid. It looks like Syd's only gone and done himself in."

"What? Because he lost his job?" Malcolm suddenly felt the tragedy more keenly. "D'you really think so?"

"That's what George reckons. He's proper cut up about it. He blames West Ham, but you can't keep someone on when things ain't right, can yer?"

"Well, no. And a lot of people get sacked without committing suicide because of it."

"And they didn't even officially sack him—they *retired* him with a decent pension an' all. But less than a fortnight later…"

"How—how did he do it?" Malcolm asked, thinking of his father.

"He drank a bottle of disinfectant. Well, not the whole bottle I don't suppose, but enough."

"Oh, dear God, no." Malcolm brought his hand up to hide his eyes.

"I know. It's horrible, innit? It said in the paper that it were an accident, but well, a bottle o' Lysol don't look nuffink like a bottle of Syrup of Figs, does it? He'd been drinking, but disinfectant don't look nuffink like whisky neither. There will be an inquest, we reckon."

"Even if you were intent on doing it, why on earth would you do it like that?"

"I dunno. Maybe he thought it would be like when they take poison in the pictures, a quick swig, clutch yer heart, and Bob's yer uncle. But instead o' that, it left him in agony and he didn't die until the next day."

"God! That poor, poor man," breathed Malcolm.

Inquests always concluded that people who killed themselves were of "unsound mind," suffering from "temporary insanity", or had acted when "the balance of their mind was disturbed". He reckoned these were easy phrases to cover the authorities' reluctance to investigate these tragedies any further, but perhaps in this case, they'd be right.

The news had affected him. Some called it a "coward's way out", but Malcolm didn't see it that way. It was not cowardly to surrender to what many people fear the most. He'd contemplated it himself but had always drawn back from those darker moments.

"Anyway Malc, there ain't nuffink you and me can do what's gonna make it any better for Syd and his family. We've got a free afternoon, mate, and I think we should spend it in this pub. What d'yer say?"

"I'd like that."

"Come on, then, let's get another pint and go and watch the river for a bit."

They carried their ale outside where all was grey. The Thames was grey, the sky was grey, and even the yellow London brick of the warehouses looked grey. Gulls glided hopefully around Wapping Old Stairs, the lower steps of which were hit by the wash of a freighter bound for St Katherine's Dock. Many of the patrons indoors must have been watermen and lighter-men judging by the number of vessels moored around the Stairs. The numbing cold and the gloom would dampen the spirit of any man, particularly given the tragic news, yet Malcolm was curiously content. He was alone with Alfie and therefore was happy. He didn't know how long it would last so he would enjoy every second they shared.

They raised their glasses to Syd King, then Alfie said, "Come on. Let's go back inside. Me fingers are that cold, I can hardly grip me pint."

Time alone with Alfie in the Ramsgate was preferable to any football match. This was the first time since the night they'd met that they hadn't been part of a crowd. As much as Malcolm liked his fantasy that he was becoming "one of the lads", this boy was the point. Boy? Man? He was both at different times. To hear this vibrant young man talk of tragedy had been a strange juxtaposition. The shadow of death enhanced appreciation of one so alive with youth, promise, and hope.

"I don't suppose you've had much experience of death before, Alfie."

"I'm afraid you're wrong there, mate. I've lost me nan, me cousin, and me dad in the last few years."

The cousin. The suits—of course. Malcolm could have bitten his tongue off. Instead, he mumbled, "Oh, Alfie, I'm so sorry."

"Don't be daft! It ain't your fault, is it? Truth is, mate, death ain't never far from you in these parts. Nan was getting on a bit, but Edward, he was only nineteen, and Dad… Well, it was an accident. They happen, don't they? Me mate Joe, when we was kids, he was very sick and everyone thought he was gonna die. The doctors couldn't even say what was wrong wiv him, they didn't know. Quite a few times I was there when everyone thought he'd gone. If he had died, I think… Well, I'd have found it hard to take, you know?" He smiled. "But he fought, and he fought, and eventually he won. And when we knew that he wasn't gonna die of whatever it was, I can't remember ever feeling so happy in all me life."

Malcolm experienced a flicker of something that felt perilously like jealousy. "Do you still see him?"

"Not too often. Even though he missed such a lot of school, he was a clever kid, was Joe. He works for a solicitor's firm up Fleet Street way now."

"How old are you, Alfie?"

"I'm nineteen. Where did that come from?"

Malcolm looked down into his drink. "I don't know. I just wondered, that's all. You haven't even been given the keys to the door yet."

"I ain't sure there *are* any keys to our front door as it goes. It's never locked anyway, 'cos we ain't got nuffink worth pinching. You ain't bothered about having a younger mate, are yer?"

"A little, perhaps."

"Well, I shouldn't worry if I was you. I've been a working man fer nearly five years now. I ain't some silly kid."

"I know you aren't. And we *are* friends now, aren't we? So, it's too late to worry about it."

"That's right. Anyways, I think it's nice to have a mate who's different from the others."

"Am I that different? How?"

"Well, you're that bit older than us and yer posh for a start."

Malcolm winced and laughed. "I'm *not* posh!"

"You are compared to me, mate. I'm proper common, I am. Common as muck."

"I think you're very uncommon." Malcolm looked directly into Alfie's shining blue eyes as he said it. Alfie smiled back and didn't look away.

They drank slowly, becoming easily, pleasantly drunk. The crowd around them ebbed and flowed, and they were both glad to be a part of it and oblivious to it in equal measure. In a way, it was just the two of them. They spoke of inconsequential things made wonderful by the beer. They relished what common ground they stumbled upon, down to their shared dislike of the cucumber and all its children. They shared thoughts they had never shared with anyone before, nothing too important, but there was an intimacy to them. Having Alfie's smile to himself was as intoxicating as the beer. Malcolm longed to reach out and touch him or remove his cap and ruffle his hair as the other boys did. But he couldn't do that because it wasn't how grown men of his class behaved. His motives would have been different from those of the others anyway, and it would be a betrayal of Alfie's trust. This new friendship was a gift to be enjoyed, and suffered, as it was.

Aside from the barmaids, the clientele consisted entirely of men who made their living on the river, lightermen, tugboat hands, and the odd skipper. With Alfie working at the docks and his own job relying on the port,

Malcolm felt a part of a great Thames community. Something bigger than them all, making sense of their lives.

""'Ow come you ain't married yet, Malc?" asked Alfie out of the blue.

The alcohol dulled his sense of alarm. He shrugged. "Who'd have me?"

"Don't put yerself down!" protested Alfie. "You're a nice-looking geezer as it goes. I bet there's plenty of gels in that office of yours who'd be happy to tie the knot wiv yer."

Thanks to Doris Finch, he did have something he could say on the matter, with a strong element of truth to it.

"There was a woman who got rather stuck on me. She was persistent. But I just wasn't attracted to her. It's rather put me off affairs of the heart, I'm afraid."

"Yes, I can see how it would. It's difficult when someone won't take no for an answer. You don't wanna hurt no one, but sometimes you just have to, don't yer?"

Alfie must have encountered the problem more than just the once, Malcolm thought. Nora was surely only the latest in a long line of disappointed women.

"Don't worry though, Malcolm. The right person will come along in their own time. You're too good to go to waste, mate." He closed his hand over Malcolm's and added with childish candour, "There's something proper lovely about yer."

The unexpectedly warm compliment turned Malcolm's face crimson, and he hurriedly deflected it. "What about you? If not Nora, you must have had a sweetheart at some point, surely?"

Alfie released his hand and sat back in his chair. "You know what? I haven't. Not really. Don't get me wrong, between you an' me I've got up to stuff I shouldn't have wiv quite a few gels. But they weren't what I'd call "sweethearts". As I said, I'm only nineteen. Mum would take a dim view of me walking out wiv someone before I'm twenty-one, I reckon."

"That's probably sensible." Malcolm hesitated before moving into dangerous territory, but the beer made it possible. "You are very, very good-looking, as I'm sure you're aware. And as you're a nice chap too, well, there should be no shortage of suitors for you."

Alfie gave one of his familiar chuckles. "'A nice chap'! So, I'm a chap then, am I? Yes well, I ain't in no hurry, I can tell yer. I like me freedom too much. I'm only just past having me mum wanting to know where I am, who I'm wiv, and what I'm up to all the time. I don't want nuffink like that again for a good while yet. I don't think you plan them things anyway—love an' that. When it happens, it happens and there won't be a bleedin' thing I can do about it."

Alfie impulsively bought them each a pickled egg with the next round. Malcolm had never had one and was extremely dubious about allowing the smelly, slimy thing to pass his lips, but he was incapable of denying the boy.

"Just eat it in two bites. don't think about it too much. Don't worry. It don't taste of nuffink but vinegar."

Once he'd got used to the explosion of vinegar and the slimy egg white in his mouth, he immediately felt more awake and somehow less drunk. He said so.

"That's what I done it for, mate. I reckon we're on a proper session here and this will help us carry on for longer, won't it?"

Malcolm flushed with pleasure. Alfie was happy in his company!

As evening turned into night and the faces changed around them, they found weightier things to share. Each had lost his father at sixteen, even though the circumstances had been different. Each felt that his friend's loss had been the crueller. It had been hard for Malcolm to accept his father's suicide, but Alfie's loss was more recent and still raw, and their relationship had been close. Alfie, in turn, reckoned he couldn't have coped if he'd thought his father's death had been deliberate.

The alcohol corroded a lifetime of caution. Malcolm less than subtly steered the conversation back to Alfie's looks. Having sidestepped the earlier compliment and despite the drink Alfie looked uncomfortable and tried changing the subject. In his state of inebriation, Malcolm would not be deflected now he'd started down that road.

"Malcolm, I ain't Rudolph bleedin' Valentino."

"You're considerably better-looking, I'd say. And you're *real*. You live amongst us."

"I can't talk about this. If I do, it makes me sound like I think a lot of meself."

"But there's surely no use in pretending you don't know. It must be wonderful to be as handsome as you are, Alfie."

He shook his head reluctantly. "It's like anything else, Malcolm. There's good and bad to it."

"Really? I'd have thought it would be a wonderful thing to have everyone look at you and be confident that they'll like what they see. You could have any woman you want, you know, and most men must at least partly wish they were you."

"Do you wish you was me?"

"Well, yes, I do in a way. Anyone would, surely?"

Alfie looked a little annoyed. "Oh, Malcolm, can't we just leave it? Don't be just another one who goes on about the way I look."

The drink had made Malcolm bolder, but it intensified his feeling that he'd somehow overstepped the mark. He was mortified. He'd had such a wonderful day in spite of the tragedy that had brought it about, but now he'd pretty much ruined it all. And he couldn't find any words to make it all right again.

Alfie saw him floundering, saw his inner turmoil if not its cause. He sighed. "I'm sorry, I didn't mean to snap at yer, Malc. Look, I know I've been lucky in some ways, but me boat gets me into all sorts of bovver. You probably don't realise how often I get attention I *don't* want. How often I have to say no to people. That ain't always easy. You shouldn't ask a question unless you're prepared to hear the answer 'no', but there's a lot what does, you know. And when I do say no, it can't be just because I don't fancy 'em. It must be because I think too much of meself, that I reckon I'm better than them. It's like I ain't entitled to me own thoughts and feelings. I don't like upsetting people, but it seems I do. And it ain't just gels neither, I can tell yer."

Malcolm was jolted by that remark. It was as though he'd suddenly and unexpectedly bitten into another pickled egg. Was this a thinly disguised warning for him? But it was perfectly understandable that Alfie would draw the eye of men who liked men.

"Mum spent a lot of time swatting women away from me when I was younger," Alfie went on. "She'd say, 'Keep yer hands off the biscuits, they've only just come out of the oven'." His smile dimmed. "I got people looking at me all the time in pubs an' that, and some of 'em want to hurt me, Malcolm. Scar me because they think I need taking down a peg or two.

Frank and the others have saved me from a few glassings over the years, but one day someone is sure to catch me when they ain't around and that'll be that. No more pretty face. Maybe they'd be doing me a favour."

Malcolm listened quietly. The disadvantages of Alfie's rare beauty now seemed so obvious he was embarrassed he hadn't considered them.

"Oh, Alfie, I'm sorry to have been so insensitive. I can't pretend I don't admire the way you look, but if that was all there was to you, I doubt we'd be friends. In fact, I don't really know why you bother with the likes of me, to be honest."

"Wotcher mean, 'the likes of you'? I'll tell yer why I bovver, shall I? It's 'cos you listen to me. It's 'cos you seem to care what I think about things. It's 'cos you don't treat me like an idiot. Even George and Frank sometimes behave as if I don't have a thought in me head. They think that 'cos I've got a face the gels like and I know me job well enough, I ain't got no use for a brain. You ain't like that. That's why I don't want to hear you yapping on about the way I look. No offence. I ain't a dumb blond. I ain't even blond."

"I'm sorry, Alfie. Truly. I think you're warm and kind and funny and honest—"

"Steady on, Malc! I've got to get me head out of this pub, you know." Alfie's smile showed that he understood, and all was well.

Chapter Thirteen

The Rum Quay

Friday, 21 April 1933

CHARLIE BROWN'S WAS often their starting point for a night out. Even though he'd seen all the curious antiquities many times by then, Malcolm had come to love the place above all other pubs. It was somewhere that welcomed misfits—and he was a misfit.

This Friday night seemed like any other as the docks emptied and the pubs filled up with dockers and seafarers, wages burning holes in their pockets. He arrived to find Sid sitting alone, lost in his paper. He liked the chap, but when it was just the two of them, he could be hard work. Sid always seemed distracted, and one never had his full attention. He was always reading for a start. He invariably had a folded copy of the *Daily Mir-ror* in his pocket, or a paperback book. By half-past seven when George and Frank arrived, they were on their second pint. Alfie wasn't with them.

*

BETWEEN THE WEST India Import and Export docks were timber sheds and rum warehouses built over a labyrinth of cool dark vaults in which wines and spirits were stored. The green and grey arches, covered in patches of white fungus that glowed in the dark, were peaceful, almost monastic. Most of the spirit housed there was rum shipped from Jamaica, which was why it became known as the Rum Quay.

Inside, the spirit issued an all-pervading, seductive scent which spread through the unending darkness, for there was no electric light beneath its cool stone arches. Coopers, like a silent order of monks in aprons made of rough sacking, groped their way through lines of plump wooden casks, "puncheons" and "hogsheads" lying on their sides, swollen with maturing rum. The glow of their oil lamps moved through the blackness as the coopers shuffled from cask to cask. They were checking that all was well, for the slumbering rum was a volatile cargo. They tapped the wood of each cask and could tell, just by the sound, whether all was as it should be. Then they moved on. Their light, the shuffle of their feet, and the noise of their tapping receded. But this evening, one distracted cooper, new to his job and eager for the pub, moved on without the lamp he'd been carrying, having failed to hear it slip between two casks. He could see no light and assumed that someone else must have picked it up by mistake. He was wrong.

*

THE AMERICAN FREIGHTER, *President McKinley,* surrounded waterside by lighters, was still being discharged of its cargo beside No 4 Warehouse on the North Quay. Tommy and his gang of stevedores were making their weary way past it towards the gates from the Export Dock where they'd been loading a ship bound for Japan when Walter Burgess approached them hesitantly, scratching the back of his head.

"All right, boys? You don't fancy a bit of overtime, I don't suppose?"

They didn't. They'd all done a heavy day's work and had plans for a relaxing evening. More work was the last thing they needed and the noises they made were not encouraging.

However, Alfie said tiredly, "I told you once that I'd never say no to a bit extra. When do you want us, Walter?"

"Right now, I'm afraid. There seems to have been a bit of a flu out-break. Either that or a nasty attack of Friday-night-itis, I reckon. I've only got a handful of men left and we'll be here all night at this rate. She'll be running up the Blue Peter with half her cargo still inside her."

"You're a bloomin' nuisance, Walter, but go on then. I'll stay and help," said Tommy. It meant his wife Rose would be half-cut by the time he got home and there would be a scene, but wasn't there every Friday night? He couldn't let his nephew show him up, and with any luck Rose would have passed out altogether by the time he pulled up in their drive.

"I can't stay," said George. "I've got Sid waiting for me at the gate and, to be perfectly honest, I'm done in. I ain't been feeling meself today at all."

Alfie was "done in" too and Malcolm was waiting for him at Charlie Brown's, but he'd once begged Walter for extra hours at a time when the family had been desperate for the money. Walter had kept his word and given him first refusal for any overtime, off the record. He no longer needed the money, still less the work, but a promise was a promise. He couldn't let Walter down just because he was the desperate one now.

"I'll stop, Walter," he said. "George, will you explain what's happened to Malcolm? Tell 'im I won't be long, but if he don't wanna wait, I'll try and see 'im tomorrow."

"Right you are," said George. Then, "He's like yer bleedin' wife, that geezer."

*

IN THE PUBLIC bar of Charlie Brown's, George explained the situation as he slumped down onto a stool beside his brother, but Malcolm decided to sit tight and wait. Sid read out an article from his *Daily Mirror* about the supposed sighting of a monster in Loch Ness, and they debated whether it was likely to be true or not. Sid was open-minded, which drew only scorn from Frank and George. Malcolm couldn't have cared less about it and didn't feel able to participate. He desperately hoped Alfie wouldn't be delayed for too long.

*

AT THE IMPORT Dock, as Walter had hoped, Tommy had imposed the organisation that had been lacking all day and Alfie displayed more gumption than the casual dock labourers. Tommy directed the men in discharging cargo onto the quayside, from where it would be moved into the sheds, while the rest of it went over the other side onto lighters to be towed elsewhere in the port. Alfie worked in the hold ensuring that only what was meant for discharge was unloaded and on the correct side of the ship. He then supervised the shifting of what remained so that it was stowed safely and evenly balanced.

When the job was done, Alfie appeared from the hold and walked briskly down the gangway. His uncle was perched on a capstan waiting for him as Walter sent the labourers on their way, with more heartfelt thanks than they deserved. Alfie didn't want to be rude, but he was anxious to get away. He was meant to have met Malcolm at seven and it was now a quarter past nine. Even though he'd sent that message with George, he knew if he'd stuck around, Malcolm would be uneasy without him. He didn't want him scared away. The unlikely friendship was coming to mean more to him each time they met.

"You got ants in yer pants, boy?" asked Tommy, having noticed his nephew's discomfort.

"I've had someone waiting for me for over two hours. I need to go."

"Oh, yes? What's her name then, Romeo?"

"Wotcher talking about?"

"Well, you ain't gonna get this agitated unless it's a bird what's waiting for yer, are yer?"

Alfie sighed in exasperation but didn't correct the misconception. "Like I said, I gotta go. Give me love to Aunty Rose."

The West India Import Dock had become dark and still. There would have been men below decks on the moored ships, but most of the crews were out on the town. Apart from the three of them, the only ones around at that end of the dock were a man securing the tarpaulin covers on a barge moored nearby and two PLA policemen pacing slowly along the lonely quay on their usual patrol.

Before Alfie could dash off, Tommy rose from the capstan and said,

"Here, I think there's smoke coming out of that shed over there!" He pointed across the water at a rum warehouse and the others peered across into the gloom. They were quiet for a moment, then there was the unmistakable flicker of a flame.

"Good God, you're right! I'll get those constables to raise the alarm." Walter was breaking into a trot as he spoke.

"It don't look like much—yet," said Tommy. "There's no electric in there. I expect some fool's left an oil lamp. You're a fit lad, Alfie. Run over and see if you can put it out before it catches properly."

Alfie didn't pause to ask questions but ran for all he was worth down the North Quay.

"But don't take no risks, boy, d'you hear me?" Tommy shouted after him.

Shortly after Alfie had disappeared into the gloom, Walter returned. "The Fire Brigade are being called. Let's hope they get here before it catches properly. Alfie's gone, has he?"

"No, I sent him over to see if he could snuff it out before it takes hold."

"You did *what?*" The normally placid man erupted in a way Tommy had never seen him do before. "You mean to tell me you've sent the boy running towards two million gallons of rum that might be about to catch fire? You stupid bastard! Are you trying to get him killed?"

The nagging concern Tommy had had since his nephew had run off now became a paralysing dread. He turned towards the end of the dock and shouted for all he was worth.

"Alfie! Alfie! Come back! *Alfie!*"

But his cries were futile. His nephew either couldn't hear him or didn't care to.

*

THE EMPTY DOCK echoed to the sound of his heavy boots as Alfie ran between the warehouses and the transit sheds. At the end of the quay, partly due to the gloom and partly due to his own reckless haste, as he hurtled around the corner, he tripped over the rope securing a lighter and fell flat on his face onto the stone. It was a shock. He was winded and had to take a moment or two to gather his wits. There was blood, although he wasn't sure exactly where from. Because he knew the urgency of his task, he struggled to his feet and, moving gingerly at first, he tried to break into a run towards the Rum Quay again. He thought he heard his uncle shout but couldn't make out the echoing words and assumed they weren't directed at him. He hadn't gone far around the corner onto the South Quay before there was a brilliant flash, followed by a tremendous explosion that knocked him flat on his back. His head banged against the stone quay, rendering him senseless. His thick cloth cap offered some protection at least, but it had still suffered a hell of a crack.

Gathering his wits for a second time, he sat up and after wiping the blood from his eyes he stared into a vision of hell. The timber shed was well alight, but so was the low roof of the Rum Quay sheds. The sky was an angry red, and it was raining sparks. He could feel the intense searing heat against his face. Thick black smoke billowed from the stricken buildings. As it reached him, he was suddenly in complete darkness. The acrid smoke caught at the back of his throat, causing him to retch. He'd have to go back. The trouble was, such was his confusion he wasn't sure where back was in this darkness.

He heard and felt a series of bangs like the sharp reports of artillery fire. The darkness abated, and he was confronted with a blaze the size and ferocity of which he wouldn't have imagined possible. The fire seemed a liquid thing, spraying everywhere, including towards him. It moved so quickly, and he was hurt and in a complete muddle. The sickly smoke was thickening again and getting more and more noxious. This time, rather than just retching, it made him vomit. He could hardly move. He could hardly see. He could hardly breathe. The angry flames must surely overtake him soon. With a rare clarity, he realised these might be his last moments of life and he thought, *I just wanna be in the pub. I just wanna be with Malc.*

*

"BOYS, BOYS! YOU gotta come out and see! The whole of the bloody docks are on fire!" A giant of a docker, in a state of agitation, ambushed the jovial Friday-night conversations in Charlie Brown's Public Bar and beckoned the patrons to follow him. At first, they were about as ready to believe him as they were the Loch Ness Monster stories in the paper. But there was a commotion outside. There was shouting, a lot of people were running about, and the distant sound of fire-engine bells was getting louder. Everyone dashed to the pub door and scrambled out into the stretch of road leading up to the dock gates, some to help if they could, but most just to see all the excitement. The West India Dock Road swarmed with people pushing to get closer for a better look, making it difficult for the pumps to get through. The first engines had arrived quickly, but even they were impeded by the growing crowd.

The block of nineteenth-century warehouses nearest them and the Dock Offices were not on fire, yet they could see flames leaping high into the sky beyond. Then there was a series of sharp reports like gunfire.

"What the fuck was that?" yelled Frank.

"That'll be some of the casks exploding," said George.

"I don't like the look of this," remarked Sid anxiously. "If it's the rum that's gone up, there'll be no stopping it."

The Dock Police were reinforced by Metropolitan officers from nearby Limehouse police station, and they began to push people away from the road up to the gates to make way for the Fire Brigade, as engine after engine arrived from stations further afield, bells clanging frantically. Charlie Brown's, located where it was, had to close so that it could be used to treat the wounded—and if things were as bad as they threatened to be, it would also become a makeshift mortuary.

In the middle of this turmoil, a cold terror crept over Malcolm. Hoping that someone would reassure him, he asked, "What about Alfie? Where's Alfie?"

The others looked at him without speaking for a moment until George said, "Malcolm's right. We've gotta try and find out."

"If it *is* the Rum Quay that's gone up, he should be all right. He don't ever work over there," said Frank.

"But he was working on a ship directly opposite. And you know what he's like, Mr bloody Helpful," said George.

Frank shook his head emphatically. "He'll be fine. I'm telling yer."

"Course he will," added Sid.

Malcolm could tell by their tone that they were trying to convince themselves, for they were experiencing the same cold fear. George used his large frame to barrel his way through the crowd towards the line of police at the dock gates. When he got to them, he shouted to one of the officers,

"Can I go in? Me mate's still in there!"

"No, sir. No one but the Fire Brigade is allowed through."

"But I can help!"

"I said no. What you gonna do, sir? Blow it out? Leave it to the professionals. You'd only get under their feet."

George considered using his physical strength to muscle his way through but reasoned that he'd be overpowered by numbers and probably be arrested, which would help no one. He felt a growing panic. Just then he seized the lapel of a docker he recognised.

"You were discharging *President McKinley*, weren't yer?"

"That's right, mate. Looks like we finished just in time, dunnit?"

"So, you was all away before this went up?"

"Pretty much. Walter was still there along with Tommy Atwood and Alfie. But it was all done and they was all of 'em ready to leave, so I'm sure they'll turn up. Maybe they've left through a different gate, through into the Millwall."

Frank and Sid had managed to get through the sea of people to join George, but Malcolm, buffeted by the crowd, had been swept to its edge. He would have feared being trampled underfoot had he not been so frantic with worry. There was no sense in him following anyway, for what use was he likely to be?

Frank pulled at George's jacket sleeve and shouted, "Come on! We can get in along the railway line."

"Where's Malcolm?" asked George.

"I don't know, and I don't care neither. We ain't got time to play nursemaid. We just need to find Alfie. Are you wiv me or not?"

*

IN GLENDALE STREET, Robert Atwood thundered down the stairs to join his mother and sister in the kitchen.

"Have you seen the sky out there? Must be a fire or summink!"

With an exaggerated roll of her eyes his sister Kitty said, "What else would it be, you dimwit?"

"I hope Alfie's all right," he said, ignoring the barb.

"Of course he'll be all right. He'll have finished hours ago, and he'll be in the pub with his mates as usual, I should think."

"I expect you're right, love," said their mother, "just so long as he don't get any silly notions about helping. You know how he is."

"I'm going out to get a better look, Mum," said Robert, moving towards the door.

"Oh, no, you don't!" Alice Atwood snapped. "It's bad enough having 'im out there somewhere without you going an' all."

"Aw, Mum." Robert was becoming almost as handsome as his brother, but his face was marred by a scowl with the unfairness of it.

"You can 'aw, Mum' as much as you like, Robert Atwood, but you ain't going and that's that."

"I'm fourteen, Mum. I could go and you couldn't stop me," he declared defiantly.

"True. I couldn't stop you from leaving. But I could stop you from ever coming back, now couldn't I? So stick that in yer pipe and smoke it!"

Robert groaned at the injustice, but having been outsmarted, he put aside his resentment and ran noisily back up the rickety stairs. At least from there he could see the dramatic red sky and listen to the excited cries from the streets.

"He'll 'ave them bleedin' stairs down before he's done," grumbled Alice. "They're only fit for firewood as it is."

"Alfie'll be all right, Mum," said Kitty, knowing where her mother's mind really was.

"I know, love. But I'll be glad to 'ave 'im indoors. I always am. I worry about you all even when the docks ain't on fire. Just you remember that, my gel."

*

DESPITE SID'S INSISTENCE that it was a terrible idea, George and Frank scaled a wall and walked along the Import Dock railway sidings, which ran beside the North Quay warehouses. Alfie's dad had been killed on this stretch, and George was determined that if he could do anything to prevent another Atwood from dying here tonight, then he was going to do it. There was confusion, with men running this way and that. A few had climbed walls to get a better view of the calamity, but most of them were quickly apprehended and hustled away by PLA constables. George and Frank avoided this fate by walking slowly with purpose as though they had every right to be there. It was easy to do, because they'd both worked at the West India Docks for years and knew every square inch of it.

*

"DEATH AIN'T NEVER far away in these parts," Alfie had said and now he was dead. Malcolm was sure of it. He sat slumped on the kerb a little way down from Charlie Brown's, where they'd first met and where they'd since spent many happy drunken hours. They were just good friends, but what a silly phrase that was. Alfie seemed to him a symbol of what little good there was in the world. He always had time for Malcolm. Always a kind word or gentle mockery that was never intended to hurt. Although they could only ever have been friends, he could see no point to his life if Alfie was gone. He had made everything worthwhile.

It was nearly one in the morning and the crowd had become sparser, even though the column of smoke and the fierce glow over the docks and distant explosions all meant that the fire still burned. Policemen filtered through the crowd telling people there was nothing to be done and they might as well all go home. The fire was under control, but they were going to let it burn out, which they expected would take days rather than hours.

Malcolm asked no questions. He sought no confirmation of what he knew in his heart to be true, but he overheard someone ask whether anyone had been hurt.

"A few firemen have needed treatment, but we don't think anyone's died. Although until the Fire Brigade can get near the places that are still ablaze, we can't be sure, can we?"

So, if he was unaccounted for, it was almost certain that his beautiful young friend had been killed; the nature of his death too horrible to con-template.

*

DUE TO A slight shift in the wind, the vile smoke that had made Alfie vomit had veered away from him again. Disorientated, dripping with blood, and gasping for breath, he struggled to his feet and stumbled back towards where he hoped the *President McKinley* was moored. The heat was so intense that the back of his neck felt like a sizzling strip of frying bacon. Although it was as bright as day, the combination of tears and blood in his eyes, the violent light and the acrid, billowing smoke made it hard for him to see clearly. He was so confused by now that he wasn't at all sure he was heading away from, rather than towards danger, because the heat seemed all-enveloping. If he should survive, he promised himself he'd never complain of the cold again.

He dimly made out what he thought might be the corner onto North Quay and as he staggered around it, he was careful to avoid the lighter rope. He wasn't about to hit the stones for a third time if he could help it, particularly as it would likely be the end of him. As it was, he had a cut over one eye that bled down the side of his face. There was a large graze on his cheek and his nose was scraped and bleeding. His cap was saturated with blood from when his head had hit the stones.

He hadn't got far along North Quay when he felt himself being seized and crushed into an embrace.

"Oh, thank God! Thank God!" It was Uncle Tommy, who didn't seem capable of saying much more than that.

"Blimey, Uncle Tommy," Alfie managed. "'Try and put it out before it catches properly', he says!"

Tommy held him at arm's length and laughed. Despite the inferno a few yards over the dock and the millions of pounds' worth of damage, sheer relief made him feel deliriously happy. He thought he'd sent his nephew to an awful death, but he hadn't. In the days to come he knew he'd be haunted by this train of events, but at that moment, he felt better than if he'd won the jackpot on the Littlewoods football pools. Eventually he said, "I thought I'd killed you, Alfie boy. If I ever tell you to do anything like that ever again, just tell me to *fuck off*. That's an order, boy."

Alfie's white smile flashed through the blood and dirt. "If you say so, Uncle Tommy."

Given the state of his uncle, he decided not to tell him that, were it not for his own clumsiness with the rope, along with a subtle shift in wind direction, he would almost certainly have been incinerated by now. It was one of the few times he hadn't been mindful of Walter's dock safety warnings, and it was a bloody good job he hadn't, because it had probably saved his life.

By this time, there were scores of fire engines along the quay, and more than a hundred firemen had arrived from nowhere. Their hoses snaked over the cobbles of the North Quay. The fire had turned night into day. Flames leaped eighty feet into a red sky, and further explosions rent the night as more puncheons of rum blew up. Burning rum merged into a river of fire, and waterfalls of flame wept into the import dock like molten gold. On contact with the water, it hissed, but instead of being extinguished, it continued to burn and spread over the dock, turning it into an orange lake of flames.

This surreal sight was tainted by the smoke that billowed from the stricken quay, and as the wind shifted again, the stench of burning rum became so strong it made them gag.

"Cover your face, boy," spluttered Tommy.

"Get away from here, lads! It ain't safe to stand and gawp at it," bawled one of the firemen as they dashed past the pair to train the hose they were dragging on the flaming water.

Silhouetted against the inferno, a wooden masted cable ship, the closest vessel to the heart of the blaze, looked doomed. "Oh, my Gawd, Uncle Tommy! The *Faraday*. She's 'ad it for sure if we don't do nuffink!"

"There's nuffink we *can* do, Alfie. And if there was, you wouldn't be doing it. I've nearly killed you once tonight already. So, fuck the *Faraday*. There ain't nobody on board 'er."

Alfie accepted his uncle's judgement. He was in no condition to do otherwise.

*

WHEN GEORGE AND Frank reached the North Quay, there were firemen everywhere, trying to prevent the blaze from spreading. Besides the obvious danger of more timber stores going up, it threatened adjacent warehouses holding goods from America and the Orient—sugar, dates, tobacco. Every ship in the dock was crawling with firemen as they trained their hoses on the water itself, to drive the burning rum away from their blistering hulls.

When they saw the rectangular lake of fire that had been the Import Dock only a couple of hours before, both young men simultaneously exclaimed, "Fuckin' 'ell!"

George and Frank's luck ran out as two PLA policemen apprehended them.

"Where did you two spring from?" demanded one, then, "No, don't tell me. I don't care. Step on the vehicle, if you please."

Reluctantly, they did as they were told, the "vehicle" being one of the electric bogies used for moving goods around the quay. One of the policemen stayed behind while the other climbed onto the cart, fiddled about with the controls ineffectively for a moment, and said, "Can either of you drive this bloody thing?"

George stepped up to the controls, and at the constable's direction, hurried the bogie down North Quay towards the dock gates. It bucked as its wheels crunched over hoses. They all had scarves tied over their mouths so they looked as if they were fleeing a bank robbery rather than a fire. George took heart in seeing the *President McKinley* was not in flames although there was a complement of firemen on her deck desperately fighting to keep it that way.

"More passengers," said the policeman as they approached three figures in the distance clinging to each other for support. They were smoke-blackened and their faces were obscured by their scarves. One was covered in blood, but he was instantly recognised by his friends, just by the way he moved.

"Oh, thank God—it's Alfie! It's them!" cried Frank as they slowed to pick them up.

"What the blazes are you doing still here?" Tommy croaked.

"You could have chosen your words better," remarked Walter dryly.

"We came back for '*im*!" said George, poking Alfie in the chest. He didn't trust himself to say any more because he was close to weeping with relief.

"Alfie, the state of yer!" exclaimed Frank, who expressed his relief with laughter.

"I'm all right, boys. Honest I am. It's exciting, innit?" said Alfie with a level of cheer that ordinarily would have only one explanation.

"Here, are you drunk?" asked George in astonishment.

"You know, I think I am?" laughed Alfie. "I dunno why 'cos I ain't drank nuffink."

"It's the fumes from the rum," said the policeman. "'Arf the bleedin' firemen are giggling like schoolboys."

"Where's Malcolm?" were Alfie's next words.

*

AMBULANCES WERE PARKED close to the gate, with nurses standing by, but there were few casualties for them to deal with. One of them stuck a dressing on the cut on Alfie's head, but he refused to go to hospital. They reluctantly allowed him to join his mates who were hanging around outside, tired and relieved.

Eventually George managed to say, "I thought you was a goner, mate, honest I did."

"Well, don't tell me Uncle Tommy, but I almost was. I ain't never come closer than that in all me born days, I can tell yer."

"You had us worried sick, mate," said Frank.

"I know. I'm sorry, boys. But now I gotta find Malcolm, 'cos he'll be proper worried," insisted Alfie.

"Oh, come off it, Alf," snarled Frank. "It's been hours since we saw him. He'll 'ave gone home, be warm and dry, tucked up in bed in his pyjamas. And even if he ain't, where are you gonna start looking for 'im?"

"Frank's right, mate. You need to get yourself home, 'cos yer mum will be climbing the walls by now," said George. "You know how she gets when her little boy's in a scrape."

"She don't know I was still in there though, does she? Malcolm does. I know you think yer talking sense, but you don't know him like I do. He'll be in a right state."

"You've known him six months," protested Frank. "And so what if he is in a state? It ain't your problem."

As though it was something that had only just occurred to him, Sid chipped in with, "Oh, if you want Malcolm, he's over there, sitting on the pavement."

"Why didn't you just say so, you fool," complained George, giving his brother a none too gentle shove.

"I just did."

"Thanks, Sid. Look, I'll see you boys tomorrow. I'm just gonna see he gets home all right, then I'll go home meself, I promise yer."

"Fuck me! You're unbelievable, Alfie. You look like you've gone six rounds wiv Jack Doyle and *you're* gonna help *him* to get home! It was us what came looking for yer, remember. Us! Not that useless—"

"Frank, I'm touched you was worried but don't spoil it all by being a silly sod, eh?"

*

SITTING ON THE kerb, head in hands, face towards the gutter, Malcolm was a picture of utter misery. Alfie approached him undetected, nudged his shoulder gently with his knee, and said, "Oy, what you doin' sitting here in the cold?"

Malcolm's pale face looked up, and he shot to his feet with an unexpected agility. He hugged Alfie to him tightly, as though he was never going to let go. He was crying, so Alfie let him cling and said nothing.

After a while, Alfie cleared his throat and said, "Blimey! It must be 'Hug an Alfie Day' today. Me uncle did the same. And I think George wanted to, truth be told. I must niff a bit with the smoke. And I've thrown up a couple of times an' all."

"I don't care. I was so frightened. I thought, I thought…"

"I know. I know. But I'm fine. I'm a bit tipsy from the rum fumes, mind, but otherwise I'm fine."

Malcolm wiped tears from his eyes. "You must think I'm such a fool."

"No, I don't," said Alfie. "It shows me you care. I dunno why you should care this much, but it's nice that you do."

"I do, Alfie. I really do."

"I'm sorry I've given you such a bad night."

"It's hardly *your* fault. And now I can see that you're all right, well, I'm all right too. But Alfie, your poor face!"

"I know. Not so handsome today, am I?"

"It would take a lot more than a few cuts and bruises to stop you looking handsome." It was out before he could stop it. Surely Alfie would see that his feelings were not in the least Platonic.

But if he'd noticed anything, Alfie wasn't letting on. "Look, seeing as I most probably won't have any work for a while, maybe we can do summink in the week? Just you an' me, eh? Make up for tonight."

"I'd like that," whispered Malcolm.

"It's late. 'Ow will you get home?"

"I'll get a taxi. And don't argue, but I'm taking you home in it first."

"All right. If you insist."

Malcolm would have loved to hold Alfie for the short journey, but of course that wouldn't have been on. Alfie asked the cabbie to drop him off outside the Manchester Arms. As he climbed out, he gave Malcolm's hand a squeeze.

"G'night, Malc," he said in a strangely intimate way.

It was probably wishful thinking on Malcolm's part, but instead of killing Alfie as he'd feared, the Rum Quay fire might actually have brought them closer together.

Chapter Fourteen

Pathé Gazette

Wednesday, 26 April 1933

GOING BY THE papers for days afterwards, Alfie had been at the heart of a drama watched by two million people, from the streets of East London and from vantage points all around the city—from Parliament Hill, from the Crystal Palace, and even from as far afield as Romford, Hendon, and Potters Bar. Although the Fire Brigade had successfully kept the blazing rum slick away from all the vessels in the dock, the fire had drifted out onto the River Thames itself, where thankfully the fire boats had been able to extinguish it.

When Alice Atwood first set eyes on her son's bruised and bloodied face, she'd had what Robert described as "a fit of the screaming ab dabs". The story of how the drama had unfolded left her not knowing whether to hit him or kiss him.

"Gawd forbid we ever 'ave another war!" she exclaimed. "You'd 'ave no chance. Not with you 'aving to show willing and help out all the bleedin' time."

Alfie didn't tell her everything, but when Tommy came around to see how he was and confessed that he had put her eldest son in peril, she flew at him like a hellcat. Alfie and Robert had to put themselves between her and their uncle, and he was lucky to get out with no more than a few scratches on his hands and face. Having lost his only son, he understood her anger even as he was fending her off; she could see how bad he felt about it, so there was no lasting damage done. Nor was there any lasting damage to Alfie's face. He bore the marks for a week or so, prompting people to make more of a fuss of him than they usually did. On first seeing him, Alice had behaved as though he'd been permanently disfigured, but to others, he was just a good-looking lad with a few cuts and bruises and a shiner.

The fire continued to burn for the best part of a week. Over four million pounds' worth of rum had been lost. The papers claimed it would have been enough to supply London for forty years. In daylight, the damage to the docks was less extensive than the spectacle had suggested it would be. The Rum Quay and the adjacent timber sheds were gone, leaving a charred and stinking mess. The crumbling vaults beneath had continued to burn like a little piece of hell. They were under ten feet of water pumped in by the Fire Brigade, which was now pumping it all out again. The damage to the rest of the dock was superficial. The *Faraday*, the nearest vessel to the blaze, had suffered little more than blistered paint. Malcolm was able to direct his attention to finding out how much of the rum that had gone up in smoke so spectacularly had belonged to the British Atlantic's clients. Although the company had arranged storage for a few puncheons, insurance made it a minor inconvenience.

Alfie chose not to meet Malcolm in a pub as had become their custom. He suggested instead that they take a stroll in the West End, then go for tea and cake at a Lyons Corner House. He mentioned the one on Coventry Street, but Malcolm was wary of it because of "the Lilypond" and the more outrageous queens.

"I know," he said. "There's a plush new one on the corner of Oxford Street and Tottenham Court Road. I think you might like it, Alfie."

They met at Charing Cross, ambled around Trafalgar Square and up the Haymarket. Alfie's face was healing nicely, and he looked nowhere near as bad as he had the last time Malcolm had seen him. As he hadn't been to work, he was smart in one of his suits, a charcoal-grey serge with a black pinstripe. His cap was pulled down over one eye, a little more so than usual because it was the blackened one. He was easy to cast as the wounded hero, and he drew as many glances of admiration as Malcolm had become accustomed to. He wasn't talkative, however, and when Malcolm's conversational efforts dried up, they walked in silence, but a companionable one.

In Charing Cross Road, Alfie had been wide-eyed at all the bookshops, which to Malcolm were commonplace. Many had trestle tables on the pavement outside bearing second-hand books with people clustering around them, eagerly scouring them for bargains. They browsed, but Alfie said, "I don't wanna be lugging anything around with me today, but I must come back and spend a few hours here."

"What type of books are you interested in?"

"I dunno. All sorts, I suppose. There's so many things out there I know nuffink at all about. If I read more, I'll know more, won't I? And if I know more, I'll be able to talk about summink besides football and boxing."

In common with many from the East End, Alfie hadn't spent much time up West. Poplar, Limehouse, Bethnal Green, Mile End, the Isle of Dogs, the Docks, and the Boleyn Ground were Alfie's small world and he seldom left it. Malcolm loved him for what he was and had never considered trying to "improve" him. His reaction to the booksellers made him seem a creature straining on the leash, desperate for new knowledge and experiences, and Malcolm wondered whether he might be able to help with that.

The large complex of cafés within the flagship Oxford Corner House might have been the Savoy as far as Alfie was concerned. He drank in the surroundings with child-like wonder. In the luxurious Mountview Café, they were directed to a table by a cheerful nippy, smart in her black uniform with a starched white collar and apron, and a cap bearing the Lyons monogram. Battered and bruised though he was, she fell under Alfie's spell right away.

The Mountview was more elaborately decorated than the usual Lyons tea shop. Its magnificent Art Deco room was lined with large marble columns, with collars of glass petals from which extravagant uplighting gave the illusion that the moulded ceiling was being supported by light. It was vast but seemed even more so because of the mirrored walls. There must have been a hundred tables, covered in crisp white linen tablecloths and spaced out over a lush and colourfully patterned carpet. Beside the staircase at one end, a string quartet played light classical music. The place reeked of gentility.

The tea was served in a silver-plate teapot, matched by the milk jug, the sugar bowl, and the salt and pepper cellars. Malcolm ordered a Welsh Rarebit and Alfie a generous piece of grilled ham. When it came, he ate with relish. Once he'd finished it, he had several cakes, and as he drank a third cup of tea, he sat back and let his eyes wander around the opulent room. For Alfie, eating out had never been more than fish and chips or a café near the docks. Apart from one or two of the grander pubs, he had never experienced anything close to this level of luxury, and he was in awe of it. That, and his untypically quiet mood, touched Malcolm.

Alfie caught his gaze and smiled sheepishly. "It's nice in here, innit? I like the way the carpet's so deep you sink in it. It ain't what I'm used to, that's for sure."

"It *is* very smart. They've spent a lot of money on it. It's certainly a cut above your ordinary Lyons."

"It's a new building, innit? What used to be here?"

"The old Oxford Music Hall."

"Blimey, I wonder if me mum and dad ever came here. Dad was Marie Lloyd's greatest fan, you know? He went to watch her funeral over Hampstead and everything."

They couldn't stay there all day, much as Alfie might have liked to, so they split the bill at his insistence and wandered out onto crowded Oxford Street.

"I know," said Alfie suddenly, "let's go to the pictures!"

"All right. What shall we see?" A visit to the picture house wasn't something Malcolm did often.

"Dunno. It don't really matter. Let's just go into the first one we come to, eh?"

There were several cinemas on Tottenham Court Road, but Malcolm was relieved that the Dominion was the first they came to. The Carlton and the Majestic a little further up both had a reputation as places where one might find men to misbehave with, and he didn't want to risk anyone trying to drape their mackintosh over Alfie's lap.

Two grand staircases on either side of a palatial foyer were enough to make Alfie's eyes wide again. The Poplar cinemas were nowhere near as grand, neither in scale nor in decor. The auditorium was enormous and seemed ridiculous for the sparse house attending the main feature, which was to be *The Good Companions*. The pair settled into sumptuous maroon velvet seats just as the cock crowed and the *Pathé Gazette* newsreel began running. They should have known the leading story would be a report on the fire at the Rum Quay. Alfie had to sit and watch something frighteningly real to him shown on the big screen, accompanied by dramatic music and a commentary delivered at a breathless pace.

Malcolm resisted the urge to lay a comforting hand on his friend's arm. "He's a tough young East End docker, not a delicate little flower," he told himself. To his astonishment, Alfie's hand found his own in the darkness and clung to it. He didn't relinquish it until the *Gazette* moved on to a news piece about the joyful release of some British engineers who'd been detained by the Russians, followed by an item on the new-fangled electric traffic lights in Trafalgar Square.

The opening feature was *The Water Gipsies*, a short film made the year before, based on a novel by A.P. Herbert about simple river folk. A girl fell in love with an artist and ignored the attentions of a dull, but far more suitable, boatman. A third suitor, who was a bit of a wrong 'un, fell into the river while trying to force his attentions on the heroine, and despite the young artist jumping in to try to rescue him, he drowned. In the end, spurned by the posh artist, the heroine settled for the dull boatman.

When the lights came on between features Malcolm said, "Was that a happy ending? I'm not sure."

"It weren't for the actor what played the artist," said Alfie grimly. "He was dead before the film even came out. He died a couple of months after they did the scene where he dived into the water. They reckon he caught sumfink from it. He were only twenty-three an' all."

"Good God! I had no idea."

"It was only a small piece in the *Herald*. They didn't make a big song and dance about it. I suppose they didn't wanna put people off going to see the film."

Of course, Alfie read every word of every issue of the *Daily Herald*. "Twenty-three?" Malcolm said soberly. "That's a real tragedy."

"Yep. You never can tell, can yer? When yer number's up, I mean."

If he'd aimed to take Alfie's mind off his own mortality, then he wasn't making a good job of it. Two usherettes carrying down-lit trays had emerged, one selling twopenny bars of chocolate and cigarettes while the other offered tubs of ice cream and choc-ices. Out of desperation Malcolm asked, "Would you like an ice cream? Or some chocolate?" Alfie didn't want anything as they had not long eaten. He wouldn't have that body if he stuffed himself every five minutes. Malcolm was relieved when the lights went down again.

The main feature was an adaptation of J. B. Priestley's *The Good Companions,* a light-hearted musical that lifted their spirits. Malcolm didn't think it all that good a film, but he enjoyed Alfie's enjoyment of it.

Afterwards, they wandered towards the Kingsway Tunnel where he could catch a tram home to Highgate.

"I've been in a funny mood, ain't I?" said Alfie. "I'm sorry."

"Good Lord, you don't owe me any apologies! You haven't seemed quite yourself, but you haven't been hard work or anything like that."

"To tell you the truth, it's that fire."

"You astound me," said Malcolm, and Alfie laughed.

"Yes, yes, I know that's probably stating the bleedin' obvious. But I could've died, Malc. I didn't think about it much when it was happening, or afterwards when me mum was fussing round me, but I ain't slept these last few nights for thinking about it. And seeing it in the pictures…" He smiled self-consciously. "I'm being a bit wet about it, ain't I?" He blushed pink. "Holding yer hand like a little boy an' all. Sorry about that."

"Alfie, I understand. I'd feel exactly the same. And you can hold my hand any time you feel the need."

"It ain't just dying I've been thinking of. It's made me think about living…about everything. We waste such a lot of time, don't we? We think we have forever, but we don't."

"That's true enough. But it would be exhausting to live each day as though it might be our last. Expensive too."

"I ain't a thinking sort of person, Malcolm, to tell you the truth. Honest to God, it's fair worn me out," Alfie said. "I'll be fine though. Don't you worry."

Malcolm wanted to tell Alfie he could talk to him at any time about anything he wanted to. He also wanted to take Alfie in his arms and hold him, but he said and did nothing. They were near to a bus stop where a Number 8 was just pulling in.

"This'll do me," said Alfie, turning towards him and placing a hand on his arm. "Thanks for this evening. It's been what I needed. You know, I don't think anyone but you would have done tonight."

And with that, making light of any aches and pains he may have been nursing after his ordeal, he sprinted athletically after the bus as it pulled away, leaped onto the rear platform, and raised a hand of farewell to Malcolm as he climbed the open staircase and ducked to disappear into the upper saloon.

Part Four

Mad About the Boy

Chapter Fifteen

Calamine Lotion

Saturday, 3 June 1933

GRACE TREVELYAN WORE a determined expression that suggested she meant business. She'd cleaned the house from top to bottom, but she surveyed the garden with furrowed brow. The lawn was neat enough and the flower beds ablaze with early summer blooms, all of which was down to her own efforts. However, there was nothing she could do about the great oak, a huge tree that was older than the house.

"Malcolm, you really must do something about that tree," she said.

"I know, I know. It's on my list of things to sort out." He was impatient with her for reminding him about it yet again. The list of practical tasks he must do in his spare time seldom got any shorter.

Mrs Trevelyan sighed. "Well, forgive me for not finding that particularly reassuring, dear. Those panes in the attic window have been cracked for months now. Every time I hear the wind, I'm at my wits' end waiting for them to be smashed altogether."

The tree hadn't been cut back since Malcolm's father had been alive. Whenever there was more than a light breeze, its branches would strike the upper floor windows. One wild night in January, Grace's fears had proved well-founded as the branches lashed the attic window and cracked several panes. There was no point in getting the panes replaced until the threat posed by the tree had been lifted. She didn't want it felled because it had been one of the things she loved most about the house when she and William had first viewed it, but it needed to have its branches severely cut back.

The idea of Malcolm climbing up a ladder with a saw in his hand was laughable, but she did think he might find someone else to do it. Her son, so assured within the precincts of his own office and confident in his dealings with clerks, wharfingers, and warehousemen, dreaded talking to tradesmen. His mother may have thought he'd pushed the problem from his mind but in reality, it loomed larger than any worries he had concerning his work, to the point that it prevented him from relaxing in his own home.

During a night out in the East End, sedated by beer and casting her as the villain, he got his mother's nagging off his chest and cited the "bloody tree situation" as an example. George, who was always on the lookout for an opportunity to make money, made an offer.

"You don't wanna let yer mum go spending good money on summink as simple as that," he said emphatically. "We'll do it for a few bob if you like."

Alfie agreed and said he'd be happy to help and even Frank expressed willingness. It seemed a perfect solution; the problem of the tree would be solved, and he could introduce Alfie into his home and more importantly, to his mother. He accepted the offer and went home elated that something which had been weighing on his mind was to be resolved so beneficially.

The Trevelyans' red-brick Victorian house was in Cranmer Avenue, a road lined with mature lime trees and rising off Highgate Hill before falling steeply down to Archway Road. Number 86 stood just before the brow of the hill and the top-floor windows afforded a spectacular view across North London, allowing Grace to look down on Holloway geographically as well as socially. The windows and front doors of all the houses in the street boasted white surrounds, rounded rather than sharply cornered, giving the architecture a distinctive unity.

A flight of steps led up to the front door, painted maroon and half glazed with stained-glass detail, opening into a spacious vestibule. An inner door, also lavishly decorated with a stained-glass design, opened into a wide hallway paved with black and white floor tiles. Three doors opened off it. The first on the right led into the drawing room, the second into the parlour, while at the end of the hall a third led through into a large kitchen, a larder, and a scullery. On the first floor, Grace Trevelyan's bedroom overlooked the street, while Malcolm's looked out onto the back garden. There were two guest bedrooms and a bathroom on that floor and three more bedrooms and a smaller bathroom on the second. These might once have accommodated servants, but Mrs Teller, the occasional help, lived in Holloway, and the days of having a cook and a maid had ended during the war.

Grace arranged to borrow a ladder from her friend Marjorie up the road, and early on Saturday morning in brilliant sunshine, Alfie and Frank turned up with two pairs of garden shears and a saw, but without George. He had succumbed to some ailment but the others reckoned they'd manage it easily enough between them. Grace insisted on making them a cup of tea before they began, and when she produced a plate of home-made biscuits to go with it, they were effusive in their praise.

The two young dockers had never been in a house this size before. Like those of tourists in a great cathedral, their eyes roamed the high ceilings and plaster cornices, and the substantial oak, walnut, and mahogany furniture.

Before they started work, Alfie visited the bathroom and said, "Blimey, Malcolm, if we had a barfroom like that you'd never get me out of it!" In fact, Malcolm had often complained to his mother about how old-fashioned it was, but the ornate porcelain bath was long enough for a grown man to lie down in, and at one end, it boasted the rare facility of a shower, with a rail for the curtain to keep in the spray. Alfie had never seen the like of it in a private house.

When the boys had started work, Malcolm would occasionally glance out of the window, only to get the impression that Frank was acting in an advisory capacity, with Alfie doing most of the work. It was a hot day, and Alfie soon discarded his shirt. Broad-shouldered and narrow-waisted, as he laboured the muscles in his back and arms moved gorgeously under smooth, unblemished skin that glistened with sweat. Malcolm had never seen this much of his body before, and it had a considerable impact on him. He was perfect. They'd known each other for eight months and now he was confronted with this new dimension. On a rising tide of despondency, he wondered why he was torturing himself like this. They would only ever be friends—and not even that, if this lovely young man ever had an inkling of what was going on in his head, in his heart, and indeed in his trousers.

The sun was relentless all morning and into the afternoon, making all physical activity uncomfortable and even dangerous. With the tree three-quarters done, Alfie clambered unsteadily back to the ground. He staggered, stumbled, and passed out on the lawn. Thank God he hadn't done it while he was still up in the tree. Malcolm took the stairs two at a time and rushed into the garden. Frank was trying to bring his friend round by slapping his face gently and Grace was fanning him with her apron. He came to and they helped him onto his feet.

Grace, who had been sceptical throughout about Frank's contribution to the task, took charge.

"Let's get him in out of this sun. Malcolm, go and phone the doctor."

"Doctor!" exclaimed Frank scornfully. "He ain't made of money. It's just a bit of sunburn, that's all."

"Well, maybe that could have been avoided if you'd done a bit more of the actual work," said Grace with a withering glance. "Poor boy. Look at his back. He's been burnt to a crisp."

That was an exaggeration. Alfie's skin was often exposed to the sun, but once they'd helped him indoors, they could see the angry red burn over his shoulders and back that hadn't been as noticeable in the brilliant sunshine.

"Oh, Good Lord! But it is just sunburn as you say," she conceded reluctantly. "Help him upstairs to your room, Malcolm. We'll let him have a lie down for a couple of hours."

"I don't want to be any trouble, missus," protested Alfie groggily.

"Nonsense. It's no trouble, dear. I'll pop down to the chemist for some calamine lotion."

Shortly after she'd gone, Frank took his leave, citing another obligation he had back in Poplar. "You'll enjoy looking after the poor wounded soldier, won't yer, Malcolm? You'll have him all to yerself," he said with an unsettling leer.

Malcolm wouldn't have been able to take Alfie up the stairs and along the landing had Alfie not been able to largely support himself, albeit unsteadily. He had to guide and steer him, which inevitably involved considerable contact with his bare skin, a wonderful agony. Despite his hours of labour in intense heat, he smelt surprisingly nice. Alfie was not in any condition to take in his surroundings but was grateful to collapse heavily onto the bed, where he lay on his stomach. Malcolm sat down on the armchair beside him until Alfie's breathing deepened as he dozed off.

The half-naked sunburnt young man lying face down on the brass double bed was a parody of one of Malcolm's desperate night-time fantasies. He was completely vulnerable. The angry red of his shoulders and back did not disguise his perfection. Malcolm could have reached out and touched him anywhere on his body as he lay there spark out and he would not have noticed. He felt dirty for thinking it. He tore his eyes away from the slumbering boy, rose from the chair, and walked out of the room without a backward glance, leaving Alfie to sleep in peace.

When his mother returned, she was clutching a paper bag emblazoned with the words "Boots the Chemist".

"Gracious me! It's very hot out now, dear. Where's that Frank one gone?" she asked in a tone heavy with disgust.

"He had something he needed to do this afternoon and he didn't think there was much point in hanging around."

"Oh, didn't he?" spat Grace. "How is the patient, anyway?"

"Asleep. I think."

She took a small blue bottle from the bag and handed it to her son. "Probably for the best. Here. Shake it well then rub the lotion onto his back."

"Me?" he said with alarm.

"Well, yes, of course you! He can hardly do it himself, and he'll find it less embarrassing having a friend do it than an old lady he doesn't know. Be gentle. Then when he wakes it will be more comfortable for him. His skin will peel, but he should feel considerably soothed by it."

Malcolm trudged up the stairs, compelled to do something he longed to do, but didn't believe he should be doing. He eased open his bedroom door and slipped quietly inside. He shook the blue glass bottle vigorously, and after removing the cork, he sat carefully on the edge of the bed, inhaling the aroma of childhood sickness. He hadn't encountered the stuff since he'd had chicken pox when he was six. He poured the thick, pale-pink liquid into his trembling fingers and let it run onto the expanse of flesh before him. As soon as it made contact, Alfie gasped.

"I'm sorry! Did I hurt you? I didn't mean to wake you," whispered Malcolm.

"Nah, I was just dozing. It's cold, that's all."

"It's calamine lotion—should help the pain. I'm going to have to rub it in. I'll be as gentle as I can."

"Go on then."

As Malcolm spread the cooling lotion over the burnt part of his skin, Alfie showed no sign of discomfort; in fact, he visibly relaxed under the touch. Malcolm caressed every contour from his neck, over his shoulder blades and right down to the dip at the base of his spine. He covered his sides, his shoulders, and arms, everything that was visible. Stroking this perfect body felt like heaven. The lotion left chalky pink smears on the satin-smooth skin.

"Are you all right?" he enquired nervously. "I haven't hurt you?"

"Nah. You've done a grand job. You should have been one of them geezers at a Turkish barf."

"Do you want me to do your front?" It came out before he could stop it.

"Nah," said Alfie quickly. "Yer all right. The sun was mainly on me back and I can't lay on it just now anyway. I tell you what, give me back one more rub, will yer?"

Malcolm was happy to oblige and before he'd finished, Alfie had nodded off again, undressed and asleep on a bed in which he'd been dreamed of so often. Malcolm sat and watched him for a while before abandoning his vigil and going back downstairs to his mother.

She looked up from her sewing as he entered. "How is he? Did the lotion help?"

"Yes, I think so. He's asleep. He drifted off as I was rubbing it in."

She tutted. "The poor boy. I'd like to give that Frank a piece of my mind, I can tell you. And what about the tree? It looks ridiculous as it is. It's all lopsided."

"Yes, Mum, but let's not worry about the bloody tree just now. Not until we're sure Alfie's all right."

"Really, darling, he's hardly at death's door. It's a bit of sunburn, that's all. It'll clear up soon enough." She added, "You know, he really is quite beautiful." Grace would often comment on men she thought "handsome", but Malcolm had never heard her call one "beautiful" before. "But I daresay that being a man you won't have noticed that."

"I can't say I have, no," he lied.

"Oh, Malcolm! You men are so *silly* about that sort of thing. You have eyes, don't you?"

"I suppose he is a rather nice-looking chap," said Malcolm weakly.

"There's an understatement if ever I heard one. He's exceptional! Why, if Marjorie was half the painter she thinks she is, I'd suggest he sit for her. But I shan't because frankly, I doubt her daubing would do him justice."

*

EVENING HAD FALLEN by the time they heard Alfie's tentative steps on the staircase, as though he had no right to be there. He pushed open the drawing-room door and diffidently poked his head around it.

"Hello. How long have I been asleep?"

"The best part of four hours, dear," said Grace, as she laid aside her sewing and rose from her armchair. "How are you feeling?"

"I'm just a bit dozy, that's all. But I feel a lot better than I did, thanks. Sorry to be such a trouble."

"It's no trouble," Grace told him. "I'm just a bit annoyed with your friend, that's all, letting you do all the work like that."

"I feel a bit guilty myself. I could have helped," mumbled Malcolm.

"Nah. Don't be daft. Why buy a dog and bark yerself, eh?" Alfie smiled at him and added, "I got to be honest, I think yer hands are better at rubbing in lotion than they would be sawing branches anyway."

Malcolm blushed. He was mesmerised by Alfie's bare chest, the dark nipples, the line of hair at his navel. He was sure no finer sight had ever graced this room in the half-century since it was built.

"I'm glad he did a good job, Alfie," Grace said kindly.

"I suppose Frank finished off, did he?" Alfie asked.

"No, dear. He didn't finish off, he just buggered off, if you'll pardon my French, and left you and the tree."

Alfie raked his fingers through his dark hair with a pained expression. "Oh. blimey! He's bloomin' useless." The sudden glimpse of the tangle of dark hair in his armpit prevented Malcolm from speaking. There wasn't much hair on this wonderful body but where it grew, it was thick.

"I suppose I'd better pay you, as nobody could fault your effort." Grace reached for her handbag.

"Nah, missus. I'll come back and finish it off for yer next weekend."

"Don't be silly, dear. I won't hear of it."

"If it ain't finished, it ain't finished. You can't pay good money for a job that ain't been done proper."

"Well, if you're sure…"

"I am. I ain't gonna take no more than an hour to finish, I reckon."

"I've put your shirt into the wash." Grace picked a clean shirt up off her sewing box. "You can borrow this one of Malcolm's to go home in. I've just sewn a button onto it."

"Oh, missus, you shouldn't have troubled."

"Nonsense. Yours was full of sweat. The salt would have aggravated your sunburn. Put it on and sit yourself down. You'll have a cup of tea, and I've made you a sandwich. Ham, will that suit?"

With that, she disappeared to fetch the promised snack. Alfie's delicious smoothness disappeared into Malcolm's shirt and as he buttoned it up, he smiled shyly at Malcolm.

"Mums, eh? They just can't help themselves, can they?"

"She likes you, Alfie."

"I dunno why. I've brung 'er nuffink but trouble. But I like her an' all, as it goes. Cor, and them biscuits! She's a character, in't she?"

"She's that, all right."

*

A WEEK LATER, on a mercifully grey day, Alfie's bike leaned against the Trevelyans' side gate again. He'd returned Malcolm's shirt, clinically laundered by his mother, and finished the tree-pruning off in an hour. He sawed up the branches and stowed them beside the shed. Once the foliage had withered and died it would be firewood for the winter months. He refused to take any money for his work because of all the drama, but Grace handed Malcolm a pound note and insisted he take him to the pub. They went to the Old Crown, a grand ecclesiastical-looking pub on the corner of Highgate Hill and Hornsey Lane, where they settled in a corner with a couple of pints of mixed.

"How's the sunburn?"

"It all peeled off, and now it's like it never happened." Alfie sipped his ale and gave a devilish grin. "Do you wanna check?"

Malcolm was alarmed. "I was only asking to be polite."

"You was good with yer hands though, mate, I'll say that for yer. With that pink stuff, I mean."

"Calamine lotion."

"That's the one. Did you…enjoy it as much as I did?"

"It was—I was—just helping." Confusion. Alarm. Malcolm felt there was something new between them and had the awful feeling that his game might be up.

"I know you was. And I was very grateful. Like I say—it felt nice. I enjoyed it."

Malcolm drank his beer, but as soon as he'd put it down, he was nervously picking it up for another sip. Their usual easy rapport was gone. He trembled slightly and hoped it wasn't visible. He'd tried to fight his own desires and behave like a good friend the previous Saturday, but perhaps Alfie had seen through him anyway. Whatever the circumstances, he had enjoyed caressing his body even through a handful of pink cream and he had thought about it every night since. He was a predator. A vile predator. If the penny had dropped, he would lose Alfie's friendship and he'd be lucky if he didn't lose some of his teeth too.

Alfie leaned towards him and looked him directly in the eye. "It's all right, Malcolm. I know."

Malcolm swallowed with difficulty. "I'm sorry?"

"I know you like me," said Alfie with a shy smile.

"Well, of course I like you—you're a very decent chap."

Alfie chuckled. "Well, I'm glad you think so, but that ain't what I mean, and you know it. You *like* me, like a man is supposed to like a woman…only I'm a man."

Malcolm gasped for breath like a landed fish on a riverbank, waiting for the fisherman's blow.

"Like I said, it's all right, Malcolm. I understand. Same again?" He picked up their empty glasses without waiting for an answer and went to get them filled. Malcolm stayed fixed in his seat, barely moving, barely breathing, until Alfie returned. When he did, he placed a pint onto the table in front of Malcolm and squeezed his shoulder affectionately before sitting back down.

"Please don't look so worried, mate. I told you: I understand."

Now he'd gathered his thoughts a little, Malcolm felt that perhaps he should test the worth of their growing friendship. He would have to trust Alfie not to hurt him physically or reputationally.

"*Do* you understand, Alfie? Really? If so, perhaps you could explain it to me."

"Explain what?"

"Explain why I'm like I am. Why am I cursed to feel like this about other men?"

Alfie leaned forward and put a hand on his shoulder again. "Look, I ain't no doctor, but I reckon it's just one of them things, mate."

"And you don't hate me for it?"

Alfie looked incredulous. "Nah, of course I don't. Why would I? You've been nuffink but kind to me. You ain't the first person in the world to be that way and I daresay you ain't gonna be the last."

"Sometimes it feels as if I am though. The only one, I mean." He knew there were others, but not anyone like him.

"Well, you ain't. Trust me."

"I suppose that someone who looks like you do would be sure to draw attention from, well, the likes of me."

"Yup."

"But you know I feel more for you than just that sort of thing, don't you?"

"After the way you was after that fire? Course I do. I wouldn't be sitting here now if I thought you was just after getting in me drawers, Malc. As you say, I get a lot of attention. But you, you see who I am. I sometimes think you know me better than the others do, even though I've only known yer a few months."

"You won't tell anyone? Not even your friends?"

"No, of course I won't. What is it they say? 'Your secret is safe with me'."

"What made you decide to say something today?"

Alfie shrugged. "I just needed you to know that I know and it's all right. I don't like to see you suffering when there ain't no need for it."

Malcolm relaxed to the extent that he visibly slumped, put his hands to his face, and said, "I thought… I thought…"

"I think I can guess what you thought, Malc. But listen—I'm a dock worker from the Isle of Dogs and you're a posh boy from Highgate. We ain't supposed to be mates at all, but we are. If anyone don't like it, that's tough—but that's how it is."

"Thank you, Alfie." It was the most genuine and heartfelt thanks he had ever offered, but his friend wasn't having it.

"Nah, nah, don't go thankin' me. I ain't doing you a big favour. I suppose I must need you in me life, posh boy, just as much as you must need me. I've got one bit of advice for you though."

"Oh? And what's that?"

"You've got to stop working yerself up about every little thing, mate, you really 'ave."

Chapter Sixteen

The Greatest Chance

AS IF MALCOLM hadn't already enough reasons to love Alfie, the talk they'd had in the Crown had given him another. In most ways, nothing had changed. He still loved a boy who couldn't love him back in the way he'd like, but he no longer had to pretend on the precious occasions they were alone. He could talk about it openly as he had never been able to do before. When they were in the pub, Alfie would even discreetly point out men he thought might oblige.

"That geezer wiv the glasses at the end of the bar—he would, I reckon."

"How on earth can you tell?"

"Just keep an eye on him. See who he looks at. Watch how he looks at 'em. I'd put money on it."

Malcolm began to see it. The best way of finding men who loved men was to have Alfie around. He was never likely to chase after anyone while he was out with Alfie though. Besides finding it impossible to concentrate on anyone else, it would have been noticed by the others. Alfie didn't put pressure on him. They both seemed content just to whisper about possibilities.

Sometimes, at Alfie's insistence, the boys would come into the City so that Malcolm didn't have as far to go home. The dockers wouldn't have been welcome in many City pubs in their work clothes, but at Aldgate, the ancient Hoop and Grapes was happy to serve them as it did on the last Friday in June. Frank started grumbling about everything from the moment he got off the tram. The beer was watery, it was too crowded, he had things to do on Saturday morning, and he reckoned he was owed money for his consultancy services on the Trevelyans' tree.

Alfie hadn't come on the tram but on his pushbike, so Malcolm had to cope with Frank all on his own for an uncomfortable quarter of an hour. Once Alfie was there, all was well. He revelled in the new warmth between them. He'd known him only eight months, and yet this young man knew him better than anyone ever had before, possibly including himself. He would have been happy for the other three to melt away, and so to compensate, he made more effort than usual to talk to them. He told Frank his mother oversaw payment for tree services and he'd only have been paid if he'd seen the job through to the end. Alfie butted in and added that Frank had been paid what his efforts had merited—nothing.

That was when the conversation took on a more worrying turn as Frank remarked snidely, "You should of been paid a few bob more, Alfie."

"Oh—an' why's that?"

"Well, for the peepshow, of course."

"Wotcher mean?"

"Well, Malcolm kept sneaking looks at you out of his bedroom window, didn't yer, Malcolm? Don't think I didn't spot yer. I reckon he enjoys seeing you wiv your shirt off, Alf."

Malcolm kept his cool. "I did keep looking out, yes," he said calmly. "But that was just to see if *you* had started doing any actual work yet."

The others laughed at Frank's expense, and he was proud of his own quick thinking, but secretly worried by the mean look in Frank's eyes. After a lifetime of being discreet, Alfie had seen through him and now maybe Frank had too.

He gradually relaxed as the conversation moved onto safer ground and stayed there. As always, he enjoyed himself in this unlikely company.

Once he got home, he had the house to himself. His mother had gone to Folkestone for the weekend to see his Aunt Hannah, as she did most Fridays. He missed the polite interrogation about where he'd been and who he'd seen, and the offer of snacks. He wasn't always happy to be alone in the big house with too much time to dwell on his problems. Having finished his cocoa, he was about to go to bed when there was a knock at the front door, which was unusual at that hour. He opened it a crack. Alfie stood there.

"Aren't yer gonna invite me in then?" he asked with a devastating smile.

"It's a quarter past eleven," was all Malcolm could say.

"I know. But I've cycled all the way up that bleedin' hill to see yer! You can hardly turn a man away when he's done that, can yer?"

He couldn't see himself denying Alfie anything at any time of the day or night. He stood aside to let him in and gestured towards the parlour, where the embers of a fire still glowed. Mrs Teller had built it despite the house being empty all evening. It may have been June, but it was England and hot water might be needed.

"I've just had some cocoa, but I can—"

"Nah, don't you worry. I ain't here for cocoa and I don't plan on staying long neither. I just wanted to see if you was all right—you know, after Frank was funny wiv you an' that."

"I think I coped."

Alfie laughed. "Yes, you did. You sorted him out good and proper."

"But will that be the end of it?"

Alfie nodded. "I reckon so. He probably don't know as much as you think he does. He's always been a bit funny about people getting friendly wiv me, no matter who they are. He gets jealous, Gawd knows why."

"I can understand that, I suppose."

Alfie contemplated his boots in silence for a moment before glancing up and saying, "I reckon he was right about one thing though, weren't he? You would like to see me with me shirt off again. Wouldn't you, Malcolm?"

He flushed crimson. "D-don't be silly."

"Oh, come on! I told yer, you don't have to pretend wiv me."

Alfie stood up, removed his rough jacket, and threw it onto the settee. His scarf followed, then his cap. There was nothing unusual in this, he'd done the same on his previous visits. But this time, he unbuttoned and took off his waistcoat, slinging it on top of his coat. He then hooked his thumbs under his braces and pulled them off his shoulders so they hung down on either side of his trousers. His smile widened as he pulled his shirt over his head.

In the cosy, familiar surroundings of his mother's parlour, Malcolm was confronted by the half-naked Alfie. Without the angry distraction of the sunburn, he was breathtakingly beautiful. Malcolm didn't look for long before letting his eyes rest on anything else—the china ornaments on the mantelpiece, the Napoleon clock ticking more slowly than his heart was beating, the bowl of fruit on the sideboard. *Why does Mum buy pears that no one eats?* he wondered. The books on the bookcase shelves—a *Bible Commentary* and ten volumes of the *Arthur Mee Children's Encyclopaedia*—the embers of the dying fire… Anything but Alfie's slim, smooth body.

"You can look at me since I gone to all this trouble," Alfie said in almost a whisper. "Look at me, Malcolm."

He did as he was told and properly took in what was before him. He'd seen it before, of course, but this time it was *for* him. The clear skin with scarcely a blemish, a tiny mole or two, a couple of light scars and a scratch. The dark nipples, hard in the cooling room, the gently undulating contours of the biceps and pectorals, the arrow flight of dark hair beneath his navel with the shadow of more under his arms. Unsupported by the braces, his trousers had slipped to hang low on his hips. His belly looked flat and firm with a tight little navel, like a neat bullet-hole. He watched it rise and fall. Rise and fall. If he had been an artist, he could have tried to capture it, in oils, or in clay, or in stone. But he was not an artist. He didn't know what to do with what he saw. This was the greatest chance that life had ever offered him, and he was ill-equipped to cope with it. He could only stand there feeling that fate had called his bluff by overloading him all at once with everything he'd ever dreamed of.

Alfie moved up close to him. Malcolm could smell him—coal tar soap, just a hint of fresh sweat, like a faint smell of grapefruit and something else indefinable but far from unpleasant. God, he was lovely. And confident of his reception, it seemed. He was teasing, but not unkindly.

"You can touch me if you like. Go on. Be a devil."

Malcolm could do no such thing. He stood rigidly upright, his arms stiffly by his sides.

"No? What about a little kiss then?"

"Don't be…"

"Go on. One little kiss ain't gonna hurt, is it?" cajoled Alfie in a whisper. "I won't tell no one. Promise."

Malcolm stayed silent, and Alfie took it as acquiescence, removing Malcolm's glasses and placing them on the piano. Without making any other contact, he leaned forward, tilting his head slowly to one side as he did so. Malcolm could feel his breath on his face. It was mostly fresh although there was a hint of beer on it. He knew that all he needed to do to stop this was to take a step back, but he remained rooted to the spot. Alfie gently pressed his mouth against his and he thought that would be that. But it wasn't his aunt kissing him. Alfie's tongue probed its way into his mouth and played with his own. He had heard of this sort of thing and considered it unhygienic. As a rule, he wouldn't even drink from another person's glass. Perhaps it was the lack of hygiene that was making his head spin, but it could hardly have been the cause of the stiffening down below. His brain may have been paralysed, his heart may have been stunned, but bizarrely, his cock was able to show a measure of common sense.

The kiss continued for a long moment or two, and he was beginning to admit to himself that it was all rather pleasant, when Alfie firmly put his hands on either side of his head so that he could probe deeper and more insistently with his tongue. Malcolm's flicker of indignation was quickly extinguished as he was overwhelmed by an even greater excitement. His head spun. He could no longer let his arms hang there like two wallflowers at a dance, so he tentatively embraced Alfie and ran his hands up the smooth skin of his subtly muscled back. Silky though his skin was, there was no mistaking the hard strength of the body it was stretched tightly over. This was a young working man Malcolm was holding. Any lingering doubt he may have had about what it was he wanted from life was banished forever. He wanted this!

Alfie unclamped his mouth and let his hands drift down to hold Malcolm by the hips. His face was close.

"You're trembling."

"I know." Malcolm offered no explanation.

"That wasn't so bad, was it?"

"No. Have…have we finished now?"

"Easy, boy," laughed Alfie softly. "We 'ave for the time being. It's late—I gotta go. But I just wanted that kiss, you know?"

He released him and retrieved his shirt. As he pulled it over his head Malcolm was again able to enjoy the incredible torso and the thickets of dark hair under his arms.

When he'd finished dressing Alfie turned to Malcolm with a lazy grin on his face. Malcolm asked, "Alfie, why? Why did you want the kiss?"

The boy shrugged. "I dunno. You feel what you feel, dontcha?"

"But I didn't realise that you… I mean, you can't be…can you?"

Another careless shrug. "I dunno. I dunno nuffink. Let's just see what happens, eh?"

"I—I won't say anything. Not to anyone."

Alfie smiled gently. "I never thought you would, mate. I think this is gonna be fun. *You're* gonna be fun." And with that, he was gone, leaving Malcolm in turmoil. Wonderful, brilliant turmoil.

*

AT THE AGE of twenty-seven, Malcolm Trevelyan was a virgin. But worse than that, he was so naive he hadn't even known that tongues entered mouths when love was being made. He appreciated now that this wasn't spoken about, not because it was a naughty secret, but because to most people, it was too obvious a thing to mention. If he didn't know about that, how could he begin to guess what else might be involved?

Over the next days, he vividly recalled every detail of the kiss they'd shared. All they'd actually done was embrace and kiss for a few brief moments, but he thought them the most wonderful moments of his life. The promise of more thrilled him, but his joy was not unbridled.

He had little doubt that he was in love, but that was the easy bit. Any fool could fall in love—it required no skill, no technique, and no stamina. It was sex that worried Malcolm. Despite adoring Alfie's face and body and loving the way he was, he longed to see what the boy had in his trousers and there was no use him denying it. At the same time, it frightened him considerably. Alfie would expect something in return, and to satisfy a young man who could have anyone he wanted could prove a heavy responsibility.

At the age of twenty-seven, Malcolm Trevelyan was in the unenviable position of having received all his sexual education from schoolboys and only second-hand at that. He urgently needed help and guidance.

Chapter Seventeen

Consulting Godfrey

ON THE WEDNESDAY evening following Alfie's advances, Malcolm headed for a dark basement pub close to Leicester Square. The place was badly in need of refurbishment, but men flocked there anyway in the hope of satisfying their "unnatural appetites".

Walking down the stairs, Malcolm felt that every pair of eyes in the place was on him. He read their faces. "Oh, not *her* again!" "My *dear*! Why does she even *bother*?" "As if *anyone* would look twice at *that*!" This crowd would be looked down on by the man in the street, but he felt that they in turn looked down on him.

Standing self-consciously at the bar, he ordered a light ale. The barmaid, an older woman, looked at him impassively.

"You're not the usual sort that drinks in here," she said.

"Oh? And what sort is that?"

She was briefly surprised. "It's for pansies, dear. There's plenty of much nicer places nearby where you can drink without being pestered by the likes of them." She indicated her customers with a sideways toss of her head.

"I'm fine here, thank you."

She sniffed. "Well, I was only trying to help, because you don't look like one of them. You must do as you please, I'm sure. But what would your poor mother say?"

Indeed. What would his mother say? She'd probably be three parts appalled and one part fascinated. Even though he didn't find effeminate men at all attractive, he remained indignant on their behalf in the face of such hostility from those making money out of them. He looked around the dimly lit room as he'd often done before, only this time he was seeking out Godfrey Chalmers.

It wasn't long before he spotted him. Godfrey was older than he was, how much older couldn't be deduced without cutting him in half and counting the rings. But it would be unwise to ask. If provoked, the man could deliver a devastating tongue-lashing to anyone who crossed him. He had a soft spot for Malcolm though, and afforded him a level of protection from the vitriol with which this bar was awash.

Walking along Cheapside in the daytime, Godfrey was indistinguishable from the thousands of other businessmen. Perfectly polished patent-leather shoes, smart Savile Row suit with a buttonhole from a flower girl outside the Royal Exchange, and pomade-slicked greying hair with a geometrically neat parting. Everything about Godfrey's appearance was geometrically neat.

On seeing Malcolm approach, he greeted him with an unconvincing smile.

"Malcolm, dear. How are we? It's been weeks! What was that miserable old cow saying? Was she bothering you?"

"I'm fine."

"Well, that's uncharacteristically garrulous of you, dear. Two whole words? Wonders will never cease."

Ignoring the mockery and his own embarrassment, Malcolm pressed on, because this time he actually wanted to speak to Godfrey. He had to if he was to have any chance at all of avoiding a fiasco with Alfie. With considerable trepidation, he said, "Actually, I wouldn't mind a private word. I'd be obliged for some advice—if you have the time, of course."

Godfrey's eyes lit up. "Of course, dear. I always have time for one of my oldest and dearest friends."

This was untrue in every respect, but Malcolm smiled his thanks and allowed himself to be ushered into an even darker corner of the room. Godfrey was impatient, and as Malcolm tried to frame some words, he prompted, "It's a boy, isn't it? It can only be a boy. I mean, you'd hardly consult me about life insurance or curtains. Tell me all! What's his name? Is he handsome? Do I know him?"

"I'm not telling you his name, but you don't know him anyway. He doesn't come to places like this."

Godfrey was mildly insulted, for if he had a natural habitat, this was it.

"He is very handsome though," Malcolm added bashfully. "One might even say he's beautiful. He's a docker."

"Hmmm! A very *young* docker?"

"Yes."

Godfrey sighed. "So, you're in love?"

Malcolm heard himself saying, "Yes, I rather think I am." He couldn't prevent a happy smile from cutting through his anxiety. It was noted.

"How lovely! And how can I advise you? You seem to have it all sorted out to me, dear."

Now the moment of truth approached, Malcolm squirmed in his seat. Anything he said from now on would expose him to ridicule, and he didn't even know if he had the words anyway.

With Godfrey, the penny dropped. "Ah. It's a bedroom thing, isn't it?"

Malcolm nodded tersely.

Godfrey's interest had finally been secured because other people's bedroom antics were a constant fascination to him. He adopted a pained expression. "So, did it hurt? Was it not quite up to scratch? I take it you have done it?"

"That's the thing really. I'm not entirely…" Malcolm whispered. "That is to say, I'm not at all sure what 'it' involves."

"My godfathers! *How* old are you? There's being a virgin and there's verging on the ridiculous. Please spare me another sorry tale of unrequited lust. If you've done nothing, are we even certain that this boy's to be had?"

"I think so," Malcolm mumbled.

"You *think* so!" scoffed Godfrey with mild contempt. But he didn't want to be unkind. "Why do you *think* so?"

"On Friday night, he came to my house, took off his shirt, and we hugged and kissed."

Godfrey's interest, which had been drifting away like cigarette smoke out of an open window, wafted right back again.

"So he's interested, all right. What happened?"

Malcolm recounted the evening in detail. It wasn't difficult because he remembered everything vividly. Godfrey lapped it up but seemed a little underwhelmed by the denouement—if it could even be called that.

"But, my dear boy, is that *all* that you did?"

"Yes. But it's clear he has more in mind, and I have no idea what to do or what he wants."

"Oh well. He is at least to be had—that's something. We may yet prevail."

"I hope so because, Godfrey, he's the most gorgeous young man I've ever set eyes on in my life. If he hadn't instigated things, I would never have guessed he was at all that way inclined, let alone inclined to do it with me. I'm not stupid. I know a boy like this isn't going to settle down and live happily ever after with me. But if I can't take what *is* on offer…how will I ever forgive myself?"

Godfrey contemplated him in rare silence for a moment, and for once, there was not a trace of mockery in his expression.

"In that case, I'll just have to take you through the basics, my dear. You know what a man and a woman do, I expect?"

"Only the theory. School was useless unless you were looking to have sex with a dead frog."

"Hmm. Perhaps to start with I'd better explain the basic act of buggery to you."

Malcolm had encountered the word but had no idea what it entailed. Intent on correcting that, Godfrey did so in a graphic and matter-of-fact way.

"And *that* is fucking, my dear," he concluded.

Malcolm, who wasn't even happy about using a public convenience if there was anybody else around, shuddered. "Under no circumstances can I do *that*. And I am absolutely certain Alfie wouldn't want to do anything that disgusting either. He's a decent boy. A nice, clean, *decent* boy."

"Keep your voice down. There's quite a few in here who *will* do that and do it with relish, dear. Present company included. Alfie, is it? Nice name." Godfrey held up a conciliatory hand. "Fine. Knowing what you don't want is one way of finding your way to what you do want, I suppose. Now tell me, do you ever indulge in a little onanism?" And when Malcolm's face remained blank: "Do you wank, dear boy? Play with yourself?"

He was squirming again. He hadn't discussed his involvement in that activity since school, and he was ashamed that he still did it, imagining that few men of his age were as energetic in its pursuit. "I don't see what that's got to do with it," he grumbled.

"It has *everything* to do with it. That's you having the only sex you've ever had—with yourself. That is the only experience you have to call on. Fortunately, as it's a man rather than a woman you're after, it may well prove enough. The next time you're sitting on your settee with love's young dream, and maybe you've had a little kiss and a cuddle, unbutton him and play with him in the same way as you play with yourself. Surely even *you* could manage that for starters?"

"Well, yes, I suppose so," he mumbled dubiously.

"Don't expect him to be just the same as you are though. They all handle differently, you know?"

"You make him sound like an Austin Seven."

Godfrey chuckled, then went on, "It is a little like learning how to handle a car, in fact. Knowing which button to press and which knob to turn. Once you've got your hand in his drawers, you can work out what he does and doesn't like. It might even be fun! Who knows?"

"But how will *I* know?"

Godfrey sighed impatiently. "If he screams in pain, then he probably doesn't like it. If he gasps with pleasure, then he probably does. He may even guide you—ask you to go slower or faster, harder or softer."

"Oh, I do hope you're right," Malcolm said wistfully.

"If it looks as though it's going really well, you'll probably be able to tell by his face, then if I were you, I'd get your mouth over it."

Malcolm looked blank again. "What do you mean by that? Kiss him?"

Tutting, Godfrey began a demonstration with his delicate, tapered fingers. "No. Make a ring of your index finger and thumb. Wrap it around the base of your boy's cock and slide it into your mouth. Like so. Then, tightening your lips for grip, bob your head up and down on it. You can probably do a little something with your tongue too, to hurry him along. And hopefully, hey presto!" As Godfrey finished his crude demonstration, he spread his arms as though he were a magician's glamorous assistant.

Malcolm looked stunned. "In *my mouth?*"

"Yes. In your mouth."

"But that's…when his…stuff comes out it will—"

"Yes, he'll come in your mouth. Or you can pull away and let him shoot it in your face. That can be quite nice too. Some people prefer to *see* it all. I know I do. Ejaculation is so gloriously animal."

Mortified, Malcolm buried his face in his hands for a few moments while he digested the information, thinking, *I really can't do this. Not even for Alfie.*

Eventually he emerged with a question. "But isn't it dirty?"

"Not if your boy is as nice and clean as you say he is. If he isn't, you'll have aborted your mission long before his manhood gets anywhere near your mouth, trust me."

"But the semen…"

"…will do you no harm at all. It's full of protein. You know, I once had an appalling sore throat instantly cured by a young bombardier from the Royal Artillery, but that's a story for another time perhaps."

Godfrey had treated this whole consultation as an entertaining diversion with which he could regale his friends later, naming no names of course, but he was conscious of the alarm his advice had inspired and he did genuinely wish to help. Malcolm was on the threshold of something that might change his life, and joking aside, Godfrey thought it admirable that he should conquer his natural diffidence to seek advice and give himself the best chance of success.

"Look, dear, you may think you're the only one who's been this ignorant of sex at your age, but you'd be wrong. Many men have been in the same boat and even more women, I should think. I mean, spare a thought for those well-bred young ladies who have only seen penises on babies and classical statues until their wedding nights, when they find themselves suddenly confronted by a great big todger! I'm rather surprised it doesn't drive most of them into the arms of Sappho. You'll have two advantages over those unfortunate girls—you know what a man's naked body looks like, because you have one of your own, and now you have been blessed with my advice. You might recoil from these acts when they're clinically explained to you like this, but your reaction may be very different when your Alfie is holding you tight. No. Hang 'maybe'—it *will* be, I promise you."

*

HIS ALFIE! ON the bus home he fervently hoped that Godfrey was right. This last hour or so had been excruciating, but with luck it would prove to have been time well spent.

Chapter Eighteen

No Mess

IN THE HOOP and Grapes on the following Friday night, Alfie didn't treat Malcolm any differently from usual. But what had he expected, he asked himself: a peck on the cheek over the dominoes? Frank made no more snide remarks, and it reassured Malcolm that there had been no real understanding behind his comments, even if they happened to be true.

It was a normal Friday night out, but Malcolm was anxious because Alfie had said nothing about coming around later that evening, or any other time. It was as though no intimacy had passed between them. When the landlord rang the bell and cried, "Time, gentlemen, please," Alfie bid him goodbye.

Trudging up the hill towards home he tried to keep misery at bay. It was a long bicycle ride from Aldgate to Highgate, much of it uphill, or it took two trams. Alfie had probably decided that he wasn't worth the effort. Or he'd met a girl. Malcolm wondered wretchedly why he had been given this hope, only to have it snatched away. All the embarrassment of seeking advice from Godfrey the other evening had been for nothing.

However, not long after he got home there came a knock at the door. It was Alfie.

"All right, Malc? Is your mum out?"

"Yes, I told you—she often stays at Aunt Hannah's in Folkestone on a Friday."

"Folkestone, eh? Good old Aunt Hannah. Well, can I come in or not? It's getting chilly out here now."

"But…it's July."

"Can I come in or not?"

As they entered the parlour, Alfie removed Malcolm's glasses and popped them onto the piano. He wrapped his arms around him and gave him a hard beery kiss. Malcolm's spirits skyrocketed. Maybe they could just stay like this, lost in a kiss forever. That would be lovely. But at length, Alfie relinquished him and sat on the settee.

"Aren't you even going to take your jacket off?" asked Malcolm.

"In good time. I've been looking forward to that kiss all day."

"I thought you weren't coming. You never said anything in the pub."

"D'you want George and Frank here for tea and biscuits an' all?"

It was so blindingly obvious, he felt a fool and smiled weakly. "I suppose not when you put it that way."

Alfie rose to cast off his jacket and cap as he had the last time, but then he sat down again.

It was bold of Malcolm to ask, "Aren't you going to take your shirt off too?"

Alfie beamed. "Steady on! Control yourself, you dirty bleeder. All in good time. Anyway, I think today it's your turn."

"What?" Then it dawned on him what Alfie meant. "Oh, no! No, Alfie," he said, shaking his head emphatically. "I'll just look pathetic compared to you. I'm all weedy, pasty, and white. I'll look like something that literally crawled from under a stone."

"It don't matter. I want to see you wiv your shirt off. So, take it off."

There was nothing he could do but comply. It was more of a palaver for him. First the waistcoat, then the tie and the tiepin, the collar and the studs, the elasticated arm bands, the cufflinks. With his braces unhooked and only the shirt left to go he hesitated. "Do I have to?"

"Go on. Let's 'ave a look at yer," coaxed Alfie.

Malcolm put his hand to his face and almost sobbed. "Oh, Alfie!"

Alfie sprang up from the settee in a fluid movement and stood close enough for Malcolm to smell the smoky pub on his clothes. He planted a few gentle kisses on Malcolm's forehead, one on his nose, then he said, "Arms in the air like a good boy. That's what I used to say to my bruvver when he was little."

Malcolm submitted, and Alfie pulled his shirt up his slender torso and over his head. He then took a step back and looked him up and down.

"I'm a pasty, skinny little runt," lamented Malcolm.

"I disagree," Alfie almost whispered with a slow smile. "I think you're lovely."

He could scarcely believe these words, but there was nothing dishonest in Alfie's expression. He sighed tremulously as he felt Alfie's callused fingers move lightly over his skin, tracing the lines of muscles he had no idea about.

"You shouldn't be so down on yourself," Alfie said softly. "Your body ain't hard like a docker's, but why would it be? You sit on your arse all day in that office doing nuffink. There's no flab on you. Everything's in the right place. Your skin is—just lovely. It's so smooth and soft. It's so white it kinda glows."

As he said all this, his fingers continued their investigation, brushing a nipple every now and again, causing tremors to course through Malcolm's body. No one had ever touched him like this before. Eventually, Alfie followed suit in removing his waistcoat and shirt. Once again, he was beautiful to behold, although Malcolm's pleasure was undermined by the comparison between his own pale sedentary body and Alfie's—darker, harder. His misgivings were swept away as Alfie took him in his arms, pulling their two half-naked bodies together. The sensation of skin on skin felt so beautiful he might have wept. He had never expected life to have anything this fantastic in store for him. The hunger in Alfie's kiss persuaded him that the compliments were not mere flattery. Perhaps Alfie did find something in him he couldn't see for himself. Still entwined, they toppled sideways onto the settee.

There was an hour, a whole glorious hour, of kissing and caresses punctuated by chat, some of it of the most mundane kind. Just to be held by another person was truly wonderful to someone who'd never been held by anyone but his mother since he'd become an adult. Alfie made no move to make it more sexual. When he said reluctantly that he supposed he'd better make tracks, Malcolm was loath to relinquish him.

When Alfie began to pull away, he was so disinclined to allow this wonderful lad to be ripped from him that he was brave enough to act. Tentatively, he reached down and began to caress the large bulge in Alfie's trousers. Within seconds, it was like an iron bar.

"You ain't helping," sighed Alfie, grinning through a pained expression.

As he made no further protest, Malcolm undid his fly buttons, one by one. It was fiddly, but he figured that it might add to the titillation. He was right.

When all the buttons were undone, he reached in and softly gripped the warm rigid column of flesh and freed it from the cotton restraining it. He studied it in the subdued light. Unlike the unfortunate well-bred girls on their wedding nights, he wasn't disconcerted by confronting the "great big todger" this certainly was. He loved it. It was bigger than his own, a little longer and thicker—smooth unblemished perfection. Like the rest of him, it was beautiful. Its warmth carried none of the unpleasantness he had feared. This was indeed a clean boy. There was a fair amount of sticky fluid at the tip, a glueyness that was inevitable after prolonged arousal. He toyed with the crisp dark curls at its base.

By seizing the initiative, he had a magnificent feeling of being in charge for the first time, if only a little. He had obviously taken Alfie by surprise. He played with his cock, not as though it was his own, but to marvel at the similarities and the differences. Drawing a gasp from Alfie, he slowly pulled back his foreskin so that the smooth bulbous head, glistening with fluid, was completely revealed. He let his fingers gently grasp Alfie's balls, gratifyingly heavy in his hands. After a few minutes of this, smiling at his own horror earlier in the week, he tasted Alfie's saltiness with an exploring tongue. *Oh, yes*, he thought. *This is most definitely something I want in my mouth*. With that, he took in as much of it as he could without gagging.

It was his first time. It was not perfect. Alfie had to ask him to mind his teeth at one point. But he could tell from the gasps and moans and from the way Alfie gripped the back of his head and stroked his hair it was a big hit with him. Eventually, his breathing became erratic, and he took his hands off Malcolm's head so that he could withdraw. "I'm gonna come," he warned simply. Malcolm was sure what he wanted by this time. He slid his hands around and clasped Alfie's smooth firm buttocks to prevent him from withdrawing from his mouth. Seconds later, with a moan that was a sob, Alfie emptied himself into him.

Malcolm's mouth was so full of the warm gelatinous fluid that it was all he could do to swallow it quickly enough to prevent it from oozing through his lips. But swallow it all he did. It did not taste bad. It did not taste like strawberry ice cream, but it did not taste bad.

Alfie was a wreck, but he found strength enough to pull Malcolm to him and hold him close.

"You're full of surprises, I must say." He was half laughing, half panting still.

"Was that all right?" Malcolm sounded congested, like he had a cold.

"I'll say it was. I can't believe you swallowed it all."

"I had to. I didn't want any mess on Mum's settee."

Alfie nudged him with an elbow, and they giggled like schoolboys.

"There was an awful lot of it," said Malcolm.

"Yes well, there usually is wiv me and I was very excited. I dunno how these legs are gonna pedal me home after that."

"Well, stay here. Mum's in Folkestone until tomorrow lunchtime."

"I can't, Malcolm," Alfie groaned. "I'd love to, I really would, but I've got an early start tomorrow. I'm meant to be up to me bollocks in molasses come eight in the morning. If I'm in bed with you, there is no way I'd get there."

Malcolm must have looked crestfallen because Alfie went on, "I want to spend the night wiv yer, and I will do. We have all the time in the world. If nuffink else, I owe you one now, don't I? I started this and I ain't even made you come yet."

That's what you think! thought Malcolm. Over the months since they'd met, bedtime thoughts of Alfie had made him come many times.

Before the door was opened to let Alfie out, he turned and held Malcolm, kissing him deeply and gently. When he pulled away, he said, "You're sexy, Malcolm, don't let no one tell you different—least of all you, eh?"

Alone in bed, although he had diligently scrubbed his teeth as usual, he could still savour the lingering taste of Alfie. It was wonderfully personal. He was astounded and delighted by his own wanton behaviour. He had the taste of another man in his mouth, and he loved it. He fell asleep with a smile on his face, and his sleep was deep and sound.

*

EVEN IN THE cold light of another day, the first sexual intimacy with Alfie gave him confidence there was something real between them. Whatever was to happen next, even if it were nothing, he would still have enjoyed that intimacy with a boy who could have had his pick of women, or men for that matter, but who for those few hours had chosen him. For now at least, Malcolm was happy, as happy as he could ever remember being.

The next Friday, they gathered in the pub, and although George and Frank might have seen no difference in them, Malcolm often caught Alfie looking at him, and when he returned the glance, he'd turn his gaze away, fighting off a shy smile. Out of earshot of their friends, he put his mouth close to Malcolm's ear and breathed the words, "I can pop round to yours after if you want." Whether it was the warm breath or the thrill of the words spoken in Alfie's deep masculine voice, it gave Malcolm goosebumps and made the hairs at the back of his neck stand up. It was all he could do to whisper in reply, "I'd like that."

When Alfie turned up, once he had checked that Mrs Trevelyan was out, he'd fallen on Malcolm like a hungry wolf on a trembling faun. He undressed him with indecent haste, but Malcolm, kissed and bitten, couldn't have given a damn as to the welfare of his smart clothing. Within minutes, Alfie had returned the service rendered to him the previous week, greedily swallowing all of Malcolm's seed and leaving him panting. When he'd recovered, Malcolm slowed the pace down and manipulated Alfie's cock slowly but firmly until he shuddered and came messily onto the smooth skin of his chest and belly. Stirred by seeing this, Malcolm came again himself without much manipulation on Alfie's part, and they lay in silence for a while breathing in the scent of their own juices. Malcolm licked the cum off Alfie's skin like a cat lapping up spilt milk off a doorstep. Alfie wrinkled his nose up.

"It's full of protein apparently," explained Malcolm. "Besides, it comes from inside you, so that's all right."

He immediately regretted saying that, but Alfie just shook his head, bemused. "You're crazy."

"Mum goes away pretty much every Friday, so…is this a regular engagement now?"

"Maybe. If you want it to be."

"Do you? Want it to be, I mean."

Alfie sighed. "Well, let's see how it goes, shall we? If it's gonna be like it's been so far, then yes. Yes, I would like it."

"Won't your friends realise that something's going on between us?"

"George and Frank? Nah. Nuffink like this would ever occur to George, and Frank probably imagines I get up to all sorts anyway."

"But you do like me, Alfie, don't you?"

Alfie looked askance at him. "Would we 'ave done what we just done if I didn't? You ain't half daft for a brainy feller at times."

"I'm sorry, but this is all new to me. Until last week, I'd never done this sort of thing with anyone before."

"What? Not even at your posh school? Not even a bit of a wank an' that in the dorm?"

"Not with anyone. Do you mind?"

"Nah. It's nice that I'm getting what no one's had before. But I am surprised."

"Really? Why?"

"Well, I know you won't see it, but you're a lovely lad." Malcolm was thrilled to hear himself described as "a lad" at all, let alone a "lovely" one. Alfie went on, "And what you did to me last week—well, it didn't feel like you didn't know what you was about, that's all."

"Beginner's luck." He wouldn't reveal the nature of his research. "What about you anyway? You're clearly not entirely new to it."

"I ain't gonna lie to you, Malc, I messed around a fair bit when I was younger."

"With boys?"

"Gels mostly, but yes, some. Nuffink important. I can barely remember any of it."

Malcolm's two encounters with Alfie were the totality of his sex life and they had electrified him, so it was hard for him to imagine how anyone could forget the details of any sexual encounter. Alfie had probably had a lifetime's worth in the few years he'd been capable, simply because he was so extraordinarily attractive. But you'd think he'd remember the boys, even if only because they were the exceptions.

*

ON THEIR FRIDAY nights out, Frank expressed surprise that Malcolm was prepared to go so far out of his way to meet up at the pub with them. Malcolm could truthfully reply that he hadn't anyone to go to the pub with over in Highgate and it was good to get a change of scenery. Privately, he was more worried that Alfie had the same journey to cover while they did what they were doing. No one was to know anything about what passed between them, so they wouldn't even leave the pub together for fear of arousing suspicion. Besides being illegal, it was socially unacceptable for the classes to mix as they were. Alfie preferred to cycle over to Highgate rather than catch the tram with Malcolm anyway, for reasons of economy and because he'd never get a tram back at that hour, leaving him at the mercy of the night service omnibuses. Sometimes, by the time Malcolm got home, he'd see the pushbike leaning against the railings and knew he'd find Alfie sitting on the top step waiting for him. He came to love the sight of Alfie's bike, almost wanting to kiss its saddle whenever he clapped eyes on it.

Spied through the net curtains of Cranmer Avenue, Alfie was a figure to be viewed with suspicion. People like him did not visit the street unless it was to deliver something or to mend something. Several of the neighbours noticed his visits. His good looks drew the eye, but they were also wary of a young man of his class loitering in a quiet well-to-do residential street, particularly if he was sitting on the doorstep late at night waiting for Malcolm's tram to bring him home. In the daytime, he could have claimed to be on a job for the Trevelyans, but not at a quarter past eleven at night, nor in the early hours if they saw him leaving. On one occasion, the concerns of Mrs Oxley from number 78 resulted in a challenge from Colonel Beresford at number 80.

"Excuse me, young man, may I ask what business you have here at this hour?"

Alfie was never an obstreperous boy, but he didn't enjoy being spoken to as though he had to justify his existence. "You can ask, mate. But the 'business' that I have would be me own business, so I won't be telling you about it, now will I?"

"I see. Now look, we take care of each other in these parts. It is rather late for you to be sitting on my neighbour's doorstep, don't you think?"

Alfie was surprised that his refusal to co-operate hadn't resulted in the old man losing his rag. It calmed him and he nodded.

"I can understand that, I suppose. I know that Mrs T is away for the weekend. I'm waiting to see Malcolm."

"At eleven-fifteen at night?" the Colonel asked, one eyebrow raised.

"We was in the pub together and he offered me a nightcap. I was on me bike but he had to catch a couple of trams."

"Where from?"

Alfie sighed. Having decided to tell the old boy nothing, he appeared to be telling him everything short of the grisly details. "Limehouse."

"I say! You've come all the way from Limehouse on your bike and yet you've still beaten him back? That's jolly good going. *And* you've been here a good ten minutes. You must be very fit."

He shrugged. "I'm a docker."

"I see. How did Malcolm wind up drinking in an East End pub? He doesn't seem the sort."

"You'd have to ask him that."

"I daresay. But without wishing to seem a snob, it does seem rather… Well, you're not the sort of chap one would expect him to know."

"We're just two blokes who got chatting in a pub and found that we got on. That's all. Is it so hard to understand?"

"You know, no, it isn't. It's actually rather nice. I'm sorry to have bothered you. I'll bid you good night, young man, unless you'd care to come and wait in the warm and have a drink while you're about it?"

"Thanks for the offer, sir. But I think this is Malcolm coming up the hill now."

Disarmed, Colonel Beresford bade Malcolm a cheery good evening and went back into his house.

Part Five

A Foggy Day in London

Chapter Nineteen

Summer Heat

Monday, 7 August 1933

THE SUMMER BANK Holiday weekend was sweltering in London. The air shimmered with the heat rising from the pavements. Sunday had been the hottest day in the capital for over thirty years and its citizens flocked to any open space they could find. Monday promised to be another glorious day, and Frank had made a loose arrangement with his mates to go swimming in Victoria Park Bathing Lake before soaking up the sun and retiring to the pub.

Frank was the first to arrive, and after putting on his trunks in the changing hut, he sat nearby to wait for his mates. The park filled up rapidly, and the lake, although large, threatened to become a vast foaming cauldron of human broth. In his mind's eye, Alfie and he, along with George and Sid, had been practically the only people there. They'd all plunged in, then he'd been the first out so he could sit on the bank and watch his friends larking about in the water. Then Alfie would climb out and drape a dripping arm around his shoulder and they would chat in an easy companionable way.

But it wasn't going to be like that.

He was tense and tight-lipped when George and Sid finally turned up in their shirtsleeves, each with a colourful towel rolled up under his arm. Frank had only been waiting for about ten minutes and he'd arrived early, yet he was irritated.

"Blimey, it's proper scorching, innit," complained George. "I'm sweating so much just through walking here that it looks as though I've already been in the bleedin' lake."

"Where's Alf?" asked Frank. "He's usually the first to turn up."

"Ah, he ain't coming today, after all," replied Sid. "He said to tell you he was going over to Highgate to see Malcolm."

Frank slammed the ground in disgust and sprang to his feet. He was overcome by a deep and burning anger that he couldn't articulate.

"I'll see you in a bit," he snapped before storming back into the changing hut.

Sid winced. "Oh, dear. He weren't too happy about that, was he, George? He had a face like thunder on him."

"Yes, well, he gets ever so possessive about Alfie." George shrugged. "Frank don't get that close to anyone so easy, so when he does…"

Half an hour or so later, Frank returned fully dressed as the brothers were drying off on the bank.

"I can't believe you came all the way up here and then didn't go in," said Sid.

"It's too crowded and I ain't in the mood no more anyway." He'd sat in the changing hut after dressing, but the excited chatter of the men and boys around him had done nothing to improve his mood. He was like a pressure cooker that needed to vent steam. He sat down beside them, leaning forward and hugging his bony knees. "It ain't on, what Alfie done. It just ain't on."

"What's he done?" asked George, puzzled.

"Well, not coming here today—what else? We had an arrangement."

George shook his head. "Nah, Frank. I was there when you put it to him, remember? He was at best a 'maybe'."

Frank was adamant. "He *was* coming—he said so!"

"He said perhaps! That was if Malcolm was busy. He said it had been a couple of weeks since he last saw him."

"Oh, so now we all have to plan our lives around that posh fucker?"

"Oh, Frank! When it comes to Alfie, you hear what you wanna hear, don't yer."

"And what's that supposed to mean?"

"Well, if yer must know, you've always been a bit funny as regards Alfie. You like to treat him as though he's yer own private property. Apart from Nora, I don't know anyone who tries to boss him about as much as you do." George affected a mocking voice. "'We're doing this, ain't we, Alfie?' 'We're doing that, ain't we, Alfie?' 'You like such and such, don't yer, Alfie?'"

"Well, he's me mate!" protested Frank, his face by now a vivid shade of pink.

"We're supposed to be yer mates too and you've known us longer, but you ain't like that wiv us, are yer?"

Sid was hardly more comfortable than Frank was by now. "Come on, George. Frank an' Alfie has always been close. There ain't nuffink wrong with that."

George sighed and spoke more kindly. "I ain't saying there is. But look, Frank, you need to get off of Alfie's back a bit. If he weren't so easy-going, there might already have been ructions between you two. You know that look he gets on his face when Nora goes on at him—d'you want him looking that way when he's wiv you an' all?"

That hit home. "No, of course I don't."

"Well then."

Frank looked desperately unhappy, and George was sorry to have spoken in anger. Like most young East End boys, they never discussed their feelings with one another. They were all close, and Alfie inspired deep affection in his friends. George reckoned one of the main reasons Alfie's mates were so important to him was that they were the only people who didn't give a stuff what he looked like. Alfie made a good friend. He never forgot a birthday. He never owned anything he wouldn't share. He'd give them plenty of his time too. George adored him although obviously he would never have said so in as many words.

After an uncomfortable silence, Frank spoke again. His tone was bleak. "Can't you two see what that Malcolm's doing?"

"What d'you mean?" asked George.

"He's taking our mate away from us, that's what I mean. It ain't right!"

"Oh, come on, Frank. Alfie ain't yer gel, is he? He can do what he wants. It's a free country."

"I don't believe you, really, I don't. Don't you care about him at all? That Malcolm is leading him astray and no good'll come of it! He ain't our sort. He needs to stay in bleedin' Highgate and find his own friends, not come round here nicking ours."

"Oh, Gawd, Frank, you sound like yer eight years old!" Now George affected a mock child's tone. "'He's my friend, not your friend, and you can't play wiv us no more so there, ner ner ner!'"

Ignoring him, Frank went on, "What do you think the likes of him wants wiv a working boy like Alfie, eh? We're his best mates and we hardly get to see him no more because of Little Lord Fucking Fauntleroy. It ain't right, I'm telling yer."

George resented Frank's frequent insinuations that there was a special bond between himself and Alfie, so in a way he was pleased that Malcolm had turned up to push his nose out of joint. Trevelyan was harmless enough. He struck George as being a timid creature who was oblivious to the waves he was making. But Alfie needed to be mindful of the effect on Frank. He'd mention it if the opportunity to do so tactfully were to arise.

"Well, Frank, maybe if you'd been a bit more friendly towards Malcolm then we'd see more of the both of them, wouldn't we?"

"Yer blind, George. Yer must be. Let me tell you, Malcolm is only interested in what Alfie's got in his trousers, nuffink more."

George was angry now. "That's an 'orrible thing to say! You take that back!" he shouted, drawing a few glances from some of the other bathers. Any compassion he'd had for Frank was gone.

"*Shhh!*" warned Sid before hissing at Frank, "You can't go saying stuff like that, mate. You could do untold harm—whether it's true or not."

Turning to confront his brother, George barked, "Of course it ain't true! There's plenty of that sort been sniffing around Alfie, I can tell yer. You can spot 'em a mile off! Malcolm ain't like that and if he was, Alfie'd have nuffink to do wiv him."

Frank held his hands up. "All right, all right. I spoke out of turn and I'm sorry. Let's change the subject, shall we, before that Malcolm ruins our day even though he ain't even here."

*

MALCOLM AND ALFIE had a growing appetite for each other. Their sexual liaisons were restricted not by lack of desire but lack of opportunity. Malcolm's mother had visited her sister less often recently. Alfie would have been happy for them to do it in the seclusion of Highgate Woods or some of the wilder areas of the Heath, but Malcolm couldn't bring himself to take the risk. Not even for Alfie. Sometimes they'd meet in town for a drink. He loved spending even an hour or so with him, but the attraction was so strong that it was frustrating to have him close and not be able to reach out and touch him. The sound of his voice thrilled him, every mannerism, the way he moved, the sheer smell of him was exhilarating.

He couldn't envisage them pawing each other in the dark recesses of a queer bar, but he didn't want Alfie to get frustrated by their lack of opportunities either. For two young men with a passion for each other, even once a fortnight was only one step removed from celibacy. When he got home, he'd invariably find himself too worked up to sleep and even a feverish bout of self-manipulation didn't much help.

No sunworshipper, he hid away in the relatively cool shade of the house. His mother hadn't intended to go to Folkestone, so he hadn't made any arrangements with Alfie. Much to his chagrin, after speaking to Aunt Hannah on the telephone, she changed her mind at the eleventh hour, leaving him alone for the long hot weekend. He was annoyed about the missed opportunity, but helpless to rearrange things as Alfie wasn't contactable. He never instigated their meetings anyway, in case he should seem over-eager. If Alfie suggested it, then he knew it was what he wanted. It had been a few weeks since they'd been able to meet, and he was melancholy about it. Perhaps Alfie was cooling on the relationship—if it could even be called that.

There came a knock at the door, and he took his time in answering. It would doubtless be someone trying to sell God, vacuum cleaners, or brushes. But he opened the door to the welcome sight of Alfie stripped to the waist, his skin glowing from the exertion of cycling up Highgate Hill in the oppressive heat.

"All right, Malc? I 'ope you got summink cold you can gimme to drink, mate. Parched don't really cover it."

"Of course! I have lemonade or ginger beer." He stood aside to admit his friend, breathing in the smell of him as he slipped past.

"I'll take some lemonade, please. You don't mind me turning up like this, do yer?"

"God, no—I'm really happy to see you. Always."

"Where's yer mum?"

"She went away this weekend, after all. I was furious because we could—well, you know."

Sitting on the sofa in the parlour, Alfie polished off the lemonade in a couple of swallows and belched. "Sorry, Malc. I'm disgusting, ain't I?"

"That's all right." If it had been anyone else, he'd most probably have thought so.

His visitor gave him a steamy look. "You know what I'm 'ere for, don't yer?"

Malcolm blushed and avoided the glittering blue eyes. "But you expected Mum to be here. We couldn't have."

"Gorn! Wiv all the parks in this neck o' the woods I'm sure we'd of thought of summink you wouldn't have minded. The hot weather makes me feel like it even more, you know. I can't 'elp it. You'd think it would slow me down, wouldn't yer?"

In a small voice, Malcolm said, "Well, you'll get no arguments from me. Shall I undress?"

"No, not yet. Thing is, after riding me bike in all this heat I'm sweating buckets. I'm proper disgusting. I can't let you near me while I'm like this. Can I be really cheeky and have a barf here? Then I'll be all nice and clean for yer and we can get down to it, soon as you like."

They went upstairs. Malcolm started running the bath and fussed around fetching fresh towels from the airing cupboard and scooping his mother's bath crystals into the steaming water to make it nice. He hoped it wasn't too feminine for Alfie. While he was doing it, he was keenly aware of Alfie stripping off his shoes, socks, trousers, and drawers without a hint of self-consciousness. He supposed that anyone with a body like his had nothing to fear from the unforgiving daylight. He tried to focus on what he was doing with a greater intensity than such a simple task merited rather than take in the vision of perfect naked youth being gradually revealed beside him.

"You can look at me, you know. I don't mind."

"I—I'll give you some privacy, shall I? I'll go downstairs and wait."

"Don't be daft! Stop 'ere an' talk to me. And Malcolm, why do I need four towels? I ain't an elephant. Just the one will do."

Malcolm perched on the green Lloyd Loom laundry basket in the corner as Alfie lowered himself into the foam. For such a hot day the bath was probably too warm, but he didn't grumble. The windows were steamed up, and the porcelain and chrome fittings were beaded with condensation. Alfie opened the cold tap up so it flowed more freely, and Malcolm leaped up to open the window a crack before settling back onto his perch. Alfie lay back in the water, letting it cover him entirely for a few seconds. When he surfaced blinking and blowing, his dark hair was slick, flattened against his head. It made him look so young that had there been a yellow rubber duck floating in the bath beside him, it wouldn't have looked out of place. *What am I doing?* Malcolm thought.

"This barf is bloomin' amazing. I'd never be out of it if I lived here, I can tell yer."

Malcolm watched as his beautiful friend lathered the dark curls in his armpits and caressed his gleaming arms, chest, and belly with the sponge. The hair on his legs was more prominent for being slicked down by the water. Without any lewdness or self-consciousness, he soaped and scrubbed his thick pubic hair and genitals thoroughly. He didn't have to try to be sexy, he just was. After he'd finished scrubbing, he proffered the dripping sponge. "D'you wanna do me back?"

"Can't you manage?"

"Yes, I can *manage*. But why should I, wiv you sitting there doing nuffink and most probably dying to touch me? I want you to."

Malcolm took the sponge and began work on the smooth muscles of his back. He loved doing it, and it was obvious that Alfie was loving it too.

At one point, he craned his neck around and offered Malcolm a hot wet affectionate kiss. As he leaned forward to accept it, he felt like the luckiest man alive. The backwashing wasn't even particularly sexual, it was just a nice sensation for them both. It brought back the memory of rubbing calamine lotion into sunburn. The big difference this time was he knew he would have Alfie at the end of it.

"You got the magic touch," said Alfie sleepily.

Half an hour later, Alfie was sitting in the parlour again wearing only a pair of Malcolm's clean drawers. Thanks to the crystals, he smelt of violets.

"Flippin' 'eck! I'm glad I won't be going back on the tram. I'd get some funny looks smelling like this, I can tell yer," he said. "Do you always keep all your clothes on even when it's this bleedin' hot?" There was more than a hint of mockery in his midnight-blue eyes.

"Yes." Malcolm wasn't wearing a jacket, but his waistcoat was still buttoned up and he wore a tie.

Alfie smiled with bemused affection. He leaned over to kiss Malcolm again. It was a sweet kiss. His tongue probed but with patience rather than passion. It was a kiss to be enjoyed for itself, not a station en route to another destination. But it made them both dizzy, giving them goosebumps even in the heat. At length, Alfie pulled away and said quietly, "Blimey."

"I know."

Alfie shook his head. "Fuck me, I never bargained for nuffink like this."

He quietly suggested that they go to bed, but Malcolm insisted they stay downstairs. Using the bedrooms in his mother's house, even his own, would have felt like a betrayal, and Alfie didn't argue. The truth was,

Malcolm was frightened by the thought of what might happen if they spent the night in bed together. Physically, he was ecstatic with what they already got up to, and he was loath to introduce the possibility of going further. Much as he adored Alfie, he wasn't inclined to have anything to do with buggery. This was more because of his own squeamishness and aversion to pain than the illegality of it.

In the parlour, Alfie stripped Malcolm slowly, garment by garment as though he was unwrapping a gift. When he was naked, he let his tongue venture just about everywhere on his body as tenderly as a cat giving a kitten its first wash. There was something different about him today. He was deliberate, unhurried, and overflowing with affection. He left Malcolm's cock until last so that when he finally turned his attention to it, it was throbbing fit to burst. Burst it eventually did, and once again Alfie swallowed the lot as though he loved it. Malcolm was by that time pumping him vigorously, and shortly afterwards, he shot his load over them both.

"I'm gonna need anuvver barf now," he said breathlessly.

"Not yet. Can we just stay like this for a little while?"

"Course we can."

Malcolm settled his head sideways onto Alfie's hard, flat belly. He could hear his heart pumping the blood through him. His nose brushed against Alfie's dark bush, and he breathed in a heady cocktail of violet bath crystals and fresh semen. Alfie's long blunt fingers toyed with his hair. Godfrey had told him all about the mechanics of sex and he had been glad of it, but the overwhelming emotion that came with it had taken him completely by surprise. The sex and the affection might have seemed like two separate things, but they weren't, they bled into each other. Even though Alfie's earlier words had strongly suggested that this was purely a sexual arrangement, both knew there was more to it than that. He couldn't envisage ever entering this level of intimacy with someone he didn't love or who didn't at least care for him. Now he'd felt this, how could he ever live without it?

Even as he lay there in a condition close to bliss, he'd sown the seed of a new fear. Never had there been anything this precious in his life. Never had he had so much to lose.

Chapter Twenty

Frank Exchanges

Friday, 15 December 1933

MALCOLM LOVED THE run-up to Christmas in London. Department stores like Selfridges were festooned in coloured lights and featured magical window displays with moving figures from fairy tales. Peter Pan would fly, Cinderella would sweep, and Hansel and Gretel would pick at the Gingerbread House. Toy hawkers walked the West End pavements with trays of cheap novelties like wooden monkeys clambering up and down sticks. On Charing Cross Road, shoppers clustered around the book stalls searching for that one perfect gift, on the flyleaf of which they could inscribe their message of love.

Butchers' shops dripped with death, with lines of turkeys and geese hanging inside and out—a celebration of plenty. Bakers' windows were piled high with mince pies and Christmas puddings, and fruiterers were well stocked with tangerines, nuts, and wooden boxes decorated with camels and palm trees, containing sticky dried dates and little wooden forks with which to pick them out.

By the time Malcolm got to the Blue Posts in Limehouse, Frank was there alone. Their mutual antipathy was plain to all by now, which was why Alfie kept them apart whenever he could. Frank greeted him with the leer of an assassin. He explained that Alfie was absent due to an overdue freighter from Cuba; it had docked a little late and there was a knock-on effect. *And yet here you are*, thought Malcolm.

The small talk didn't last long.

"Look, I know what your game is, Malcolm. You can play the innocent as much as you like, but I'm on to yer. Just you remember that."

"I'd try to, if I had any inkling of what you're talking about."

"So, you're telling me that you ain't a pansy?"

"Of course not," was Malcolm's deliberately equivocal reply.

"I gotta tell yer, it fair makes me sick the way you creep round 'im, it really does. I dunno how he can stomach it. Mate, you ain't the first brown 'atter to have a crack at 'im, trust me, and you won't be the last neither. But you won't get nowhere, mate."

Malcolm wanted to blurt out that he'd already made considerable progress on that front, but he didn't want to turn Alfie into a trophy as he'd seen so many bragging men make of women they were meant to love and respect. Frank was perceptive in his way, and Malcolm's lack of reaction helped him reach a conclusion, which by the look on his face was a body blow.

"You fuckin' 'ave, ain't yer?" He put a hand over his eyes "Oh, fuck me, Alf, wotcher gone and done?"

Malcolm didn't want to deny what had happened between him and Alfie, but he said, "Look, I don't know what you think you know, but whatever's between Alfie and me will stay that way. It's no one else's business and I'm not discussing it with you."

Frank's reply died on his lips because the door swung open, and there was George. He got some pints in, including one for Alfie, who was meant to be hard on his heels. Malcolm had never been so pleased to see the man. When Alfie turned up, Malcolm was tense in case Frank decided to blurt something out, but he didn't. All evening, Frank glared at him with real hatred, and he found it deeply unsettling.

It was too late for Alfie to go over to Highgate and his mother wasn't in Folkestone anyway, so it had never been the plan, but he walked Malcolm to his tram stop at a leisurely pace. This gave Malcolm the chance to share his fears.

"Frank knows about us."

"Nah, he don't—not unless you've said summink." Alfie turned to look at him.

"Of course I didn't. Nor did I admit anything. But believe me, he's guessed and he isn't very happy about it."

Alfie sighed. "Oh well. It don't really matter."

"How can you say that? You don't know what's he going to do."

"I can handle him—don't you worry yourself about it."

"Alfie, you didn't see the way he looked at me."

"Oh, yes, I did," said Alfie with a grim chuckle. "I just wasn't sure why."

"He could make big trouble for me," said Malcolm unhappily. "Alfie, he could lose me my job. He could even get me sent to prison."

"Trust me, 'e won't. This is the East End, remember. Whatever happens, it won't involve the law. Look, whenever I've taken up with gels in the past he's always played up. He's just jealous, that's all. Thinks he's losing his pal. He don't mean no harm. Is yer mum away next Friday?"

"Yes, I think so."

"I'll come round then, shall I? Make you forget about silly old Frankie?"

"Oh, gosh, I wish it was tonight," Malcolm breathed.

Alfie gave his shoulder a playful shove. "Shush! Me an' all. I wish I could hold you right now as it goes, but…well, there we are."

As they crossed the Dock Road, a gaggle of ragamuffins outside Charlie Brown's began to yell "Away in a Manger", for yelling it surely was. They were dressed in tattered clothes, nowhere near stout enough to keep them warm in mid-December.

"It's nearly ten. These kids should be in bed, surely?"

"Yes, but people coming out of the pubs are likely to be a lot freer wiv their change than usual, Malc. These little entrepreneurs know that."

"But their parents…"

"…are most probably in the pub drowning their sorrows, mate. Gawd!" Alfie chuckled. "The little Lord Jesus might lay down His sweet head, but He wouldn't get much kip with this racket going on, would He?"

The smallest child in the group, a grubby-cheeked little fair-haired girl who couldn't have been more than four, walked up to Alfie and said in a tiny voice, "Penny for the Guy!"

"No, Dora! It's Christmas, you idiot!" hissed an older brother, judging by their physical resemblance.

Alfie crouched so that he was at the little girl's level. "Don't you listen to 'im, darlin'. Was that you singing 'Away in a Manger' for us?"

She nodded solemnly.

"Well, that was beautiful, that was. I think that's worth more'n just a penny, don't you?"

She nodded again, more emphatically this time. Alfie dug into his pocket, pulled out a shilling, and pressed it into her filthy little hand. "There you go, darlin'. You have a lovely Christmas now, d'you hear?"

She nodded again and returned to the choir with her bounty. As they walked away, one of the older kids shouted, "Cor, fanks, mister. Merry Christmas."

"That was a nice thing to do," said Malcolm. He'd have been happy to part with the money, but he'd have been too embarrassed to offer it. He made generous charitable donations towards the less privileged every Christmas, far more than a single shilling. But somehow, he felt that Alfie's kindness would be remembered long after the shilling had been spent.

Alfie shrugged. "It probably just made me feel better. 'Lovely Christmas!' It's hard to know what to say. You can't ask what they want Santa to bring 'em because in all likelihood he ain't gonna bring 'em nuffink. It fair breaks my heart, you know."

"Were your Christmases like that?"

"What? Gawd no! Mum and Dad used to put a bit aside all year so we at least had a good Christmas. We never had much in the way of toys an' that, but they saw to it we had plenty of fun and games and plenty of stuff to eat an' all." He smiled. "Don't be thinking I was a little street urchin,

Malc. If I was out after six o'clock, me mum would be combing the streets for me, and if it was me own doing, there'd be hell to pay. She'd give me a right telling-off and believe me, that weren't nice. Mum and Dad never beat me or nuffink when I was a kid." Then he sighed as something occurred to him. "Dad did once lamp me when I was a bit older. Just the once. And he went to his grave regretting it."

"Why did he do it?"

"I'd tell yer, Malc, but this is yer tram coming. I'll see yer on Friday, mate. You look after yerself, all right?"

Malcolm boarded his tram feeling that he wasn't ever likely to find out why Alfie's father had found reason to hit him. He couldn't imagine anyone wanting to hit him for any reason, ever.

*

GRATEFUL THAT THE tram had whisked Malcolm away, Alfie went back to the Blue Posts knowing Frank was likely still to be there. He arrived just as George was leaving and bade him goodnight. He then went in to join Frank.

"What you bin saying to Malcolm?"

"Me? Nuffink. Why, what's 'e said?"

"I just get the impression you gave him an 'ard time tonight, that's all."

"Nah. I told him you'd be late, bought him a pint, and that's all. I wouldn't want to offend a mate of yours, Alfie, you know that." His display of injured innocence was too exaggerated to convince.

"Really?" Alfie waited.

Then the counter-attack. "Straight up. 'E's a funny one though, ain't he? It's almost like he wants to cause trouble between us."

"I don't think it's him what's set on trouble, Frank. I dunno what you think it is yer playing at, but pack it in. *Now.* If you upset him, then you and me is gonna fall out. I don't want that and I'm sure you don't neither. I know he ain't lying 'cos he's rubbish at it."

"Really? Well, it worries me that you reckon you know him that well. Are you doing him, Alf?"

"None of your fuckin' business."

"Yes, I thought so."

They glared at each other for a tense few moments, and it was Frank who looked away first. "Look, Alfie, you're me mate. I care about yer. I look out for yer. That's what mates are meant to do. This thing with him, whatever it is, it ain't good for yer. *We're* yer real mates—George, Sid, and me. Remember that."

"An' you just remember that if you say one word out of turn to Malcolm from now on, then I won't be yer mate, real or otherwise. Don't talk to no one about it. Not George, not Sid, not me, and certainly not Malcolm. I know you don't like him and there's no law says you have to. But I do and there's an end to it. Now you can finish my pint if you like because I don't feel like it no more."

With an abrupt lunge, Alfie was out of the door, letting the cold December air rush in. As he went for a bus, he found he was trembling. To outsiders their argument must have looked like the light-hearted play-fighting that came with friendship in these streets. He'd never had a real argument with Frank, and this one had left him shaken. He'd had to act the tough guy and it didn't sit well with him. Alfie was a gentle soul in a neighbourhood where many were not. He would usually do or say anything Frank wanted him to for a quiet life, but today, he'd made a stand for Malcolm.

As he calmed down, he reckoned he'd done the right thing, even if it had rubbed Frank up the wrong way. Something about his relationship with Malcolm felt right, even though Alfie couldn't put his finger on what that was.

*

THE BLAST OF cold air had cleared Frank's head a little. He poured the rest of Alfie's pint into his own half-empty glass, figuring he might as well get as drunk as possible because it was the only way he'd get any sleep that night. He was desperately unhappy to have Alfie, of all people, think badly of him. But along with this great sadness was the equally great resentment of the outsider who'd invaded their cosy world and ruined everything. If he and Alfie were doing what he believed they were, then it wasn't on. And if he ever felt like he had nothing left to lose, then he had a pretty good idea how he could bring it all crashing down.

Chapter Twenty-One

What the Eye Doesn't See…

Tuesday, 9 January 1934

CRANMER AVENUE COMMANDED many spectacular views over London, but tonight the city was blanketed in a freezing "peasouper". You couldn't see your hand if you stretched out your arm, nor your feet if you looked down at the ground. Omnibuses edged slowly through the murk, their conductors walking ahead of them waving a hurricane lamp slowly from side to side. Many vehicles came to grief because of the poor visibility, becoming barriers that added to the muddle. The trams struggled to gain traction on the hills, and the ice made it hard for them to stop. People would die in London because of this evil weather.

Grace Trevelyan cursed the arrangement she'd made to visit Hannah midweek to help plan a winter fair. It was foolish of her to leave the house at all, she knew, let alone make her way to London Bridge station for a train to Folkestone. But if she could just get to Highgate underground station, she reckoned she'd manage.

The frosted flagstones crunched beneath her shoes, and she nearly lost her footing several times. She could hear little and see nothing. She might have retreated had she not dreaded struggling back up the treacherous hill. She came upon a dimly lit tram from which passengers were being discharged onto the pavement because it had been unable to climb the hill. Nearby, a flaming brazier warmed a boy selling the evening papers, his disembodied face glowing like a ghostly angel, and she knew she had found the entrance to the tube.

"Evening News! Standard! Star! West End Final!" bellowed the newsboy. "Fog brings London to a standstill!"

"You don't say," commented the tram conductor wryly as he waited on the pavement to usher the last of his passengers out from the tram, crouching like a cricket fielder in the slips, ready to grab one if there was a tumble.

*

ALFIE WAS HARDLY ever in control of his pushbike as he cycled all the way from the West India Docks to Malcolm's house in the fog. He suffered several tumbles and banged his knee hard on a bollard near Highbury Corner, but he found himself in the mood for Malcolm, so he pressed on. Cycling up the hill past the Archway Tavern proved impossible so he wheeled the bike along the gutter, ringing his bell periodically to sound an ineffectual warning that he was there.

"Christ, it's cold," he muttered to himself. "I need me fuckin' head read but fuck me I want him tonight. I dunno what's come over me."

An hour or so later, in a room lit only by firelight and an oil lamp, Alfie sat naked on the sofa, which had been covered with a blue candlewick bedspread, watching Malcolm undress. Self-consciousness was making the process awkward. He struggled with his waistcoat buttons and with his collar studs, and at the climax of his striptease—if that was what it was meant to be—he caught his foot in his drawers and nearly toppled over. He steadied himself on the mantelpiece just in time. Alfie, undaunted by his own nakedness, gently rubbed his bruised knee and watched the whole performance with a curious smile, which would have been recognised as great affection by anyone other than Malcolm.

"Come here, you," said Alfie, spreading his legs and patting the seat between his thighs. His cock lay pale against its crisp dark bush, but it was already stirring. As Malcolm approached, Alfie reached for him, seized his spare waist, and spun him around, before easing him down between his thighs.

"What do you want me to do?" whispered Malcolm.

"Nuffink. Just relax. I'm taking over your body for a bit. It's mine, all right?"

"Whatever you say."

He didn't understand, but he did as he was told. It was easy. He leaned back against Alfie's smooth chest, the position in itself sufficient to inspire a stiffening between his legs. He felt warm breath on his neck, then slow kisses and painless playful bites. He giggled and squirmed a bit as his ears were nibbled. Alfie's fingers raked through his hair, and he moaned with pleasure because he had found he loved that. Alfie kneaded the muscles at the front of his thighs firmly enough for him to gasp, but he surrendered to it, realising no pain was intended. Alfie slid his hands up and let his brutal-looking fingers skim through the edges of the soft blond bush, dwelling around his navel and stroking his belly until they made the briefest contact with Malcolm's pulsating erection. His anxiety about performance had abated over the last months and he was more or less hard from the moment he set eyes on Alfie.

The same hands moved up his chest and toyed with his nipples until they were as hard as his cock. By now, Malcolm's whole body was trembling, and he was aware that Alfie must feel it too, pressed together as they were. That was probably the point of it. Alfie was handling him as he might handle himself, making it feel intensely personal. After twenty minutes of this exquisite torment, Malcolm's cock had expanded as far as it possibly could and lay flat against his belly, weeping clear fluid. He knew Alfie was similarly stirred because his breathing was unsteady and he could feel his hardness pressed against the small of his back.

Alfie groaned into his ear and said gruffly, "Oh, Malc, this must be what it's all about, mate. Feeling like this."

With that, he gave Malcolm's nipples a final twist and slid his hands back down to find his erection. At first, his touch was light, he barely grazed it, but it pushed into the palm of his hand like the head of an affectionate cat and so he seized it firmly and began to masturbate him slowly.

All Malcolm could do was writhe and push back against Alfie who chewed at his neck as he firmly wanked him off, increasing the rhythm, but only slightly, prolonging the sensation.

"Oh, please," Malcolm begged, urgently needing release. The pace increased again until he was right on the edge, then Alfie tightened his grip and returned to a longer stroke and a dead slow rhythm. Malcolm gasped and whimpered until he arched his back, shuddered, emitted a great sob, and emptied himself volcanically over the pair of them. It was a mess worthy of Alfie. Malcolm fell back against his lover like a drenched corpse. He was always greatly affected at the point of orgasm but this time he was beside himself. When his breathing had calmed, he turned around to see that one salvo had hit Alfie in the eye, which was half closed with the acid sting of it.

"Sorry," said Malcolm weakly.

"Don't be. That was lovely," breathed Alfie with a devilish smile. "Fuckin' 'ell, you and me together don't 'arf make a mess though!"

This was probably only the opening session, so it was hardly worth them peeling apart, mopping up, and getting dressed again. They decided not to budge but just to lie, limbs entwined, dozing in the flickering firelight, the heat of their bodies drying the fluids they'd spent. They were like two animals, snug, safe, and warm in the dark house shrouded in treacherous, freezing fog.

Unfortunately, that's how Grace Trevelyan found them. Her train had been cancelled. She had been forced to return by an inability to see anything, but she was able to see this only too clearly.

*

WHEN MALCOLM SIDLED in to face the music, she was sitting at the kitchen table with a glass of sherry in front of her and the bottle, still uncorked, close by. He hovered in the doorway.

"Mum, I'm so sorry."

"I'll just *bet* you are," she snapped.

"I don't know what to say to you."

"Well, I should think of something. Heaven knows it's taken you long enough to come in here and face me."

"I was getting dressed."

Grace noted that Malcolm's clothing was correct in every detail, tie, tie clip and all. It was as though he thought if she saw him meticulously attired, she might doubt what she'd witnessed not fifteen minutes ago. But there was no chance of that.

"Have you *no* excuse to offer me?"

He had racked his brains while they'd been dressing, but he'd reached the conclusion that any excuse would insult her intelligence. It was strangely liberating to be left with no other option but the truth. He had the inappropriate urge to burst out laughing.

"Well, there really isn't any other explanation for what you've just seen but the obvious one, is there? Alfie and I had been making love."

"*Making love!*" she spat. "Is that what you call it? 'Making love' was what we used to say when a man bought a woman a bunch of flowers or a box of chocolates and pecked her on the cheek. Clearly times have changed."

"Mum, I'm sorry." He couldn't help smiling, which didn't help matters.

"Yes, so you said. Most of all I expect you're sorry to have been caught. Or perhaps you're sorry that I've found you having…*relations*…with another man! Not even a man, a *boy*! Maybe you're sorry because you know it's wrong." Her voice changed. "You realise it's quite illegal."

"Of course I do."

"Oh, do you, my lad? Oscar Wilde served two years' hard labour for this very crime—and that was only thirty years ago! Attitudes haven't changed a bit in that time. And it would be worse for you, because that boy is much younger than you are and your social inferior by some way."

"Oh, Mum!"

"Don't 'Oh, Mum' me! I know you have modern ideas about society but don't expect a jury to be so enlightened. They will assume you've corrupted the boy."

"Alfie! Alfie! Can't you even say his name now?"

"I don't want to say his bloody name. And he's skulked away, I notice."

"He hasn't skulked anywhere. I sent him home, despite the fog. He was quite prepared to face you."

"It's a good job he didn't because I'd have slapped his pretty little face for him. I may not listen to every word of the Reverend Greene's sermons, but I have heard enough to realise that the face of evil can be seductively attractive."

"Oh, Mum, you know Alfie's not evil." Malcolm sighed. "What are you doing back anyway?"

"If you must know it's because of the bloody fog. I was unable to get to London Bridge in time and the trains aren't running anyway. So, I came back only to be confronted by"—she shuddered—"that!"

*

THE NEXT DAY, after a fitful night's sleep Grace lay in, leaving Malcolm to attend to his own breakfast. Once she was sure he'd left for work, she bathed and went downstairs to make her own breakfast of tea and a slice of toast which might have been made of balsa wood for all the pleasure it gave her. She hadn't cried since William's funeral, but she felt close to doing so now. But no, that wouldn't do. She felt she needed to make this a trouble shared and so she took her hat and coat from the hallstand, adding a suitably stout scarf. The fog had lifted, but remnants of it lingered in dips in the road and the frost also remained. It wasn't a nice day to be out, but she was only walking the few hundred yards up Cranmer Avenue to her good friend Marjorie's.

Marjorie was a woman of independent means who dabbled in oils. She may have had only modest abilities herself, but she moved in a Bohemian circle and numbered several notable painters among her friends. Her studio was in the attic, but the rest of the house was vibrant with exotic-coloured fabrics and lush green plants. The drawing room in which she entertained guests was opulently Edwardian, softened by strategically placed ferns on a grand scale. A Napoleon mantel clock's Westminster chimes sounded the quarter hour as Grace concluded her summary of this scandalous development.

"Stark naked!" exclaimed Marjorie, her incredulity turning her mouth into a crimson circle.

"Yes, and worse than that—but I'll spare you the details, dear."

Marjorie looked slightly disappointed to be spared. She flapped about Grace, her silver bangles rattling as she did so. "But Grace dear, he's your son, your little boy, you've seen him naked before…"

"Not like that! I haven't seen him naked since he was a boy. Not since before we sent him to boarding school—and if this is anything to go by, God only knows what he got up to there! Besides, nudity in the parlour isn't really the issue as I'm sure you can appreciate."

Her friend perched on the edge of an armchair. "Well, what do you propose to do, dear?"

"I really have no idea."

"You can hardly turn in your own son, can you? Even if you were just to report Alfie, he would inevitably be drawn into it. As you say, the authorities would be likely to assume that Malcolm had led the boy astray."

"And supposing he did?" she wailed. "Oh, Marjorie, supposing he did! Alfie seemed like a down-to-earth, hardworking young man. I wouldn't say he was God-fearing exactly but he's clearly good to his mother, he takes pride in his appearance, and he's—well, *kind*. What if my son has ruined that boy's life?" Grace nearly wept. "I shouldn't be able to bear the shame of it."

"I shouldn't think along those lines, dear, not yet. I've only met Alfie a handful of times, but he didn't strike me as being all that impressionable. Rather a self-assured young man, I'd have thought. Let's concentrate on your options. You could demand that they stop this nonsense, and if they agree, you'll say no more about it. Pretend the whole sordid episode never happened. You could even forbid Malcolm from seeing Alfie ever again, using the threat of the law as a sanction."

"Oh, then I'd forever be the wicked witch, wouldn't I? And he'd know full well that I wouldn't go to the police and report my own son, bringing disgrace upon myself in the process."

For a while, the women were each lost in their thoughts on the matter.

"The thing is," Grace went on eventually, "I've never known Malcolm to be as happy as he's been since he met Alfie. He was always such a sad young man, and I was worried for him, particularly when you think of how his father…well, you know. I was so delighted to see he'd found a friend he got on with so well, that I pushed aside any reservations regarding social class. But I had no idea what they were up to, not until last night."

Marjorie said gently, "You could just turn a blind eye, Grace dear. What the eye doesn't see the heart doesn't grieve over. Make it clear that you don't wish to know anything about it, and you certainly mustn't have to witness them carrying on under your own roof again, but that aside, they're free to do as they wish out of your sight."

"That's all very well as far as it goes, but I can tell you're not a mother, Marjorie. Every moment they're out of my sight, I'd be afraid for them— for both of them. I'd be afraid of the law catching up with them, or even worse. You hear such terrible things, don't you?"

"You're only a mother to one of them, dear, but I do take your point."

Grace had surprised herself. For the first time, she had tacitly acknowledged that she had a relationship with Alfie and if anything awful were to happen to him, it would be as painful for her as if it were to befall her own son.

"Marjorie," she said, and cleared her throat. "Do you know anyone like *that*?" She made a limp-wrist gesture.

"Oh, heavens, yes of course, Grace! I move in artistic circles, don't forget. Some of my dearest friends are 'like that', as you put it."

"And are any of them *happy*?"

"Well, some are and some aren't. Just like everybody else, really."

"I wonder if there are any older ones. Ones I might be able to speak to?"

After pausing for thought, Marjorie said, "I know just the person— Victor. He lives in Chalk Farm so if he's free I expect he could come right over. I can offer him a spot of lunch. You too, dear, of course." With that, she headed for the telephone in the hall.

*

MALCOLM'S DICTOGRAPH BUZZED, and he plucked the receiver from its cradle and flicked the switch. Miss Hassell had a Mr Atwood on the line. It was rare for Alfie to phone him, let alone at work.

"Ah yes, from the West India Docks. Put him through, would you?"

"Malcolm? Are you all right?"

"Hello, Alfie. Yes, of course I am. What about you? I'm so sorry I sent you back out into that wretched fog. I've been worried…"

"Oh, mate, it was awful! Took me hours but I got there. And I understand, of course. How is it at home?"

"Honestly? I don't know. We had a set-to about it last night. I apologised that she had to find out like that, but not for you and me. She isn't happy about it, of course, but I think she knows I've no intention of stopping."

"What d'you think she'll do?"

"I don't know that either."

"I don't reckon she *can* do much. She ain't gonna report us, is she? I mean, my mum would never report me. She might kill me, mind."

"I shouldn't have thought she would, no. But Alfie, watch what you say on the telephone, won't you? No one is meant to be listening, but you can never be sure."

"Gawd, yes. Sorry. Flaming things. I just wanted to check you're not too upset about it, or in trouble or nuffink."

"I'm glad you did, if only to let me know that you got home all right.

You know, in a way I'm glad she has found out the truth because I don't like deceiving her. If it comes to the worst, I'll simply move out and find somewhere else to live. I have ample means, after all."

"You don't wanna do that though, Malc. You're all she's got, mate. You can't leave her all alone in that big 'ouse."

"Well, it's rather up to her. I mean, that's what would happen if I followed her wishes and got married, isn't it? In all likelihood, my new wife wouldn't want to be saddled with her mother-in-law, would she?"

"You'd have to choose yer wife carefully then. Yer mum is good to have around. I like 'er. I think she liked me an' all, but now she's seen me stark bollock naked and covered in—"

"Yes, yes, I'm only too aware of what she saw, thank you very much." He spoke more tartly than he'd intended, worried about someone listening in.

"Look, can you come to the Hoop and Grapes on Friday after work?" Alfie said. "Maybe you'll know more by then."

*

VICTOR PAGET RELISHED a crisis and was pleased to be summoned to give assistance as though he was one of the emergency services. When he arrived at Marjorie's, there were hugs and kisses and it sounded to Grace as though each was the other's favourite person in the whole world.

"It's so good of you to pop over at such short notice, dahling Victor," gushed Marjorie.

"That's perfectly fine, dear. I *must* say I'm intrigued."

"This is my dear friend Grace. Grace wishes to seek the benefit of your experience in matters…well, you know."

"I don't, but I'm sure she'll enlighten me. How do you do, Grace?"

"Yes, hello." She was unaccustomed to having her hand kissed and was taken with Victor's manners, which seemed to come from an age gone by.

"As I don't detect a whiff of the Sapphic and I'm far from being an expert in that area anyway, am I to assume that you have a son?"

"Yes, I do. Malcolm."

Victor raised his eyebrows. "I see. And are there some tell-tale signs that lead you to believe young Malcolm may be *so?*"

Wishing to hurry things along a bit, Marjorie interjected, "She walked in on him naked in the arms of an equally naked young docker, dear, and if that isn't a reliable enough tell-tale sign then I don't know what is."

This information was enough to have Victor sink onto the sofa next to Grace and place a hand on her arm. "A docker, you say? Oh, my! Tell me all."

Grace gave an account of the whole sorry incident. Perhaps given her audience, for the first time she began to feel as though she might have overreacted. However, Victor seemed sympathetic.

"Silly boys. Why were they thus engaged in your parlour anyway? Are there no bedrooms in your house?"

"Yes, there are plenty. But they were drawn to the warmth of the fire, I imagine. We don't always light fires in every single room, so it is rather chilly in the rest of the house—particularly if you've a mind not to wear a stitch of clothing," she added bitterly. "I was meant to be out of the way in Folkestone, you see, and that's where I would have been were it not for that blasted fog."

"Shocking, wasn't it? I was a prisoner in my own home last night.

And this other young man—had you encountered him before?"

"Oh, yes. Alfie's a frequent visitor and he's always been most welcome. I must admit he's a good boy to have around. He's very useful about the house, you see; if something needs mending or a fuse needs changing, he'll do it without even being asked. Not like Malcolm who's a clever boy but useless at anything practical. Alfie has always been nice to chat to. There's the light of mischief in his eyes sometimes, but he never seems to get up to any."

"Until now," Victor murmured.

"I don't think that 'mischief' is a strong enough word, do you?"

"Dear lady, I'm sure you'll have guessed that over the years I have indulged in copious amounts of such mischief, and worse besides. If it's advice on a cure you're after, I'm hardly your man."

"Yes, you're quite right. This is all terribly new to me. I feel I'm having to do a lot of thinking very quickly indeed. It's making me quite giddy."

"It does you great credit that you're doing it at all, Grace. Many parents wouldn't even try to understand. Your son may not appreciate it yet, but he is a fortunate young man."

"Oh, I have considered the 'never darken my doorstep again' approach, but Malcolm is all I have, you see? I only ever had the one child, and I lost his father eleven years ago, longer really because he was overseas with the war for five years. Even if I was to send Malcolm packing, I'd spend all my time worrying about him."

"From what you were saying, it sounds as though you are rather fond of his friend too."

"I am—or was. I no longer know. But you see he's a few years younger than Malcolm. Alfie's only twenty, I think, and I'm terribly afraid that Malcolm has led the boy astray. It would be a terrible thing if he's ruined that boy's life as well as his own. Alfie is not of our class and should surely be able to rely on his social superiors to lead by example."

Victor guffawed and spluttered, "I beg your pardon, but I do find that idea inordinately funny."

Marjorie interjected again. "Victor, you should know that Alfie is rather beautiful to look at. I mean, quite spectacularly so. Sublime even. That being the case, I personally would find it hard to believe that Malcolm is the first man to have tried his luck."

"Really?" Victor's eyes lit up. "I must meet him. His does sound like a visage that should be shared if Marjorie here is to be believed anyway. She does have an eye for such things, you know. In fact, I'm surprised she hasn't already had him decked out in a toga holding a bunch of grapes for her work." He became more serious. "But Grace, I may be able to help you here. If a twenty-year-old boy is what you would call normal, then no amount of persuasion or cajolery would get him to enter into a full-blown queer relationship, not even with 'the squire from the big 'ouse'. I know from experience, at sixteen they'll almost all try it, but at that age, they would try it with inanimate objects, and often do. At twenty, they haven't been given the keys to the door yet, but they aren't children any more. In short, Grace, I doubt that Malcolm has forced anything on this boy."

"There you are, dear!" Marjorie said triumphantly. "That's what I said, isn't it?"

"Victor, is it at all possible for…people like that…to ever be happy?" Grace asked timidly.

"People like me, you mean. Yes, it's possible, Grace, but I wouldn't say it was probable. There are couples who live their lives together happily without drawing attention to themselves, but they're pitifully rare, in London at any rate. The conflict with the law and society's attitudes are formidable barriers, of course, but they're not the only ones. In London, we're talking about a community of desperately unhappy, often damaged individuals. If they spot anyone who looks as though they may be within touching distance of paradise, that person will soon find themselves dragged back screaming into the rabble. The queer world can be a very bloody one, I'm afraid."

*

WHEN MALCOLM GOT home from work, he and Grace ate dinner in silence apart from the scraping of cutlery against china and simple requests to pass the condiments. As they concluded their meal with a cup of tea, he felt it was his responsibility to try to break the ice.

"I *am* sorry about what you saw last night, truly I am. I expect you'd have had to know some time, but I wish you hadn't found out in the way that you did."

Grace's mood was hard to fathom. She didn't look angry any more, but she didn't look thrilled to bits either.

"I love him, Mum."

Grace's expression was one of weariness and mild pain. "Oh, Malcolm, I can see why you might, obviously. But it isn't on, is it? Darling, you can't just take up with a young working-class boy. You must see that."

"I pretty much have done. It's a *fait accompli*."

"So, you think that's it, do you? You think it's all done and dusted and there's nothing anyone can say or do to change it?"

"Yes. That is what I think."

"I'll wager his family haven't been told about this…arrangement of yours. How do you expect they'll take it? Are the working-classes all right with this sort of thing nowadays?"

"It will be fine."

"Do you really think so? When you take up with someone seriously, you aren't just taking them on, you know. You're taking on their lives—their family, their friends, their world. It can be difficult at the best of times. It's almost always a challenge even in the case of normal relationships. But with a boy like that… What are you going to do if they disown him? They might, you know. How would you be able to cope with the guilt of having taken a young man away from his family, from everyone and everything he knows?"

"All we need is each other," he insisted.

"Oh, Malcolm, please grow up for heaven's sake! I'm sure you think that now, and perhaps he does too. But being *everything* to someone is a heavy burden to bear, no matter how fond of them you are. You scarcely know each other. You don't know all that much about him, or his past. And you're both young, particularly him. I'm afraid that you'll run the risk of hating each other before too long."

"Look, we've no plans to tell anyone. We had no plans to tell you just now."

"So, you were going to carry on in your own little world? As if nothing and no one else mattered?"

"Yes! That's it precisely. I don't know whether it will last, but it's already given me more than I ever expected from my life. I've found some happiness, Mum. If it doesn't last, I'll be broken-hearted, but at least I'll have had it, don't you see? What's the alternative? Am I to end it and make us both miserable now?"

"When his family do find out—and they will, you know—they will assume that you've corrupted him, and they may well report you to the police. He's at an age when young men are impressionable."

"Be reassured, East End families do *not* report things to the police. And he isn't impressionable, Mum. You don't know him at all if you think he is."

"I don't know him, it's true, but neither do you, not really. As for the police… Well, you'd be surprised at how far a mother will go to protect her child."

Chapter Twenty-Two

Egg Custard Tarts

Thursday, 11 January 1934

GRACE TREVELYAN HAD been waiting outside the dock gates for a long time. She knew she was conspicuous, dressed in pastel shades in a bleak landscape of warehouses and the quayside derricks that reared up and poked the sky. If this was the reality faced daily by Malcolm's young plaything, no wonder he was looking for a way out.

Alfie was easy to spot among the drab river of humanity that flowed through the dock gates at five o'clock. The rumble of traffic and the sound of ships was usurped for a spell by gruff voices and the tread of heavy boots on the cobbles from a procession of men in dark clothing and cloth caps. Although dressed similarly, Alfie stood out like a pearl in a box of buttons. When he saw her, he was bewildered at first, but the penny dropped and his expression clouded over. Grace was sad to see it, let alone be the cause. Then, stifling any sympathy, she asked him tersely if there was anywhere nearby they could go "for a chat". He led her to a shabby café on the West India Dock Road.

She consented to a cup of tea which he bought for her, along with a very yellow pastry on a plate.

"What is that?"

"It's a custard tart, what's it look like?"

"Well, thank you."

"It's a pleasure. If we'd been here last month, I could have got us an opium cigarette each. But Mr Pereira, the guy who ran this place, was banged up for selling 'em."

"Was he a Chinaman?"

"Nah, they get the blame for everything round here. He was Portu-guese or sumfink, I dunno. And don't worry, I was only joking. I ain't never bought nuffink more dangerous than a custard tart in here. I promise yer."

There was much stirring of tea as Grace tried to find words to ex-press her foreboding, without making her seem like a Victorian matron. It was Alfie who spoke first, and he blushed as he did so.

"Look, I'm really sorry for what you saw the other night, missus, I really am. It must of been an 'ell of a shock."

"Well. It's done now. I'm not here to berate you."

He raised his eyebrows "So, wivout wanting to be rude, why *are* you here exactly? I thought I was banished."

"Look Alfie, you seem like a nice enough boy. You've been kind to me. I was very impressed with your attitude during that business with the tree and you're always helpful and pleasant. That's why I was so surprised that you…you know."

"Yes, well, I'm a bit surprised meself, to be honest." The colour rose in his cheeks again as he smiled sheepishly and, like most people, she found it enchanting.

"There you are, you see? That is what I'm most worried about. You're an attractive boy, that's clear for all to see. You're always going to get a lot of attention, not all of it welcome."

He shrugged. "That's true enough. I certainly can't argue wiv it. We all have our crosses to bear, eh?"

"If Malcolm is…afflicted with this "vice", then that is bad enough. I don't want to carry the burden of seeing my own son corrupt someone else."

"Meaning me?"

"Well, yes. As I said, you're a lovely-looking boy and it's no surprise that he'd be tempted. But to draw you into this sort of thing—well, it's just too bad of him."

Alfie seemed at a loss to know what to say. Grace went on, "I dare say you're flattered by the attention. He's older than you, he's bright and from a more affluent background. I'm afraid he might have seduced you and—"

Alfie held up his hand. "Missus, let me stop you there. No offence, but you've got this all wrong. If I'd waited for Malcolm to seduce me, we wouldn't be having this chat, because nuffink would ever have happened. I don't rightly know what's going on, to tell you the truth, but I *do* know that whatever it is, I started it. I liked him from the off, and yes, he's not the sort of person I normally knock around with and, I dunno, that might be part of the attraction. But when one thing led to another it was *me. I* started it. So, don't you go putting it all on him."

"Yes, but are you sure he didn't manipulate you, make you think it was all your idea? They can be very devious, you know."

"Ha. I'm sure 'they' can. But if I'm wrong then he ought to be on the stage, missus."

"He's…"

"I know, cleverer than me as well as richer and older and higher up in the world."

"Goodness me, I must seem such a snob." Grace looked contrite. "I don't mean to be rude to you."

"No, I know you don't. An' I can see that it's big of you to be thinking of me rather than him, your own son. Some people would assume I was just after his money, which I ain't."

"I'm his mother, Alfie. If I'm absolutely honest, walking in on you both is not the first inkling I've had about this. You were the shock, not him. There have always been signs that he's more drawn to male company. Whenever Malcolm talks of work it is always men he talks about. The newspaper photographs he dwells on… A mother takes all this in, you know. When he started seeing you, the alarm bells did ring somewhat, but for the first time since he was a small child, he seemed happy. I've never been able to say that before these last months. I also reasoned with myself that a boy like you would hardly be likely to have anything to do with that sort of thing."

"It's probably a lot more common than you think, missus. And you know, it ain't such a big deal in the end. I like Malcolm. I like him a *lot.*

Family aside, I ain't never been this close to anyone before, let alone another geezer. But in the end, one or other of us, both probably, will meet the right gel, settle down, get married, 'ave a family. That's what happens. That's normal."

Grace sat back in her hard wooden chair. "Oh, Alfie, do you think so?"

"Course I do. I really think that's what'll 'appen. It's only natural, innit?"

"I do hope you're right, for all our sakes."

"Course I'm right. Now eat your custard tart."

"Well…" She eyed the yellow pastry dubiously.

"*Eat* it. You look all in. I bet you ain't had nuffink since breakfast wiv all your worrying. You're like 'im, or maybe he's like you."

*

MALCOLM WAS SITTING at the kitchen table when she waltzed in, plonking a paper bag onto it as she passed.

"What's in there?"

"They're egg custard tarts, dear. Try one, they're really rather delicious."

"You don't eat shop-bought cakes."

"Well, I tried one of these and I liked it."

He read the name emblazoned on the side of the paper bag. "West India Dock Road? What in God's name were you doing there?"

"I went to see Alfie, if you must know."

He flung the bag none too gently back onto the table with a mild curse.

"Careful, dear, you'll break them. And that's not the sort of language I like to hear in my own house, thank you very much."

"You were warning him off, I suppose."

"No, dear. We had a perfectly amicable chat over tea and egg custard tarts."

"A chat? What could you possibly have to say to each other, without discussing that business the other evening? Hardly likely to result in a so-called amicable chat."

"If you absolutely must know, I wanted to make sure he knew what he was doing and that you weren't exerting any undue pressure on him."

"Pressure!" Malcolm was outraged. "I never have! And I'm your son—what about me?"

"You're older than he is. You're more educated than he is."

"Oh, yes, those lessons in elementary seduction techniques I had at school have really paid off!"

"Don't be facetious. And I know it's not fashionable to say so, but you are also his social superior."

"Oh, *Christ!*"

"Yes, well, don't let's bring Him into it." Grace let a moment pass before saying, "It's all right, Malcolm. He has reassured me that you haven't led him astray or taken advantage of him. Indeed, he said it was rather the other way around, but I took that with a pinch of salt. He may just have been being loyal. He does strike me as the type."

Her son looked her in the eyes. "So where does this leave us?" he asked quietly. "I suppose you want us to stay out of your way: what the eye doesn't see and so on."

"Yes, so long as I don't have to witness anything untoward, Alfie is welcome here and you may carry on as you were. I'd really rather you didn't have relations under my roof. I mean, I trust you would show me the respect of not going to bed together here or anything like that. But I don't mind you expressing affection for each other."

"Should we draw up a list of what is and isn't permitted?" Malcolm said ungraciously.

"I don't think that will be necessary." And Grace had one more thing to say before she was done. "Don't consider it a seal of approval, Malcolm. It's far from being that. As you are aware, the world outside frowns upon this sort of thing. But if it's what you want and it's what Alfie wants, then I don't see that your relationship is anyone else's business really. It's not what I'd want for you, but I'd rather know that you were out of harm's way here where although the Good Lord can see you, the public and the law can't. And if nothing else, at least you've chosen a decent sort. Alfie's a nice boy."

Malcolm could see all sorts of problems with this arrangement, but he had to concede that it was a start and a much better outcome than he had expected after the *in flagrante* drama that foggy night.

"Mum!" He embraced her. "You're not such a bad old stick. I don't know what to say, except thank you."

"Well, you can start showing your gratitude by never calling me an 'old stick' again."

*

ON FRIDAY, THEY met at the Hoop and Grapes as arranged. Although the immediate crisis seemed to have passed, Malcolm was uneasy about the way his mother had been so easily disarmed by Alfie. What might he have said to defuse her outrage?

Since Frank had confronted Malcolm before Christmas, they hadn't been out with the gang as often, not to the pub nor to watch West Ham, preferring to spend the time alone together.

"Is this all right, Alfie?"

"What d'you mean?"

"Us meeting like this. I rather feel that I'm taking you away from your friends and I don't want to do that."

"It's fine. I can go out with them any time. I'm not 'aving you exposed to any more of Frank's nonsense like you was at the Posts that time."

"Thank you. But we can't hide away."

"I know. And we won't, honest. If I'm not around as much as he'd like, perhaps he'll realise that he should of kept his trap shut."

"Do you mind my asking what you said to convince my mother to drop the subject of—well, of us?"

"Not a lot. I just had to get her away from the notion that you'd seduced me wiv your fancy ways." Alfie smiled at the recollection.

"Is that all?"

The expression on Alfie's face suggested it wasn't, but he was reluctant to say anything more. He sighed and said, "Malcolm, I love the time we spend together. I love what we do together. But you *do* know…" Then he changed his mind. "Ah, forget it."

"No, go on. What were you going to say?"

"Look, nuffink's 'appening that you don't know about and maybe nuffink will change for months, years even."

"I have no idea what you're talking about."

"I ain't surprised—I ain't doing a very good job of it. What it is, I just worry that you might come to depend on me too much. We're about as close as two blokes can be. We'll always be friends, I hope. But one day one of us, both of us even, will probably meet a gel and—"

"A girl? I don't understand."

"Malcolm, one day I'm gonna meet a gel and settle down. Get married and 'ave kids. And you're probably gonna want to do that too. It's what happens. It's what men do."

Malcolm froze inside. Even as he recovered, he didn't trust himself to react. When he did, he spoke calmly.

"Alfie, I hadn't been at school more than a fortnight before I realised that I'm queer. I won't ever be settling down with any girl. I'm queer, do you understand?"

"You can't know that!"

"I can and I do. It's the way I'm made."

"But you ain't like them, Malcolm. I've got nuffink against them, but if you was like that, then we wouldn't be doing what we been doing. I could never."

Malcolm realised that Alfie was referring to the more effeminate men one could hardly fail to notice in the West End. He had referred to them in the abstract because he didn't know a word for them that wasn't in some way derogatory. Even during this tense conversation, Malcolm was impressed by Alfie's restraint, for he himself had used those words and used them often.

"Look, I'm not like them apart from the fact that I'm just a man who is attracted to other men, that's all. It's simple. Like I said, I'll always be this way. I'm queer."

Alfie looked troubled at hearing this. "Well, I ain't. I'm sorry, Malcolm, but I just ain't. I know that what we do is against the law, but I don't mind being a naughty boy every now and again if it feels good and it don't hurt no one. But one day, Malc, I *will* meet a gel and that'll be that. It's human nature. It's what I want—wife, kids, the lot. You must see that."

Malcolm managed a tight smile. "I do. I'm sad about it for my own part, but I do understand, Alfie. Honestly."

"So, we ain't gonna fall out over this?"

"Of course not. The last thing I want to do is to argue with you. Thank you for being honest with me. Now, can we talk about something else?"

*

ON SATURDAY MORNING after Grace had picked up her wicker basket and gone out shopping, he sat and pondered that conversation. He was fond of rerunning their chats, but he wasn't as keen on this one. He sat by the fire with a cup of tea and stared into the flames as he was wont to do when he was thinking. His mother often said that a fire was good company.

He hadn't been shocked by what Alfie had said. Of course, Alfie was a normal young man. Of course, he'd eventually want to settle down. As he had said, it was only natural, and his finding the woman he wanted to spend the rest of his life with wasn't necessarily imminent. Malcolm had been moderately alarmed when Alfie mentioned Doreen, a new secretary in the Dock Office, several times. According to him, she was ever so glamorous but wouldn't take any nonsense and was keener on her career than she was on any man, so Malcolm relaxed. Good for her. Alfie had said he reckoned that if she did ever consent to walking out with someone it wouldn't be with some scruffy docker.

There would be someone, of course, sooner or later, but for now, he was a young man who'd found a way to sow his wild oats without the risk of getting some girl into trouble. Malcolm would harvest as many of those wild oats as he was able. Whether he had years, months, or weeks more of Alfie, he'd take them. He hadn't expected to ever be as happy as he had been this last year or so, and if there was more to come, then he'd take it and cherish it. That a boy as good-looking and good-natured as Alfie had bestowed that privilege on him was wonderful, and he was going to savour every second even if it was tinged with the sadness of knowing it wouldn't last forever and might not even last that much longer. He didn't know whether he could bear to continue the friendship once the inevitable had happened, but that was a bridge he'd cross when he came to it.

Part Six

You Made Me Love You

Chapter Twenty-Three

Plans

Wednesday, 7 February 1934

AS GRACE KNEW about them, Alfie came around more often, even when no "shenanigans" were on the cards. One evening when Malcolm had been delayed at work, Grace found herself alone with him for the first time since their afternoon tea on the West India Dock Road. At first, it was awkward, but rather than banishing him to the drawing room she seated him in the kitchen so they could chat as she pressed on with her chores. The days of the cook and the housemaid were long gone.

"I say, Alfie, I made a Victoria sponge yesterday, would you care to try a slice? It's rather scrumptious, even though I say so myself."

"Oh, yes please, missus. Don't mind if I do."

"As it seems that we will inevitably be seeing more of each other, do you think I could prevail upon you to stop calling me "missus"? My friends call me Grace. And I do hope we're to be friends."

"All right, Grace. I 'ope so too."

As she opened the door to the larder to fetch the cake, she winced at its creaking. "It's like a haunted house," she observed impatiently.

"It just needs a drop of oil, that's all. 'Ave you got any? If so, I can sort it out for yer."

She looked dubious. "If we have any, it will be in the shed with all my late husband's tools. That means it will have been there for twelve years." She made a face. "Does oil last that long? It doesn't evaporate or anything like that?"

"No, Grace," said Alfie with a smile. "It don't evaporate."

He was gone for longer than fetching an oil can merited. Clutching it on his return, he said, "There are a lot of pretty decent tools in there, but they could do with cleaning up a bit."

"There'd be no point, dear. Malcolm's not a bit of use at practical things. I doubt he's been in that shed at all since his father died."

"I can believe that. I've just 'ad to spend five minutes brushing cobwebs off me. They was all stuck in me hair an' everything."

Alfie oiled the hinge on the larder door and opened and closed it a few times to let the dark-brown lubricant work its way through.

"There you go. Easy."

"Oh, thank you, dear. That's much better. It was one of the many little things around the house that irritate me. Malcolm has stopped even pretending he'll ever get around to them, but it wasn't really bad enough for me to call in a tradesman."

"You don't need a tradesman to put a drop of oil on a bleedin' hinge!" scoffed Alfie. "Why don't you make a list, Grace? Your son may be useless, but I ain't. I might as well make meself useful when I'm round here."

"Oh, Alfie, I can't treat you like a hired handyman."

"I don't mind. I do it for me mum all the time. I like fiddling with things, to tell you the truth."

He washed his hands at the sink and sat down at the kitchen table. Grace cut him a generous slice of the sponge and served it on a bone china plate with a pattern of pink roses. She had some silver cake forks that were ideal for a sponge, but she decided one of those might bewilder him, so she left them in the drawer.

Alfie took a bite, and Grace noted his perfect teeth with approval. "Oh, Grace, that is just *lovely!*" he exclaimed.

"I'm glad you like it." She was taken aback by his enthusiasm.

"Honest to God, I ain't never tasted a cake as good as this before."

"Don't let your mother hear you say that."

"Mum don't really bake cakes. She's got too many other things to do, I suppose. She's been known to make jam and even fruit tarts after we used to go blackberrying when I was a kid. But never cake. I doubt she could manage anything like this."

Pleased and embarrassed, Grace moved to change the subject. "Let's have the wireless on, shall we? Henry Hall will be on in a minute. I do like his show, don't you? Do you have a wireless?"

"We do 'ave one now as it goes, but I ain't often in to listen to it. I know who he is like. I hear all the tunes up Alexander's. That's a dance hall in Poplar."

"Ah, I used to love to dance, even though it was a lot more straitlaced in my day, of course." She smiled at the memory.

"I can just picture you cutting the rug. We'll 'ave to go sometime. All three of us."

"Don't be silly, Alfie. You wouldn't want me tagging along."

"Why not? I can hardly dance with Malcolm, can I? People would take a dim view of that, I reckon."

Now she knew about them, Alfie wasn't even going to pretend in front of her that Malcolm and he were "just good friends" as the expression went. She found his transparency refreshing but hoped he'd be more circumspect in company.

"Alfie, you know what you said—about you eventually meeting a girl and settling down?"

"Yes?"

"You do care for Malcolm, don't you? I mean genuinely. It's more than just—you know."

"Of course, I do, Grace. I couldn't do any of this if I didn't. Nor could I sit here and scoff your cake if I was just using your boy, now could I?"

"I suppose not. It's just that I…I'm not quite sure what the attraction is for you."

"Grace! 'Ow can you say that? He's your son!"

She was touched by how quick he'd been to defend him. "I know, it's just that—"

"I ain't even gonna start telling you about fancying him. What muvver wants to hear that, eh? But it's far more than that anyway. He sees into me, Grace. He knows who I am. I've had a lifetime of people clocking me face and looking no further. Malcolm talks to me properly; he listens to me. He cares what I think about things. He can tell what mood I'm in. He's proper nice, your boy."

This speech brought the tears to her eyes and made her wonder whether she knew her son at all. Seen through the eyes of another, he did seem "proper nice", and in a way, it made her prouder of him than any of his achievements at the British Atlantic.

*

Wednesday, 20 June 1934

ALFIE WAS COMING around more often, and Malcolm was thrilled about it. It couldn't all be down to his appetite for his mother's baking. Now he'd got to know her better, Alfie regarded Grace with reverence. Having agreed that they shouldn't share a bed in Cranmer Avenue, he told Malcolm he wouldn't have been comfortable going to bed with him in his mother's house even if Grace hadn't said anything. "It wouldn't feel right," was all he said. So, sex continued much as before, as something that happened by the fireside in the parlour whenever Grace was away. And it was wonderful. What was more, Alfie showed no signs of tiring of it, which instilled in him a growing confidence.

He recalled his elementary lesson in sexual matters from Godfrey and how emphatic he had been then about what he would and wouldn't do, and what he thought Alfie would and wouldn't want. Godfrey had been right about the reality of making love to Alfie being a lot better than a clinical explanation of the practicalities had promised, and he wondered if he could go further now. The more he thought about it, the more he felt he wanted to do that—but would Alfie? Sex happened when Alfie decided it would, and he also tended to decide what form it would take. Older by a few years, Malcolm was reluctant to instigate anything lest it feel like molestation. If Alfie started it, then he knew he wanted it. Fortunately, Malcolm knew how easily triggered the boy was. A kiss or a caress at the nape of his neck was usually enough to get him going.

He became preoccupied with the notion of giving himself to Alfie, submitting himself, allowing the boy inside him physically as well as emotionally. It would be worth any pain or unseemly consequences. But Alfie had never suggested that it was something he'd like to do.

As they snatched a couple of pints in a dark corner of the Hoop and Grapes, Malcolm plucked up the courage to broach the subject.

"Alfie, it would be nice if we could share a bed for a whole night sometime, wouldn't it? You once said we would, remember?"

"Yes, I remember. I'd like to as well, but we ain't doing it at your house. We agreed."

"I know. But surely we could arrange something, somewhere?"

"Yes. We could go on holiday or sumfink. Camping maybe?"

Malcolm made an uncertain noise and pressed on. "Alfie, would you be prepared to—I mean, would you like to, er, bugger me at all?"

A slow smile spread across the young man's face. "Bugger?" and he laughed softly to himself.

"What's wrong?"

"Bugger—it's such a funny word, innit?"

Malcolm gulped. "Sorry. It was a bad idea. Forget I spoke." His face burned. As far as sex was concerned, he was more comfortable doing it than he ever would be talking about it.

Alfie put a hand on his shoulder and moved closer to ensure he wouldn't be overheard by any of the clerks and messengers around them. Malcolm felt his warm breath against his face as he said, "If you're asking me whether I'd like to fuck you, then yes, Malcolm, I would. I would very much like to fuck you. If you're sure that's what you want. It weren't so long ago you was scared of a kiss—remember? Now you want me to give it yer up the arse?"

Malcolm was thrilled and appalled in equal measure by Alfie's words. After hastily looking round to make sure that no one had heard the Anglo-Saxon vernacular, he said, "That's true, but I got used to the kisses, didn't I?"

"Yes, you did that all right," said Alfie, grinning. "It'll take a bit of thought though. I don't think we can be doing *that* on your mum's settee."

"Good God! No, indeed."

"And I ain't fucking you over a bin round the back of a shop neither."

"I'm relieved to hear it," said Malcolm primly before adding after a pause, "although perhaps we shouldn't rule that possibility out entirely."

"You dirty bleeder!" laughed Alfie. "We ain't alley cats. I'm sure we can do better than that. Leave it wiv me, eh? I'll sort sumfink out, don't you worry." He punched Malcolm's shoulder playfully. "Bugger!" he chuckled.

The relationship had shifted subtly. Malcolm had always been a private man, jealously guarding his solitude. Now he burned with a need to give himself to this young man and savoured the thought that what so many other people so obviously wanted, he was going to get, sooner or later.

*

ALFIE WAS NO muscleman, but because he did heavy work he was athletic, energetic, and strong—and of course he was young. Beside the fire in the parlour, Malcolm had plenty of opportunity to contemplate his manhood. Contemplating it was one of his favourite pastimes, but each encounter carried the added frisson of knowing that if all went to plan, it was going inside him. A coward about pain, Malcolm feared that the penetration would really hurt, but to have Alfie inside him would be such a wonderfully personal thing for them to share. Another precious memory to store away for darker times.

At home in the evening and for large parts of his working day, he found his mind wandering back to the prospect until it became an obsession.

Chapter Twenty-Four

Key To the Door

Friday, 20 July 1934

"WILL I SEE you at all on your birthday?" asked Malcolm as they looked over at the still-busy Limehouse wharves from the Angel Tavern in Rotherhithe.

As far as the law was concerned, this was the last weekend of Alfie's boyhood, for on Monday he would turn twenty-one and become a man. There was sure to be a celebration on the Isle of Dogs, and Malcolm was as afraid of being invited as he was of *not* being invited. If he wasn't, he'd wonder whether he was all that important to Alfie. On the other hand, if he were to go, the ill-feeling between him and Frank might sour the occasion. But if he was invited and didn't go, Alfie might feel hurt.

"I dunno, mate. I got the day off, but me mum has arranged for me an' Robert to help out with the opening of Tower Beach. We'll be keeping an eye on the nippers to make sure they ain't swept away. That's for the afternoon. I'm sure she's got some surprise party planned for the evening but I ain't sure where it'll be. The Manchester, most probably. Whatever it is, looks like you don't know about it, eh?"

"No, I don't know anything. But look, I don't expect to be invited and it's probably better if I don't come, the way things are between Frank and me."

Alfie nodded sadly. "I ain't happy about that though, mate. If there's gonna be a do, I'd want all me mates to be there, including you. Especially you."

Malcolm sighed. He'd probably have been uncomfortable with Alfie's family anyway. How could he exchange pleasantries with Mrs Atwood given what he got up to with her son? He didn't want to cast a shadow over the occasion. "Look, I'll bring the car into work. Then, if you can get away from beach duties, I'll take you somewhere for tea. Or we could even have a picnic in the car. Just so that I can give you your gift."

"You got me sumfink?"

"Of course I have. It's your twenty-first and I… Well, you're im-portant to me. You know you are."

"I'll speak to Robert and see if I can sneak off at four. How's that?"

"Perfect."

"We'd best make it a picnic in the car though. I'm gonna be all sandy, ain't I? In fact, I'd better warn you that if I have to go in the river after some drowning nipper, I'll be worse than just sandy. No one's gonna want that in a nice caff, are they?"

Malcolm was happier for having made this arrangement, but Alfie had more to make.

"Talking of beaches, I've been thinking about, you know, what we talked about. 'Ow do you fancy going to Brighton over the Bank Holiday? Just you and me?"

Malcolm's brow furrowed. "Won't it be ridiculously overcrowded?"

"It will, but that could work in our favour. Normally it's bad, with people sleeping under the piers and all along the beach and that, but we won't 'ave to. Wilf and Ada from our street go every year to the same guest house, but Ada's expecting any day now, so they've decided not to risk it. They don't want to lose their deposit, but everyone in their family already has plans so they've given me the chance to take the booking over. 'Take a mate,' they said, 'as long as you don't mind bunking up together'." A twinkle in the eye. "Well, I don't mind if you don't."

"A *guest* house?"

"Yes. A big house in one of them streets what leads down to the front. No one will bat an eyelid at two gents sharing on a Bank Holiday, not when there's people sleeping all over the shop outside."

"I don't know," said Malcolm cautiously. "A *seaside* holiday? It's not very me."

Alfie was exasperated. "Oh, come on! Where's your sense of adventure? I used to love going to Southend when I was a kid. Mum used to take us there for days out. Brighton's a bit classier than that, they say. I ain't suggesting you bring your bucket and spade or nuffink. We can go and have tea and scones and do all the stuff that you toffs like to do. Don't you want to share a bed with me for three nights? And mornings? And afternoons?

And we can, you know—do buggery an' that." Alfie was still tickled by the word.

Whatever Malcolm had pictured for their new intimacy, it hadn't been this. But he accepted the plan and later, the thought of waking up with Alfie, lying with him, touching him, warmed him to the idea. The East End pubs and the Boleyn Ground had not been him, but he had loved both experiences. Alfie had the knack of making him see things differently, so maybe he could transform a trip to the seaside too.

*

ON HIS BIRTHDAY morning, Alfie didn't have to get up because both he and Robert had the day off work. His brother rose early anyway but returned to the bedroom they shared at nine-thirty and patiently waited for him to stir.

"Happy Birthday, Alfie." Robert handed him a card and a parcel wrapped in brown paper bound with coarse string. Alfie sat up, rearranged the bolster and the pillows to support himself better, smiled his thanks, and opened the card. It featured a tea clipper in full sail.

Inside the package was a gleaming tankard of untarnished pewter, engraved simply with his name in copperplate along with his date of birth, 23 July 1913.

Alfie beamed and ruffled his brother's hair affectionately. They lived on top of each other so there could easily have been sibling rivalry, but there had never been any of that. Robert was the nicest, kindest, calmest of brothers. Although six years his junior, Alfie reckoned he was the wiser. It was an aura he had. He experienced a pang of guilt when he thought of his brother saving every penny he could lay his hands on to buy this tankard when his own Post Office savings account was so healthy.

"Happy birthday, darlin'." His mother hugged him, and after he'd washed in the yard, she served up a breakfast of bacon, eggs, sausage, fried bread, and black pudding. A rare treat. There was a pile of cards to be opened from family, friends, and neighbours. His mother had bought him a silver key about eight inches long from Chrisp Street Woolworths, the symbolic "key to the door". It was hardboard covered in foil and had it been real it would have looked like something more likely to open the door into a church rather than their modest terraced house. There were two ties and five pairs of socks from her, "grown-up" presents, she called them, and a fine leather collar box from his grandad. A package from Uncle Tommy and Aunty Rose contained a brand-new three-piece suit in the darkest blue serge. His mother's fixed smile tightened at their extravagance, but Alfie knew that Rose wanted him to have a suit of his own, rather than Edward's hand-me-downs, as well as they'd served him.

"Seeing as you've got the day off work, it's good of you to help yer brother over the Tower. It'll be lovely having a beach so close to home, won't it, wiv you being such a water baby."

"Mum, I ain't a baby no more. And I won't be swimming in that river neither. It's full of all sorts. It's disgusting."

"Well, you won't have to go in most probably. They asked Robert to go along to help keep an eye on the little 'uns, wiv him being a good swimmer. I expect it will be ever so busy so they'll be thrilled to bits to have you an' all, Alfie."

He shrugged. He'd end up going in if anyone was in difficulty, but he wished they hadn't chosen his twenty-first birthday to open the bloom-ing beach. Reading about it in the *Daily Herald*, it was a nice idea, he had to admit. The King had decreed that the Tower foreshore should be opened up for kids whose families weren't able to afford a day out at the seaside. Fifteen hundred barge-loads of sand had been deposited there, forming a narrow beach with Tower Bridge looming over the eastern end of it. It would disappear at high tide, so they'd have to know when to close the two flights of stone stairs leading down to it. A new iron ladder had also been added between the beach and Tower Wharf and they promised to always have an attendant on the beach itself and a waterman in a launch nearby to help anyone who got into trouble. The bigwigs would be there for the grand opening and that meant there'd be speeches that were sure to suck some of the joy out of the occasion. Alfie and Robert steered well clear of the ceremonial rigmarole.

Alfie loved to swim. Part of the reason his build was so admired was because he was often at the public baths or the Island Lido. As he grew into adolescence, swimming had offered a better way of keeping clean than trying to stuff his growing body into a zinc bath in front of the kitchen fire. He'd come to love it, and that was why his mum called him a "water baby". Alice Atwood was proud of the young man he'd grown into, as a person and also as a fine physical specimen. She took credit for his lovely skin and his beautiful teeth because she'd taught him to look after himself. The thick head of hair and the handsome face may have been down to nature, but the body was mostly his own doing through the effort he put into his work and into his swimming. He was so good at it she reckoned he could have won medals, but he never showed any interest in being competitive.

"I love swimming, Mum, and I wanna keep it that way. I don't wanna make a chore of it. I like it being just me and the water, with maybe a mate or two to lark about with. I don't want no coach hollering at me even if I was to get me boat in the *Topical Times* because of it."

He decided he wouldn't be troubling the disgusting grey-brown soup that was the River Thames unless someone desperately needed his help.

"Don't you go in neither," he warned Robert. "Not unless you have to. There's oil and chemicals and all sorts in that water. And when someone has a shit on them ships, where d'you think that goes?"

His brother nodded grimly. "It's a shame though, innit."

On a Monday afternoon, it was mostly mums with their kids crawling all over the narrow strand. The grey walls of the Tower of London loomed over the path swarming with excited nippers in various stages of undress, and the tourists were treated to more than the odd flash of a little white bum. East End kids weren't bashful and they'd have been happy to run their pale, bony little bodies around stark naked had they been allowed to. As it was, all sorts of tattered garments had been pressed into service as make-shift swimming trunks, with old school gym shorts being the most com-mon. Some of the kids were using the Tower's empty sentry boxes as chang-ing huts. Alfie and Robert had the good sense to wear their bathing trunks underneath their trousers, having anticipated there would be little privacy.

The harassed beach attendant gave the brothers each a handful of leaflets listing a series of *Danger Don'ts* and told them to issue them to eve-ryone before allowing them down onto the sand.

The beach was hardly visible under a seething mass of humanity. Al-fie was first called into action when a kid of about eight who'd been romp-ing nearby let out an almighty yelp and began to cry.

"Oh my gawd, Albert! Wotcher gone and done now?" shouted his mother shrilly.

"It's me foot! I've hurt me foot! Look, it's bleeding an' everyfink!" he howled from his reddening, tear-stained face.

Alfie knelt and inspected the damage. It wasn't hard to see what had happened because the wound still had a jagged piece of brown glass projecting from it, most probably from a broken whisky bottle.

"Get it off me! Take it out!" wailed Albert.

"Nah, mate. We've got to leave it in for a doctor or a nurse to take it out. You've gotta be a brave lad."

Albert wailed even louder, disinclined to display any courage.

"Aw, mate! Don't cry. It's like wiv an Apache arrow in a Tom Mix picture. If you snap it, it's harder for 'em to get it all out."

Mention of the cowboy actor and arrows captured the boy's imagination enough to turn the wail into a whimper, and it was his anxious mother who now seemed the more distressed.

"Don't worry, darlin', he'll live," said Alfie cheerfully. "I'll carry him up to the Tower and they'll see to him. D'you wanna grab yer stuff and follow us up?"

The kid was all skin and bone, like a scrap of nothing in his arms. "You'll be famous," Alfie told him. "The first person ever to cut his foot on Tower Beach. You sure as hell ain't gonna be the last."

"Will they 'ave to cut me foot off, mister?" asked Albert.

"I should think so," said Alfie. "They've got that big axe they used for chopping people's heads off, ain't they. One chop should have it clean off, I reckon." A flash of alarm ignited in his charge's eyes and his face began to crumple. Alfie hastily went on, "No, of course not! I'm only kidding yer. You may have to get a couple of stitches though."

"And a plaster?"

"Not a plaster. I think this is important enough for a bandage, mate."

"Cor!" Albert was obviously impressed by the idea. He'd be the envy of his pals, all bandaged up like a wounded hero. "Will I walk wiv a limp?"

"I expect so. For a few weeks maybe, not forever though."

Albert was left in the care of a Yeoman Warder pressed into helping with any casualties. The boy's mother, confronted by the colourful and imposing uniform, was all apologies for taking up his valuable time, in her best English. Alfie winked at Albert, ruffled his unruly mop, and left them to it to go back to the beach. The area above the narrow strip of sand was busy with hawkers trying to make money out of the venture. There were deck chairs for hire, ice creams and sticky red toffee apples for sale, and the canvas stage was set for a Punch and Judy show. Down on the beach among the mayhem, a small fleet of rowing boats were available for hire at thruppence a time, and kids could be taken on a launch under Tower Bridge and back for the same price.

The beach attendant, unhappy in his work, returned often to remind them of whatever rule concerned him most at the time.

"Don't let the little perishers dive off Tower Pier, lads. There's soft mud all around it and we don't want 'em stuck in it headfirst! And even if they can swim, tell 'em not to go too far out 'cos of the currents, see?"

"I know, Bob," said Robert dryly. "It's all in the bleedin' leaflet, mate."

"I'm only saying. Watch out for 'em chucking stones an' all. Not only is it dangerous, but we need all the pebbles to stay on the beach or it'll be gone in no time. Whose bloody awful idea was this, for Gawd's sake?"

When he'd hurried off again Robert said, "Blimey, he's cheerful, isn't he? I take it he never volunteered for this."

"He ain't wrong though, is he? Poor little Albert hadn't been down here five minutes before he had arf a bottle stuck in his foot."

"Aw, but look at the little uns' faces, Alfie. It's a bit mad today, but once it settles down it will be lovely, I reckon."

Alfie listened to the shrill cries and screams of excitement and answered with a nod and a smile. It was far from perfect, but it was something, and it was something for people who had next to nothing.

A stout middle-aged lady hawking coloured paper windmills gave them the glad eye. "Blimey, look at you two! Yer look good enough to eat, you do. There's a couple of lucky girls out there wot don't know it yet. When yer old enough, o' course."

"He *is* old enough, Ma," Robert said, jerking a thumb at his brother. "He's twenty-one today as it goes."

"What? Happy birthday, darlin'. Here, come an' have a birthday kiss from Hattie."

He permitted her to crush him to her well-padded bosom with a grip so tight it wouldn't have shamed an all-in wrestler. Her hands were all over his back and shoulders like she didn't know which bit of him to grab first, and she planted a big slobbery kiss on his mouth and another two on his cheeks for good measure.

"I'm gonna send my daughters down here to look for you two, I'm telling yer. You'd look lovely in the wedding photos. There'll be fighting mind, 'cos there's four of 'em and only two of you, but still…" Her sentence dissolved into a high-pitched cackle that scattered the gulls.

"Thanks for that, brother dear," said Alfie wryly, wiping his face when she'd gone.

"It's your day, mate," he replied with a shrug and a smile.

*

AT FOUR, ALFIE left Robert on the beach knee-deep in toddlers and climbed the steps onto Tower Bridge where Malcolm was to pick him up. The blue Humber pulled up at the kerb promptly and Alfie hopped into the front passenger seat. On the steps, away from the prying eyes of most pedestrians, he'd managed to struggle into his shoes, socks, and bags but he remained shirtless because he wanted his shirt to stay as fresh as possible.

Trying to keep his eyes on the road as he eased the car over the bridge Malcolm said, "Happy birthday, Alfie. I have a small picnic in the boot. I thought we could go to Southwark Park and eat it to celebrate."

"Sounds good to me. Me mum did me a proper breakfast but I ain't had nuffink since, so I'm 'arf starved."

"Did you have to go into the river in the end?"

"No, thank Gawd. Most of the casualties were cut feet 'cos of all the broken glass there is down there."

"I'm not surprised. You know, it seems to me a rather dangerous venture. I mean, a lot of people have been drowned there over the years."

"Maybe. But you should of seen the nippers. Their faces! They don't care about no broken glass, nor nuffink else. And at least this way there's people watching over 'em."

Malcolm couldn't help noticing Alfie's face soften as he spoke of the children, and it stung a bit. He would want his own, and he should have them. Malcolm wouldn't want to get in the way of that. But Alfie was only twenty-one; there was time yet for it to sort itself out.

Alfie was impressed with the wicker picnic hamper even before it had been opened. Beneath a tartan groundsheet, it held sandwiches, both ham and tomato and cheese and onion. There were grapes and a banana each, plus scones with a jar of strawberry jam and a tub of Devonshire clotted cream. Most impressive of all was a bottle of Moët & Chandon.

"Cor, Malc, you've really pushed the boat out, ain't yer?"

"You're only twenty-one once, Alfie."

"Can I keep the cork? Me Aunty Rose keeps one in her make-up bag to remember sumfink or other."

"Of course you can. I'll pop it in your make-up bag myself if you like."

"'Ere, watch it!" warned Alfie, grinning.

Stripped to the waist in a public park he was drawing plenty of eyes. He stretched languidly, his glistening arms raised. Here on the green grass, beneath a rich blue sky in golden sunshine, the birthday boy looked preposterously handsome. Malcolm basked in reflected glory and almost wished that people knew of the intimacies they'd shared and would share again.

"Thought any more about Brighton?" Alfie asked, aware of the nature of his thoughts.

"I've thought about precious little else."

"Good." Alfie flashed him a smile and there was just the hint of a blush. Could it be that he was a little shy about it? "I'll be telling Frank tonight that I ain't going to White City wiv him. Wish me luck. I never promised nuffink anyway. But…"

Malcolm could see that his stock would fall even further with Frank once he heard their customary Summer Bank Holiday afternoon had been torpedoed again. "You can still go with them, you know," he said.

"I don't want to though. I wanna go to Brighton and—you know"— he lowered his voice—"do buggery wiv you."

Chapter Twenty-Five

Fuss

THAT NIGHT, ALFIE wasn't surprised to be led into the Manchester Arms by his brother, but he was taken aback by the number of people waiting for him. Half of Cubitt Town must have been there, with a fair portion of the workforce of the West India Docks. He could scarcely finish a pint safely for having his back slapped, and an impressive pile of cards grew taller every hour. There were sandwiches and pork pies and a birthday cake, the handiwork of a beaming Mrs Grodzinsky, who reckoned he still wasn't too old to have his cheek pinched and be called *bubbeleh*. The room was hushed as he was made to blow out the twenty-one candles and make a wish.

Sid muttered to George, "You know, I've never met anyone who needs a wish less than Alfie does."

"What d'yer mean?"

"Well, he can have any gel he wants. He's a shoo-in for becoming Master Stevedore after Tommy. Everyone likes him from the tiniest nipper to the oldest granny. Apart from good health, what's he got to bleedin' wish for?"

"West Ham for the Cup?" suggested George.

Nora turned up, already under the influence, and she made loud ribald remarks, many of them within earshot of his mother, about Alfie having been "a big boy" for some time. He stayed out of her way, but Alice had heard enough. She made a beeline for the girl.

"Look, darlin'," she said, "you're making an exhibition of yourself. I'm sure you and Alfie have messed around a bit, but you ain't bin round ours for your tea, 'ave you? That's because he ain't walkin' out with you. Nor would he."

"I only meant that, well, we've been ever so close…"

"There's some things you got to be 'ever so close' to do, dear. But you ain't bin anywhere close to his heart and don't you forget it, madam."

At that point, Rose stepped in and steered Alice back to her table. To Nora, she said, "Don't take it to heart, gel. She's his mum. It ain't like he sits down and discusses his love life with her. But you know, a boy who looks like Alfie is gonna play the field, isn't he? You know that, don't yer?"

"Of course, I do. Five years I've loved him. But he's twenty-one now. He's a man. It's time for him to make a few decisions and when he does… Well, I wanna be there for him to choose if he wants."

"Oh, darlin', I think you know in your heart of hearts that it ain't likely to be you he chooses. You know, sometimes I feel like he's a cruel joke on us all. He looks so lovely, but there's sumfink—oh, I dunno, sumfink dark inside of him. It's like everyone wants him, but no one's gonna have him."

"Blimey, gel, you don't 'arf talk some rubbish!" It was Tommy. Rose was mortified that her husband had sneaked up on them and caught what she'd said. "You wanna stop getting those bleedin' magazines. That *Woman's Weekly* 'as a lot to answer for, I reckon."

She bridled. "A gel needs some help in finding her way round a man's world, Tom. You're probably as proud as punch seeing your nephew tomming around Poplar leaving a trail of broken hearts…"

"Oh, leave off! Alfie ain't like that."

"Huh. That's all you know."

"Mr Atwood's right," interjected Nora. "Alfie ain't like that, not really. He ain't been wiv nearly as many gels as he could've."

"Oh, yes? Who told yer that then? Alfie?"

*

ALFIE TOOK HIS pint outside to escape the stuffy Saloon Bar full of people who were all over him. He was feeling emotional. Even though he didn't like a fuss, he was touched that so many had turned up for him. The Manchester Arms had been a suitable choice. The pub had hardly changed since he was a scrap of a boy whose feet hardly touched the floor while he was in there for people picking him up and fussing over him. Twenty-one years old and he'd had a pretty good time of it, all told. Even though the family didn't have much in the way of material things, he hadn't gone short of love. He got it from his blood family, his street family, and many more besides.

Now he was officially a man, he'd be expected to take up with a girl and that didn't sit too well with how he was spending his spare time at the moment. He couldn't see past Malcolm. Maybe he should put all his energy into making the Bank Holiday in Brighton a wonderful weekend but then cool it down and call it a day? It might be easier for them both in the long run. But when it came to it, he doubted he could walk away from the man so easily. The thought of waking up one day and realising he'd never see Malcolm again was enough to bring him out in a cold sweat.

And there was Doreen. She was a cut above, she was, and after a false start, they got on like a house on fire. He wasn't close to walking out with her, but people at work noticed how well they got on. And they did. They'd been to the pictures together a few times now. She wasn't some silly girl who'd think that meant they were courting. She was just what he'd want from a girl. She was lovely and he was proud to be seen with her, but she was also clever and not afraid to stand her ground. West Ham United aside, she was happy to talk about whatever he and his mates talked about. She was even a member of the Labour Party and could match George in any political discussion. He got the impression that if she couldn't find the right man for her, then she just wouldn't bother getting married because she was Doreen Wilkes and that was enough. She didn't need a man to carve out a place in the world. So, she'd been out with the lads just as though she was one of them. Because of Frank's behaviour, she hadn't met Malcolm, but he was sure they'd like each other. He was struck by how often the two made the same remarks.

He wasn't on his own for long, and he wasn't surprised that the presence behind him turned out to be Frank. He seemed in particularly high spirits.

"No Malcolm today, I see," he said, scarcely able to conceal his glee.

"Looks that way, dunnit?"

"Well, it's for family and close friends really, innit? A twenty-first, I mean."

"I saw him earlier on, as it goes. We had a picnic, wiv champagne, and he gave me my present." He lifted his arm to reveal the gleaming gold lozenge cufflinks. Frank gave them a cursory glance.

"Very nice. Very expensive too, I expect. But then he's got plenty o' dosh, ain't he, so it don't mean nuffink to him, does it?"

"Maybe not. He still took the trouble to get me initials engraved on 'em though, didn't he?" Alfie showed the cufflinks again, moving his wrist to highlight the letters A.L.A. etched into the gold. "It's just as well for you that I couldn't arrange me own 'surprise' party. Make no mistake, Frank, if *all* me close friends were here, Malcolm would be here too."

"Course," said Frank dismissively before changing the subject. "Anyway, all set for Bank Holiday?"

"Wotcher mean?" *Here goes*, thought Alfie.

"Well, we're gonna go over White City to watch the British Empire Games and then go drinking in Shepherd's Bush, ain't we—around the Green and along Goldhawk Road. Should be a good night."

Summer Bank Holiday had become a time when the lads all did something together, and this pub crawl outside of their regular stamping ground was the outing that Alfie vaguely remembered them discussing. He couldn't recall them making any firm decisions though. Normally, they might decide in his absence, and he'd be happy to go along with it. He'd bucked the trend the previous year by visiting Malcolm instead of bathing in Victoria Park with them and because of that, he had felt a little guilty for abandoning them again. But now, he didn't feel well-disposed towards

Frank, having endured his spiteful pleasure at Malcolm's absence. He was almost pleased to have a reason to bring him crashing back to earth and did so without apology.

"I can't do it. I've got other plans."

Frank's face was a picture of scorn. "Wotcher mean, 'other plans'? We always do Summer Bank Holiday! It's always been just the four of us— or at least it was until you stood us up last year."

"Well, I'm not coming this year neither. Wilf and Ada from our street had a room booked in Brighton and they can't go. So, I'm going there instead."

"What? Yer going to fuckin' Brighton on yer own?" Frank asked incredulously.

"No, of course not. I'm takin' a friend."

For one happy instant, Frank thought he'd be going to the seaside with Alfie and wondered how he was going to break it to George and Sid, but it was only for an instant.

"Malcolm's going wiv me."

"Malcolm! So…you're gonna share a bed wiv him all weekend?"

"Of course. There's only the one room and they're like gold dust."

"Honest to God, don't you even care what people will think of yer?"

"Frank, it's Bank Holiday, it'll be crazy. No one will blink an eye at two men sharing, if that's what yer worried about."

Frank seemed beside himself. "I ain't worried about what anyone thinks—you're the one what needs to be worried. The bloke's a pansy! You'll be sharing a bed wiv a pansy!"

Alfie's handsome features darkened. "You don't know that."

"*Course* I fucking do! And what worries me is, *so* do you!"

"We're just mates. That's all."

"So, you don't let him mess about with you then? Is that what you're saying?"

"I've told you before, whatever him and me do or don't get up to, it ain't your business, Frank."

"Oh, yes, it is! I'm yer best mate."

"So you keep saying."

"I can't stand by and watch him turn you into a fuckin' pansy!"

"I ain't a pansy, Frank. And neither is Malcolm."

"Do me a favour! You let him mess about wiv you and it ain't like he's paying for it. Sounds pretty pansy to me. And him? I'm telling yer, he won't be happy until you're up to your nuts in his guts." Even in the darkness Frank could sense Alfie's blush and he realised instantly what the main weekend entertainment would be. "Oh, my Gawd! You're after bumming him in Brighton. Tell me it ain't true."

Recovering from the impact of Frank's rage, his own began to smoulder. "True or not, it ain't yer business, Frank," he told him again. "Now it's me birthday, so let's go back in and have a drink."

"I don't wanna fuckin' drink! The thought of you an' that filthy little creep together—it makes me wanna spew."

"Well, don't think about it then."

"How can I *not?* Me best mate is turning into a fuckin' Nancy boy! I should tell your mum, shouldn't I?"

"I can't stop you, Frank, but I'd make sure she ain't holding nuffink sharp when you do."

The bitterness was etched on Frank's face as he almost cried with rage, "Me best mate, a *pansy.* A fuckin' Nancy boy!"

"If you want us to stay mates, I'd shut up now if I was you."

"I don't want a fuckin' pansy for a mate!"

"Then there's nuffink more to be said, is there?"

With that, Alfie turned and headed for the Saloon door and Frank stormed off into the warm Island night. Pausing at the door, Alfie stepped back outside, needing a moment to gather himself after the row.

But within moments of Frank's stormy exit, all thoughts of the row were pushed out of his mind as he became aware of a rumbling sound. At first, it was so faint that he wasn't sure he'd heard it at all, but it grew to become the roar of aircraft engines. He looked to the sky and saw one, then three, then five, then countless shapes against the moonlight. Aeroplanes. Dozens of them. Soon there were fingers of yellow light feeling around in the darkness, the beams of searchlights rising from around the docks.

Alfie was bewildered. As far as he was aware, the country wasn't at war with anyone, but this looked like an attack. Drawn by the noise, others began to file out of the Manchester to look up at the spectacle as it unfolded in the night sky. Dixie and Walter were at his elbow.

"Shouldn't we be running for cover? Finding some place to shelter?" he asked them.

"No, son," said Dixie, placing an avuncular hand on his shoulder and giving it a squeeze. "It's just an exercise. They're testing out the air defences."

"I ain't heard no guns."

"Well, of course not! They ain't gonna be dropping any actual bombs and we don't wanna be shooting 'em down neither."

Walter said, "Go inside and sit with yer mum, Alfie. The planes have shaken her up a bit."

Even though he found it hard to believe that a woman as strong as his mother could be upset by a little noise, he did as he'd been asked and found Alice loudly protesting to all around her that she didn't need a brandy. However, she accepted one, and he could tell she was rattled. Eventually, when only he was paying attention to her, Alice admitted that the idea of bombing from the air terrified her.

"I can remember the bloomin' Zeppelins over the Island when you was just a toddler. They frightened the life out of me well enough, but then they sent them big aeroplanes over and killed all those little kiddies in Upper North Street School, only a year or so older than you was, Alfie. The Germans have had nigh on fifteen years to think of worse ways of killing even more people. And we live near the docks—and you and Robert work in the docks. You're all grown up now, but yer still my babies. I can't think of nuffink worse than someone up in the sky, someone we can't do nuffink to stop, trying to kill you all, to blow you all to bits."

"It's just an exercise, Mum. It's just so that if it was to happen, we *could* do sumfink about it."

"Yes, love. I expect yer right." But she didn't sound convinced.

*

ONCE THE EXCITEMENT of the "air raid" had abated, Alfie was still shaken up by his argument with Frank. He wondered whether he was being wise in doing the Brighton trip at all now his so-called "best friend" knew so much about it. Since he'd been at the docks, Bank Holidays had been spent with his mates. George and Sid would think it odd that he wasn't going to White City even if they didn't share Frank's suspicions. It might seem even more of a betrayal without knowledge of what the attraction was.

He was worried too about the strength of his desire to go. Since he and Malcolm had first discussed what was going to happen in Brighton, he'd hardly been able to get it off his mind. It bothered him how much he wanted the whole weekend, not just the obvious. He'd never spent this much effort in arranging an assignation with any of the girls he'd been with, but he reasoned that he might have done so, had an opportunity like this one dropped into his lap. Still, what kind of a man was he to arrange to sleep with another man? Perhaps Frank was right and he was some kind of… But he didn't want to think about it. It was just a bit of fooling around. It made no difference in the grand scheme of things.

He thought of young Albert on the beach that afternoon and longed to be that age again, with nothing more to worry about than a shard of glass lodged in his foot. The sky had always been blue and the sun had always shone. When he was even younger than Albert, the men would toss his little body in the air in the Saloon Bar of the Manchester for no other reason than to see him laughing like a drain. He remembered going with his dad to see the Hammers play the first FA Cup Final at Wembley Stadium—a day of enchantment for him despite the result. How he missed his dad. Then, hanging around the wharves with his mates, watching the ships being unloaded. Sometimes a crate of fruit would shatter on the quayside, having been dropped accidentally on purpose by the dockers, and all the kids would pounce and run off with as many oranges, lemons, or grapefruit as they could gather in their jumpers.

Now here he was, anticipating a weekend doing something illegal with a man in a strange guest-house bedroom. According to everyone, he'd been a lovely little kid, but now he sometimes felt about as dirty as a boy could get.

Was it even what Malcolm wanted? After all, he had sounded in two minds about it. Perhaps all he wanted was the fuck and didn't really want to go to Brighton. It might be better all round if they were to sort something out in London so that they could both walk away if it didn't work out. He could do Malcolm *and* the British Empire Games.

He got so uptight about the situation that he stepped into a telephone box at lunchtime next day and called Malcolm at the office. After charming his secretary, he heard the familiar voice at the end of the line, sounding surprised. But hearing his friend calmed him.

"I won't keep you long," Alfie told him. "I just wanted to say that we don't 'ave to go to Brighton if you don't fancy it."

"Why do you say that?"

"Well, you didn't sound too keen on the idea when I first suggested it. I'm frightened I might have got carried away and forced it on you a bit."

"No, I'll admit it's not the sort of holiday I'd normally take. But it isn't really about where we go, is it? I just want to spend the time with you, Alfie. I just want to spend a whole weekend with you."

Alfie looked at the silver dial with an intense, slightly troubled face, but said nothing.

"Unless you've changed your mind?" Malcolm went on. "I mean, if you don't want to go any more, just say. Perhaps you want to do something with the others instead? White City, wasn't it? I will understand. Honestly. That would be perfectly all right."

Alfie heard the disappointment in Malcolm's voice as he selflessly offered this escape route. He pondered his reply quietly for a moment but gradually a smile lit him up, and he said, "Nah. Brighton it is. And buggery it shall be."

"Shhh! Switchboard!"

Frank aside, Alfie was sorry to disappoint his old mates, but the bottom line was that he wanted to spend the time with Malcolm as much as the other way around. It was just one weekend. Where was the harm? The previous evening he'd let it get all out of proportion in his mind and had worried about nothing.

Chapter Twenty-Six

You Made Me Love You

Friday, 3 August 1934

"READ ALL ABAHT it!" cried the newsboys in their breaking voices as they hawked the early editions. Every newspaper stand around Victoria station screamed *TRUNK MURDER—LATEST.* A few weeks before, the torso of a woman had been discovered in an unclaimed trunk at Brighton station's Left Luggage office, and the papers were still full of it.

Inside Victoria, it seemed that few people had been deterred from their Bank Holiday trip to the seaside by this grisly episode. Alfie queued for the tickets, and Malcolm's heart sank when he saw that the two little pieces of card he returned with were marked Third Class.

During the long, tiring day ahead, he would often ask himself what he had let himself in for. Most employers required staff to work on Saturday morning but, because there wasn't a ship, Alfie had been released at lunchtime on Friday, allowing them to catch an early afternoon train. Unfortunately, an awful lot of other people seemed to be doing the same thing, and it was bedlam, a whirlpool of humanity shrouded in steam and smoke. A cacophony of young women in cloche hats chattered excitedly. Shrill long-suffering mothers admonished their overstimulated offspring in vain. The chatter had to be loud to be heard over the noise of slamming doors and the powerful percussion of departing locomotives.

Malcolm wanted to get into a compartment as soon as possible to grab a seat so he could close his eyes and forget they were there, but Alfie's good nature, enhanced by his holiday humour, inclined him to help just about everybody, with just about everything.

"For goodness' sake, come *on*!" urged Malcolm.

"All right, keep yer lid on!"

"We'll be standing all the way at this rate."

"Well, so what if we are? It's only an hour or so and we're young and fit. We should stand really."

"I should have insisted on bringing the car," Malcolm said, more to himself than anyone else.

"Don't be such an old misery guts," said Alfie. He wasn't perturbed by the busy station. On the Saturday, they'd most probably have had to queue even to get into it, then queue to get onto the platform and would probably have had to stand all the way.

As it turned out, they didn't have to stand at all. A Third-Class carriage that had seemed impossibly full of young women miraculously rearranged itself to accommodate them. It was Alfie they were obliging, of course, but they did the same for Malcolm with good grace once they understood he was a part of the package. The train was one of the new electric ones, so even Third Class was relatively plush. Shortly after they'd sat down, the train's humming gathered strength. It lurched and edged forward, and they could hear the last few doors slamming shut before it made its way smoothly out of the station.

The two girls beside them produced a wooden crate of brown ale, eliciting tuts of disgust from older, more "respectable" passengers. Although it wasn't ladylike, they were undaunted and happy to share with the boys.

"D'you always drink brown ale, gels?" asked Alfie with raised eyebrows.

"Ooh, no, love! But beggars can't be choosers, and Beryl got these free from her old dad, didn't yer, Ber?"

"Oh, yes, Cyn. Well, he don't know about it yet, like, but I daresay he'll 'ave calmed down by the time I get 'ome."

They all screamed with laughter at Beryl's audacity.

"Here, boys! 'Ave you got somewhere to stay?" Cyn asked.

"Yes, we're all fixed up, love."

"We haven't and it's a bit of a worry, what with this trunk murder. Innit awful? A girl don't feel safe no more."

"I think they've arrested someone for it. But you should maybe stick together to be on the safe side."

In a low voice, Cyn continued, "Just think, that poor woman did this very same journey, in pieces, in a box!" Her eyes opened wider. "Maybe it was this very same train! Maybe this very same carriage!"

"Nah, if it was a trunk she'll have been in the goods van," Alfie assured her.

"Most of us gels are struggling for beds. You wouldn't have room for a couple of little ones, would yer?" she asked. "You could be our protectors. We could top and tail. No funny business, mind."

Malcolm was alarmed, but Alfie just grinned and said, "Sorry, love, we're having to share a bed as it is, ain't we, Malc? It's gonna be ever so poky."

"Oh well. I was only asking. Sumfink will turn up, I'm sure."

"We can't go anywhere too far from the station, Cyn," said another girl. "I've heard the buses in Brighton will be on strike on Monday. I hope that don't put the kibosh on any of your plans, boys."

Malcolm considered this yet another blight on a doomed venture, but Alfie smiled at him as he said, "It don't matter to us, love. We're right in the centre and we won't be wandering too far."

"Well, if you see us about, come and say hello, won't yer? You'd have ever such a good time wiv us, you know, boys," said Cyn, leaning into Alfie as she spoke.

"I don't doubt it, gel, but me an' Malc are after a quiet time, ain't we?" He glanced at Malcolm with a twinkle in his eye. "You know, a bit of a dip, some fish and chips, a drink or two an' I reckon we'll be ready for bed. The sea air always gets me that way."

At Brighton railway station, they were scarcely able to put one foot in front of the other. Malcolm hated crowds, and yet here he was in Brighton for Bank Holiday weekend! He tried to fight it, but a rising tide of misery welled inside him. Alfie could see it and placed his free hand on his shoulder.

"Slow down. Relax. Most of these people don't know where they'll be sleeping tonight, but we do. We'll be fine once we're in our room. Snug as two bugs in a rug."

Burgundy and cream trams and red and cream buses were lined up outside the station. They were so busy that a band of pirates brandishing cutlasses would have had trouble boarding them, so Alfie cheerfully suggested they walk. Each carried a brown leather suitcase of modest size. They weren't full to capacity because it was only a weekend trip. When Malcolm had asked Alfie whether he should pack his dinner suit, Alfie had looked at him as though he was mad. Then he winked and said, "I shouldn't. You'll be wearing yer birthday suit most of the time."

The streets leading down towards the seafront were packed with people, a few looking as irritable as Malcolm felt, but most high-spirited and in the mood for fun. White herring gulls circled overhead, cawing loudly, ready to swoop for any sandwich or bag of chips left unattended. Unlike Malcolm, they loved a crowd and behaved as though they were entitled to any food they could pinch from it. Alfie saw him looking at one perched on a cast-iron lamp standard nearby, arrogantly surveying the throng.

"That one's a big bugger, innit? Mean-looking an' all."

At the Beau Regard guest house, Malcolm was beside himself with trepidation. He felt that everybody with half an ounce of intelligence would be able to see what they were up to. They'd perceive him as a vile lecher, bringing a much younger man to Brighton for immoral purposes. Had Alfie been a girl and this a traditional "dirty weekend", it would have been bad enough, but this was a criminal matter. When he had watched Alfie chattering away happily with the girls on the train, he looked so young, and it was easy to see him as vulnerable. He should have been with one of those girls, and if Malcolm were a decent man, he should encourage him to go back onto the straight and narrow.

He needn't have worried about their reception at the guest house. Alfie was like a crisply folded five-pound note. His introduction allayed concerns, overruled objections, changed attitudes, and made the impossible possible. It wasn't all down to his handsome face; he "had a nice way with him". Perhaps that was why his disposition was so sunny. Thanks to his looks, he lived in a different world to mere mortals. He would always be accommodated somehow, whatever he did, wherever he went.

Mrs Turner, the guest house landlady, who struck terror into the hearts of many and who had been distinctly uncomfortable at the thought of two young London lads taking one of her rooms, felt all her scruples melt away like an ice cream left out in the Brighton sun the moment she set eyes on Alfie. She was mortified that the two young men would have to suffer the inconvenience of sharing a bed, but sadly, there was no forgotten room that could be hastily prepared this Bank Holiday weekend, not even for Alfie. He consoled her with, "It's fine. I think we might even enjoy it. It'll be like going camping, won't it?"

"That's the spirit, dear. I'm so terribly sorry, I don't have anyone to take your cases up at the moment," she simpered in her best voice, patting her perm as she did so. "If you leave them in the hallway, I'll get the boy to bring them up, directly he returns from his errands."

Alfie picked up both cases with little effort and beamed at her. "I'm a docker, love, these ain't nuffink, trust me."

*

THE ROOM WAS dominated by a gleaming brass bedstead, plump white pillows, and a cream candlewick counterpane. A bay window overlooked the street down to the seafront. A tiled washstand bearing a white basin and ewer were provided for a quick wash, along with fresh green towels. As he wandered around the room, Alfie seemed touchingly impressed by everything. Mrs Turner told them that a shared bathroom at the end of the corridor was also at their disposal.

Once she had left them, Alfie threw aside his cap and flung himself backwards onto the bed to lie with his hands behind his head, looking at him with a curious smile. Malcolm felt like a nervous virgin from an Elinor Glyn novel, confronted with both her seducer and the scene of her undoing. It contrasted sharply with how he'd felt only moments ago as they'd checked in. He doubted anyone would be reluctant to succumb to this particular seducer. Lying on the pale eiderdown, he looked like a dream come true.

"It's proper nice, innit?" Alfie said happily.

"It's all right." Malcolm shrugged. "The wallpaper's a bit busy for my liking."

"You're used to better. I ain't. I think it's good wallpaper because it ain't peeling off the wall. Anyway, sod the bleedin' wallpaper. Come here an' give us a kiss." He spread his arms wide and waited for his command to be obeyed. Malcolm lowered himself primly onto the edge of the bed and leaned down to give him a brisk dry peck on the cheek, but Alfie pulled him down on top of him.

"What was that meant to be? Pathetic!" he said, before kissing Malcolm unhurriedly and with great tenderness. Pulled against his firm warmth, Malcolm's head spun a little. Somehow, something between them was changing. The intimate embrace aroused them both, but Alfie made no move to make it sexual, and when the kiss was finished, they lay in each other's arms, heads together. It was warm, intoxicating affection. Were it not for the impracticality of it, Malcolm would happily have stayed like that all weekend, provided his hands could wander into Alfie's trousers occasionally.

"All that worrying for nuffink, see?" Alfie said.

"Thank you for being so patient with me."

"S'all right. I must think yer worth it, mustn't I?"

*

AFTER SETTLING IN for half an hour, hanging up their clothes, and having a wash, Alfie insisted that they take a walk along the Palace Pier. It was madly busy, and they couldn't have found a vacant deckchair if they'd wanted one.

Beneath the hoards engulfing it, the Palace Pier featured an enormous pavilion at the seaward end, with exotic Moorish cupolas mirroring those of the nearby Royal Pavilion. There were smaller ones containing dining rooms, grill rooms, smoking rooms, and reading rooms. An electric tramway ran the length of the structure and overhead were ornamental arches festooned with coloured lights. There was a place for bathers right at the end of the pier, and a landing stage for pleasure craft. At the centre, a newer ornate pavilion and a glazed winter garden stood, along with a theatre, hosting one of Jimmy Hunter's *Summer Shows* with Tommy Trinder and Betty Driver. Malcolm was relieved when Alfie said they'd have no time for one of those.

They fought for space as excited children thundered up and down the boards and the air was pierced by exhilarated screams from the dodgems and the Ferris wheel. Malcolm's good humour had been restored by their cuddle, and he tolerated the crowd with better grace than he'd managed earlier. They queued for fish and chips, then found a stretch of railing to lean on. Malcolm was unaccustomed to eating fish and chips at all, let alone straight from a copy of the *Argus,* but it helped him understand why it was so popular a meal with the working classes. Perhaps it was because he was ravenous, or maybe it was the sea air and the company, but it was one of the finest meals he had ever enjoyed. White cod flaking out of golden, crispy batter; thick chips fried in lard, well-salted and drenched in vinegar that stung the lips. All for a measly fourpence, including a bottle of Vimto with a striped paper straw. They polished off their food looking down at the calm turquoise sea and over at a beach rapidly filling up with people who didn't seem inclined to bathe.

"It will be getting dark before long and a bit chilly, I shouldn't wonder," Malcolm observed. "Why would anyone decide to go to the beach now?"

"They ain't as lucky as us. They got no place else to go, so they're staking out a patch to spend the night on," explained Alfie. "The early birds are settling as far from the sea as they can, look, so's the tide don't get 'em when it comes in."

Malcom saw that many had nothing but the daily newspapers to serve as bedding. "Good God. Rather them than me."

"They'll be fine, all snuggled up. Unless it rains."

After they left the pier, Alfie led him through the narrow Lanes until they found a welcoming-looking pub. It was busy, and as Alfie bought the beer Malcolm searched for seating. He found an empty table from which all the seats had been removed, and after politely asking several groups, he managed to acquire two upholstered iron stools. Alfie congratulated him, and he was pleased with himself about it.

After some light-hearted small talk, Alfie asked, "Are you nervous about being here alone wiv me? About doing stuff that's against the law. Mostly about what I'm gonna be doing to yer, at some point."

"You've probably realised by now that I'm a rather nervous person and I'm a coward. So the answer is yes, of course I am."

"It's coming on for two years now since we met. We've spent a lot of time alone together."

"Yes, but this weekend is different."

Alfie nodded. "Yes. It is."

"I'm always worried about the law, but I have a choice: either pretend to be someone I'm not or break the law. I've always done the pretending. I was a fortress of pretence, until you crept up under cover of the night and stormed my ramparts."

Alfie laughed quietly, and Malcolm saw that he had no need to explain.

"You ain't no coward either. You're afraid but yer doing it anyways. That's brave. And we don't have to do it at all if you ain't sure."

"I am sure though. A great many people engage in this activity, but I've never yet seen it on a gravestone."

Alfie nearly choked on his beer. "Well, they wouldn't, would they? Even if it was what killed 'em."

Malcolm grinned. "No, I suppose not. I expect they'd put *Fell Asleep* or something like that."

Alfie chuckled. "It's nice, being here wiv you. And like I said, we don't have to do nuffink if you don't want to. I could just hold you if you want."

"Thank you for saying that." Malcolm smiled, and it was straight from his heart. "But if you honestly think I can lie next to you for three nights without anything happening, then you're dafter than I thought."

Their conversation was interrupted as an indifferently tuned piano chimed up, and a sing-song tentatively began. Had it started before they arrived, Malcolm was sure they'd have turned away and gone elsewhere, but they would have to endure it for as long as it took them to finish their pints. Alfie had other ideas. He joined in with the next chorus as the crowd got less self-conscious and the volume increased. He would never have made his fortune as a singer, but he carried a tune better than most around them.

It was smoky, and as the sing-song gathered momentum, the place became noisy. The customers were remarkably jolly, through holiday excitement or inebriation, or in most cases both. Three pints and seven or eight songs in, Malcolm relaxed and began to enjoy the moment. Alfie's arm was draped companionably over his shoulder and stayed there. Ah, the smell of him—soap, beer, youth. To the high-spirited, well-oiled clientele, they looked like drunken companions, and nothing more. And when the pianist played the first bars of "You Made Me Love You", Alfie turned and looked at him, then sang every word, making it more poignant than any music-hall song was expected to be.

Alfie looked happy and unguarded. There were stars in his midnight-blue eyes, and his face was slightly flushed in the heat of the crowded bar. He looked ridiculously handsome. Malcolm was affected by hearing him sing about being reluctantly in love, even though he had to remind himself that it was only a silly old song. It was familiar to him, but it had never sounded as good as it did being belted out by this lovely young man backed by a pub full of drunken people.

When the song ended and cheers filled the saloon, Alfie gave Malcolm a squeeze and brought his smiling face close, as though to kiss him, before pulling away saying, "Better not, eh? I don't 'arf feel like it though."

So, Malcolm spent a couple of hours in circumstances that would once have appalled him, a sing-song in a pub being a bit lowbrow for someone of his background. But he'd loved almost every minute of it, because of this new intimacy between them which Alfie didn't bother to hide, but which nobody was taking any notice of. He didn't even want to hurry Alfie back to their room. He just wanted to savour every second of this wonderful evening.

They sank a couple more pints before heading back through crowds of excited, happy, often unsteady people to the Beau Regard guest house. Mrs Turner viewed their early return with approval.

"Hello, boys. I trust you've had an enjoyable evening? I must say I'm surprised to see you back so early. The pubs aren't even shut yet."

"It's been a long day," said Alfie. "We don't wanna spoil our holiday by overdoing it on the first night, do we?"

"Well, if I may say so, that is *most* sensible of you. If only our other guests were as wise. I think some of them will have to take their chances on the beach tonight, because this door will be locked at eleven forty-five sharp."

As soon as the door of their room had closed behind them, Alfie pinned Malcolm up against it and kissed him deeply, for a long time. When he came up for air he said, "I've been wanting to do that all night."

"I want to do that every time I set eyes on you," Malcolm whispered.

Alfie took off his jacket and flung himself backwards onto the bed.

"So," he said. "You and me. In bed together. I ain't never done this before, you know. Spent all night with someone, I mean."

"You share a bed with your brother, don't you?"

"That ain't the same thing at all. At least I bloody hope not! I ain't never even stayed in a guest house before."

"Are we going to—you know—tonight?"

"Buggery? Nah, I don't think so. Not tonight. Let's just do what we normally get up to on yer mum's settee and then get some sleep, eh?"

"Actually, that sounds perfect to me. Perfect."

Chapter Twenty-Seven

Lovers

IN THE EARLY hours of Saturday morning, Malcolm had luxuriated in being able to share a bed with Alfie. Having never shared one with anyone in his life before, he had known it would be nigh on impossible for him to get much sleep, but it was a small price to pay for that ecstasy. They'd made love in an affectionate, unhurried way before settling down. Having Alfie's warm, smooth nakedness lying there beside him was overstimulating. He wanted so much to touch him all the time but was wary of becoming a nuisance. "Mate, once I've nodded off you can hire a jazz band to play at the bottom of the bed and it won't make no difference," Alfie assured him.

Alfie had only rarely had a bed to himself in his entire life, and once they were spent, he dropped off quickly. Even in this, which offered so many potential ways to irritate, he was perfect. He lay still, and the only sound from him was his slow, quiet breathing. When Malcolm plucked up the courage to embrace him, Alfie adjusted his body to accommodate him without properly waking. Malcolm was able to cuddle and caress him to his heart's content without fear of disturbing him, but in doing so, he disturbed himself considerably.

It wasn't just his physical and sexual presence that kept Malcolm awake, it was the fact they'd made it this far. Being with Alfie was everything to him, which gave him everything to lose. On the other hand, he'd expected nothing—and to have this astonishing boy lying beside him was so much better than nothing. To and fro the pendulum swung.

Eventually, as first light began to turn pale shapes into objects around the room, he drifted off to sleep for a few hours until awoken by his own desire, the smell of grilled bacon, and the melancholy cawing of the gulls. Alfie was still spark out, his lovely face close. Would that he could wake up to that face every morning for the rest of his life, Malcolm thought. In sleep, Alfie looked so young and so innocent. One might even say angelic, if unaware of his unholy intentions.

When he did at last open his eyes, it was to see Malcolm still looking at him intently.

"What?"

"Good morning."

"Good morning. What yer looking at?"

"The most beautiful boy in the world."

"Get away wiv yer! You soppy ha'porth!"

Now he was awake, he stretched languidly, diverting Malcolm's attention away from his face to his body. His skin looked darker against the crisp white linen sheets. The paisley-patterned eiderdown, the blanket, and the candlewick bedspread had long since been kicked to the floor. His tan hadn't been acquired by any decadent lounging, but by working stripped to the waist at the docks and swimming at the Island Lido. Mid-stretch, he mischievously pushed his hairy armpit into Malcolm's face. If it was meant to repel him, it failed. He breathed in the smell of him, his favourite fragrance bar none. He rested his hand on Alfie's chest and toyed with a nipple, drawing a gasp as he pinched it. He let his hand slide slowly south, threading it through his thick pubic hair and seizing his already rising cock.

"Uh-oh. Here comes trouble," said Alfie, smiling.

Malcolm manipulated him slowly, loving the feeling of control it gave him. Alfie pulled the sheet off himself, fully exposing his youthful, clear-skinned nakedness.

"Go on, get yer chops round it." Malcolm did not need telling twice and descended onto him to suckle like a hungry pup.

Afterwards, as they lay in each other's arms, Alfie said, "It smells really strongly of sex in here, don't it?"

"I know. I hope whoever does the rooms doesn't recognise the smell."

"I shouldn't worry. They'll be used to all sorts in a place like this. We can open another window. And if you put that oh-di-Cologne stuff you use on, it should hide it a bit."

"But what if it doesn't?"

"It will. And even if it don't, they won't know that it weren't me 'aving a wank while you were out getting the papers or buying a post card or sumfink. Will you stop worrying about every little thing?"

Mrs Turner had given them a pleasant table in the dining room where they were able to enjoy a full English breakfast of excellent quality. She fussed over them far more than she did over any of the other guests.

When they were replete, Alfie said, "Come on, let's go for a walk along the prom. Then we can go down on the beach. I've got you a present. You won't like 'em, but you'll need 'em."

*

MALCOLM DISMALLY CONTEMPLATED his new pair of brown swimming trunks. If he'd been forced to buy some for himself, he'd have gone for a costume that included a vest as well as trunks, to cover up as much as possible. Alfie had gone for the cheaper option, and it would have been churlish of him to complain. As Alfie had shelled out for them, he would at least have to wear them, even if he didn't go near enough to the sea to get them wet.

"I'll go back to our room and put them on."

"No need. You can change right here. I'll hold the towel round yer."

"Oh, Alfie no! People might see!"

"I'll be holding the towel round yer—no one will see."

"*You'll* see."

"Yes, but I've seen it all before, ain't I?" Alfie grinned lasciviously. "I've had most of it in me mouth, come to think of it, mate."

When, after much hopping and stumbling, the awkward task had been accomplished, Malcolm sank onto the sand and embraced his legs in front of him. He'd never felt so exposed, so puny, so white, like a pile of raw tripe in a butcher's window. It had been bad enough when Alfie had first seen him unclothed in the subdued light of the parlour, but here in the full glare of the afternoon sun, he felt as though the whole world was judging him.

"Blimey," said Alfie. "Me mum can never get her whites as white as your back."

"Well, thank you very much," grumbled Malcolm. "You were the one who forced me into this display of near nudity."

"I'm only kidding yer. It's all right. Nobody's looking at yer."

"Only because they'll go blind if they do."

Alfie laughed. "Well, I think you look proper nice in them trunks, Malc, honest I do. Now come on, let's go for a dip."

"You go ahead. I'll join you in a moment. But I'll only be paddling, up to my ankles and no further. I can't swim, remember."

"All right. Don't be too long about it though."

It was mid-afternoon, and the beach was crowded. The young bathers had a sizeable audience as they frolicked in the surf. Those who chose not to bathe were in their shirtsleeves and many sported khaki shorts. The air was pierced by the screams of overexcited children. In the shallows, carefully marshalled toddlers in sun hats fetched bucketfuls of water for sandcastle moats or brandished shrimping nets that were never likely to catch anything other than strands of slimy green and brown seaweed. At the top of the beach in an irregular line of striped deck chairs sat survivors of the Edwardian age. Many of them wore what looked like their Sunday best as they snoozed or otherwise engaged in the grim business of having a good time.

He'd seen Alfie naked before, in darkened rooms lit by the fire and a single oil lamp. Here in the bright sunlight, in his trunks, any flaws would have been ruthlessly exposed, but there were none. Disregarding the odd bruise or graze sustained at work, his skin was unblemished. He wasn't bulging all over with muscle, but you could tell he was a manual worker. When he stretched, he looked like an anatomical illustration of what men were meant to be.

In comparison, Malcolm felt a milksop, a runt, and at the age of twenty-nine, he already felt old. But he enjoyed the quiet satisfaction of knowing that, for the time being at least, Alfie was his. All those ladies whose eyes followed his every move probably imagined how lovely a kiss with him would be, but it was Malcolm who would get the kiss and that would just be for starters, because the whole point of the trip was for them to be as intimate as two men could possibly be. Come hell or high water, he was going to be "fucked" by the most beautiful boy in the world.

Tired of messing around in the sea on his own, Alfie picked his way back up the shingle to his friend. His body was beaded with water, his hair plastered against his head, which again made him seem disgracefully young. Malcolm rose to his feet assuming Alfie would dry himself off and they would leave, but the boy had other ideas. He shook his hair vigorously, like a dog, so that Malcolm was hit by the spray. This was annoying enough, but he followed by seizing him around the waist before he could evade his grasp and hoisting him up into a fireman's lift. The young docker was used to carrying weights far heavier than Malcolm.

"Alfie! Whatever are you…"

The protest was futile, as Alfie turned and ran back down the beach with Malcolm screaming protests all the way, a burden of little consequence over his shoulder. The feeling of Alfie's skin against his was exciting, but any pleasurable aspect ended abruptly when he was shrugged off into the surf. The shock of the cold water took his breath away. His spectacles were swept off his face. His eyes, nose, and ears filled with salt water, and his heart with panic. He tried to scramble to his feet but found no purchase in the fine shale. A strong pair of arms dragged him spluttering back into the sunlight.

"You're all right. You're all right," soothed Alfie. "I'm sorry. It's a bit deeper there than I thought it was."

Malcolm fought for breath and for words, spluttering out sea water and mucus. He was angry and frightened and embarrassed. Alfie tried to hug him, but he fiercely shrugged him off, and nearly toppled back into the water. Alfie tried again, and this time, he succumbed to the embrace, for physical rather than emotional support.

When his eyes and nose and one ear were clear, he pulled away. "I've lost my glasses," he said, looking helplessly around the water at his feet. It seemed futile. Shaking with fear and rage, he staggered the few yards to the shore and made his way up the sand with as much dignity as he could mus-ter, which wasn't a great deal. Everyone around them had seen the incident and watched his progress in case there'd be any further drama. A few paces up, a young woman intercepted him with a hand on his forearm.

"I say, are you all right? I saw it all. What a beastly thing to have done. Your friend should be ashamed of himself, and I shall jolly well tell him so. Here, would you like a handkerchief?"

She proffered one, and he accepted it gratefully. It was nice to feel that, for once, someone was considering him ahead of Alfie.

The culprit caught up with them and handed Malcolm his glasses, having retrieved them from the shallows. Malcolm's new friend turned to admonish him.

"You bully!" she squeaked indignantly. Disconcerted by a wet, un-clothed, and conspicuously handsome young man, she paused for a moment, clearly calculating where she could decently strike him, before slapping him hard on the chest. "You could have killed him with your silly nonsense! You *brute*!"

Alfie seemed more amused by this genteel dressing down than anything.

"You're right, darlin'. I've said I'm sorry and I'll keep on saying it till he forgives me."

"Don't you darling me!"

*

A CONTRITE ALFIE left them sitting on a bench on the prom. Malcolm's new friend Constance was staying at the Grand Hotel on the seafront. She told him they could go back there, have some decent food, and if he felt like ditching Alfie, he was welcome to share her room, which contained a couch of generous proportions. He assured her that he was all right and they should wait for his friend. Now the panic of his soaking had subsided, he feared he might have overreacted and it might sour the rest of their stay. If they couldn't get back to how they'd been with each other the previous evening in the pub, he would never be able to forgive himself.

Alfie returned with fish and chips and bottles of Vimto for the three of them. Constance snatched her portion and ate hungrily, but she didn't thank him, just so he knew she still considered him a brute. Despite his gloom, Malcolm savoured the meal and wondered how it was that he had avoided fish suppers all his life.

Afterwards, they packed up and headed into the nearest public house. The wireless behind the bar was turned up, so that the patrons could listen to the BBC broadcast of speeches from the opening ceremony of the

Empire Games from the White City. He wondered whether Alfie was wishing he'd gone there with his friends after all. There was nowhere to sit at first, but eventually they got a small table that would seat three next to a door into the saloon. The speeches were replaced by the music of Mantovani and his orchestra.

When Alfie went to the bar, Constance said grudgingly, "He is *very* good-looking, I must admit. Aren't brutes always?"

"He isn't a brute. Not really," said Malcolm softly.

"I don't understand why you're such good friends with him. He isn't really our *sort*, is he?"

"What do you mean by that?"

"Well, he's very working class, darling, isn't he?"

"I'm not sure *I'm* your 'sort' if it comes to that. I'm very middle class and I suspect you're not."

"Be that as it may, you and I can converse on the same level."

"He…he's my lover." He had never used that word before, let alone uttered it to a stranger. He was at once thrilled and terrified by his own daring. Constance was temporarily dumbstruck, and Alfie's return with the drinks stifled any further reaction from her.

It was all quiet at their table until Alfie said, "You've told her about us, ain't yer?"

"How did you know?" asked Malcolm, surprised.

"Well, she ain't shut up until now, has she? What else could it be?"

Constance wasn't about to be diverted by the insult and said, wide-eyed, "Malcolm says that you're his lover. Is that true?"

Alfie glanced at Malcolm, but he didn't seem angry. Rather, he was smiling. To Constance, he said, "How can it be true? I'm a *boy*!" After a pause, he went on, "I'm only kidding yer, of course it's true. I've just never heard him call me that before, that's all."

Constance leaned back in her chair. "I'm not sure I believe you. Either of you. You wouldn't tease a girl?"

"Yes, we would, but we ain't. We'll deny it all if you tell anyone else, mind."

"I wouldn't—truly, cross my heart. I think it's rather thrilling."

From then on, any antipathy Constance had for Alfie was swept away by her fascination with them. It was all they could do to dissuade her from buying a bottle of champagne to celebrate their daring, but they shared a drink or two more with her before she reluctantly had to tear herself away and go to meet the rest of her party for dinner. She tried to persuade them to "meet up with the gang" later, but Alfie told her they'd done their socialising for the day.

As they sat finishing their drinks, Malcolm said, "I'm sorry, Alfie, about earlier. For making such a fuss, I mean."

"Don't be daft. It's me what's sorry for being such an idiot. I treat you like one of me mates sometimes an' forget you're a proper grown-up."

"I don't know about that. I wish I wasn't such a big baby."

"I shouldn't have done it. You can't swim, after all. And you weren't no baby telling Whatsername about us, was yer?"

Malcolm put his hand to his face. "Oh, God! That was reckless of me. I'm so sorry about that too."

"Don't be. Lovers. I liked it. It's what we are after all, innit?"

*

AFTER SUPPER, THEY retired to their room and enjoyed a long cuddle, fully clothed until Alfie said, "Look, what we talked about. I do want to, but you know, this is the really illegal bit, the bit that people find hardest to forgive. I have to be really sure it's what you want."

"It is! Do you want me to write a declaration on a piece of paper and sign it for you?"

Alfie pulled a face. "Wouldn't be very romantic, would it? 'I, Malcolm Trevelyan, hereby allow Alfie Atwood to do buggery to me'."

"I never had you down as a romantic."

"Yes, well—I'm full o' surprises, I am. For me as much as you."

Alfie started to undress, but Malcolm made no move to follow suit. He just loved watching Alfie's beautiful body being gradually revealed. He particularly loved the moment that he pulled his shirt over his head. Every time. It was exciting, but there was also something touching about it. It was as though the young man was giving himself as a gift, and it was as special to Malcolm now as it had been that first time in the parlour.

When all that remained were his trousers, braces dangling, he paused and said, "Are you getting stripped or what? We can't really do buggery wiv you still done up like a dog's dinner."

"I enjoy watching you undress, that's all."

Malcolm allowed himself to be pulled into an embrace. "Ain't you sweet?" whispered Alfie before kissing him deeply. When they pulled apart, he said, "Now get 'em off, Mr Trevelyan, 'cos I wanna 'ave me wicked way wiv yer."

"Will it hurt?"

"It might. But only for a very short while."

"You will be careful, won't you?"

"Look, if it's worrying yer, we don't have to do this. I don't want you to do nuffink you ain't happy wiv. But I would like to do it, yes. I got to be honest, I've not thought of much else since it first came up. I'm shocked by how much I want you, Malc. I really am proper shocked."

Malcolm's fear of pain and of embarrassment receded. This gorgeous young man wanted him and that trumped everything. He undressed and lay face down on the bed, assuming what he thought the required position would be, bracing himself for the act. He heard Alfie make a slightly impatient noise.

"Turn over, Malcolm."

"But I thought…"

"Trust me. Please. I wanna see yer face when I do this. That way will be nicer. And I can be sure I ain't hurting yer too much if nuffink else."

He did as he was told but felt a fool. He was so apprehensive there was no hint of an erection and his cock looked like one of the less impressive items on a seafood platter.

"I'm sorry, I…"

"*Shush*. Bring your legs up. That's it." Alfie leaned against Malcolm's knees and, parting his legs a little wider, began to stroke his thighs, around his hips, and up his belly. He reached further and spent a good few minutes toying with his nipples until they were impressively hard. Malcolm had been quietly reignited down below, and his cock throbbed gratifyingly against his stomach. Alfie lightly brushed it with his knuckles, which made it lift off his belly and pulsate even more.

He grinned at him. "There, it don't take much, does it?" He reached over to the bedside table where he'd left a little round flat yellow and silver tin of petroleum jelly. Malcolm had seen one before, at home in the bathroom cabinet. Heaven only knew what his mother used it for, and it was best not to speculate.

"This is going to feel a bit funny at first, but it won't hurt, I promise. I'm just going to put some of this stuff up yer arse, to help me slide in easier."

For a man as fastidious and private, this should not have been an easy thing to hear, even from someone he adored. But although the language used and the matter-of-fact way in which he used it could have sounded ugly, it didn't. It thrilled him. Last night, he'd reflected that he'd never previously shared a bed with anyone before, and he certainly hadn't come close to sharing this part of his anatomy with anyone.

As he felt the cold invasion, he tensed.

"Relax! It's only me finger," murmured Alfie.

He tried not to clench and breathed deeply, eliciting a "That's it, mate" from Alfie. The finger circled gently and very gradually went deeper inside him, eventually beyond the second knuckle. Then Alfie withdrew and reinserted it and continued moving it slowly in and out. The initial discomfort abated, and the sensation became pleasant. Maybe this wouldn't be so bad because Alfie's fingers were long and brutal.

Eventually, Alfie reached for the tin again and said, "Take a couple of fingers full of this." Malcolm did as he was told and scooped out a dollop of the amber-coloured jelly. He didn't much like the consistency of it. "Rub it onto me." He moved hesitantly towards Alfie's bare chest, but Alfie grabbed his wrist to stop him. "Not there, you fool," he laughed, not unkindly. He adjusted himself to bring his now massive-looking erection closer and nodded at it. "*There*."

He did as he was bid, drawing a gasp from Alfie as the cold jelly first touched his cock. He liked the stuff a whole lot more now, as he slowly rubbed it into Alfie's hardness, feeling a dorsal vein moving beneath his fingers.

"Oh, God, you're good at this," Alfie groaned after a while.

"Probably because I'm loving doing it," Malcolm replied.

"Yer gonna 'ave to stop now or I'm gonna come before I've even got into yer."

Reluctantly, Malcolm ceased his ministration. He still had qualms at the thought of what he'd just been holding entering him. It seemed obscenely large and likely to do him internal damage, but they were already past the point of no return as far as he was concerned.

Alfie leaned back, took Malcolm's ankles, and lifted up his legs. He put them over his own warm, strong shoulders.

"It'll hurt a bit at first. But if it's too much, just say, and I'll stop. I don't wanna hurt yer."

"I trust you."

"I know you do."

Malcolm looked up at Alfie, his beautiful face smiling gently, his smooth chest pale in the lamplight. His hard flat belly and the arrow of hair down to the explosion of dark curls from which his cock jutted, glistening with the fluid his own caresses had coaxed from it.

Steadying him with a hand on each of his hips, slowly Alfie pushed his cock into Malcolm. He was right, it was painful, and Malcolm made a sound, although scarcely more than a whimper.

"All right?"

"*Yes.* Yes," breathed Malcolm as he adjusted to the new sensation.

Gradually, Alfie eased in the rest of his length and the pain receded.

As it did, it was overtaken by a pleasure the like of which Malcolm hadn't dreamed existed. Alfie started to thrust his pelvis slowly and rhythmically. Malcolm opened his eyes, looked into his lover's face, and saw that this was for both of them. Alfie was breathing erratically, his eyes fixed on what he was doing and his expression somewhere between concentration and pleasure. The rhythm stayed slow and the sensation in Malcolm grew in waves until he felt he'd explode. He began to moan with it, but Alfie shut him up, murmuring, "We don't want old Ma Turner bursting in with the First Aid box!"

Alfie released one of Malcolm's hips, subtly shifting the sensations, and he began to slowly wank his cock. Then he increased the pace and thrust harder into him. The physical sensation was enhanced by the thought of what it was he was doing, or what was being done to him. It felt wonderfully animal. Alfie was vigilant for any signs of pain, but by this time, Malcolm's only problem was keeping quiet. He panted without crying out until with a groan he came and came and came onto his belly, wondering if he would ever stop. The resulting spasms within him ensured that Alfie wasn't far behind, and he emptied himself into Malcolm.

When Alfie had recovered his wits, he pulled out and slumped on top of Malcolm.

"Bloody hell! That was fuckin' *lovely*," he breathed. "*You're* so fuckin' lovely, Malc!"

Alfie rolled off but pulled him into an embrace and kissed him on the forehead, the temple, the ear. Malcolm had half expected him to become more distant after they'd both come, but he was sleepily affectionate. Before long, the even sound of his breathing suggested that he was sound asleep.

Malcolm disentangled himself from his young lover's body, pulled on pyjama bottoms, and padded barefoot along the landing to the lavatory. Recalling his perusal of *Everybody's Family Doctor,* he thought he understood the rectal inflammation cross-reference now, although hopefully it wouldn't apply in this case. It would be jolly bad luck after just the once. He smiled, realising that if it was up to him, they wouldn't be stopping at just the once.

When he returned, he sat in a chair for a while and watched Alfie, sleeping like a child. He marvelled at his own audacity in describing him as his lover to Constance and even more that Alfie hadn't objected. They were *lovers.*

He thought back to the first time he had set eyes on him in Charlie Brown's, that wet October evening in 1932. He'd been happy just to spend time in his company, and he'd only aspired to be his friend. Alfie had seemed just about as unobtainable as it was possible for anyone to be, but now they were *lovers.* Even though he knew it would hurt, Alfie had been inside him. Despite being a fiercely private person who cared about hygiene to the point of obsession, he had let Alfie ejaculate inside him. Yet there had been none of the awkwardness or embarrassment he had expected to endure. Instead, there had been passion, deep and dirty, but it had been laced with affection and humour. He'd loved every second of it and was certain that he wanted to do it again. But even if fate were to conspire against it ever being repeated, he would still have had this. An episode that would disgust most who considered themselves "decent people" had been the most precious moment of his life. He was a lonely young man and he expected to be alone, always, but for this weekend at least, he wasn't. And he would have the memory of it to warm his future solitude.

When he climbed back into bed, he kissed Alfie on the temple and switched off the bedside lamp. With a scarcely audible moan, Alfie folded himself around him without properly waking. In contrast to the previous night, he felt comfortable entwined with his lover, and counting blessings rather than sheep, he was soon sound asleep.

Chapter Twenty-Eight

Cracks In Alfie

WHEN MALCOM AND Alfie stirred the next morning, they were as shy with each other as two men naked in bed together could be. At first, they couldn't look at each other without turning away again, smiling. Eventually, Malcolm settled on his side to face Alfie who lay on his back, his hands behind his head, staring at the ceiling.

"I can never be this happy again," Malcolm said. "I should die right now, here in your arms."

"Don't talk daft. It wouldn't be very nice for me, would it? It would also leave me wiv a lot of explaining to do."

"I grew up convinced that what I felt about boys was wrong—that it was against nature," said Malcolm. "That first time you came around to my house and kissed me, everything changed. And now, when I'm lying in your arms like this, it feels like the finest thing I've ever done in my life. Do you think we're doing wrong, Alfie?"

"I don't think about things like that too much. It ain't really for me to judge, is it? I mean, the law says it's wrong, I know, but the way I look at it is: if you wanna do it and I wanna do it and it ain't 'urting no one else, then it ain't nobody's business but our own."

"True enough. Even when Mum walked in on us, I felt embarrassed, of course, but I wasn't in any way ashamed." He blushed at the memory. "Obviously, the poor woman shouldn't have had to see her son in that situation, but even at the time, my first thought was thank goodness we spread something over the settee. What if your mother had walked in on us like that?"

"I ain't gonna lie to yer, she'd of been after you with the carving knife, mate. Gawd's truth she knows I ain't no saint, but she'd still see you as interfering wiv her little boy most probably."

"In a way I understand that. I'm a timid sort of fellow, but if anyone looked like hurting you, I think I could possibly become a killer."

Alfie smiled and hugged him tighter. "Let's hope you don't have to kill no one on my account then, eh? I don't much fancy prison visiting, or having you swing for me."

They fell into silence for a few minutes, then Malcolm sighed. "You are beautiful, Alfie, both outside and in. You're gentle and kind and considerate, and I love the way you are with people, the way you give them your time, think the best of them. I'd love to be like that but I'm just not. You haven't had any of my advantages, my education and so on—but you're the better man, Alfie. I genuinely think you're better than I am."

Alfie gave a groan. "I dunno so much, Malc. I ain't nearly as nice as a lot of people seem to think I am."

"I just wanted to let you know that this isn't all about your face. Not for me."

"Thanks, Malc. I've been looking at the same old mush in me Dad's cracked shaving mirror all me life. I know by what other people say that I've been lucky—but I don't judge people by the way they look so why would I judge meself that way? So, I'm really glad you don't."

"Well, I do a bit," Malcolm teased him. "If I didn't, I'd be no better than those annoying rich people who insist that money doesn't matter."

*

THEY ENJOYED THEIR full English as Mrs Turner once again made sure they had the best of everything. All tension gone, they were in high spirits and their fellow guests appreciated their company. No one had any inkling of what these two personable young men had been up to behind a locked door. They strolled around Brighton, taking in the older West Pier and wandering around the absurd opulence of the Royal Pavilion. They had tea and pastries in a small café, but by then, the sky was stained with black clouds. The resulting downpour gave them an excuse to sprint back to the guest house, scamper up the stairs, and rip off their damp clothing.

After their lovemaking, this time with Malcolm in charge, Alfie pulled him close and said sleepily, "I never dreamed it could be like this. What you done to me, Malc, eh?"

*

ON THE BANK Holiday Monday, sex and sea air meant that despite lying entwined with another man, Malcolm slept well. When he awoke, he was filled with melancholy, because this incredible, joyous weekend was drawing to a close, but he was determined not to let his feelings spoil the day. He leaned towards a kiss, but Alfie jerked his head away, cupped his hand, breathed into it, and recoiled. "You don't wanna be kissing that, mate, I promise yer. Stinks like a badger's gusset."

"I'm not sure badgers have gussets," Malcolm observed. "In fact, I don't think they even wear drawers."

"Well, use yer imagination, can't yer?"

Alfie catapulted himself up out of the bed and took the couple of steps to the washstand. There, he set about brushing his teeth vigorously, leaving Malcolm free to admire the tall, lean body before him. His mother had often said that unlike women, men did not look their best when undressed. "Untidy and awkward" had been her words. It would have been indelicate to ask her whether she'd revised her opinion, having been confronted with his lover's naked body. She'd quickly come around to caring about Alfie, and that was far more important. The two got on so well together that Malcolm doubted she'd wish to swap him for the daughter-in-law of whom she'd once daydreamed.

The springs vibrated as Alfie flung himself back onto the bed, fresh-breathed, bright-eyed, and ready for action. As he moved to pounce, Malcolm laid a hand on his chest to prevent him from coming any nearer.

He said ruefully, "I have breath like a badger's gusset too."

*

THEY BREAKFASTED AND went out for a stroll, but the weather was indifferent. Tired Londoners traipsed the streets in search of further amusement before they boarded their trains. They stopped at a café for a cup of tea, and Alfie suggested that they return to the boarding house to make full use of their room before checking out. Women wandered the landings with piles of fresh linen to make a start on the rooms already vacated. They were careful to make sure that their door was locked.

Seconds after the door shut, Malcolm set about pleasuring Alfie with new confidence, and he was determined to take his time over it, for in pleasuring Alfie he was pleasuring himself. He instinctively knew when Alfie was gathering himself to come, so he took him to the edge time and time again, stopping at the last possible moment. He had never expected to be good at this, but he was. The tough young man was again reduced to a twitching, panting, whimpering wreck, his hands clenching and unclenching. After forty minutes, the lad was begging to be allowed to come and Malcolm set to it again and did not stop. Alfie gasped and moaned; his face contorted in ecstasy. "Oh, fuck me! Oh, fuck!" he breathed as his body arched and when the moment of release came it was explosive, drenching the pair of them and leaving Alfie fighting for breath.

When his breath had steadied, he lifted himself up onto his elbows and surveyed the mess that glistened on the skin of both their bodies. "That's ridiculous! Sorry. I like shooting it out, but I ain't so keen on it once it's here."

"I love it. I'll think back to this a lot when you're not around, in my quieter moments."

"When you're having a wank an' that?"

Even now, Malcolm could be shy about it. "We all do it, I suppose."

"I don't do it much as it goes," Alfie told him. He shrugged. "It ain't like I don't feel like it. But I share a room and a bed wiv me brother, the walls are paper thin, and the lav ain't a very nice place to do it in. That means I pretty much have to walk all the way up Mudchute to do it. That ain't good at the best of times, so I dunno, I prefer to save it all up for you nowadays."

*

ALFIE'S MOST COMMON exclamation during sex was "Fuck me!" Malcolm wondered whether it was merely an unguarded expletive or whether there was desire behind it. Was he meant to return the favour he'd been rendered the night before? He had never pictured himself as the dominant sexual partner, but the closeness that had grown between them on this holiday had made him wonder whether there should be any barriers at all between them. He wanted to experience Alfie in every imaginable way.

As they lay idling on the bed, he said, "Alfie?"

"Yes?"

"How about me doing buggery to you?"

Alfie didn't look at him and didn't reply for a moment but then said, "Nah. Nah, that ain't how this works."

"All right. That's fine. I was just wondering."

"Well, don't. I do you. That's how it's got to be."

He was quite sharp about it. Malcolm was taken aback, and there was an awkward silence between them, which made him furious with himself for having raised the possibility. This weekend had been the best of his life, far better than he had any right to expect—yet still he'd reached for more. He was an idiot, and he was afraid he might have ruined everything.

It was Alfie who broke the silence. He sounded disappointed. "I thought you liked it, what we done. I thought you was happy."

"Oh, Alfie, I *am* happy. I've never *been* so happy. I've loved every second with you and I want more, lots more, as much as you're prepared to give me. I'm sorry I even brought it up. It had never even entered my head before and it need never do so again. Please forgive me."

"Oh, bleedin' hell, Malc, there ain't nuffink to forgive. I'm sorry for snapping at yer. You only asked a question, after all. Come here."

Malcolm was so relieved to be taken into his arms and kissed tenderly on the side of his head.

"We just need to keep it the way it is, if it's all the same to you?"

"Yes, of course."

*

THESE FEW DAYS at the seaside had taught them about each other and about themselves. They were subdued on the train home, dreading the moment when they would part. At Victoria, they shuffled with the weary crowds onto a District Line train. Malcolm would soon need to change to the Edgware to Morden Line to Highgate, but Alfie had a much longer journey ahead of him to Mile End. The quick handshake they managed before Malcolm got off at Embankment station felt inadequate to them both.

When he got home, Grace made Malcolm a cup of tea and asked him about his break. The highlights were severely edited down to anecdotes about piers, gulls, sing-songs in pubs, and fish and chips.

During the weekend, the reality had surpassed his dreams, and now despite his own natural pessimism, his thoughts were flirting with the notion of "forever".

*

AT MILE END station, Alfie hopped on a number 56 to Cubitt Town which took another ten minutes or so. He was less happy than Malcolm. It wasn't that he hadn't enjoyed the weekend, it was more because of how much he *had* enjoyed it. He was coming to the point when he would have decisions to make, and he wasn't prepared for it. He almost always went with his instincts in any situation. He didn't like to agonise about things as he found himself having to do now.

The house was deserted, and a note had been left on the table by his mother. It told him that Ada had had a little girl, so it was a good job she and Wilf hadn't gone to Brighton. It also said they'd all gone to the Bank Holiday funfair on Hampstead Heath, and if he needed food, he could fetch himself fish and chips. He was wondering whether he could be bothered or not when there was a knock on the door. He opened it to the lumbering figure of George, who as always had to stoop under the jamb to follow Alfie into the kitchen.

"How was the Games?" inquired Alfie.

"They was all right. Athletics ain't really my thing." George sat heavily on a kitchen chair and leaned forward onto the table. Alfie sat down beside him.

"White City's good though, innit? Me dad took me to the dogs there once."

"Yeah, well, anuvver reason the day weren't too successful was 'aving Frank wandering around with a face like thunder. At first, he didn't seem to wanna tell us nuffink, but in the end he did."

"Oh."

"Yes, so I won't be asking you about your weekend, that's for sure."

Alfie was tired and he didn't feel up to an argument with his mate, but there was surely one brewing and he saw no way of evading it.

"What's he said?"

"Well, he told me what you an' Bertie Wooster was going to be up to by the seaside—and it weren't eating whelks and making sandcastles by all accounts."

Alfie shook his head wearily. "What do you want me to say, George?"

"I want you to tell me that you was winding Frank up. Or that he's got the wrong end of the stick. Then we can have a good laugh and forget all about it."

"I can't do that."

"I'm very sorry to hear that, Alfie. I dunno what to say to yer. Honest I don't."

"I dunno what to say to you either, so it ain't gonna be much of a conversation, is it?"

"This thing with Malcolm—it ain't right. It ain't you."

"I dunno who I am any more."

"Well, I know who you are. You're Alfie Atwood, the best mate I could ever have hoped for. You're gonna be my Best Man and I'm gonna be yours. We always said! Our kids are gonna play together, look out for each other, like we do."

"That's what I always thought."

George stood up and leaned to loom over his friend. "That's how it's got to be, Alfie. You've got to get rid of him, mate. It pains me to say it, but Frank was right. He's turning you Nancy. I defended you last Bank

Holiday when he made a big fuss about it all, but it looks like he was right all along, don't it? Malcolm meant to turn yer head right from the start. He's just like one of them blokes who used to eye you up at the pool," he said bitterly. "They're devious bastards. You do know I'm right, don't yer, Alfie?"

"Like I said, I don't know nuffink no more."

"*Talk* to me. Talk it through with me."

"Are you having a laugh, George? After what you've just said to me, you want me to try and tell you what I'm thinking, what I'm feeling? You ain't prepared to listen, mate. The only story you wanna hear has Malcolm as some kind of pantomime villain and it ain't fair. That geezer tortures himself over every little thing. He ain't devious. He's a nice man. I may not know much, but I do know that."

George held both his hands up in a pacifying gesture. "All right, all right. Maybe he's just sick—ill, I mean. He's got plenty o' dosh so he can find some specialist to help him, can't he? You can't though. You can't afford to catch what he's got. You gotta steer well clear of him, mate."

"Come off it! When have you ever known me drop a mate?"

"A mate? You ain't known him five minutes!"

"It's been nearly two years. Anyway, that ain't the point, is it? I may be in trouble here an' you ain't helping. Yer supposed to be me best mate. But yer just making everything ten times worse."

George glared at the ceiling for a moment, then sighed and sat back down at the table. "All right, tell me. About Brighton. I'll hear you out. Just try not to say anything that'll make me spew."

"I ain't gonna tell you no details, don't worry. That's between him and me."

"Go on, then."

When it came to it, Alfie had no idea what to say, particularly as they'd spent so much of the weekend in bed together. After pausing for thought, he said simply, "I had a really lovely time with him, that's all. I ain't never felt that close to no one before. I didn't want it to end, that's the God's honest truth. We didn't do nuffink much besides the obvious, but it all felt right, you know?"

George's face became distorted again. "No, of course I don't know! How can it be right? The law says it's wrong! And it's in the Bible, innit?"

"Really? Which bit?"

"Well, I don't fuckin' know! But it is there."

"George, when did you last go to church without it being a wedding or a funeral?"

"What's that got to do with it?"

"It's got everything to do with it, because you can't just turn to God to support what yer saying when you don't take a blind bit of notice of Him the rest of the time."

"You don't go to church neither."

"That's because I don't believe in none of it. I'd tread more carefully if I thought you did, but 1 know you fucking don't." He looked at his pal. "Them church types demand to have their bleedin' beliefs respected but they ain't so hot on respecting the beliefs of those what don't believe what they do."

"We've got off the point a bit."

"We usually do, mate."

George smiled reluctantly. "Ain't that the truth. But tell me, if you had such a good time with Malcolm, why d'you reckon you're in trouble then, eh?"

"Look, I dunno how to explain it properly. It's like I went to Brighton thinking I was one person, but I've found out that's not who I am at all. And you're right, I had me future all planned out, wife, kids, the lot. But now…" He went on sadly, "It's what I *want* to want, but is it really what I want?"

"Of course, it is! And you can still have it, mate. You can have yer pick of the gels. I've never met one yet what'd say no to yer. What's happened with Malcolm has turned yer head, that's all it is. You got Doreen. She's a smashing gel and she's clearly crazy about yer. Even if it's not her, you'll meet some gel up Alexander's; yer head'll be turned back again and that'll be that."

"I dunno. Maybe yer right, but it just don't feel like that at the moment. And Malcolm ain't gonna meet some gel, I shouldn't think."

"You don't know that. He might bump into some posh bird called Felicity at a garden party or sumfink. Their eyes will meet over the scones."

"I don't think Malcolm's life is quite what yer picturing."

"Yes, well, I don't give him much thought, to be honest with yer. He ain't our sort, an' you know he ain't. Even if he was a bird, you'd be getting plenty of grief about it."

"Say you're right—and you might be, if that's the way it works out, then fair enough. But what if you're wrong? Where does that leave us—you and me?"

"Honestly? I dunno, Alfie. I don't know any pansies except Malcolm and we ain't exactly bosom buddies, are we? We'll just 'ave to cross that bridge when we come to it. And I hope we don't never come to it, mate."

Alfie wanted to be left alone. George had brought things to a head, but he'd have had plenty to think about even if he hadn't turned up. He'd wanted to mull over how it had been with Malcolm, not how to keep George sweet. He saw a way to engineer his solitude. "I'm going up your way to the chip shop. Coming?"

Part Seven

Stormy Weather

Chapter Twenty-Nine

Fighting "Forever"

Thursday, 9 August 1934

MALCOLM FOUND IT difficult to concentrate on his work. His mind often wandered and got lost in Alfie. He made minor errors but laughed them off rather than fretting over them as he would usually have done. Peter Burkett, now a senior clerk, could see that something had changed with him. Whatever it was, it must have been something good, because his boss loved the world all of a sudden. A lady friend perhaps? He had always been appreciative of his staff's efforts, but now he acted as though each successful transaction had saved his life.

His grand mood may have been obvious to all around, but he was trying to tone it down. When he thought of the things Alfie had said and the way Alfie had been with him, he began to believe their relationship could last. Alfie's insistence that one day he would marry had been before that weekend. Malcolm had shared more of himself than he had ever thought he could with another human being, and Alfie had shared plenty of himself in return. Surely this must be love.

All these good feelings tumbled about inside him, but he had no one he could discuss them with, apart of course from Godfrey. He arranged to meet him in the Swiss Hotel on Old Compton Street. More of a pub than a hotel, it was a well-known gathering place for those seeking others who were "so". It seemed a little better than the other queer places, or his happy frame of mind may have helped him view its patrons benignly. The room was divided into two narrow corridors by an island bar, meaning one had to push through the crowd on one side or the other. He found Godfrey ensconced in a raised area at the back, from where he was able to survey the rest of the pub as though it was his domain, which in many ways it was.

"So, how was the Bank Holiday for you, dear boy?" he asked after the first sip of the gin that Malcolm had bought him.

"It was magnificent. More wonderful than I could ever have dreamed possible," Malcolm blurted out. He couldn't have wiped the goofy smile off his face even if he'd tried. "Alfie was very, dare I say it, loving."

"Really? Am I to have any details?"

Malcolm blushed violently. "No. It's all rather personal."

Godfrey knew that a couple of drinks would loosen his tongue, but for the moment, he was content to raise his most expressive eyebrows and say, "Well, you are a lucky boy, aren't you? You know, it's high time I met the young fellow, don't you think? I do hope you'll bring him along to my birthday drinks."

Malcolm looked doubtful. "Oh, I don't know. I could ask him, I suppose. When and where?"

"It's on the twenty-fifth of August at the Caravan Club in Seven Dials—Endell Street. Nothing formal, just a few drinks with some of the usual crowd from about eleven, after the pubs shut. You must come, of course, but I really hope Alfie will be able to join us too."

"I'll do my best. I should like you to meet him. After all, if it hadn't been for your sage advice, I wouldn't have had the last year or so with him. I shall be eternally grateful to you for that."

"Nonsense, dear boy. Love will always find a way. So, all was up to scratch by the seaside, I take it?"

"It could hardly have been better." Malcolm gave him an account of the weekend. Without being too graphic in his description, he made it clear what had befallen.

"Well, dear, things are going well!" said Godfrey. "Quite often the limitations of these little *affaires du coeur* are exposed by a whole weekend in each other's company, but it sounds as though there was no friction at all… Well, not of that sort anyway."

"I wasn't too happy when he picked me up and tossed me into the sea. We had a bit of a falling-out over that, I can tell you. He was most apologetic about it afterwards though."

"Just affectionate horseplay, I expect."

"Quite. There was another rather tricky moment when I raised the possibility of my, er, doing unto him what he'd done unto me."

"Malcolm! You *didn't!*" He'd imagined Godfrey to be unshockable, but judging by his expression, this wasn't so.

"Well, yes, I did. But he made it clear that it wasn't on."

"And that, my dear boy, is hardly surprising. What were you thinking?"

"I don't understand why that's so bad. He did it to me, after all."

Godfrey sighed in exasperation. "Oh, Malcolm!" he exclaimed wearily. "I know you imagine that your little affair is unique, but it isn't. It is, in fact, rather a common arrangement you have. Many a working-class lad has a similar one with a gentleman of means. Don't ever lose sight of the simple truth that you are 'musical', my boy, but he is not. He is a normal boy off the street who is prepared to indulge in a few 'musical' acts: surely you can see there's a world of difference?"

"Not really, no."

"He is prepared to do the business with you because, I don't know, I presume that you do him favours, make it worth his while."

"I don't pay him, if that's what you're getting at," Malcolm said indignantly. "Whenever I do pay for something, he pays in his turn."

"Really? That is a bit of a departure, I'll grant you, but the whole arrangement will hinge upon his masculinity not being questioned."

"Godfrey, no one who sees Alfie could ever question his masculinity."

"If he were to allow you to bugger him, then *he* would question it himself, don't you see? As far as he is concerned, he's a normal young man who sticks it into a hole and he's not too concerned about it being the wrong hole."

"Well, that makes me feel really special," said Malcolm disconsolately.

"Oh, don't be such a silly goose! As he's taking no money off you, then he clearly enjoys doing it, which does you great credit and makes you very lucky indeed. But if you try and change the dynamic of it all, and in so doing you upset the balance, well, then you will, in all probability, lose him. I'm certain of it. Honestly, you're the one with the education and you're the one with the money and status. To all intents and purposes, you should be the one who's in control of this affair. But if you're not giving him money or showering him with expensive gifts, you should at least afford him a modicum of control in the bedroom, so as not to damage his ego."

Malcolm's elation following the idyllic weekend had been shaken. "Of course. I've been rather stupid, haven't I?"

"Yes, you have. But it sounds as though your weekend recovered, so you must have got away with it."

"I apologised and told him I'd never ask him about it again."

"Well, be sure you don't. These working-class boys are simple creatures and if handled correctly, your arrangement could hold good for months. Years even."

He hated to think of what he had with Alfie as being an "arrangement" but felt he had to ask, "Do they ever last…forever?"

"Good Lord no. Not in my experience. Sooner or later these boys all want to settle down and that's usually the end of it. You weren't hoping for more?"

"No. He's told me that's what will happen. It's just that—oh, never mind."

"Even if he doesn't find a girl, you may just find he gets too old for you."

"It isn't like that!"

"Just as you say. Just as you say."

The meeting had not gone at all well. Rather than sharing in his rejoicing, Godfrey had deflated him. But Godfrey didn't know Alfie. He hadn't seen them together. Despite what Godfrey said and what Alfie had said before the weekend, he still felt things might be different for them. He'd be cautious thanks to Godfrey's counsel, but he would remain hopeful.

By this time, his companion had become distracted by someone he'd seen across the bar. After gazing into the middle distance for a moment, he said, "I say, Malcolm, have you ever seen that young man in the dark-green Fedora before? The one leaning against the wall beside the cigarette machine?"

He turned to look at the object of his friend's curiosity. He was a tall, slim, upright figure with what might have been a pleasant face, had it not been marred by a grim expression. "No, I don't believe I've ever seen him before, here or anywhere else. But of course, I'm hardly a regular myself."

"Hmm. When we go our separate ways, would you do me the favour of not kissing me goodbye?"

"I wasn't going to, Godfrey. I never do," he said drily. "Why, anyway? Do you have hopes in that direction?"

"Yes, in a manner of speaking. My hopes are that he isn't Lily Law on the prowl. As you can see, he's rather good-looking, but I just have a hunch that the only thing he's looking for a feel of is someone's collar."

Malcolm was alarmed and glad he was about to leave anyway. He glanced over at the man again. Now that he thought about it, Godfrey's suspicions were certainly plausible. "Shouldn't we get the hell out? Both of us?"

"Heavens no. We mustn't do anything that suggests we may be up to no good, my dear. Besides, I have seen him a few times lately at my regular haunts, and if I'm right and he is a policeman, then I think they're up to something a little bit grander than the odd arrest this time."

"Such as?"

"I've no idea. But perhaps it would be wise of you to pursue your policy of keeping your boy safely indoors until the threat passes. Not that it ever really does for the likes of us. And of course, you absolutely *must* come to my birthday drinkies. The Caravan Club is quite new so I'm sure that will be fine. It's one of Iron Foot Jack's and he's well acquainted with the ways of Lily Law."

*

ALFIE WAS STILL affectionate whenever he came around to Cranmer Avenue, but he wasn't the happy-go-lucky young man he'd been before. Malcolm couldn't forget how he'd reacted to the prospect of being the passive partner, even just once. He hadn't been right since. Could an affront to his ego be the reason?

One evening, Malcolm walked up behind Alfie as he stared through the nets at some children playing in the street. He wanted to slip his hands around his waist and embrace him. He wanted to kiss his neck, but he hesitated.

"Go on, then," said Alfie quietly without even glancing back.

"What?"

"Do whatever it is you wanna do. You can touch me, Malcolm. You know that, don't yer? Yer mum ain't around."

"I know. It's just—I'm afraid."

Alfie turned to look at his lover. "Afraid? Of me? You wasn't afraid of touching me in Brighton, was yer? You're never afraid of touching me when we're—you know."

"Not afraid of *you* exactly. I'm afraid of doing the wrong thing. That I might touch you when you don't want to be touched."

Alfie nodded. "I see. But you have to trust me to tell yer if you do anything I don't want. 'Cos I will, you know."

"Look, Alfie—you seem unhappy about something and I'm afraid it's down to what I asked you in Brighton."

"What? Nah. You asked about fuckin' me and I said no. But asking me was the right thing to do. You had every right to ask me. Malcolm, you and me 'ave been about as close as two blokes can get. Would that of 'appened if I was worried about you touching me? I want you to touch me. Sometimes I need you to touch me."

"But what is it that's upsetting you?"

"Nuffink," Alfie said gruffly. "I've just got a lot on me mind, that's all. I can't go round smiling all the time. I ain't a bleedin' clown."

"I'm sorry." Malcolm felt wretched. "I'm just no good at all this."

"What? Don't be ridiculous. You know, if somebody else talked about you the way you talk about yourself, I'd probably punch 'em on the nose." He smiled. "Well, if I was Frank I would." There was a pause, then he went on: "Look, I'd never banked on being like this wiv anuvver bloke. It was never the plan. But when you can bring yourself to touch me, somehow all me plans go out of me 'ead. When you touch me, I never want you to stop. Not ever. It scares me how much I feel like that. I…I just don't have the words to explain to you what's going on inside me. If I tried, I'd get it all wrong and make it worse. You just have to be patient with me and trust me to sort it all out, in time."

Alfie turned away to look out of the window again, and as he had expected, Malcolm came up behind him, slipped his hands around his waist, and kissed him on his neck. Alfie pushed his body back into him, and they stayed like that for some time.

"Sometimes, being in your arms feels like home," Alfie said quietly. "It feels right even though most people would say it's wrong. I feel comfortable. I feel safe. I feel like I could sleep for a year and only have nice dreams."

Malcolm steered Alfie's head around and kissed him tenderly.

Alfie said, "Don't ever be afraid of touching me, Malcolm, not ever."

*

AFTER THEIR TALK on the way to the fish and chip shop on Bank Holiday Monday, Alfie had reluctantly agreed with George that he should further prepare Malcolm for the probability of him wanting to settle down and start a family. Despite George's disapproval of Malcolm, he had a sense of fair play and believed that Alfie needed to be honest with him for both their sakes rather than just for his own. To that end, Alfie spent a fair amount of time rehearsing conversations, ranging from simply urging Malcolm to be careful to breaking it off with him before they got in too deep.

The trouble was, they were already in too deep. His half-baked plan to split up straight after the Bank Holiday weekend had been a non-starter because he just couldn't drop Malcolm after they'd been so close. Nor did he want to. Brighton had changed everything. Whenever Alfie turned up at Malcolm's house, any thoughts he had about warnings that would cast a shadow over their relationship were banished the moment the door was opened to him. He just wanted to sit with his lover under the tree in the garden, shaded from the August sunshine and hidden from the neighbours, playing with his soft fair hair, stealing the odd kiss. Then when twilight fell, he wanted to go indoors to the sofa in the drawing room, or the one in the parlour, and make love. He wanted to feel Malcolm's skin against his own and to hold him as he shuddered through his crisis. He wanted to fuck him too, any chance he got.

It had been a nasty moment when Malcolm had asked that question in Brighton, but he was touched by how apologetic and how angry the poor bloke had been with himself afterwards. He didn't want Malc to feel like that.

*

MALCOLM HAD ASSUMED that every Londoner had visited the usual attractions at some stage in their lives, but he was wrong. Alfie had hardly been out of the East End apart from for boxing and the odd London derby. Though initially appalled, it did mean he could offer Alfie a whole range of new experiences. Over the last months, he'd taken him to the South Kensington museums, Madame Tussauds waxworks, the Tower of London. They visited the zoo in Regent's Park where he was nonplussed by the level of Alfie's enthusiasm, particularly for the penguins at the newly opened modernist Penguin Pool. He was bouncing off the walls with joy, and it underlined the fact that in many respects, he was still an innocent boy.

Looking at things through Alfie's eyes, Malcolm enjoyed them anew and sometimes came to think about them in a different way. At the British Museum, he was keen to show his friend the exhibits that had particularly fascinated him as a child—the mummies in the Egyptian Hall.

As they stood looking at one example, Alfie frowned. "There's one thing I don't understand," he said.

"What's that?"

"When does it get to be all right to dig someone up from their grave and stick 'em in a glass case for people to gawp at?"

"Well, these are thousands of years old."

"So? What's the time limit for being left in peace? Where's it written down? I mean, I wouldn't want anyone to do this to me dad. And this geezer's from bleedin' Egypt! What's he doing here? I mean, I know he ain't likely to wake up or nuffink, but if he did, he'd be ever so confused, wouldn't he? Waking up in fuckin' Bloomsbury!"

When he thought about it, really thought about it, Malcolm concluded that Alfie was right. Every day threw something up to make him respect him a little bit more.

They did all this because he cared about Alfie's experience of life. He wanted him to have the opportunity to do all the things that he had done. And he also loved being with him, sharing whatever they were doing. It bound them closer.

Malcolm had brought so much into Alfie's life, with the unspoken promise of so much more, that Alfie didn't want to spoil it. He wondered whether one day he'd take his own son or daughter to the zoo, look down at the penguins playing on their spiral ramps, and think fondly of Malcolm, a ghost from the past. Right now, he didn't know which was more difficult to picture, the as yet unconceived children, or a life without Malcolm.

Chapter Thirty

Godfrey's Birthday

Saturday, 25 August 1934

HE HAD BEEN in two minds about taking Alfie to the Caravan Club, the intimate basement in Seven Dials where Godfrey was to have his birthday drinks party. On the one hand, he was afraid that Alfie would take one look at the assembled queens and walk right out again. On the other, albeit wary of parading him around like a prize, he couldn't help feeling a little thrilled by the thought of being seen with such a scintillating "catch" by those who once sneered at him behind his back for being so cripplingly shy. Whatever faults a queer place might have, lords could socialise with grooms in them, vicars with shop assistants, and a handsome young docker would be currency of a high denomination indeed.

The Caravan Club had opened in Endell Street the previous month. Malcolm hadn't been there yet, but he knew it would be full of the usual crowd. When he first suggested it, Alfie seemed unenthusiastic, but he had relented in the face of Malcolm's transparent disappointment. They resolved to show their faces, hand over the gift of a decent bottle of brandy, have a couple of drinks to be sociable, then leave. They popped into the Angel on St Giles High Street first, so that they weren't stone cold sober when they entered the club, knowing all eyes would be upon them. As they walked down to Seven Dials, if Alfie was nervous, he wasn't letting on.

Malcolm was certainly nervous as they approached the narrow alley to the entrance. On those rare occasions that he attended an illegal drinking club, he always worried about someone he knew seeing him go in. London may have been the largest city in the world, but it was surprising how often you could bump into people you knew, especially when you didn't wish to. The potential humiliation of being denied entry also worried him.

Close to the Swiss Church, they turned off Endell Street into the dark alley and went down the few steps into a basement. The man at the door was a familiar and outrageous figure. He was a large, powerful-looking fellow with dramatic long black hair that was elaborately braided. One leg was shorter than the other, and he wore a crude metal contraption of a boot to compensate for it. He was known as "Iron Foot Jack" and, having encountered him presiding over some of his earlier short-lived ventures, Malcolm was intimidated by him.

Tonight, admission proved easy as, once again, Alfie's countenance met with approval. If you were running a club for homosexuals, having that handsome a boy in it would be good for business. They paid their one and six each and went through into the subdued light and thick smoke of the club.

It was a long narrow basement with bare floorboards serving as a dance floor at one end, while the other, covered in worn Persian rugs, was scattered with tables fashioned from wooden casks and rough seats of bare wood informally covered in loose velvet. The ceiling was obscured by swathes of hanging fabric so that it resembled the interior of a sheik's tent. However Bohemian it was meant to look, Malcolm thought it a dreadful fire risk. One dropped cigarette could ignite this tart's tinderbox and incinerate them all, for the stairs they had just descended appeared to be the only exit. However tawdry the decoration, it was mostly obscured by people, smoking, laughing, drinking, and bouncing about to the music of "Charlie", who was squeezed into the corner playing an accordion. The tiny dance floor hosted several dancers, all male couples apart from a single, heavily made-up woman who danced alone.

Although Malcolm had never set foot in this place before, it was occupied by the old familiar faces, with a scattering of "fresh meat". Anyone new tended to cause a sensation; there would be whispers and arch looks, often followed by blatant attempts at a pick-up. Godfrey had warned his friends that Malcolm was bringing his young man and made it clear that any efforts to pounce on him would result in excommunication from his circle; in their small world, this was no mean threat.

Because the club was crowded, people didn't all set eyes on them at the same time, but Malcolm observed with some pleasure that Alfie's introduction to the room was rather like an outbreak of fire: a flicker here, a flare-up there, then a rapid escalation to a roaring conflagration. Godfrey, holding court at the centre of the crowd as they arrived, welcomed them and gushed about his birthday card and the bottle of brandy. He insisted on getting the two newcomers a drink, and at the first opportunity he had to address Malcolm privately, he hissed, "You lucky, lucky devil! I had assumed you'd been exaggerating, but he is quite divine. Couldn't you take the delightful brandy back and let me have him instead? It is my birthday, after all."

Malcolm drifted off to the lavatory, and on returning, he stood apart for a while, recalling how miserable his visits to places like this used to be. He'd go to them to try to find some people with whom he had something in common—but instead felt more alone than ever, as well as inadequate, conspicuous, ridiculous, and desperate.

Now, two years down the line, although many of the faces were the same, he viewed the crowd differently. The eye was still drawn first to the flamboyant queens in their camp finery, with their own language, Polari, and their own codes of behaviour. They had filled him with revulsion at the time, but he didn't hate them any longer. Some were naturally effeminate, and he saw nothing wrong in that. If that was who they were, then they were right not to hide it. And they were brave. They didn't have the luxury of becoming invisible whenever they chose, for personal safety and to fit in with convention.

It was easy to overlook all the others there—the men who drank quietly alone or with friends, or who lurked in the shadows waiting for love, sex, friendship, understanding, something...*anything.* He had assumed they were sneering at him, while just like Malcolm himself, they had been trying to play a game the rules of which weren't printed anywhere.

He hoped that in coming here with Alfie he wasn't twisting a knife in the heart of some lonely soul in the crowd. The thought made him ashamed of flaunting his good fortune. He would have preferred his relationship with Alfie to inspire hope, rather than deepen someone's misery.

There *were* people here who would be pleased for him, who would marvel at the change in him and see it as a sure sign of hope. But there were other badly damaged people present who would do anything to break them up, not just through a simple desire for the man he had, but also through envy and spite.

Brandon Farley, or "Brenda" as he styled himself, was one such bitter old queen. He was enraged that such a plain mousy individual as Malcolm Trevelyan had managed to snare such a magnificent boy. He studied Alfie with hungry eyes, taking in the angelic face and the rougher edge of his accent and his unaffectedly masculine mannerisms. As far as Brenda was concerned, the boy was a wet dream come true and such a rare treasure should not be squandered on a grey, hopeless nobody. He said as much to "Nevina", more usually known as Neville Gowling, his regular lady-in-waiting.

"Of course, it simply won't do, dear," he said. "We have to get that divine boy off Trevelyan. I mean, the very idea! Ugh! It's such a *waste.*"

"That's a bit mean, Brenda, if you don't mind my saying."

"Well, I do mind. Auntie Brenda has to put things right. It's the natural way of things."

"Godfrey says they're devoted to each other."

"Tosh. Boys like that are out for what they can get—and looking as that one does it should be hobnobbing at the Savoy with Prince George himself rather than slumming it here with a shipping clerk or whatever he calls himself. I mean, how can that dull little nobody hope to satisfy such a splendid animal's needs? I mean to intervene for the greater good, Nevina, and I mean to do so right now."

Brenda, with his nose haughtily in the air, flounced away and made a beeline for Malcolm. Neville had assumed that the young lad would be the target, but extraordinarily, it seemed Brenda was intent on giving Malcolm a piece of his mind. Surely even a quiet little wallflower wouldn't stand for that? The crowd parted for Brenda's calculatedly exaggerated mince, because no one wanted to risk getting the rough edge of his tongue. Neville trotted obediently in his wake like a doped poodle, fearing that his friend was about to be a bully.

As Brenda approached, Malcolm could see that he appeared intent on opening a conversation with him—something he had never previously condescended to do. He considered taking evasive action, but that would have been awkward in such a small club. In the end, he turned towards him with what he hoped was a neutral expression on his face.

"Malcolm…" began Brenda as though he was addressing an inefficient servant for his own good. He paused for effect, and to make sure all those assembled were listening. This delay proved fatal, for it was the only word he was to utter during the exchange. Alfie appeared from nowhere and pushed between them.

"Sorry, mate." He glanced dismissively at Brenda before looking intently into Malcolm's eyes and telling him, "There's sumfink I've just gotta do."

He put his hand behind Malcolm's head so there could be no retreat and kissed him slowly, lingeringly and deeply. As always, the kiss made Malcolm's head spin. It was as though from a position of peril he had stumbled through a portal into paradise.

"*Bravo!*" said an impressed voice from one of Godfrey's friends, and there was even a ripple of applause.

Once Brendon Farley had recovered his wits, he exclaimed, "Well, *really*!" and flounced away like an affronted dowager with Neville scampering at his heels, his devotion rather undermined by an irrepressible smirk.

When he emerged from the kiss, Malcolm was blushing violently, while Alfie smiled at him, pleased with himself.

"What on earth prompted you to do that?" Malcolm managed.

"Well, I dunno what that geezer was gonna say to yer, but it didn't look like nuffink you'd wanna hear. So I said to meself, 'I can kiss 'im in 'ere an' no one will care.' So, I did. Nice, weren't it?" His brows knitted in mild concern. "'Ave I done the wrong thing?"

"No, Alfie. You've done exactly the right thing. It couldn't possibly have been any more perfect. Thank you."

"Don't mention it."

Not long after the incident, Malcolm noticed Brenda sneaking up the stairs and out of the club, and he experienced a pang of guilt. But he and Alfie had simply kissed, so why should he feel bad about that?

After they'd done a reasonable amount of socialising, they settled at a small table that was convenient for the exit so they could leave without any lengthy goodbyes. They were no longer in a hurry, having enjoyed the night more than they'd expected to. After an hour or so's good-humoured conversation over the music and general hubbub, Alfie's brow furrowed. He looked as though he had something he needed to get off his chest.

"Malcolm, you know I always said that I'd meet a gel one day?"

Malcolm froze. "Yes?"

"Don't worry, nuffink's 'appened yet, I ain't met anyone. I just need to be sure that you understand. I mean, we got so close in Brighton, didn't we?"

"Please stop. Please don't tell me any more."

All the elation of the public kiss had gone, and a wave of despondency washed over Malcolm. It looked as though Godfrey had been right to pour cold water on his dreams. One of the things he loved most about Alfie was how normal he was, a regular working-class East End lad, so of course he was going to meet a girl and settle down. Malcolm couldn't blame him for it. But for the moment, he couldn't trust himself to utter a single word more in case he burst into tears. They sat in silent sadness as though oblivious to the revelry around them, which suddenly seemed tawdry and silly.

Eventually, Alfie said, "Please don't shut me out, Malcolm. I've only told yer this 'cos I care about yer. I may be wrong and it may never 'appen, who knows?"

"Oh, it'll happen," said Malcolm quietly.

"It might be years. You might get sick of me well before it does."

"Will you please do me the courtesy of not saying things you don't for one moment believe?"

"All right. I'm sorry. I can see that you love me, more than I've ever known anyone love another person. It's an honour but it's a bit frightening too. I ain't saying I can match it, but the way I feel about you ain't no small thing neither. Falling in love with a bloke weren't never the plan. But it's 'appened. I admit that. I love you, Malcolm."

How he had longed to hear Alfie say those words. The circumstances were all wrong, but even now, laced though they were with sadness, they warmed him. "Don't say that just to make me feel better. Please."

"I'm saying it 'cos I mean it. And it's important to me that you know that."

With a superhuman effort, Malcolm pulled himself back from the edge of the pit of despair. He knew that Alfie had warned him again out of concern, and he could not blame him for wanting a normal family life. He also believed his declaration of love and understood that it hadn't been an easy thing for him to say.

"I do know that, but thank you for saying it. I'm not going to worry about it, not until it actually happens. One of us could be run over by a bus tomorrow, so why worry, eh?"

"That's it. Look on the bright side." As a gesture of gratitude for his understanding, Alfie leaned forward and kissed Malcolm tenderly. It was a kiss for comfort, but it became passionate. Unfortunately, it was a kiss that was to be rudely interrupted.

*

THERE WAS A kerfuffle at the bottom of the stairs into the room. "*Ladies and gentlemen, stay where you are, please!*" shouted the voice of authority as a dozen or so dark-uniformed policemen filed into the room. There were shrieks of outrage and howls of indignation and even the odd scuffle. "*Be quiet! Can somebody get the bloody lights turned full on?*"

Normally, such a declaration would be the cue for those assembled to scatter, to find fire escapes, windows, rear entrances, or any other possible means of escape. But the Caravan Club had just the one exit. When the lights came on, the place looked even more scruffy and squalid, with any magic having been banished with the shadows. Malcolm recognised the officer issuing commands by his green Fedora. If this was his moment of triumph, it hadn't made him look any happier.

"I'm ruined," said Malcolm simply, and he sank back onto his stool beside Alfie.

"What d'you mean?"

"This will be in the papers. One whiff of this and I'm finished at British Atlantic. And what about you? Oh, God, Alfie, why did I bring you here?"

"Don't you worry about me."

They fell silent among the bedlam that surrounded them, but Alfie was thinking, looking for a way out. After a while, he said, "Listen. We're right near the door. I'm gonna make a bit of a fuss to distract the coppers on that side and when I do, walk out. Don't run, just walk like everyfink's normal."

"But I'll get stopped!"

"Maybe. But if you are, it ain't gonna make things any worse, is it? There's a chance you'll get out. It's worth a try."

"But what about you?"

"I told yer, don't you worry about me. I'll be fine."

He necked the rest of his drink and followed it up with abandoned drinks from nearby tables. Nobody noticed because of the furore. He went on, "You know that Batista's? The all-night café on Charing Cross Road? Wait for me there. No more than an hour, mind. If it's longer, you can assume I've been carted off to Bow Street."

"Oh, Alfie, I don't think I should leave you."

"Trust me," he urged. "Right—count to five and *go*."

With that, Alfie rose to his feet. Affecting the unsteady gait of a drunkard, he lurched over to the nearest officer. He deliberately stumbled and allowed all his weight to come down on the constable, which brought them both crashing to the floor. Thinking one of their number was being attacked, all the policemen near to them converged on Alfie and tried to prise him off their fallen colleague. Alfie didn't kick out or punch, but he affected confusion and stuck to the policeman like a limpet to a rock.

Appalled with himself, as Alfie was being roughly handled, Malcolm did as he'd been instructed. After a count of five, he walked slowly but purposefully out of the room and towards the stairs. Iron Foot Jack was not "coming quietly" as they say and was expressing his outrage to three very wary policemen, so they were oblivious to Malcolm as he sneaked past behind their backs. Two officers were coming down the stairs but they pushed past him, and before he knew it, he was out in the alley. There was a constable posted there too, but before he could utter his challenge, Malcolm said, "Your sergeant said I could go." This was enough to make the officer hesitate and before he could ask for clarification, without breaking his stride, Malcolm had taken the few short steps onto Endell Street, pushed through a crowd of rubber-necking porters from nearby Covent Garden, and turned towards the hub of Seven Dials. Alfie's plan for him had worked—but at what cost to him?

*

ALFIE SAT NEXT to Godfrey as they waited to be interviewed by a police officer, in order to decide whether it would be worth taking them around to Bow Street police station and charging them. They could hear all the protests and excuses those before them were making, none of which got them anywhere other than into the back of a waiting Black Maria. Some of those apprehended seemed to be relishing the drama, and there were plenty of witty exchanges and constables' blushes to be enjoyed. But there were those who sat quietly with ashen faces, contemplating the same ruin and disgrace that Malcolm had feared so much. Alfie was glad that he seemed to have got him out of it.

Now it was himself he needed to worry about. He had never been an accomplished liar, but under these circumstances, he gathered himself to give the best performance of his life. To Godfrey, he muttered, "No offence, but I'm gonna say whatever I think will get me out of this. Some of it may not sound too good to yer. It'll be a pack o' lies, but I'm gonna say it anyway."

"You go ahead. Say what you need to," Godfrey reassured him. "I shall be doing much the same, although realistically I think I may have to rely on my legal friend to get me out of this one."

Alfie was beckoned to the interviewing constable, a grey-haired, moustached man who couldn't have been all that far off retirement.

"All right, mate?" said Alfie, swaying a little. The constable glanced at him impassively before looking down at his notebook again.

"Sit down. Name and address."

"Alfie. Alfred Atwood, forty-two Glendale Street, Cubitt Town East."

"Age?"

"Twenty-one."

"Occupation?"

"I'm a stevedore, sir."

The officer looked at him again, leaning back slightly in his chair, his eyebrows raised. "What have you got to say for yourself then? What's a young lad like you doing in a place like this?" He sounded tired and a little disappointed in the boy sitting opposite him.

"I'm asking meself the same question, sir."

"Perhaps you could answer me and yourself at the same time then, son."

Alfie sighed before beginning. "It was like this. I was a bit the worse for wear, to be honest. I'd 'ad a row with me gel, see? So I just come up near 'ere to get drunk. I went in the Chandos, where I weren't likely to bump into her, or any of her stupid mates. Well, when the pub shut, I was walking up St Martin's Lane and these three fellers started chatting to me. They said they knew a place I could carry on drowning me sorrows, so o' course, stupidly I says yes. That's 'ow I got to be here." He made as if to burp, and the officer moved his chair back.

"So, you'd never come here before?" the constable asked, still keeping his distance.

"No, sir."

"We've had this place under surveillance several times in the last fortnight, you know. So, if you have been frequenting it…"

"On my life, I ain't never been here before, sir. Nor nowhere like it neither. Honest to God."

The officer's face looked pained. "Could you not see that it was an establishment full of homosexuals? Did you not see men dancing together? Touching each other?"

"I could 'ardly see me own feet, sir. It was like a fog in 'ere, what wiv all the smoke and me being so drunk."

"You expect me to believe that you were oblivious to the kind of place it is?" said the officer sceptically.

"Oh no, sir! I could tell right enough. Just a few minutes before you arrived, I felt an 'and in me trouser pocket and I don't think he was after me small change if you get my drift. Before I 'ad a chance to say, "Ere, wot's your game?'—the swine touched me!" Alfie shook his head grimly and emphatically. "'E touched me where he really shouldn't oughter 'ave."

The officer rose. "Right. You wait here, sonny."

He went away, and Alfie glanced over at Godfrey who gave a little silent clap and mouthed, "Bravo!" Alfie suppressed a smile, but he did treat him to the briefest of winks.

The constable returned shortly with a sergeant who said, "Well, son, it seems like we saved your bacon tonight, don't it?"

"Yes, Sergeant. I'm ever so grateful for it an' all. I musta bin the only bloke in this place what was pleased to see yer."

"We have your details, but I don't think you need to come to the station. If we need you to give evidence against these 'ladies', we'll be in touch."

"O' course. But I don't think I'll be much help." Alfie made himself shudder. "I didn't see who it was what was messing with me. That made it all the more creepy, I can tell yer."

The sergeant adopted an avuncular tone. "Yes, well, if I were you, I'd make it up with your girl, son, and steer clear of the West End. These types prey on nice-looking young chaps like you, you know."

"Well, if I didn't before, Sergeant, I sure as hell do now."

Just as he rose to leave, the tall plainclothes officer wearing a green Fedora came up to speak to the sergeant, who told him, "This one's more of a victim than a culprit, Mr Taylor."

The detective inspector looked Alfie directly in the eye and held his gaze for a long moment. Alfie suddenly realised that he'd seen him before—in the club earlier that night. He'd pushed past him in order to give Malcolm the big kiss that had saved him from Brenda. There was absolutely no chance this man hadn't seen him do it. He'd been totally in control of himself throughout the ordeal, but now he felt a cold sweat on his back.

After a long moment, Detective Inspector Taylor smirked and gestured towards the door with a nod.

"Better run along then, sonny boy, before the sergeant thinks of something else to nick you for."

*

A SKIN HAD formed on the surface of Malcolm's coffee, which stood cold on the table in front of him. He was frantic. Any relief he felt at his own escape from disaster had been eclipsed by the shame of having abandoned Alfie to his fate. After an hour and twenty minutes, he was about to call it a day when he was startled by a rap on the window. He turned to see Alfie grinning at him through the glass.

Alfie came in and plonked himself down on the chair opposite, as though he hadn't a care in the world.

"Told yer," he said. "I'm right as rain, and you ain't ruined."

"Oh, Alfie. I don't know what to say."

"Don't say nuffink. Just get me a coffee and a sticky bun if they got one, I'm starving." He looked at Malcolm's barely touched cold coffee and turned his nose up. "Best get yerself one an' all."

"I've got a better idea, Alfie. If you're starving, we'll take a taxi back to Highgate. I'm sure that Mum will have something more substantial in the pantry. I'll pay for another cab to take you home afterwards too. After what you've done tonight, it's the least I can do."

*

AT NEARLY 4 A.M. their cold feast was interrupted by a tetchy Grace, looking formidable in a hairnet, dressing gown, and slippers. Malcolm explained the circumstances because he was too weary to concoct a story. She was furious with him for having gone to such a place and for taking Alfie. She launched into a monologue cataloguing the perils of which they were well aware, but they were too tired to interrupt and argue about it.

Eventually, Malcolm said that they should see about getting a taxi for Alfie.

"Don't be ridiculous!" snapped Grace. "You're hardly likely to get one at this hour. He must stay here." Her tone was kindlier towards their guest. "You don't have a ship tomorrow, do you, dear?"

"Erm…no."

"I'm afraid that none of the beds are made up in any of the guest rooms."

"The settee is very comfortable though," said Malcolm.

"No. You can't expect Alfie to sleep on that," Grace reproved him. "You'll just have to share Malcolm's bed, dear, if that's all right. It's a good size so it should be plenty big enough for the two of you."

The pair were dumbstruck, so she continued, "There, that's decided then. Good night, boys, or rather good morning. Don't be too long and try not to make a noise when you come up." With that she was gone.

When Malcolm found his voice, he sounded cross. "This is unbelievable. So infuriating! She always has a room ready and aired for Aunt Hannah—always! I looked in only yesterday and it was fine. There were even bloody flowers in it—just in case Aunt Hannah turns up unannounced as she tends to do. Well, she isn't going to turn up at four in the bloody morning, is she?"

Alfie was smiling. "Malc, calm down, mate."

"Why should I calm down? If she thinks her precious guest room is too good for you—"

"Don't be a fathead. That ain't what she thinks. Can't you see?"

"See? See what?"

"Well, that this was yer mum showing us that she's all right with us doing what we do."

"At this hour?"

"You ain't half daft sometimes, Malc. She did it so's you and me can be together. I mean, she probably thinks we're too tired to get up to much mischief tonight and she's right about that. But she knows we ain't gonna play Tiddlywinks when we wake up in the morning, don't she?"

"Do you really think so? I mean, why didn't she just say?"

"'Cos it's hard for her, of course. Accepting you and me is sumfink she can't bring herself to put into words, I reckon, but she's shown us instead and you should bloody well love her for it. I do."

Malcolm sat back down at the table, and a big smile broke out on his face. "My God, you're right. It's fantastic!"

Alfie got up and embraced him from behind. "That's more like it. Now, I think you should let me have a wash and get into your nice big bed. You can do the same. Then I think you should snuggle up to me and hold me for what's left of the night. I ain't got no pyjamas, but I don't expect you'll mind that. And in the morning—well, then we'll see, won't we?"

By the time Malcolm had finished in the bathroom, Alfie was sound asleep. He climbed gently in beside him and did exactly as he'd been told. It felt so wonderful to have *his* boy in *his* bed. He doubted he'd get a wink of sleep.

Why worry about forever? The human heart, the human mind, and the ever-present shadow of death meant there really was no such thing as "forever", so he would train himself not to fret about the future. The present was far too beautiful for that. He would fall back on his plan to take as much of Alfie as he was willing to give, because it was the only plan that made any sense. Whatever its risks, the affair had made him happier than he'd ever been or ever believed he could be. In the morning, he would make love to a man in his own bed for the first time, always assuming his mother didn't burst in with a tray of breakfast.

Malcolm drew him closer and murmured, "I love you, Alfie. I can't believe that someone like you could ever be for the likes of me, but here you are, lying in my arms. I can feel your heart beating and hear your every quiet breath."

"An' I can hear you rabbiting on," mumbled Alfie. "I love you too. Now shush, will yer!"

"Sorry. Good night, Alfie."

And before he could think of any words to capture the perfection of the moment, he slipped away to join his boy in the Land of Nod.

Acknowledgements

Joan Deitch who helped turn a pipedream into a prospect. David Noad, Eileen O'Hare, Ed Brovelli, Helen Smart, and Rich Howgill whose input and encouragement have been essential.

About the Author

Chris Simon is the youngest son of a headteacher and was born and brought up in North Wales. He attended college in Liverpool and Manchester studying Geography and English and returned to Wales to work at a holiday camp, doing everything from chalet allocations to scrubbing grill pans in the off season. He did this over three summers before moving to London to join the civil service, starting in North London benefit offices and ending with the Department for Transport in Westminster.

As well as football and music, Chris has a great love of social history, particularly that of London. After visiting the capital at the age of twelve his desire to live there became the first certainty of his life. He settled in Walthamstow in East London and is a keen supporter of Manchester City and, of course, Wales. It had always been his intention to write a novel whenever he found the time—and now he has.

Facebook
www.facebook.com/chris.simon.3152

Twitter
@FleemingHell

www.ninestarpress.com

www.facebook.com/ninestarpress

www.facebook.com/groups/NineStarNiche

www.twitter.com/ninestarpress

www.instagram.com/ninestarpress

bsky.app/profile/ninestarpress.bsky.social

www.threads.net/@ninestarpress